Daddy's Boyz

Tales of Intergenerational Adult Gay Sex

Literotica Edited By

Bob Condron

A STARbooks Press Publication

Copyright © 2006 by STARbooks Press
ISBN 1-891855-63-8

This book is a work of fiction. Names, characters, places, situations and incidents are the product of the author's imagination or are used fictitiously. Any resemblance to actual events, locales, or persons, living or dead, is purely coincidental. All rights reserved, including the right of reproduction in whole or in part in any form.

Published in the United States
STARbooks Press
PO Box 711612
Herndon VA 20171
Printed in the United States

Many thanks to graphic artist John Nail for the cover design.
Mr. Nail may be reached at: tojonail@bellsouth.net.

Book and text design by Milton Stern.
Mr. Stern can be reached at miltonstern@miltonstern.com

Cover model and image provided by Raging Stallion Studios
http://www.RagingStallion.com

Contents

Introduction	i
Dave's New Puppy	1
Fruit of the Vine	9
Going Back for Thirds	17
Summer of Truth	33
Hired Hand	45
Saturday Punk	57
About Gordon	63
Rampage	71
The Center of Gravity	77
As Good As It Reads	95
The Big Dog	105
Eating Fugu	117
Getting the Message	131
Politics Unusual	141
Victim of Pleasure	155
The Kid from Left Field	169
Love in the Arms of an Older Man	187
Boy in the Pool	197
Encore	205
Elegant	217
A Man of Taste	227
Trey	235
Learning the Ropes	253
Me, Daddy — You, Cub	265
Even Daddies Need Daddies	271
The Contributors	277
About the Editor	281

Acknowledgments

My special thanks to:

Every author included in this anthology for their valued contribution(s). Had it not been for their enthusiasm, skill, expertise and patience *Daddy's Boyz* would have fallen by the wayside long ago. Sincere thanks also go to the many, many talented authors whose work I was unable to include.

James C. Johnston and Adrienne at The Erotic Readers & Writers Association for sending out the call and for valued advice.

Karen T., a.k.a. my Muse, and my encourager for being there with a positive ear at all times.

Dale E. and Lesley C. for their loving kindness — I consider myself blessed to have yous in my life.

Milton Stern for his skilled and sympathetic formatting of the manuscript.

And last but certainly not least, T-Baer without whom there would be no Bob Condron, no Author's Biog. of Literotica and no *Daddy's Boyz*.

Introduction
Bob Condron

Daddy's Boyz is a project close to my heart. The idea was born of my own personal experience of being a gay man who has always found older guys attractive — a reality for many gay men I don't generally see reflected in a gay media that most oftentimes equates youth with sexual potency and desirability. Promoting this stereotype unremittingly, to my mind, is neither accurate nor fair, nor does it reflect my experience. Hence: *Daddy's Boyz*.

The original call for submissions contained the line: "Time to shatter the stereotype!" — a reference to the insidious and pervasive "sad, old queen" archetype. This prompted an indignant and vociferous response from one recipient who wrote to complain: "Don't you realize that 'the stereotype' was shattered years ago, Dumb Shit?"

I will concede that, perhaps if one is privileged enough to live in a gay capital like New York (as my critic does), it might seem that way; but out in the sticks? That is simply not my experience. I did, nonetheless, remove the line from the call.

I have been fortunate to spend the last decade of my life as an out gay man in two of Germany's gay capitals, Berlin and Cologne. The latter, it is claimed, is the European "Bear" capital, while the former has a Leather and Fetish scene that is second to none. Naturally, older gay guys are both visible and considered desirable in both locations, but not so in my hometown in the North of England. Despite being the fourth largest city in England, what scene is there revolves around youth and the young. In the land of the disco bunny, the big 3-0 looms large, and at 40, one is considered well past the "sell by" date.

But times are indeed changing — however slowly. The queer status quo is finally being challenged, as the city now boasts a regular Bear Night on the first Friday of every month, progress of a sort. It attracts guys from all over the region. And certainly the emergence of the Bear community worldwide has contributed significantly towards providing atmospheres conducive to a positive self-image and a sense of belonging for many older gay

Bob Condron

men — not to mention a viable community where the Bear/Cub dynamic is celebrated. Sometimes a significant age difference is a feature of these couplings, sometimes not. Oftentimes discrepancies are defined through role-playing. In any case, what is clear is that age, maturity, and experience can be an asset, not a liability.

The stories that comprise *Daddy's Boyz* have real meaning for me. The sports arena, for example, is a theme that features prominently here and prompted the most submissions — a testament to its potency as a sexual fantasy. My first crush ever was on the obligatory physical education coach. He must have been in his mid-forties, and I was around 15 or 16. I can still remember the longing I felt for him, remember the heartache that manifested itself physically. Not surprisingly, the relationship did not develop beyond the context of my own head, though he — Brian — was something of a prototype for the kind of men I would continue to find attractive.

Even so, I found it necessary to make clear in my call for submissions that all characters represented must be 18 years of age or older, and that underage sex and/or incest were not to be considered acceptable themes. I did not, and do not want to fudge this issue. Having worked as a counselor with numerous men who were sexually abused as adolescents, I know that the reality of sexual abuse is anything but erotic, and I have no wish to perpetuate the fantasy that it is. Despite this, submissions exploiting that theme duly arrived. I can only conclude that some writers cannot read. Fortunately, the majority could.

I will finish this introduction with an anecdote:

I met a guy in a Cologne bar recently: a short, stocky muscle-packet all the way from Costa Rica, who insisted on calling me 'Papi' both in and out of the bedroom, despite the fact that he was only two years my junior! The Daddy/Son relationship was a state of mind, or was I coming into my own Daddy years? Either way, I was not about to complain. Growing older is a fact of life and one to be embraced. The positive aspect of lusting after older guys is that, eventually, you will become the object of your own affection.

Dave's New Puppy
Thom Wolf

Dave called last Tuesday night to talk about the new piece of ass he was sticking. He'd known the boy a week, having met at Lush.

"I was standing at the bar, waiting for a beer, when this kid walks over and starts slobbering over my nuts. It was amazing — no come-on or anything — he just drops to his knees, plants his mouth on my crotch and starts chewing."

"How old is this kid?" I asked. Dave wasn't the kind of guy who ran around chasing chickens. In the years I'd known him, I couldn't recall seeing him with anyone noticeably under 30.

"19."

"You've got to be joking. It'd be like fucking a fetus," I said.

"This boy knows what he's doing. I want you to meet him. Come round on Thursday night."

I wasn't keen on the idea, but neither could I think of a good enough excuse to drop out. I wondered if this was the start of Dave's mid-life crisis. He was in his early 40s, just the right age for a gay. I'd known plenty of guys who suffered their gay-induced identity crisis earlier than that; I was one of them myself. It's not our fault; finding hot older guys when you're at a prime age yourself is not easy. The last man who made me call him daddy was 34 — two years my junior.

Dave was so hot for Mike that he had already started sticking him when I arrived at the house. The front door is never locked when Dave is home. I let myself in, calling out his name.

"Upstairs," he hollered.

His house is airy and modern with light walls and stripped floorboards. Dave did all of the work himself. I ditched my jacket at the bottom of the stairs and followed the sound of grunting to the second-floor bedroom. From the open door, I saw Dave's hairy legs sticking over the edge of the bed; and the kid was on top of him, riding his hard pole. I caught the side of the boy's face as he arched his back, his suntanned skin glistening with sweat. From the sheen of his skin and the dampness of his short blond hair, I guessed they'd been at it for some time already. He wore a red tank top, which was dark with perspiration, and solid black boots. The contrast of his white ass and suntanned limbs was surprisingly erotic. I might not be a chicken lover, but I can appreciate a decent piece of ass when I see one; and this was especially fine.

He rode Dave's cock with skill, rising three or four inches and dropping back. Dave wore a cock strap, and the sight of his hairy nuts pressing against the boys butt was beautiful. I could see the kids pucker glistening and bulging as it stretched around the thick pole.

He tipped his head a little, his brow knotted with ecstasy, and managed a smile. His face was tanned with a broad forehead and straight nose. It was a face that still had some growing to do, but was not unattractive. A feeling came over me. I was looking at a boy, a face, so fascinating that given time, he could absorb me whole. What pleasure did fate have in store for me by bringing this boy into my life at that moment. I could fully understand Dave's infatuation.

"Hey," Dave called from beneath, "glad you came." He gave Mike's butt an open palmed slap, and the boy rose all the way off his pole. As Dave's big head popped free of the kid's anus, I was delighted to see a long dribble of lube ooze out of the open hole before it slowly closed back up. Mike reached behind, giving his ass a slow stroke, fingering the juice back inside himself. I knew then why I found the boy so attractive, despite his youth, he was a beautifully slutty bottom. This would be fun.

I pulled open my jeans and tugged out my dick, which was hard and dripping a healthy drool. Mike didn't need to be told what to do. He bounced off the bed, giving me my first sight of his perfectly sized dick, and got down on his knees in front of me. Both hands curled around my cock, and he raised his face to look at me. His blue eyes sparkled with lust. I stroked the side of his face, feeling soft skin, trailing my fingers through the sweat, and brushing the sun-kissed freckles that formed a light pattern across his forehead and brow. A pink tongue darted from his mouth, wetting his lips, before he opened them wide to work my head. He sucked the tip, mingling cock juice with saliva and then, using it as lube, sunk my cock down his throat. I felt blood surge into my organ, getting harder and thicker. Mike's breath rasped through his

Daddy's Boyz

nostrils. I curled my fingers around his damp blond head and pulled him all the way, feeling his nose in my pubes, his chin pressing against my balls.

Dave watched from the bed, his hairy shoulders propped up on pillows, a broad smile on his bearded face. His mammoth thighs were spread wide, framing his fat cock and hairy low-hangers. The angle of his hips showed just a hint of dusky brown asshole. I had fond memories of the night that Dave, drunk on beer and whisky, rolled back his chunky thighs and begged me to eat his funky ass. I even wriggled a couple of fingers into his impossibly tight chute before he started screaming bloody murder. His asshole is sealed so tightly I've often wondered how he shits through the fucker.

Mike was working a nice rhythm over my cock, sucking like a pro to the depths of his throat. I kept the pressure on the back of his head, each time waiting until I felt him gag before easing up.

"Ass," I said when it was time to slow things down, not wanting to cum yet.

Mike dropped back onto his knees, his cute brow creasing. "You want me to rim you?"

I shook my head, "Your ass. Back on the bed."

He nodded obediently and did as I asked, getting up on all fours, back arched, his ass high and proud. Dave came forward and planted his massive paws on Mike's butt, spreading him. His hole was perfect, shaved of all hair, slightly enlarged like all pig bottoms are. His pucker was reddened and swollen from the fucking he'd received earlier, still juicy with lube. I bent down and kissed the tender rim, feeling its heat against my lips, feeling it quiver. I licked all the way around the rim, savoring the taste of ass and lube. Dave stretched his cheeks wider, distorting the shape of Mike's anus, allowing me to taste the most intimate region of this beautiful body.

I sat back and slowly teased him with a couple of fingers, entering the hole easily, following the curve of his ass, deeper into the rectum. He worked his ass muscles, chewing at my fingers. "Good boy," I said, withdrawing, giving his anus a short, sharp slap with the flat of my hand. Mike moaned, and his asshole quivered, pursing like a mouth. The hole pouted, and I slapped it again, and again — each time Mike made a little "Oh" sound, tipping his head and arching his spine a little bit more. His tank top clung to his sweaty torso like a second skin. His asshole flushed an angry shade of red.

I told him to move to the edge of the bed while I undressed. Dave got on his knees, in front of him, feeding Mike his cock, which the boy gobbled up greedily. I stood behind him, getting one foot onto the bed for leverage and plunged my dick into his moist, welcoming asshole. Dave winked across Mike's back as I pushed all the way in, holding his hips in both hands until his butt cheeks pressed against my pelvis. I grabbed a handful of his T-shirt, twisting it tight and rode him like a horse. I was filled with a desire to possess him, to break and dominate his sweet white ass.

He worked his asshole all the while, squeezing my dick, sucking it into his rectum, wanting me to fill him entirely. Dave pulled out of Mike's mouth and with a few hand strokes splattered the boys face with his heavy load. Three long spurts coated his face from brow to chin. As the forth and fifth, weaker spasms, emptied Dave's dick, he wiped his cum into Mike's damp blond hair. I tugged at his tank top, forcing him to rise and give me a look at his come-drenched features. White rivulets, as thick as paste, coated his skin, a striking contrast with his suntan.

I pulled out and told him to turn over. Mike scooted round onto his back, hitching his knees into his chest. I lay on top of him, slipping my dick back into his hole and began licking the sticky seed from his skin. Mike turned his head slowly from side to side as I fucked him, giving me full access to his face. I mashed my dick into his guts, fucking deep into that slut ass, and kissed him, sharing the taste of Dave between us. I came with a roar, holding his perfect body tight and spewing my cream into his ass.

When I withdrew, I sat back to admire his hole. It gapped open for a moment in a vacuum left over from my dick, before it slowly began to draw in on itself, closing shop. An amalgam of spunk and lube dribbled down his crack. Mike's hand moved quickly into the crevice, rubbing the liquid into his skin like an expensive body cream.

Dave wanted a beer. We stuffed a large black plug into Mike's ass, keeping the fucker loose for later and told him to get dressed. He moved quickly, retrieving his clothes from the chair in the corner. He stepped into a white jock and pulled his baggy jeans over the top of his boots. His face, beneath the tan, was flushed.

Daddy's Boyz

Anyone looking at him now would know without doubt that this kid had just been fucked.

We went to a bar in the village, which was reasonably busy for so early on a Thursday night. It would really get going around midnight. At that stage, we had no idea if we would stay that long; it would depend on Dave's willingness to share his new toy with anyone but me. The bar was long and dark with bare wood floors. A leather movie played on multiple TV screens around the bar — Jackson Price getting it in a sling with a huge black dildo — the soundtrack lost below blaring disco music.

We found an empty booth and sat down with a jug of beer and three glasses. Mike was looking at Dave and me, full of youthful candor and interest.

"How's your ass feeling?" I asked, stroking his face, following the clean line of his jaw to an exquisitely cleft chin.

"Hot," he said, sipping beer and licking the foam from his upper lip. "The plug feels great."

"Good. It's supposed to," I said.

We finished the jug of beer and order another. The place began to fill up. Mike listened with interest as Dave pointed round the bar to all the men we'd had. I watched him as he listened, squirming in his seat as Dave regaled him with one hot story after another. I imaged his pretty ass chewing down hard on the plug as he listened so attentively. I could see the hunger for experience in his eyes, a wild desire to know everything about life and sex, a desire I used to think would mellow with age, for, if that were true, then I was yet to reach the age myself.

"Take off your jeans," I told him.

He was off his seat in a heartbeat, shoving down his jeans, discarding them on the dusty floor. "Get on the table," Dave ordered. "Let's see how that ass is doing."

A conversation at the next table ended, unfinished. At the bar, a couple of guys who had noticed the impromptu strip, elbowed their friends. Mike had captured the attention of the bar. He climbed up onto the table, standing straight and then squatting to show us his rear. The flat black base of the plug protruded from his ass, obscuring his hole. I stroked the back of his thigh, which was smooth, shaved, like his butt. "Push it out," I told him.

He shifted, shoving his ass closer to our faces, wriggling: a true showoff.

"As nice as that looks from here, that's not what I meant. Push that plug out of your ass," I commanded.

He steadied himself, bending over, his hands on his knees. The base of the plug shifted as his asshole pouted and pushed. It bulged slightly, but his effort was not enough and the plug settled back into place. Dave smacked his ass, leaving a stinging palm print in Mike's delicious white flesh.

"Shove that fucker out of there. I want you to work that hole harder, cause we're gonna fuck it," I said.

Mike took a deep breath, gripped his thighs, and bore down, pushing hard. Like a heavy black torpedo the plug shot out of his hole, landing with a thud on the wooden tabletop. His luscious asshole oozed a clear white juice. Just like before, Mike's hand came round to sensuously massage the orifice. A rumble of approval ran round the room. A group of interested observers began to gather round the booth. Reveling in the attention, Mike worked his hole, pouting and tightening, finger-fucking his chute.

Dave swiped the boys hand away. He stood, grabbing his ass in both hands, holding him like a ripe piece of fruit, and brought him to his mouth. Dave licked and sucked on his well-seasoned hole, thrusting his tongue deep into the pink interior. Mike moaned, digging his fingers into his thighs, turning his head to watch his daddy burrow in his ass.

I reached between Mike's thighs and tugged the pouch of his jock aside, freeing his cock, which fit snugly in the palm of my hand. He was sticky on my fingers. I slipped his foreskin back and forth across the head, caressing the crown, smearing it with his precum, then putting my fingers in my mouth to taste his subtle essence.

Dave pulled back from the boy's ass, his beard matted with saliva and lube.

"I think he's ready for more," Dave said as Mike lay down on the table and wriggled his butt over the edge. Dave opened a sachet of lube with his teeth and squirted the contents into the boy's hole. Mike hooked his arms around the back of his knees and offered his ass. Dave unbuckled his jeans, shoved them to mid-thigh and, holding his cock at the base, guided it inside. Mike

Daddy's Boyz

ignored the men who were watching and looked directly into Dave's eyes as he fucked him. Dave's dick made a noisy squelching sound as he shoved it in and out of that eager hole. I leaned over to watch as he pulled his fat piece all the way out, hovering for a moment at the edges of his rim, and shoved back in. He repeated the action again and again, to a satisfying rhythm. Dave's face was set in an intense expression as he jacked his hips faster and faster, pounding that hole. I slipped my cock out of my jeans, tugging a lazy rhythm as I observed the show.

With a loud grunt, Dave slammed his dick deeper and screwed his face, spewing his load into Mike's rectum. He withdrew, his hard cock dripping and wet. We wasted no time trading places. I instructed Mike to change position. I got him face down over the table and slipped easily into his fuck-worn ass. He lay forward, pressing the side of his pretty face against the wood. Despite the pounding he had already taken, Mike's ass was still working. He tightened his sphincter around my cock and shoved his butt towards me. I was filled with love as I hammered his ass, pulling all the way out, tearing back in. His hands gripped the edge of the table, the knuckles showing white, the muscles in his shoulder bunched beneath the tank top. I held his ass tight and emptied my balls into his guts, thrusting until the last drop of sperm had left me.

I withdrew and watched the milky white fluid dribble from his beautiful hole and trickle down his thighs, like white chocolate sauce on his golden skin. One of the men who had been watching, a stranger, could not resist the delight. He rushed forward and devoured our spunk, recklessly sweeping Mike's ass with long strokes, not stopping until his juicy pucker was shiny and clean. It was madness, insanity, but Mike seemed to have that effect on everyone. I well understood the stranger's compulsion to have a piece of him. His ass — second or third hand — just had to be had.

Mike's eyes were wide and brilliant, triumphant as the man ate the deposits we had left in his cum-dump of an asshole. Dave smiled and sat down to finish his beer. The crowd around us began to thin, heading back to their drinks.

When the ass licker was done, I helped Mike to stand and gathered him to my chest. I took him to the bathroom, leading him naked through the crowd. More than a dozen hands reached out for him, desperate for his ass, but I drove him away from them; I didn't mind sharing him with Dave, but wasn't ready to turn him over to a bar full of horny bastards — not yet. I ran the water and washed his face and body, drying him down with paper towels before re-plugging his ass with the black toy. As the torpedo re-entered his bowel, Mike growled and fell trembling against me. He shot a high arch of come that splattered against the opposite wall and dribbled slowly down the cracked, discolored tiles.

Fruit of the Vine
Peter Eros

Out of the Northwest, a summer squall raced through the Sonoma Valley. The sky darkened, changed to sapphire, then switched to a kind of gray-green. The atmosphere, already thick with humidity, turned aqueous, making the air so heavy it seemed as though I was breathing underwater.

I ran from the upper ridge of the vineyard down to the verandah of my Daddy's house as the downpour hit. The storm rattled windows and shuddered the wisteria against the corner posts. Daddy Kai stood in the doorway of his bedroom, wearing only a brief pair of shorts. He beckoned, grabbed my shoulder with his right hand, and he led me towards the inner sanctum.

He shuffled his boxers to the floor, kicking them into the corner of the room. I slipped out of my sandals and tore off my tank top and shorts, my prick already leaking its excitement. Daddy Kai lay back on the bed and spread his thighs. I crouched between them. My hair brushed his belly as I worked over him. Sweat lay on us like seawater; we seemed oiled with it. He groaned out loud, feeling his cock swell, quivering for release as I slowly, delicately, utilized my nails, fingertips, lips, tongue and hot breath to excite him.

I savored each moment, reaching out with the flat of my palm to feel his heart pounding against his ribs. His breath came short and hot from the back of his throat. He gasped intermittently as I added a delectable fillip here and there, tweaked his distended nipples. His eyes were closed; he was immersed in the heat of his own desire. He groaned, reached down and gently drew my hungry mouth away from his engorged cock. His eyes opened, and he drank in my slick nakedness riding atop him: my swollen prick, my sturdy thighs, my narrow waist, the flare of my ribcage, my pumped pectorals.

Daddy Kai's eyes, smoldering, heavy-lidded with lust, inflamed me. With ease his strong arms pulled me upward, like a doll to be arranged, straddled across his face. He slurped my bobbing cock. I cried out at the contact, my fingers entwining his

Bob Condron

hair as I pressed my hips forward and back, establishing a rhythm — slow at first — as I savored the hot lick of his tongue, the nibbling of his lips. I was dripping with need, groaning with ecstasy, my body quivering in anticipation as he sucked me deep into his throat and greedily nursed my pre-cum.

I held my pelvis immobile, felt the pleasure rippling through my musculature in uncontrollable waves. I felt the tide pulling me onward and at last gave myself over to it completely. I bucked my hips against his mouth with frenzied need, my thick, curly hair flying around my head as if I was in the midst of the storm that was raging outside. It was what Daddy Kai was waiting for. He eased me away from his mouth, forced me to sit back squarely onto his swollen, spit-slicked prick. I gave a wail of delight as, with one long, ecstatic thrust, he plumbed me to my depths. The heated contact was all I needed. Kai convulsed inside me. My fingers stroked his cheek. My head fell forward and our tongues dueled, my stiff cock jetting its heavy load over his heaving belly. A reflex I could not hold back any longer.

We lay at length, listening to the rain drumming on the roof above. It diminished with the same slowness that our pulses took to return to normal. He lit a joint and took a deep drag before handing it to me.

"How long has it been now, Pedro?" he asked.

"Three months," I answered.

"Thank God you found me. You make me very happy. Are you happy?" he asked.

"¡Si, si! I like it here very much. You know I love you, Daddy Kai. You have given me a home in this lovely place, and money, and good food and clothing, your loving companionship, and the best sex I have ever known. Why wouldn't I be happy?" I asked.

It was true; three months since I had left Acapulco and headed north to find my El Dorado. I am 22 years old. My mother raised her five children alone. Somehow she earned the money to provide her boys a good education with the Jesuits and I, unlike my brothers, was sensible enough to concentrate on learning English. But English isn't much use in Mexico unless you have contacts among wealthy and influential people. I had work, but it was only menial. I'd been an agricultural worker in the vineyards and a busboy in restaurants, but my only chance at a real life was to head north.

Since my teens, I have been a diver off the cliffs of Acapulco, thrilling the tourists but gaining little for myself except the adrenaline rush of the moment and exposure to the wealthy men who were willing to take their pleasure from my well-formed and agile body. Most of them were married men, wealthy enough to afford a double life. I didn't mind. I enjoyed their mature company and their practiced certainty about what they wanted from me. It was so much more satisfying than the fumbling, embarrassed and inexperienced efforts of boys my own age. These randy Daddies taught me a lot about how to pleasure a man as well as financing my journey to "al norte" with their gifts. Fucking tourists for profit also enabled me to expand my English, to learn the necessary words and phrases that the Jesuits never taught me.

Finally, it was time to make my escape. I took the usual route North, through Tijuana. In that ramshackle town, I made contact with the coyotes who arrange passage for illegal immigrants. They aren't hard to track down. I found a cell-phone toting coyote right at the bus station, standing next to a police wagon, loudly quoting prices of $400 to $800 for transportation to Los Angeles, with custom trips available to anywhere in the United States for a negotiable, higher fee.

We traveled at night. I don't know where we crossed the border, I only know it was somewhere in the desert. There were ten of us crammed into the back of a small van. I was still poor, but felt delivered from poverty. I had hope and ambition and was away from the scrutiny of family and friends. I was free among strangers in the eventful world where I could practice being someone else until I was someone else.

Offloaded by the side of the road, I quickly thumbed a lift. A trucker offered to take me cross-country to the wine capital for the price of a blowjob or four. I accepted; it seemed cheap at half the price.

Jobs done to both our satisfaction, my burly "compadre" gave me a Santa Rosa newspaper, and I perused the classifieds, hoping that a vineyard needed staff. The Ratzinger Winery was the only one advertising. At journey's end, I changed in the back of the cab into my best jeans and a tight T-shirt. True to his word, my trucker dropped me at the gates of the vineyard.

All my possessions were packed in a duffel bag. It was a weekday and regular winery tours were being conducted. A sort of tram was being pulled behind a tractor as it threaded though the fields. The wine shop was open, and the staff was friendly, but they said the boss was away till later in the day. When I explained that I had no transport, they said I could take a tour and then wait in the shade outside the gate to his residence. They gave me a sandwich and a soda.

When I first saw Kai Ratzinger, he was piloting his Harley Soft Tail Classic down the steep canyon road towards the ranch house gates. He had silver rimmed riding goggles clamped tightly over his eyes. He was wearing threadbare and skintight 501s, scuffed work boots, and a dark blue silk bomber jacket over a tight white lycra T-shirt.

I saw him before he saw me, his head held high as he captained the behemoth cycle around a corner. He looked hell-bent and happy. He noticed me standing in front of the gates. The motorcycle pulled to a stop. He slid the driving goggles onto his forehead and looked me over, revealing his unusual, almond shaped, cobalt-blue eyes under hooded lids. There was a questioning glimmer in those eyes.

Then, above the roar of the motorcycle echoing through the valley, something clicked. His full, moist lips spread into a smile that said many things. It said, "I like what I see." It said, "We can get along." It said, "I think I'd like to screw you."

"Need a job?" he asked.

I could only nod. Brush my crotch with my thumb.

Then he did something totally unexpected.

"Push the code!" he yelled above the roar of the cycle.

"The code?" I asked.

He dictated the code, which I punched into the keypad. The electric gate opened across his driveway. I'd known him less than five minutes and he'd already given me the keys to his Kingdom!

He propped the bike in the open garage next to his Lancia then crossed the forecourt to join me. He had the tall, broad-shouldered bearing of a power lifter. The bulge of his crotch was prominent and full, firm buttocks stretched the ass of his jeans. He was maybe 45 but in tip-top shape. He gestured for me to go ahead of him up the path to the entrance of his sumptuous home.

"Do the honors, Kid," he said as we arrived at the door. "Can you remember the combination?"

Again, I pressed the buttons on the keypad, and he pushed open the ornate, paneled door. A muscular hand grasped my shoulder and thrust me ahead of him. As the door slammed shut behind us, he spun me around and into his open arms. Pressing me to him, he engulfed my mouth with his own. Startled but happy, I relaxed in his masculine embrace and enthusiastically responded with my agile tongue. He drew his head back and held my shoulders firmly, gazing into my amazed-but-excited face.

"Son," he whispered softly, "I guess you need love as much as a job ... and this Daddy sure as hell does."

He pushed me ahead of him into his bedroom, both of us stripping our clothes off as we went, my eyes quickly taking in my surroundings. The bed was huge and covered with a paisley-patterned quilt. The headboard was mirrored and a built-in wardrobe with mirrored doors ran the entire left-hand length of the room. Until I was flat on my back, I didn't notice the mirror on the ceiling above the bed. Another large mirror adorned the right-hand wall, beside the French windows that opened onto a verandah. We sure made a beautiful couple.

Daddy Kai knelt over me, held me at arms length, appraising my body. I gazed at his pumped, hairy pecs, his large dark-brown nipples standing proud of his chest. His skin color was like milk chocolate. He was totally hairy save for his groin, which was shaved smooth like a prepubescent. But Daddy Kai was totally adult, with the largest cock I had ever seen. Like mine, his was uncut, standing proud above his big, low-slung ball sack that was also shaved hairless. His prick, twitching upwards to greet me, was drooling freely, throbbing and impatient to release its fertile juices.

He reached out, took hold of my hand, and guided it to the hardness of his belly. My hand traveled right down to the base of his stiff prick. I made a fist around his cock and moved it all the way along its silky length. I left one hand on his prick, not wanting to let go of this new toy, and stroked his nuts with the other, fondling each one under their hairless, smooth sack.

"Oh yes, Sweetheart!" he murmured, "Daddy's gonna love his sweet baby!"

I looked up at Kai's face and smiled at him; I then returned my gaze to his ball sack, marveling at the size of the huge nuts nuzzling beneath my fingers. I felt his fingertips lightly brushing my ass. My manhood tingled with delight. I could smell a mixture of cologne and perspiration on him. Our lips made contact, our bellies crushed together, and our hands clutched each other's buttocks.

I flipped him onto his back and shuffled onto my knees. I spread his thighs and lapped his silky smooth cock with my tongue. I then took as much of it as I could into my mouth. My tongue traced its length and slipped under the foreskin. He squirmed as I flicked my tongue against the sensitive tip, after which I swallowed his entire cock without gagging, his exposed glans stuffed all the way down my throat. I pumped and slurped, slid my wet lips along his warm length as my hands continued to fondle and squeeze his balls.

He quivered with delight and tilted his head back against the pillow, licking his lips. His deep breathing soon transformed into moans of pleasure and excitement, as he took the initiative and started fucking my face. I gripped his smooth ass cheeks tight, helping him to ease in and out of my mouth. Each time he pushed in, I held my tongue just at the tip of his prick, catching his foreskin and rolling it all the way down his shaft, massaging the sensitive head with every inch of my throat as I swallowed him whole.

I wanted him to cum in my mouth so badly. I began to squeeze his prick between my lips as my tongue furled around him. My right hand massaged and squeezed his smooth, shaven balls, while the fingers of the other hand probed his tight, hairless asshole. He shot a huge load within seconds. I gulped and swallowed, hardly losing a drop, exulting at the feel of his milky ooze in my throat and gullet — Daddy sperm, feeding me his fertile love.

He relaxed back, emptied, and dragged me up to rest in his arms. I lay beside him, ever obedient, my heart still pounding hard and fast against my chest. I snuggled close to him as his hand caressed the curls at the back of my neck.

I kissed him tenderly on his forehead, eyelids and nose. Our lips met, and my tongue forced entry. He responded passionately, chewing on my lips as his tongue dueled with mine, thrusting to the back of my throat.

Disentangling himself somewhat reluctantly from my embrace, he stood naked and proud. Stretched like a cat. Strode across the room and opened one of the mirrored doors to his bathroom. He took a piss. I watched through the open door. Watched the golden arch splash onto white ceramic. My turn next.

When I returned from the bathroom, he was on the bed, kneeling on all fours, waving his smooth, taut buns in the air.

"Fuck my big Daddy ass, Son. Show me what you can do," he said.

He took one of his hands off the bed and spread his ass cheeks for me, giving me my first glimpse of his smooth ass crack and his rosebud-puckered hole. I buried my face right into his crack. Teased and tantalized it with the tip of my nose and tongue. I pulled his cheeks wider, inhaling, licking and sucking on his beautiful hole. He groaned and grunted, and I could feel him jerking his dick with delight as I thrust my tongue ever deeper into his asshole. It tasted wonderful, tasted of man. Then I knelt erect. Took my seven inches and tickled his buns with it. My prick was so hard and full that I could have cum just from that minor friction, but I held it in.

He lubed himself up. I watched his slick fingers slipping in and out. I then took one of his hands and placed it on my pulsing dick so that he could guide me into his ass. He sighed with pleasure when I entered him. Buried deep, I pumped in and out. His breathing increased sharply as my thrusts accelerated. He pushed back when I pushed forward. I moved harder, faster, exultant at the feel of my heavy foreskin rolling back along my shaft as it slid deep into Daddy Kai's tight, aching hole. I reached beneath him and stroked his hard, throbbing cock. Just then, I felt a tightening in my balls. I grabbed his hips and, pounding into him, experienced the most powerful orgasm I had ever had. His arms thrust behind him grasping my buttocks, holding me in, he fell forward as I emptied my load of spunk into his ass.

Bob Condron

Sated, my cock slid out of him. Our breathing gradually returned to normal. Kai flipped over onto his back and pulled my mouth to his. Kissing me deeply, lovingly, he grinned.

"I'm your Daddy, and you're my butt-fucker and my cock-sucker now, my beautiful boy. Mine and mine alone. Do you think you can handle that?"

"¡Si, si, Padre!" I said as I rested my face in the hollow of his neck.

"And your name?" he asked.

"Pedro," I told him.

"Pedro. That's a beautiful name."

It has been three months now, and Daddy Kai has taught me a lot about the running of the vineyard. He bought me a wardrobe full of handsome clothes, a lightweight motorbike so I can get around, and he has initiated an adoption process through his lawyers. But principally, he has taught me that love knows no boundaries. I feel like I belong to him, that his flesh and my flesh are one and the same. I have become that someone else I have always wanted to be. I am now my Daddy's baby.

Going Back for Thirds
Hank Edwards

The bleacher beneath me is cold, hard and uncomfortable. I usually enjoy sitting on hard objects, but when the temperature is hovering in the 40s and the object happens to be made of aluminum, everything changes. I shiver in a fresh gust of wind and wrap my arms more tightly around myself, wondering just why the fuck I had agreed to this in the first place.

On the field below, the players break their huddle and line up. I take a long, lingering look at the young, firm ass cheeks hugged by tight fitting uniform pants before the ball is snapped and the play commences. The quarterback falls back, searching for a viable target. He finds an open man, cocks his arm and sends the ball spiraling down the field to his teammate. The receiver catches the ball with ease, tucks it into the crook of his arm and sprints to the end zone as the crowd, myself included, gets to their feet screaming with joy.

The kid who just scored is my ex's nephew, Brady. He's attending college across the country from his family and, at my ex's request, I came to watch his game today. The first time I met Brady was at a Fourth of July family gathering that my ex, Robert, had dragged me to. Back then, Brady was pretty much the prototypical, healthy teenager — a stocky, sports loving kid with more energy than two suns and a broad, slightly awkward smile. He was the third of five kids pumped out by Robert's sister, Madeline, and her husband Greg. Robert and I had been going out for six months, and this was the first time I was meeting his entire family. A little overwhelmed and feeling out of sorts by all the familial conversation going on around me, I stepped out into the yard for a moment to myself. I found Brady punting a football, chasing it across the yard only to turn around and punt it again. The kid cajoled me into tossing the ball with him, and we spent an hour laughing and playing catch until Robert stepped out on the deck and called us in for dinner.

I saw Brady a few times after that, all within the year Robert and I dated. We bonded a little because we both felt like outcasts at those gatherings: him the middle child and me his uncle's reluctantly acknowledged male date.

And so, here I sit, watching as Brady, now 20 and playing college football, struts off the field. I wait a bit for the stands to clear before I make my way down and into the hall outside the locker room. The place smells of college man sweat, soap, and fresh dirt from the field, a mixture that shoots straight to my crotch and gets me half hard in minutes. I may be 44, but the plumbing works just as well as it did 20 years ago.

I wait for half an hour, talking with the quarterback's parents who are smiling so broadly I fear their faces may split in half. The door to the locker room bangs open, and a muscular group of players pours out, yelling and whooping and punching each other as they head for the exit. They all smell of soap and cologne and, just lightly, of clean, fresh sweat. My cock swells even more, and I turn to watch the group of them run off down the hall, squinting to see if Brady is mixed in with them.

"Mike?" The voice is deep, tentatively hopeful.

I turn and feel a flutter in my heart at the sight of him. Brady has grown into a hot young man. Wide, hazel eyes, dark, red hair, broad smile filled with white, even teeth, square jaw shadowed with stubble. He stands 6' 3", an inch shorter than I, but his shoulders are broader.

"Uh, yeah," I say, caught off guard by my reaction to him. "I'm surprised you recognized me."

"Are you kidding? You were my hero!" He moves up to throw his strong arms around me, hugging me tight. I hesitate then hug him back, my hands feeling the muscles in his back even through his jacket. He steps back, and his eyes take in my face.

"Wow, it's so great to see you. Uncle Robert told me you lived out here now. I told him I'd love to hook up. But I didn't hold out much hope. I'm honored," he says.

I shrug, embarrassed and turned-on and flustered.

"Well, as you can see, he did pass on your message, and here I am. Today was his suggestion. Thought it might be a good idea for me to come watch the game so you'd have someone representing your family. I hear no one back home could get away," I tell him.

"Yeah, I was bummed about that." He takes a breath and turns to wave as a few more guys file out of the locker room and pat him on the back then he looks back to me and asks, "What are you planning to do now?"

I blink and stuff my hands in my pockets to try and disguise my erection.

"Um, well, you know. Probably head back to my apartment and get some things done around the house. I'm sure you've got parties to go to, I don't want to keep you, just wanted to let you know someone from your past saw your amazing play," I tell him.

He grins at me, "Well, there is a party later, but how about we go to dinner and catch up? It's been a long time."

I catch myself nodding without realizing it and say, "OK, sure. Dinner would be great."

I drive us to a steak house and am amazed at how open and comfortable Brady feels around me. I only saw him a handful of times the entire year I dated his Uncle Robert, and I broke up with the mutual decision that we made better friends than lovers, but have kept in touch ever since. I've heard about Brady's exploits as the kid grew up, saw the occasional school photo framed on Robert's desk, but never saw him in person again until today.

"When did you move out here to California?" Brady asks as he slathers butter across a thick slice of warm bread.

"About five years ago. I got a promotion and was able to transfer to the Los Angeles office. I miss Boston the city, but not the weather," I tell him.

Brady grins, "I hear that." He tears the buttered bread apart, thoughtful. "So, do you talk to Uncle Robert a lot?"

I shrug, "Sure. We're still good friends. We decided we were better friends than ..." I let my voice trail off, not sure how much Brady knows about his uncle's personal life.

He looks up with a smirk, "It's OK, Mike. I've known Uncle Robert is gay for a long time." He arched an eyebrow. "Not many adult men bring their friends to family get-togethers, you know?" He sits back as the waitress places a thick, sizzling steak before him. When she leaves he looks me in the eye and says, "I really liked you. I was bummed when you stopped coming to our family gatherings."

I don't know what to say and struggle for words, "Well, sometimes things just don't work out between people."

"Yeah, sometimes," he says as he carves into his steak and pops a piece into his mouth, closing his eyes and moaning. "God, this is so good. I never eat like this."

"Welcome to college, here's your boxed macaroni and cheese and pizza coupons," I say, and he laughs.

"Yeah, really. That should be part of the orientation." He focuses on cutting his meat, quietly, then asks, "So, are you dating anyone now?"

My stomach clenches at the hint of interest in his voice and manner. What the hell is going on? Brady is 24 years younger than I am; I dated his uncle. Surely that makes, what I cannot help conjuring up in the back of my mind like an endlessly looping porn film, somehow wrong.

"Um, no. No one special," I say as I tuck into my own steak, and we fall silent as we both eat.

Later, I drop Brady off at his dorm and hand him a card with my various phone numbers listed, "Here. If you need something, give me a call OK? I know it's tough to be so far away from your family."

He leans down into the car and smiles at me as he slides the card into the back pocket of his jeans. I envy that card for a brief moment, tucked so close to the firm swell of his ass, then turn my attention back to his bright, hazel eyes.

"Thanks for dinner, Mike. It made the game a lot more special knowing you were watching. I'll talk to you soon."

"Take it easy, Brady."

I watch him take the steps to his dorm three at a time and imagine those long, strong legs wrapped around my waist, imagine driving my cock into his tight, willing ass faster and faster.

Shaking myself from the fantasy, I shift into Drive and head for my apartment. The moment I let myself in the door I begin to strip and move right to the bedroom. My cock is at full mast, precum dribbling down the pulsing shaft. I lie back on the comforter, wrap my hand around my aching dick and begin to stroke furiously. Images of Brady's young, strong body flip through my mind as I reach down with my left hand and stretch my balls out between my legs. I can see Brady's tight, pale ass cheeks spread wide as I bury my face between them, my mouth and tongue working over his throbbing anus then flash to his hard, strong cock, standing tall and proud over his dark red bush. Runners of my spit glide along the length to pool on his balls and in his pubes as I suck him hard and fast. My cock, in turn, is stuffed in Brady's mouth, his full lips clamped tight around it as I thrust into his throat, fucking his face.

I grunt as my balls fire off their pent up load and cum splatters over my flat, hairy belly and up to my broad chest. I squeeze the slick, fat head of my cock, milking the last few drops of my spunk from the slit.

Afterwards, I stand beneath the hot spray of the shower and try to stop thinking about Robert's nephew, focusing instead on the pile of paperwork I brought home with me on Friday. The trick works; my erection fades and I turn off the water, determined to get my mind off Brady.

A few weeks later, I find myself staring at the calendar in disbelief. Good God, how did it get to be the Tuesday before Thanksgiving already? I've been consumed by work and have not had a chance to attend any more of Brady's games. I have called his dorm room a few times, left a couple of messages on his voicemail and received messages back from him, but we have not yet been able to connect. As I contemplate the image of another Thanksgiving dinner spent eating alone in a restaurant and maybe going to see a movie by myself, I keep thinking of Brady. The kid has to be lonely this time of year. He's away from his family, his old friends. True, he has new friends, but most college kids go home for Thanksgiving to be with their families, unless their families live thousands of miles away.

I shake my head as I open my address book, pick up the phone and dial his number. This is ridiculous. He's going to have plans already, and I'm going to appear to be a pathetic and lonely old man, which, apparently, I have become.

"Yo, Brady here, bust me a rhyme."

Thinking it is the voicemail again, I pause and wait for the beep.

"Hello?" It's his voice, questioning but friendly.

"Oh, Brady?" I stammer. "It's Mike. Mike Nelson."

"Hey, big Mike! How's it going?"

The kid sounds excited to hear from me and the tone of his voice lends me courage. "I'm well, thanks. Look, I know it's short notice, but I just realized this Thursday is Thanksgiving and I wanted to check and see if you had made any dinner plans. I thought I might whip us up something if you didn't have anything else going on."

"Oh wow, that would be great," Brady replies. "That's so cool of you to invite me over. All I had to look forward to was cafeteria food, and 'look forward to' is really a euphemism for 'Oh dear God, please let me die now,' you know?"

We both laugh, then he tells me he'll grab a cab or a bus over and not to worry about picking him up. I give him my address and tell him I'll supply all the food then hang up, simultaneously cursing myself and looking forward to Thanksgiving.

Thanksgiving morning I start to make dinner. I don't normally cook a lot, being single makes it tough, but I'm no slouch in the kitchen. I lather a 10 pound turkey with butter and seasonings, all the while trying not to imagine Brady himself stretched out on rubber sheets and covered with butter. I busy myself even more, keeping my mind distracted as I whip potatoes, slide the yams in the oven, and cut up bacon for the green beans.

Right at 3:00 p.m., the bell announces Brady's arrival, and I buzz him into the building, popping the hall door open and returning to the kitchen.

"Gobble, gobble," Brady calls, and I turn to take him in. He's the picture of young health, wearing his leather jacket over khakis that fit him like old denim, and a green button down shirt left open to reveal tufts of dark red hair on his chest, the material's color bringing out the green in his eyes.

I swoon a little at the sight of him then smile as innocently as possible. "Hey there, Happy Thanksgiving! Come on in and make yourself at home," I tell him.

Brady drops his jacket on a chair and comes into the kitchen to stand behind me, a hand pressed against my back as he looks down to where I'm cutting celery for appetizers. He places a bottle of wine on the counter and I narrow my eyes at him.

"How did you buy that? You're only 20."

He shrugs and grins, snatching a piece of celery to munch as he looks around at the dishes I've dirtied so far. "I've got my resources. Jesus, did you use every dish in the place?" he asks.

"Not yet," I reply. "But it's on my to do list."

Brady starts rolling up his sleeves and moves toward the sink, "Looks like I'll earn this dinner."

"Hey, Brady, you don't have to do that. I'll clean up later."

Brady shakes his head, "After dinner is for visiting and getting to know the host. I don't want a pile of dishes waiting once the tryptophan from the turkey kicks in."

We work well together in the small kitchen; Brady cleans each dish and utensil and places them in the dish rack to dry as I bustle around him chopping and basting and stirring. I try not to stare too often, but his ass is a thing of beauty snuggled beneath the light khaki material, and I cannot help myself. Once or twice he catches me looking, and I feel myself blush.

"Sorry, it's just that you look so much like Robert," I explain, and he does.

"Yeah, I get that a lot," he says.

Dinner is finally ready, and as Brady is returning the last mixing bowl to its rightful place, I set the turkey on the table and light the candles. He stands beside me, his hand on my back again, and looks at the table setting with shining eyes.

"Mike, this is so great of you," he says quietly. "I've been feeling really lonely out here this year. For some reason, this year is worse than my freshman year."

"Well, don't worry about that today. You're with a friend," I tell him.

He turns to look at me, his face serious, and he says, "Thanks, that means a lot."

I tear my eyes from his and wave him to a chair at the end of the table. "Please, sit. I'll pour us some wine if you'll carve the turkey," I say.

The meal is delicious, more so than I had hoped, and between the two of us we devour the turkey and most of the trimmings. Conversation runs from my job to his classes to the goings on of his family back home, but never once does he mention a girlfriend or, for that matter, a boyfriend.

We leave the dishes to soak in the sink and move into the living room. I light the gas fireplace and several more candles scattered around the room. Brady chooses several classical CDs from my collection and loads them into my player, and we both sit on the soft leather couch.

"So, anyone special in your life?" I ask, ignoring the warning bells going off in the back of my mind.

Brady grins and stares down into his wine glass, "No, not yet."

"Haven't found the right girl?" I ask.

He shrugs, keeping his eyes from me, "Something like that." He's quiet a little longer then says, "It's hard to find the qualities I like in the people around me."

I raise my eyebrows at this, "Oh? Qualities like what?"

"Oh, you know. Stuff like life experience, maturity, personality," He says as he glances at me then darts his eyes away. "Things that most college kids won't have for years."

My cock begins to harden at the ideas running rampant in my mind, and I chug the last of my wine, getting up to pour myself another glass as I say, "Sounds like you're attracted to older women."

"I wouldn't say that exactly, but you're getting warm," he smirks, downs his own wine and holds out his glass for a refill. I turn away to set the wine on the table, and when I turn back he has moved closer to my spot on the couch. Not much closer, but enough that I can tell he has done it.

I sit in my same spot, aware of the waves of heat coming off his strong, fit, youthful body.

"Brady, let me ask you a personal question."

He puts his head back against the cushion and smiles at me, "Sure, ask away."

"Are you gay?"

He is quiet, his eyes staring right into mine, then he nods and looks away, "Yeah. But don't tell my folks or Uncle Robert. They don't know yet. And I'm not ready to tell them."

"You know, it's not such a bad thing," I say.

"Oh, I know, it's just ... they'd have trouble with it at first, and I want to get some more experience under my belt first."

"More experience?" I ask.

He nods, spinning his wine glass slowly in his hand, eyes watching the swirling liquid. "I've fooled around with a few guys, but I've never gone all the way." He looks back at me. "I've been waiting to do that with someone I trust. Someone I care about."

My cock is a raging spike of flesh in my pants, precum leaking into my boxer briefs and threatening to soak through my wool pants. I keep my eyes on Brady's face as I ask, "What are you trying to say, Brady?"

Instead of answering me, he slides quickly across the slick leather cushion, hesitates momentarily, then presses his mouth to mine. The stubble on his jaw scratches across my smooth skin and sends shivers down my spine. His tongue pokes roughly at my lips, begging for access, which I grant him, opening my mouth and taking it in. He groans and leans into me, his big hand falling into my lap where he encounters my rigid cock and gasps.

"Oh fuck," he moans against my mouth, "You're so fucking big and hard. Oh, fuck."

I put my hands on his shoulders and push him back a little, looking him in the eye and ask, "Are you sure you want to do this?"

"Oh yeah," he says in a breathy voice, his pupils dilated and his lips slightly swollen from the force of our kiss. "I've had a crush on you since I was eight."

I shake my head, "I feel like the priest in *The Thorn Birds*," I mutter.

Brady frowns, "Who?"

"Never mind," I say as I lean forward, slowly, and cup his face in my palms. "You are a very attractive and outgoing kid. You could have anyone you want. Why me?"

He shrugs, "Why not?" He places my hand squarely on his straining basket. "Come on, it's OK. I'm not going to change my mind once we start."

I take a breath then lean forward and kiss him, hard. My tongue fills his mouth, wrestles with his own, then eases back over my lips, inviting his in for more. We kiss for a long time, tongues battling back and forth, mouths gasping, practically chewing at each other. I feel the muscles in his back move with his body and then slide my hands around to his chest. Football has filled him out, built up his torso. I unbutton his shirt and run my hands through the dark red hair on his chest, over his square pecs to pinch his small, round nipples. They harden into points, which I tug on as Brady gasps and moans against my mouth.

"Oh, fuck," he says, leaning back to allow my hands to caress him. "That feels really good."

"You've got an amazing body," I tell him, my eyes roving his pale, muscular torso. His stomach is flat and ripped with muscle, the hair narrowing to a happy trail that disappears beneath the waist of his pants. I plant my fingers around his navel and press down to open it up then lean forward, darting my tongue into its salty depths. Brady gasps and lays a large, warm palm on the back of my head as I lick and suck at his navel. I move my mouth slowly up his stomach to his chest where I take each hardened nipple between my lips. I suck them, hard, and tug on them with my teeth as he squirms and moans beneath me.

Brady, meanwhile, has pulled my shirt from my pants and unbuttons it, spreading it open and sliding his hands inside to massage my hairy chest and belly. His fingers twist my nipples, and I grunt against his chest.

"You've got a hot body, Mike," he says. "You must work out."

"Gotta keep the goods in shape, so they can be put on display once in a while," I reply and he laughs.

"Let's go into the bedroom," he suggests. "I want to see you naked."

My mind is no longer screaming for me to stop, throwing up warning klaxons and flashing neon signs. My cock has overridden whatever logic may have existed and guides my body as I push up from the couch, my shirt hanging open. I take Brady's hand and lead him down the hall to the bedroom where I switch on a couple of low watt lamps in the corners and turn back to where he stands beside the bed, still clothed, waiting for me.

"You're gorgeous," I say as I step up to him, my voice quiet and eyes serious.

"Funny, I was just thinking the same thing," Brady replies.

"What, that you're gorgeous?" I murmur, running my tongue around his ear.

He chuckles, "No, that you're gorgeous." His fingers slide beneath my shirt and ease it from my shoulders to fall on the floor. He moves his hands down over my chest and belly, parting the hair before his fingers and stopping to twist my nipples and squeeze my pecs.

I mirror his move, sliding his shirt off and feeling his chest, and lean forward to kiss him, softly at first then more insistently. He wraps his arms around my neck and pulls our bodies together, his hips grinding against mine and pressing his firm cock alongside my own erection.

Unable to take it any longer, I break our embrace and fall to my knees before him. My mouth is dry as I fumble with the buckle on his belt, finally getting it open and undoing the button and zipper on his khakis. His pants fall around his ankles, and I find myself staring at the overflowing pouch of a jockstrap.

"Oh, God," I groan. "That is so fuckin' hot."

"I thought you'd like it," He moves his hips forward, pressing the thin, stuffed cotton against my mouth. "I wore it while I was working out this week. Haven't washed it yet."

"Seems you had this all worked out beforehand?"

"Kinda," he grins.

My own cock jumps as I open my mouth and run my lips and tongue over the sweaty pouch damp with his precum. I bite softly along the length of his dick, pressing my tongue against the straining cotton as I move up and down the shaft. He is at least seven inches long, and thick. I reach the top of his jock and find the fat, bulging head peeking up from beneath the waistband. The smooth, silky skin glistens with precum, inviting me to run my tongue across its surface. Brady groans, pressing his hands against the back of my head.

I peel the waist band of his jock down and release the confined serpent. His cock stands straight up along his belly, almost reaching his navel. The dark red bush around the base spreads out to a thick forest that runs down along his muscular, powerful legs. I stare at the gorgeous dick before me as I reach down to lift each of his feet and pull the jock and his pants off. I then peel off his socks and run my hands along the tops of his large, handsome feet, up along the bulges of his calves, across the hairy expanse of his thighs until they meet at the V in his crotch. I tightly grab hold of his pulsing cock and pull down until it is pointing right at my face. Leaning in, I open my mouth and take him down my throat, tasting the slick of precum left behind along my tongue.

"Oh, fuck," Brady gasps. "You sucked that fucker right down to the root. Oh God."

His hips begin to move, and soon he is fucking my face, his fingers snarled in clumps of my hair. I reach down to free my own cock from its prison of boxer brief cotton and stroke myself as Brady's dick slides in and out between my lips.

He grunts, a deep, animal sound that makes my balls clench with desire, and suddenly my mouth is filled with the sharp taste of his cum. He pulls my face in tight against his body, my nose buried in his sweaty bush, and empties his balls down my throat. I greedily swallow his load, relishing the taste of his spunk as my hand moves faster along my cock.

"Don't cum yet," he gasps. "I want you to cum on my face."

He slowly pulls his cock from between my lips and helps me to my feet. His hands push my pants down, and I step out of them as he leads me to the bed where he stretches out on his back. I kneel on the mattress and position myself over him in push up position, my stiff cock pointing down right over his open, eager mouth. I ease my hips down, and he closes his lips around my shaft, sucking hard as I begin to fuck his face. He reaches up and begins to pull on my nipples, an act that pushes me even closer to the edge of orgasm.

Just as I'm reaching the point of no return, I sit up and back on his chest, pulling my cock from his mouth. He watches as I stroke my dick, slick with his spit, my eyes locked on his. His mouth, full lips wet and parted, is open, ready to take my load, and the sight flips my switch.

"I'm cuming," I moan and feel Brady's hands tighten on my thighs in anticipation. My stroking narrows to the magic spot just beneath the head of my cock, and I aim it down just as the first surge of semen spurts forth. The shot splatters across his cheek and he groans. The rest of my load floods his mouth and halfway through I stuff my cock between his lips, leaning back as he suckles it greedily, eyes closed, fingers gripping my sweaty thighs.

A few minutes go past, and I finally roll off him, reluctantly pulling my dick from his soft, sticky lips. I lie beside him, my arm around his shoulders as he rolls against me, his head on my chest and shoulder in my armpit. We are a perfect fit.

"Do you want to clean up?" I ask through a yawn. The turkey and the sex have ganged up on my middle aged stamina: I am exhausted.

"No, I like the feel of your cum drying on my face," Brady says as he kisses my chest and reaches down to squeeze my softened cock, releasing the last few drops of clear fluid up out of it.

We fall asleep like that and lie peacefully until I awake with a start several hours later. The room is darker, the sun has set by now, and I look down at Brady's soft, unlined face, so young, so open and calm in sleep. He stirs a little, and his eyes blink open, confused for a moment until he raises his head and sees me, then he smiles broadly and my heart jumps in my chest.

"Hi," he says, running his tongue over his teeth. "How long were we asleep?"

"A while," I say vaguely. "Want to take a shower?"

He nods and follows me into the bathroom. I have a large, glassed in shower with two shower heads and a built in bench along the side. We step beneath the hot spray and take turns lathering each other up. His large hands, so nimble with the football, are soft and find all the right places to get me hard again.

I turn him to face away from me and run soap over his wide shoulders, down the ridges of his spine and over the round, tight mounds of his ass. I nudge the pulsing wrinkle of his anus with a soapy finger and Brady immediately lifts a foot to the bench, opening his ass cheeks and allowing me access to his asshole. With slow, delicate movements, I slide my index finger into him and watch as he tips his head back, the hot water bouncing off his firm chest.

"Oh, yeah," Brady groans. "Get it in deep."

I oblige, fucking his ass with my index finger as I reach up to turn his face so I can kiss him. We stay that way for several minutes, my finger pumping into his ass while our tongues grapple together between our mouths.

"I want you to fuck me," he sighs. "I want your dick to be the first one inside me."

Eager to satisfy his request and my fantasy, I switch off the water and grab two towels. We kiss as we dry off, our hands straying to touch, fondle, squeeze each other. My eyes devour the sight of his muscular, long limbed body as my cock twitches and leaks precum.

Bob Condron

Brady drops to his knees to suck my cock deep for a moment, licking it clean of precum. He gets to his feet, kisses me, then leads me back to the bed.

"What do you want me to do?" he asks, his eyes glowing.

I do not hesitate to tell him "Lie on your back and raise your legs."

He follows my orders, and I lean down to feast on his tender, virgin asshole. My fingers spread his anus to allow my tongue admission to the hot, damp darkness hidden behind his beautiful rosebud. I lick and suck, spitting into the reddened opening and slipping one, two, then three fingers into him.

"God damn," Brady groans, turning his head side to side. "Get those fingers up inside me. Yeah, that's it."

"Ready for something bigger?" I ask, my voice deep with longing.

"Give it to me," he says and looks up at me. "I want your cock in me. I've fantasized about this for years."

I don't need any more convincing. I grab a condom from the nightstand and roll it onto my throbbing prick then squirt a large helping of lube across it. I pull Brady to the edge of the bed and take hold of his ankles, pushing them back over his head to lift his hips and bring his asshole up to the height of my crotch. Brady reaches down to take hold of my cock, wraps his fingers around its girth for a moment before directing it to the spit slippery threshold of his body.

I take it slow, pressing firmly into him for a few moments then pulling back, feeling his body gradually relax around my invading member. Brady keeps his eyes on my face and concentrates on loosening the muscles in his rectum as I slide slowly in and out of his hole.

"Does that feel OK?" I ask.

"Yeah, it feels good. Go deeper," he replies.

I press harder on my next thrust and stop three quarters of the way inside him at a muscular blockade. Brady gasps and closes his eyes then laughs a little.

"Sorry, I guess I wasn't ready," he says.

I pull back, the head of my cock just inside his sphincter, and ask, "Ready now?"

He nods and closes his eyes as his fingers tighten their grip on his legs just above the knees and says, "Yeah. Drive that fucker in."

Slowly, very slowly, I penetrate his spreading sphincter. His rectal muscles part before the rounded head of my cock, and with a last, deep push, I am embedded completely within him.

"Oh, fuck," he says. "You are fucking huge. Oh, God!"

I pull back and begin to fuck him, my hips starting slow but picking up speed until I find myself banging his ass like some kind of porn star. Sweat flies from my forehead, and I watch his balls bounce with each of my thrusts. Brady takes the brunt of my fucking with his mouth gaping open, eyes closed, hard cock bumping up and down along his flat belly.

"Oh, God," he moans. "You're fucking the cum right out of me. Oh, fuck."

I look down to watch as his dick jumps and cum sprays up to his chest. He has not touched himself; his hands are still clasping his legs. The sight of his hands-free cum shot gets me going, and I throw back my head to groan as I plow deep between his round, pale ass cheeks and blow my load into the condom buried high up inside his ass.

I lean my head against his leg as we catch our breath then slowly pull out of him. His asshole is red, gaping, and I hold his legs up to watch it slowly close as I peel off the condom. Brady finally lowers his legs and pulls me down on top of him, his cum and our sweat mixing together. We kiss for a long, slow time, and then he runs his hands through my hair and smiles up at me.

"Happy Thanksgiving, Mike."

I laugh and kiss him, "Happy Thanksgiving, Brady." I get up and lead him back into the bathroom where we shower quickly. Afterwards, I loan him one of my terry cloth bathrobes, and we sit on the floor by the fire eating pumpkin pie with real whipped cream.

"Thanks for inviting me over for dinner," Brady says around a mouthful of pie. "My bird really needed to be stuffed. I can't wait to do it again."

I shake my head and grin at him, "Are you sure you want to pursue this?"

He nods and sets his plate aside then gets up off his knees and walks to me, untying his robe to expose his erection and says, "Oh yeah. I'm sure."

I open my mouth and start to suck his cock once more, trying to remember the last time I'd gone back for thirds at Thanksgiving.

Summer of Truth
Michael Rivers

My last test of the semester was in psychology. As a psychology major, three of my five classes were in this area. By semester's end I had had enough of Freud and his friends. I was ready for summer.

After turning in my test, I went back to my dorm. Earlier that day, my roommate and I had finished packing up our room. My car was already loaded, and the only thing left of mine was my backpack and a duffel bag. My roommate was still taking his final test so I ripped out a page of my notebook and scribbled him a quick note, "Hope the test went well. Talk to you this summer. Have fun. Sean."

I grabbed my duffel bag and backpack and headed to my car. Putting on my sunglasses, I picked out a CD, turned up the volume, and started my four-hour drive home. My singing voice, at least so I thought, blended perfectly with the sounds coming from the speakers.

Yes, I was ready for summer.

"SEAN!" my mom smiled as she ran out of the house to hug me. "I'm so glad you're home."

Mom always acted like it had been years since she'd seen me. Her actions showed how much she loved me.

"How did the tests go?" she asked, hugging me tightly.

"Hoping for all A's again."

"Great," she beamed. "Let's grab your stuff and then you can clean up. I'm making your favorite dinner and dessert."

"Sounds good, I'm starving." This was another of Mom's traits. During the first few days of any vacation she felt the need to feed me nonstop. I'm not sure she believed I ever ate at school. I ate everything she cooked because it made her so happy.

We unpacked my car and put the boxes in my bedroom. It always felt so weird going back to my old room for the summer. I felt so independent at college, but moving back into Mom's house every summer made me feel less grown up. It wasn't a bad feeling, just the childlike security of being in a parent's home.

Mom went downstairs to finish dinner and I started to clean up. After stepping out of the shower, I wiped the steam from the full-length mirror and looked at myself. I did a few bodybuilder poses then laughed. My five foot, ten inch frame was looking fit. A semester of light weight-training class plus a swimming class had given me the lean definition I wanted.

As the towel rubbed each part of my physique, I made observations: My blonde hair was cut short on the sides but longer and spiked on top. The previous year I had gotten contact lenses, so my blue eyes were no longer hidden behind glasses. My chest was naturally smooth, and my legs had a light covering of hair.

I stared at the reflection of my dick; I loved the way it hung after a warm shower — long and relaxed. Giving it a few gentle strokes, it started to respond. Looking at my body, my hand holding my hardness, made me feel so grown up. At 21, I was starting to fill out, to look more like a man. My hand continued working my erection, my eyes transfixed on the mirror's image.

"Dinner's ready," Mom called up the stairs.

This broke my concentration. I got dressed and headed down to the wonderful smells coming from the kitchen. Roast beef, mashed potatoes, green beans, fresh baked bread, and apple pie. Over dinner Mom quizzed me about the semester and then caught me up on everything that had been happening in her life.

"The hospital is the same. Nothing changes there," she explained. "Too many patients and more cutbacks." Mom was a registered nurse and even though she complains about the corporate functioning of health care, she loved it. Taking care of people was what she enjoyed most.

I was four when my parents divorced after my dad was caught having an affair. After the divorce, Mom decided to go back to school and get her nursing degree. Mom finished college, got hired at the hospital, and bought us a small two-bedroom home. Now she was nursing supervisor in the intensive care unit. I don't see my dad too often. He remarried shortly after the divorce, and his new family started to play a bigger role in his life. He lived three states away.

"Grandma wants to see you on Saturday," Mom said, putting another piece of apple pie on my plate. "And Mr. Carlson is excited to see you, too."

"Geez, Mom, he's been our neighbor for 13 years; I think you can call him Paul."

She laughed, "I never have, have I?"

"Nope."

Paul — Mr. Carlson, lived next door. He was the first person in the neighborhood to introduce himself. I remember standing by the moving van when he came out of his house and walked up to us. His jeans and T-shirt were blotched with a variety of paint colors. Small patches of blue paint were on his arms and hands. A little was on his forehead.

"Hello, I'm Paul Carlson, nice to meet you," he said shaking my mom's hand.

"Hello, Mr. Carlson. I'm Jean Wilson. This is Sean."

"Hey buddy," he said shaking my hand. "Welcome to the neighborhood. If you need anything, let me know. I'm off to work now, but I'll be glad to help whenever I can."

"Thank you," Mom said. "I'll let you know."

I watched Paul walk over to a pickup that had the words "Carlson Construction and Painting" airbrushed on the side. He got in and drove off.

Mom and I switched our attention back to the moving boxes, not realizing what a good friend Paul would become over the years. My best memory of that day was the first time Mom and I walked into our house. She started to cry because she had done it by herself. "We're home," I remember her saying so proudly.

At first Mom called Paul only in a professional way. There were a few minor things in the house that needed fixing, and he was always happy to help: some tile in the kitchen, a pipe in the bathroom, a piece of molding in the living room. Mom always insisted on paying him, on calling him Mr. Carlson.

Whenever Paul worked on things in our home, he asked me to help. "Next time you can fix it," he always teased, placing a hand on my head and messing up my hair. I liked spending time with him. Paul was my main interaction with an adult male, and he never talked down to me. He would explain what he was doing as if I fully understood. When asking me to hand him a hammer, wrench, screwdriver or tape measurer, he made it seem as if it were vital that I was there helping him.

After living in the house for several months, Mom finally invited Paul over for a social dinner. When he left, we began doing the dishes.

"You should date Paul," I said, taking the last of the dirty plates to the sink.

"What?" Mom asked, swinging around and looking at me. "Why would you say that?"

"He's 26," I said.

"I'm twenty-seven."

"That's not too young for you, and he's a cool guy," I said.

"Yes, he's very nice, but that doesn't mean I should date him," Mom said.

"Don't you want someone?" I asked.

"I don't have time for that now," she answered.

"Dad remarried," I said.

"Sean, I have no interest in dating Mr. Carlson. Don't be silly. We're friends and that's it."

"But don't you think he's ..." I continued.

"Drop it," she interrupted.

Looking back, I think she was afraid of getting close to a man again. She wanted to protect herself. Not get hurt. She'd rebuilt her life without a man's help. I never again brought up her dating Paul. It made her too uncomfortable.

Instead, Paul's friendship became a constant over the next 13 years, a fixture in our lives. And I was always excited to see him. It was a ritual to stop by his house on my first day back. This summer was no different. After finishing my mom's dinner, I told her I was going over to say hi to Paul before it got too late. I was tired from the endless studying, final exams, the long car drive, and wanted to get to bed early.

I cut across the grass like I had for years and jumped onto his front porch. The jump became less and less difficult as each year had passed. Now, I could almost step up onto the porch with no effort. I pressed the doorbell and waited for Paul to answer.

"Sean, welcome home," he smiled.

"Hey old man."

"Who are you calling an old man?" he laughed, hugging me, giving my back a few strong pats. "I'm 29, you little shit. I've got lots of good years in me yet."

"I know, I know," I smiled. "You look great."

"So do you; college agrees with you. Come in."

"How's the business going?" I asked as we entered the living room.

"Things are going great. The business continues to grow. I have seven people working full-time."

"Cool. I figured you were doing well. I saw the new pickup out front," I said.

"A treat to myself. Makes me get out and work now and then," he said.

"Keeps you out of trouble, huh?"

"Right," Paul laughed. "Speaking of trouble, do you want to help me out tomorrow? I could finish up a job early and then we can catch up."

"Gee, thanks. I've been here five minutes, and you're already putting me to work," I said.

"Hey, it would be like old times."

"Sure," I agreed. "I'm spending Saturday with my grandma, otherwise I don't have much planned the next couple days."

The next morning I helped Paul finish his project as planned. It felt great to be working beside him again. We conversed about old times, what was going on currently, and future plans.

"Want to come over for a bit?" he asked as we climbed into his truck. "We can eat lunch, drink some beers and checkout the TV."

"Sure, why not. I'm meeting up with Randy and David for a movie later tonight, but I'm free until then," I answered.

"That is...if you don't mind hanging out with an 'old man.'"

"You're only thirty-nine, remember," I said.

"To a 21-year-old, that must seem ancient."

"Naw. Not at all. But after you turn 40, that will be completely different," I assure him.

"I have a college smart-ass on my hands."

"You know it!" I said.

We drove back to Paul's house. The air conditioning felt so refreshing against our sweaty skin. "You can shower first," Paul said, pointing to the bathroom. "I'll dig out some clothes for you."

"OK," I said. Taking off my dirty clothes, I piled them in a corner. Then I stepped under the warm spray of the shower and let out a slow sigh. The water felt great flowing down my skin. I was soaping up my body when I heard Paul's voice on the other side of the shower curtain.

"Sean, here's a fresh towel and also a pair of my sweatpants."

"Thanks," I said sticking my head around the shower curtain. "I'll be done in a few minutes."

"Take your time," he said.

I finished showering and dried off. Doing my habitual mirror check, I noticed that I was already starting to get a tan. A blond-haired, blue eyed, tanned college guy would be a hit at the bar that weekend. I smiled at the thought and pulled on the sweatpants.

"All yours," I said, walking into the living room.

"About time. I thought I'd have to come in after you," Paul laughed, getting up from the couch. "I put a frozen pizza in the oven. By the time I'm finished, it should be almost done."

"Sounds good; I'm starving."

"Be right back," Paul smiled and then patted my back.

I dropped onto the couch and grabbed the remote control. After deciding on a TV channel, I picked up the magazines that Paul kept beside the couch. My attention was divided between glancing at the TV and the magazines, but as I flipped to the forth magazine my attention froze. My eyes could not move from the cover. In my hands was a copy of Hard — a magazine that reviewed new releases of gay porn videos. I purchased issues of the same magazine at the adult bookstore near campus.

In the lower right-hand corner was a mailing label with Paul's name and address. I opened the magazine and my eyes were flooded with images of hot men sucking, jerking, licking and fucking. I was shocked. I almost felt panicked, like I should run out of the house and never return.

Paul was gay.

My god — Paul was gay.

Why hadn't I seen it? I had known him for 13 years. Why didn't I realize it? Since starting college my gaydar had developed to a point where I could sit in class and figure out who was gay and who wasn't with ease. What had blocked me from seeing this? Or didn't I want see to see it? My mouth got dry and my palms started to sweat as I flipped through the pages.

"I smell pizza," Paul said, walking into the living room. I quickly dropped the magazines back onto the floor. Paul noticed the sound and glanced beside the couch.

"Smells good to me," I answered. "It must be done."

"Um…yeah…we better check it," he said slowly.

We went into the kitchen and sat at the table, finding myself looking at Paul in a way I never had before. He was only wearing jeans and as he bent over to get the pizza out of the oven, I realized how well he filled them out. He was six feet tall and had the kind of body acquired only through manual labor. His years of landscaping, painting and construction had kept him in great shape. The time spent outdoors had given his skin a nice glow. His slightly receding brown hair was cut close to his head, and he had a very light dusting of chest hair.

The man was handsome.

Why hadn't I ever noticed all this? Why hadn't I noticed the deep brown color of his eyes? Why hadn't I noticed his lips? I did suddenly notice that I had a pulsing erection hiding in Paul's sweatpants, however.

"Here you go," he said, placing a plate in front of me.

"Thanks," I said unable to look him in the face. I was certain that I was blushing

"We got a lot accomplished today," he said.

"Yeah, we did. Not much left to do," I answered.

"Want to finish it tomorrow afternoon?" he asked.

"Sure," I answered.

We made small talk while eating and when we were finished Paul asked, "Do you want to watch a movie?"

"No," I said, hoping that I hadn't responded too quickly. "I better take a nap before tonight."

"OK. Let me get your clothes," he said.

Paul went into the bathroom and put my dirty clothes into a plastic bag. "You can bring back the sweatpants tomorrow," he said.

"Will do," I said, holding the bag in front of my waist. Standing close to him was making my dick grow again, and I didn't want him to notice. My mind was full of thoughts that I tried to ignore. What would our bare chests pressed together feel like? How well would he kiss? His hands looked so strong; how would they feel, touching me?

"Have fun tonight with your friends," he said.

"I will," I answered as I left.

Leaving Paul's house, I ran home, went right to my bedroom and locked the door. An uncontrollably urge to masturbate had overcome me. I pulled down Paul's sweatpants and my erection sprang free. Climbing onto my bed, I reached into my nightstand for a bottle of lube. I squeezed the lube into my hand and massaged it onto my erection, loving the feeling of my palm sliding up and down its length.

I closed my eyes and tried to pull images of guys from my fantasies, but the only one that would come was Paul's: his white smile, his brown eyes, his toned body, strong hands ... his chest ...

My hand worked faster and faster until I heard my own breathing, until I felt my warm orgasm landing high up on my chest — almost onto my neck.

The moment was over, but I was scared to open my eyes and come back to reality.

I had just fantasized about Paul.

The next afternoon I was supposed to be at Paul's, so we could finish the painting job. For the first time, I was nervous about going to his house but knew that I could not act any different. I was gay. He was gay. But we'd never confided it to each other. Part of me wanted to run over and tell him. It would be so wonderful to finally be my true self around him.

Another part of me was afraid to tell him — as I had always been. Why tell him now? Just because I'd found out he was gay too? What if he accused me of invading his privacy? He obviously didn't want me to know or he would have told me.

I put on some jeans and a T-shirt, grabbed Paul's sweatpants and headed over to his house. "Hey, Sean," Paul said, opening the door.

"Here are your sweatpants," I said.

"Thanks," he said, taking them from my hand. Our fingers touched in the same way my fingers touch Jayson's at the gas station; I was unsure if they touched by accident or if I'd done it on purpose.

Daddy's Boyz

"Ready to go finish the job?" I asked.

"Yeah...but first I want to talk to you about something," he replied. "Let's go into the living room."

I followed him in. My mouth got dry. "OK. What did you want to talk about?" I ask.

"We both know you saw my magazine yesterday."

"Yeah," I mumbled, suddenly feeling like a teenager in trouble, my cheeks turning red.

"I thought so," he said.

"Sorry for going through your things. I didn't mean to look at your stuff. I was just trying to find something to read before we ate. I won't go through your ..."

"Sean, it's OK," Paul laughed, placing a calming hand on my shoulder. "I wanted to apologize for putting you in an uncomfortable situation. I shouldn't have left it out. I'm sorry," he said.

"I ... wasn't uncomfortable. I just didn't know what to do," I answered.

"Well, I'm sorry; it won't happen again."

"Why didn't you ever tell me?" I asked.

Paul was quiet and then finally asked, "Why haven't you ever told me?"

Now I was the quiet one and asked, "So you know I'm gay?"

"Sean, I've known since you were a teenager. I guess that's part of the reason I never told you. I never wanted you to feel uncomfortable around me, to run away from me. You had to be comfortable with yourself first."

My vision got blurry with tears. "I was so confused. I didn't know what I was. I was afraid to ask questions. I didn't know what people would think of me. I didn't know if people would still like me," I said.

"I know," Paul said. "We all go through it at some point." He grabbed me and hugged me tight. "It's OK."

I embraced him just as strongly, and it was the first time I realized that we were now almost the same height.

For years, I had looked up at his face; now I was eye level with him. He hadn't changed much. There were a few lines around his eyes, some on his forehead, and a little less hair, but otherwise he had remained the same.

"You've grown up so much," Paul whispered. "You're not that eight-year-old boy anymore."

I nodded. "Thanks for always being there. I could always trust you. Maybe this is why."

Our stare continued. At the same moment we both leaned forward and our lips touched for the first time. Soft. Warm. We stayed that way for a few seconds and then parted.

"Are you OK?" Paul asked.

"Yeah."

Paul smiled slightly and then leaned forward again. We started to kiss with more intensity but it remained slow and deliberate. Pulling our bodies closer together, I felt our erections growing and pressing against each other through our jeans. My heart was pumping blood at a fast rate.

Paul broke our embrace again. "Are you sure you're OK?"

I nodded and glanced down at the obvious tent in his pants. I wanted more of him, so I leaned in again for another kiss. Then, I placed my lips on his neck, hearing him sigh as he held me close.

"I want you to be comfortable," he whispered. "Don't do anything you don't want to do."

"I won't," I smiled. This should have seemed so weird, so wrong. But it felt so right. I was dizzy. How was this happening? We had barely done anything, and already it was my most romantic experience. Previous experiences that had seemed so intense now did not. I had two college friends that I'd hooked up with often. There was Patrick — the closeted guy on the basketball team. And there was Curtis — a music education major. These friends brought me great intimacy. Then there were the typical one-night stands. I won't deny these were all hot sexual experiences because they were. But what was happening with Paul was completely different.

There was meaning behind it. Being held in the arms of someone who cared deeply for me, someone for whom I felt the same way. Kissing lips that kissed back with real emotion was so different: full, not empty, knowing, not anonymous, caring, not indifferent. A real person, not an object.

Paul's hands started to rub my body and I followed his actions. It felt so natural, like our hands were feeling what they had secretly known about for years. I took initiative and removed

Paul's shirt. He did the same to me and pulled our bare skin together. The feel of my smooth chest mixing with the light hair covering of his inspired thousands of goose bumps to surge over my entire body. After kissing again and again, our lips naturally moved to each other's chests and nipples.

I felt Paul's fingers at the snap of my jeans. As he got down onto his knees, he pulled my jeans to my ankles. He then kissed my erection, which was still covered by my blue boxer briefs. My pulsing length was begging to be released from the constraints of the fabric. Paul put his fingers under the waistband and slowly pulled down my underwear. My erection felt cool in the free air.

Paul reached out and took my length in his hand. I jumped at the feel of his fingers wrapping around my hardness. He looked up at me. I nodded down at him, letting him know it was OK. He nodded back then gazed at my erection. I watched as it slowly disappeared into Paul's mouth.

The warm wetness moving along my hardness sparked a rhythmic pleasure. My eyes closed and my head leaned back. Paul reached up with one hand and laced his fingers into mine. I squeezed his hand tightly, letting him know how much pleasure he was giving me. Paul responded by sucking with more drive, and my legs started to shake. I was close to climax and my moans signaled this to Paul. He moved my hands to the back of his head and put his hands on my butt. His palms pressed me deeper into his mouth and my hands matched his motion accordingly.

My breathing became more rapid. "I'm close…I'm close…"

Paul didn't break his speed.

"I'm close," I warned again.

Paul didn't stop.

I couldn't hold out anymore and forcefully released my orgasm into his mouth. Screaming out, I braced my hands on Paul's shoulders to prevent from collapsing onto the floor.

Paul stood up and pulled me close. He started kissing me, passing my fluid back and forth between our mouths. I felt high, as if I'd taken a powerful drug. I hungrily kissed him back, never wanting the feeling to end.

We finally stopped kissing and Paul reached up and took my chin into his hand. We smiled at each other, and I felt for the snap on his jeans. Paul stopped me.

"What?" I asked. "I want to please you, too."
"You already have," he said.
"But I want to give you what you gave me."
"Next time," Paul smiled.

Hired Hand
Mark Wildyr

Spring is a busy time on the farm — nature's birthing season — so I was looking at dawn-to-midnight days. I'd counted on hired help to do the land preparation while I took care of selecting my bean seed as well as tending the animals. I put out the word I was looking for reliable help, but since half the countryside was looking for the same thing, I didn't hold out much hope.

Salvation arrived in the form of a slender, sandy-haired kid a couple of days later, but I didn't recognize it as such right off the bat. Still, the lad was a warm body, so I climbed down off the tractor and mopped a thick film of dust from my face with a bandana. I was working two gangs of chisels behind a row of 22 disks, and the sun was climbing fast. I can't disk when the dirt gets too hot, so my mood wasn't the best, and it showed.

"What can I do for you, young fella? Spit it out! I've got a lot of chiseling left to do," I asked.

The kid's Adam's apple bobbed a couple of times before any sound came out. When it did, it made me take a closer look. It was a man's deep baritone. "You … you can give me a job," he stammered, taking a step backward as if rebuffed by my gruffness. "I heard in town you were looking for help," he added a bit more firmly.

"Me and everybody else in the township," I muttered. "What's your name?"

"Lonnie. Lonnie Hydrack."

"You got any experience?"

"Uh-huh," he replied. "Plenty."

There are a few times in a man's life when he experiences an epiphany. Lonnie Hydrack asking for a job was one in my life, although it took awhile to understand that. An unpolished gem, well-grounded in the basics on his uncle's farm, he brought some welcome experience in irrigation practices. His true genius lay in working with animals. Even the meanest sows, trailing strings of piglets, followed him around the farrowing house like friendly puppy dogs. The boy knew how to strip and repair a gearbox better than most professional mechanics, but operating the equipment was something else. On his first try, he left so many rabbit tracks, I made him disk the field again. Missed spots, like weeds in a field, are signs of a poorly run farm.

But once shown something, Lonnie fixed it in his mind and rarely had to be told again. He never complained about the hours, the dirt, mucking out a barn, or even the Crock-Pot sausage and sauerkraut that was our staple for lunch in the field. He just plugged his ears with the headphone from a Walkman radio, set it at a C&W station, and went to work. In short, he was simpatico, as they say in these parts.

I'll never forget the jolt I got that first day when, having worked up a sweat, he peeled off his sodden work shirt. He was a deceptive youth. He'd seemed thin and kind of small when I'd first looked down on him from the tractor seat, but stripped to the waist, he revealed a solid physique with powerful shoulders and arms, narrow hips and lean belly. The kid had an open, honest face saved from being pretty by a small Z-shaped scar on his cheek below the left eye. His smooth skin rippled with muscles that weren't evident in his clothing.

Yet I knew without doubt that here stood the potential for disaster — even destruction and ruin. This handsome, innocent-looking, eager-to-please young man was as much a danger to me as I was to him. My heart and my head counseled caution. But the overriding concern was that I needed help during the busy spring season. Plenty of time to let him go when the crop was in the ground and the calves had dropped, I told myself. All it required was steely self-discipline on my part for all to be well.

Many times over the next few months, I was to silently curse that handsome youth for being such a pleasant, hard-working soul. He woke up slowly and tended to be non-communicative early in the morning, but other than that, he was a paragon. We worked hard all day, him at his chores and me at mine, once I grew to trust him. At night we cleaned up, ate, watched the news and weather on my satellite TV system, and turned in for a sound night's sleep. He was shy but pleasant company. My respect and liking for him grew despite my unspoken determination to send him packing as soon as possible.

Daddy's Boyz

Lonnie didn't once go into town in the evenings after work or on the rare day off. He even remained behind to tend the animals when I drove into town for church on Sundays. About a month after he first came, I found myself sitting in a pew, fidgeting through the sermon, and instead of taking my seat again after Communion, I walked right out the door and climbed into my pickup. I couldn't explain it to you, but it seemed important to be with Lonnie. Twenty miles straight down the road, I pulled into the barn, which served as my garage, and checked the farrowing house. Lonnie was nowhere in sight. He'd already finished his chores.

I entered the house by the kitchen door and stopped dead in my tracks. The boy lolled naked on the living room couch, his hand holding a fist full of thick, hard cock. His eyes were closed as he slowly beat his meat. He'd just started, hadn't even found his rhythm yet. I stood and watched shamelessly, taking in all the delicious details. His hard, ridged belly heaved from his efforts. The thick, flat pads of his smooth, hairless pecs rolled as he pumped himself faster and faster. The crown of his cock appeared and disappeared beneath its sheath of loose foreskin. The tip of his tongue played across his lower lip. His big toes slowly curled and uncurled as he worked toward orgasm. The fat balls jiggled as he moved.

Suddenly aware of my own reaction, I tried to back away, but was frozen. My cock hardened. My nipples rose and tingled with an itch that demanded scratching, but I was afraid to move. Afraid he would see me. Afraid to interrupt the beautiful, erotic scene. Afraid I wouldn't see him spill his precious seed. Afraid.

Working faster, Lonnie gave a series of small "huhs," and stiffened. His feet arched downward, his thighs opened slightly. His belly took a dive toward his spine. His eyes came half-open, and that mighty cock swelled with the passage of his semen. He spurted a white arc that reached his chin. The second was even stronger, splattering his cheek. Successive gushes marched down his torso until finally, the thick viscous fluid simply oozed out of the end of his engorged cock. With a sigh, he opened his eyes, swiped at his cheek, and looked down at the puddles of come on his torso. As he reached for his towel, I ducked out of sight, but a loose floorboard gave me away.

"Is ... is somebody there?" The fear in his voice was palpable.

I opened the kitchen screen and let it bang. "Lonnie?" I called loudly. You here?"

There was a sudden, frantic scrambling before he answered me from the bathroom at the back of the house. "Mr. Fellner? That you? You're back early."

"Yeah," I said and grabbed a cookie off the stove by way of delay before strolling into the other room. I was rewarded by a small dollop of semen on the back of the couch. I swept it up on my index finger. The tangy, erotic taste almost cost me my self-control.

A moment later, I heard the cistern flush and water running in the sink before he came into the room in a pair of denim cutoffs and an unbuttoned cotton shirt. A slightly guilty look was on his face.

"Don't you think you can drop the Mr. Fellner and call me Zip?"

"Zip?" he asked, wrinkling his nose, seductively. "What kind of name is that?"

"Mine. Actually, it's Zachariah, but when I was a kid I beat up anyone who called me Zachariah or Zach. So somebody came up with Zip, and it stuck."

He smiled. "Zip. I like that. It's all right to call you that?"

"It's mandatory you call me that."

It took another two months to realize what was happening. Ever since I discovered how he relieved his sexual tension, I dawdled after church on Sunday to give him some precious privacy. To be honest, I knew that if I walked in on him again, I'd lose control. So I drove the back roads over my farm every Sabbath and masturbated in a grove of cottonwoods out of sight of the house. But it wasn't working; the pressure, the need for physical human contact, built inside me. I caught myself watching the boy and fantasizing over the line of his tanned jaw, the curve of his chest, the lean sturdiness of his thighs, and that full basket. I became the watcher in the woods. And it was driving me crazy.

The time to let him go came and went. The crops were in and growing satisfactorily. The calves were on the ground and thriving. The workload slackened. And still I could not bring myself to accept the cruel necessity of sending him away. His odd mixture of sweet innocence and physical earthiness prevented me from doing what needed to be done.

It suddenly dawned on me that he had matured in my mind from an incredibly desirable sexual object into a comfortable companion. By merely envisioning him gone, I experienced an ache of loneliness. Who would I share my day with? Who would make shy suggestions about solving some problem or the other? Weed with me? Handle the irrigation gates? Clean out the storage bins? And the equipment! This was the time of year to undertake the major overhaul jobs. So I attended my heart instead of my reason and kept my mouth firmly shut, despite the fact that his presence brought almost as much pain as pleasure.

The boy brought things to a head himself after dinner one night while we were doing the dishes.

"Uh ... Zip."

Something in his tone caused me to turn and look at him. "Yes?"

"I ... I ... uh, think it's time I moved on," he said.

"What?"

He gave a little shrug. "Somebody was saying they're looking for help on the Bryce Farms up near Albuquerque," he continued.

Flabbergasted, I sagged against the sink. "Albuquerque! I thought you liked it here."

"I do!" the boy came back immediately. "But this is a slack time, and you don't really need me. So I thought I'd give Albuquerque a try."

"When?" I asked, bowing to his superior wisdom.

"Soon's I can," he said, hanging his head.

"Finish the week. We need to get the planter overhauled and put away. I want to service the combine and make sure it's ready for the fall. And my pickup needs a tune-up. You can help with those things before you leave, can't you?" I asked.

"Yeah, sure, Zip. I can do that."

"Sorry you aren't happy here, Lonnie."

The boy gave me a look that pierced my heart. "It isn't that, Zip," he said and turned away. Puzzled I watched him go to his room.

Bob Condron

I puttered around for a while longer, but he didn't come out again, so I turned in to spend a long, miserable night tossing and turning. A dozen times I sat on the edge of the bed and fought to keep from going to him. Fear of the consequences kept me from following through.

My fertile farm seemed like a barren desert within minutes of Lonnie Hydrack's departure. I was shocked at the depth of my feeling. Judging from the ache in my gut and the depression that gripped me, he would prove to be more trouble absent than he had been present. Perhaps it was my imagination, but even the animals missed him. One old sow he named Penny chased me out of her pen when she realized I wasn't Lonnie.

Work never ceases on a farm, and that was my salvation. Day by day, my loneliness and self-pity lessened, only to come crashing down again when I'd come home from Church and picture him naked on the couch.

A month after he left, I was still leaking tears and missing him terribly. One Sunday afternoon, the phone rang. I answered it, grateful for the diversion.

"Mr. Lonnie Hydrack is calling collect. Will you accept the charges?"

"What? Yes! Yes, I'll accept them. Lonnie! Are you there?"

A curious hollow echo sang across the wire, and then came that mature voice so out of character in such a young man. "Hello, Zip. Sorry to call you collect, but ... but that's the only way I could call."

"That's OK. Good to hear your voice," I answered, my heart pounding so hard I thought I was having an attack. "How you doing? Get that job?"

"Naw. They already had all the help they needed."

"Sorry. I should have let you go right away," I said.

"Don't worry about it," he said.

A long pause developed. I could hear the banging of metal and male voices in the background. Afraid he would hang up, I blurted out a question.

"So what are you up to? Find another job?" I asked.

"Yeah. Worked on a construction crew," he answered.

"That oughta pay better than farming," I tried to joke, but couldn't quite manage a jocular tone. It came out sort of strangled.

Daddy's Boyz

"Not really. Not after I pay for a place to live and stuff," he said.

"Making new friends? Got a girl yet?" I asked.

There was another pause. "Naw. Met a couple of guys on the job. No girls so far," he said.

His tone was down. My stomach plummeted. "You don't sound right, Lonnie. You wanta come on back? I haven't hired anyone to take your place yet."

"I can't right now, Zip. Maybe soon. I'll let you know. Better go, I guess. Just ... just needed to hear a friendly voice. I really miss you. You know, the farm and all."

"And I miss you. Old Penny won't let me in her pen!" I said.

That brought a half-hearted laugh, interrupted by a loud clang. "Gotta go now, Zip. Somebody else wants to use the phone."

"Wait!" I cried, panicked. "Don't go, Lonnie!

"I gotta ..." he said.

"Don't go yet. Oh, Lonnie, come on back. I ... I love you, man," I said into the phone.

Half sobbing, I paused for an answer, but the line was dead. I don't know if he heard me or not. I don't even know if I wanted him to hear me!

I spent the rest of the afternoon brooding. My mood whipsawed all over the place. One moment, I was glad he was thinking of me, the next I missed him so much my gut felt like it was on fire. He was thinking of me? He missed me? Yeah, but he'd abandoned me, bailed out, left me in the lurch! Fuck him! Who needed him, anyway?

I did.

My subconscious figured it all out and woke me in the middle of the night. Those metallic clangs. Those echoing voices spoken in commanding tones. The boy was in jail! Oh, God! Lonnie was in trouble.

I took care of the animals the next morning, dumping an extra load of slop in Penny's pen to her obvious delight, and then settled down with the telephone. By noon, I'd learned that he was in the Bernalillo County Detention Center, but not much else. A quick trip to town got me a meeting with my lawyer who put me in touch with an Albuquerque attorney named George Festoon. Within a couple of hours, Festoon determined that one Lonnie Hydrack was serving 45 days for drunk and disorderly and fighting. He was doing time because he couldn't pay his $500 fine. In short order, I engaged him to spring my young friend, agreed to meet at his office the next day at noon, and wired the required funds.

    I spent the rest of the day locating someone to cover for me on the farm for the next two days. Four a.m. found me tending the animals and doing the irrigating. I turned the nose of my truck north for the 150-mile drive to Albuquerque far too early, and I had to kill a couple of hours before meeting Festoon. He proved to be a short, plump, bald, good-humored man of about 50. He was also efficient. At two o'clock sharp, a thin, haggard kid with dirty-blond hair walked through the thick, bullet-proof door of the detention center into the reception area. He stopped short at the sight of me. After a moment, he came over to where I stood and accepted my outstretched hand. His throat worked for a moment.

    "Zip! You the one who got me out?" he asked.

    "None other," I said, my heart melting. Here was a young man obviously under stress. For the first time, it occurred to me that I might be the cause of it.

    "I finally figured out what those background sounds were and got Mr. Festoon here to find out what was going on. Drunk? Fighting? Doesn't sound like the Lonny Hydrack I know."

    "Maybe you don't know Lonnie Hydrack," he said in a low voice, drawing a sharp glance from the lawyer.

    "I know him well enough," I said confidently. "Come on, let's go home."

    I could have been riding with a mummy. He claimed he didn't have anything worth the trouble of recovering at the boarding house where he was staying and settled back in the seat to stare out the window, making no protest as I turned south on I-25. When we stopped for something to eat, I had the feeling he wanted to talk, but didn't push him. We had gassed up and hit the highway again before he mumbled something.

    "What?"

    "Aren't you going to ask me why I got in trouble?" he asked.

    "No. If you want me to know, you'll tell me. If you don't then it's none of my business," I answered.

    "From all the money you just laid out, I guess it is your business," he said.

I took the next exit and parked on the frontage road. Turning in the seat, I faced my young friend. His month away from home had not been kind to him. He was thinner and frayed looking.

"I don't want any misunderstanding, Lonnie. I helped out a friend. A good friend. That's all. I didn't ask him if he wanted any help. I just did it. I didn't put him under obligation. You don't owe me a thing. You're free to come back to your job if you want, but you can go back to Albuquerque or El Paso or Timbuktu, if you want to. If you feel any obligation, then there's only one way you can pay me back. Don't ever do this again! That's all I ask." I was reaching for the gearshift when his voice stopped me.

"I was flirting with this guy at a bar, and when he tried to follow it up, I beat his ass. Don't know why. Just did," he recited it in a flat, dead voice.

There wasn't much to say to that, so I held my tongue.

"Did you mean it? What you said?" he asked finally.

"Of course, I meant it. Didn't you know you're my friend?"

He sighed deeply, "Not that! Did you mean what you said over the phone? What you said when I was hanging up?"

My heart skipped a beat and then began thudding. "I usually mean what I say," I hedged.

He looked at me, his eyes sparkling with anger. "Then why didn't you show it? Why'd you leave me in misery all those months? I couldn't take it any longer! I had to get out or else I'd make a ... a fool of myself."

"Oh, Lonnie! What are you saying?"

"Did you mean it!" he insisted.

I closed my eyes and nodded my head. "Every word of it. I love you, Lonnie Hydrack. I think I have from the minute I set eyes on you."

"Then why didn't you say something? Do something?" he asked.

"I was afraid it would happen all over again," I said in a small voice.

"What would happen?"

I took a deep breath and looked him dead in the eye. "Lonnie, there was a guy back home ... good-looking and a real flirt. All the girls were after him. Hell, I wanted a tumble with him, too. And he made it pretty clear he was up for that. So we eventually

Bob Condron

got it together. Suddenly, the guy goes nuts. Claims he didn't know he was gay until then. And he couldn't handle it. That was the Bible belt, and hellfire and damnation was the local religion. He 'repented,' and I got fingered as the local pariah. In the end, I was literally forced to sell and come out west."

"Shit," he breathed softly. "And you thought I was some lame brain like that?"

"I didn't think anything! I just reacted to what happened in the past. Lonnie, I wanted to throw you down in the field that first day … and every day after that, but I couldn't take the chance. I didn't know how you'd react. It was agony, man. Painful to be around you. But not nearly as painful as being away from you. It took a long time for me to admit to myself that I was in love, and that made me even more cautious about doing something you might not like," I told him.

He gave an even deeper sigh, "Man, I got half-hard every time I saw you. I never set foot off the farm, never went into town to see any of the guys … or gals," he said sadly. "I thought you'd make your move sooner or later. When you didn't, I figured I'd worked it out all wrong."

"And I figured you just needed the work," I said.

He took a long time to reply, "I did … but not only. I saw you at the feed store and figured you were about the handsomest man around. Thought maybe you'd get to know me and like me. I … I didn't figure on falling in love with you."

My breath caught in my throat; my hands shook on the wheel. "Did you?"

He hung his head, "Yeah."

"Lonnie, have you ever been with a man?"

He met my gaze and said, "A cousin and I used to get together until my uncle lost the farm and went back to Oklahoma."

"Why didn't you go with them?" I asked.

"Because he took to courting this girl, and things weren't the same after that. He wanted her more than he wanted me. They were planning on getting married," he said.

"I see. Well, what do we do now?" I asked.

"I want to fuck you, Zip," he said simply. "If you'll let me, that is."

"I'll not only let you, Lonnie, but it's mandatory," I answered with a smile as I put the truck in gear and burned rubber. The farmhouse and privacy and blessed intimacy were still a long way down the road.

We didn't make it. I parked out on the desert within sight of the busy Interstate and took his fantastic cock up my butt for the first time. Then I hauled ass getting back home so we could do it again and again.

Saturday Punk
Bob Condron

Larry stuffed his hands deep into his pockets and headed away from Dublin Town center, towards Rathmines. He needed to clear his head. A brisk walk would do the trick. He was 18 years old and in a semi-permanent state of arousal; all sexed up with nowhere to go on a damp Dublin day.

It began spitting rain and the wind was up. At first, he found it bracing, but he quickly began to wish he had brought a hat of one sort or another. His head was shaved, and his skull was beginning to ache with the damp and cold. Still, he kept walking, singing to himself, the B-side of The Clash's *White Riot*. "1977 ... I hope I go to heaven ..." while he was every inch the Saturday punk in his torn school blazer and bondage pants.

He had had no intention of going into Toban Street toilets. None. But there it was just up ahead, set back from the road. The street was deserted but for a van parked opposite. On impulse, he snuck in out of the rain. One man was standing stock still at the stalls. Larry took up position alongside him, undid his fly and stared at the wall straight ahead. No sound of pissing, no movement from either party.

The other guy must have been in his mid-forties, thick set and chunky, with a full, thick beard and moustache. There was nothing manicured about him. A man's man. A Garda? The bearded guy turned his head to the side almost imperceptibly and cast an eye over Larry. Larry paused, not knowing if he should risk making a move. After a moment's hesitation, he bottled out, zipped up and made his escape.

He got no more than ten feet from the exit before looking back. The burly guy had followed him out. Another ten feet, another look. The elder's eyes once again met the younger, so Larry turned around and waited. His pursuer was over like a shot.

"Hello. How are you doing?" The man's eyes now checked Larry out from head to toe while his face split in a big, friendly grin.

"That's not a Dublin accent now?" Larry asked him.

"No. I'm up from the country. You live around here though, do you?" the man asked.

"Yeah ... but not on my own," Larry added quickly.

The man looked up into gray storm clouds. "I've a couple of hours to pass, but the weather looks none too good."

"You're right there. Pity. I've a couple of hours to pass myself. Don't fancy getting cold and wet," Larry said.

The man's eyes danced down to Larry's basket. "Would you like to go for a little drive in my van?"

"You mean now?" Larry asked. Larry waited until the man looked him straight in the eye and nodded, "Sure, why not."

They drove towards the university accompanied by the sound of the engine and, above this, the wipers sweeping drizzle from the windscreen. It gave Larry the opportunity to size up his companion. His hair was cut fairly short but tousled, curly and sandy blond. The hands that clutched the wheel were bigger than average, as were his feet. "Big feet, big meat?" thought Larry, and he smiled to himself. The man wore heavy brown boots, brown corduroy trousers, brown check shirt and had big, brown eyes to match. He put Larry in mind of a woolly mammoth. Big and strong and tough, a throwback to some former time. Yeah, he would do; he would do very nicely.

The campus grounds were quiet on a weekend even at the best of times, but on this rain-gray afternoon it was totally deserted. The man parked up near a quiet wooded spot and, fixing the hand brake with one swift hand movement, he let go one knob and clutched another — Larry's. Purposefully, he rubbed Larry's fly. Larry sighed and as the air eased out of his lungs, the blood rushed into his dick. Stiff and swollen in moments, his mickey throbbed as the stranger worked his fingers deep into the grooves of Larry's bulge.

"I bet you've got a right big cock on you. I bet you've got a big, fat mickey," the man chuckled, lustily.

"Take it out and see for yourself," Larry urged.

"In the back," he said as he tipped his head toward the rear of the van. "More room to get comfortable." The man already had the driver's door halfway open.

Outside, the stranger threw wide the double doors at the back of the van to reveal a makeshift bed; foam cushions covered by a

Daddy's Boyz

blanket. Larry put one foot up to climb in, and the man cupped both his buttocks, hoisting him over the threshold. Larry landed face down on his front. Climbing in behind him, the man pulled the doors shut and fastened them securely. Pitch black. Then he flicked the switch on some kind of portable lamp. The stranger's face was flushed and glistened in the yellowish glow.

Larry flipped over onto his back and relaxed, his hands behind his head as the man knelt over him. The stranger's fingers fumbled with Larry's belt buckle, the button on the waist of his jeans, and then trembled as they tugged the zip down over the pronounced curvature of Larry's bulge. No underwear meant all obstacles had been removed and Larry's cock burst forth.

The man chuckled, "I'd have won that bet! Fuck! Will you look at the size of that! What a beauty!" His thick fingers now encircled Larry's pulsing girth and retracted the heavy coverlet of foreskin. Helmet exposed, the stranger lowered his salivating mouth slowly down.

The man hesitated, eyes closed, wet tongue half hanging out, and then he dipped the pointed tip into Larry's drooling piss slit. Lapping up the clear, sparkling juice, he savored it in much the same way as a connoisseur of fine wine might test the first sip from a fresh bottle. Then, reverently, he kissed Larry's knob head, allowing his lips to part and slide over the helmet. Lips fixed around the rim, he sucked for a while, taking time to unbutton his own fly and yank free his distended organ. Clasping it in his fist, he began to jerk the foreskin back and forth, back and forth.

It was raining heavily now, pounding on the metal roof above their heads. Inside, the van smelled of the country, of straw and earth. The stranger's mouth worked up and down the full length of Larry's shaft, his throat relaxed to embrace him fully. Sensations of pleasure rippled through Larry's entire body as the man's beard tickled his balls. He clasped the back of the stranger's head and let his hand rest there, moving in rhythm as the stranger's eager mouth plunged forward and back.

This guy is desperate, thought Larry, but it was a desperation that delighted him. The man was cock-hungry, and Larry's dick was the sole focus of his ravenous and seemingly insatiable appetite. Something profound struck Larry as he looked down upon the rapturous expression on the man's face. His need was primal. Sucking cock was as basic and fundamental as the need to breathe or eat or piss.

Now the stranger was whining through lips clamped tight around Larry's member. Larry knew he couldn't hold off much longer, couldn't even if he had wanted to.

"I'm close ... close to cuming," Larry said.

The man pulled back, and gasped, "Can I swallow you?"

"Yeah ... yeah ... just don't fuckin' stop."

Massaging Larry's bollocks, the man redoubled his efforts: moaning with his mouth full, clobbering on his own dick, urging Larry to cum. A searing white light flashed before Larry's eyes as aching balls lifted to expel his payload. The stranger gulped and snaffled and squeezed the juice from Larry's plums. Larry's body convulsed, and his cock continued to spasm. The man hungrily consumed ever drop. And continued to suck on Larry's softening tool as he pumped his own, whilst his free hand clutched his own balls and tugged. He was whimpering as his lips held onto Larry's dick. Larry raised himself on his elbows. He reached forward and unbuttoned the man's shirt and let his fingers swirl over the man's hairy chest before finding his nipples. The stranger let out a squeal as Larry tweaked on an erect node. A moment later, the first arch of boiling lava sprayed the blanket. Then a second spurt, then a third and a fourth.

Cum was everywhere, over his hand, over the blanket, and most of it over Larry, soaking into his clothes. He really didn't care. Exhausted, the man collapsed beside him and Larry hugged him.

"That was fucking beautiful," the stranger said, rubbing his beard over Larry's cheek. "Fuckin' beautiful!"

Larry took the man's hand and licked up the sperm from gnarled skin, tough as leather. "Are you a laborer?" he asked.

"Farmer," the man replied.

The stranger had sucked Larry's cock, and Larry didn't even know his name. Now, in the comfort of Larry's arms, he let loose his intimacy.

"Are you married then?" the man asked.

"Nah. Why?" Larry asked.

"Only you said you didn't live alone," the man said.

"Oh, that," Larry thought quickly. "I share with a mate." It was a lie born out of necessity. He could hardly tell this big bruiser that he still lived at home with his mammy.

"A mate you fuck with?" the man asked.

"And then some!" One lie begetting another.

"Lucky young bastard! Thought you were too young to be married. How old are you?" the man asked.

"Not so young. Twenty one," he was getting good at this.

The man sighed, "It's a good age."

"And are you married?" Larry asked.

"Married with ten kids," the man said.

"Ten?!" Larry said with surprise.

"Had the first three by the time I was 21," the man said.

Silence.

"And how long have you been ... having sex with men?" Larry asked.

"Long before. But we didn't talk about such things back then. Didn't give it a name. No one knows about this ... side of me," the man said.

"You must feel pretty isolated?" Larry asked.

"You're not wrong there," the man answered.

The man held tight onto Larry. For the longest while, or so it seemed, they kissed and cuddled like a courting couple. Eventually, the stranger said it was time to make a move.

On impulse, Larry reached into his blazer pocket, producing a scrap of paper and a pen. He scribbled his name and address and handed it over. "In case you want to keep in touch," Larry said.

The stranger looked at the scrap of paper for a long moment. "My name's Liam by the way." He folded the scrap, stuffed it in his shirt pocket, and said, with a melancholy air, "Seeing you again would be grand, but it just might make things a wee bit too complicated."

The clinic was down a back street. Hidden away from prying eyes. Larry had made an appointment but still had to take a seat and sweat.

"The doctor will see you shortly," said a starched nurse with all the warmth and understanding of a fridge-freezer.

Larry felt sick.

First, the irritating itch began under the foreskin then the rash had appeared shortly after. A rash of tiny red pimples across his cockhead. Where did he get them from? The possibilities seemed endless — he had been putting it about a bit. Had he got it from the farmer or given it to him?! Shit! Shit! Shit!

"The doctor will see you now," grunted Nurse Face-ache. "Go down the hall, first room on your right."

"Thanks," Larry replied with no conviction.

He entered the room to find a woman doctor; hair pulled back in a severe bun, black plastic half-moon glasses perched on the end of her nose. She was seated behind a desk. As he approached she looked up from a chart and smiled. At least her face was kindly. She must be used to abject terror in her line of work, thought Larry.

"Take a seat," she said, "Now what's the problem?"

He explained the symptoms and she said, "We had better have a little look."

Usually, he would have had no problem presenting his pride and joy for inspection but in these circumstances? It was excruciating! He pulled back the foreskin and waited to be told the worst. She examined it, then, raising her eyebrows, she looked directly into his eyes.

"Nothing to worry about, Mr ...," She checked her register, "... Smith. It's just a little touch of beard rash."

About Gordon
Simon Sheppard

Gordon, he thought, wasn't much of a name for a bottomboy. Which is why he figured the kid was probably telling the truth. If he'd called himself Jason or Chad or Shane, then there'd be a shooting chance he was just making stuff up. Seems unlikely he'd invent "Gordon."

Not that it mattered much, not really. Gordon was hundreds of miles away. Supposedly, of course. He could be on the other side of the globe. He could be around the corner. Online, there was no way to tell, just as there was no way to tell if the pictures Gordon — or whatever his name really was — had sent really were of him or not. But once again, a probable. The boy in the pictures had a nice, big hard-on, but he was wearing glasses, was certainly on the nerdy side. Not the kind of pic anyone would steal and use as his own, unless he was going after gentlemen with specialized tastes. Hal had those tastes — a yen for thin, nerdy young men — but he hadn't indicated that before Gordon had sent the pictures.

"Am I too geeky?" Gordon had typed out after the pics were exchanged.

Hal's heart had given a little leap, "Not at all."

And he wasn't too geeky. He was just perfect. OK, at 19, he was less than half Hal's age, young enough to make Hal nervous. But Gordon wasn't proposing they move in together or anything; he just wanted to call Hal for phone sex.

"I won't be able to talk very loud, though," Gordon had typed out in his Instant Message. "My Dad is asleep in the next room." The words sent a slightly queasy feeling through Hal's stomach at the exact same time it sent a thrill through his hard dick. He didn't want to tell Gordon that that might be a problem, that his hearing wasn't as acute as it used to be.

Something else kind of scared Hal, as well. When he asked Gordon what he was into, the reply was, "All sorts of sick stuff."

Hal took his hand off his dick long enough to type out a question: "Like what?"

Bob Condron

The answer he got back made him wonder about 19-year-old boys nowadays.

"Extreme CBT (and I mean EXTREME), piss, fisting, animals, little holes, 666, hangman. U name it."

Well, "animals" Hal didn't want to know about. Piss had never interested him, and though he'd fisted a guy or two some years ago, he hadn't really enjoyed it. He wasn't sure what "little holes" meant. He knew that "666" was the name of the Beast of Revelations but couldn't imagine how that fit into having sex with a 19-year-old boy. And "hangman?" He could just imagine. He gave a little shiver.

He looked at the picture of naked Gordon lying on his back. At the wide, seductive half-smile, the shapely hard dick anchored in a veritable forest of jet-black pubic hair, shaft resting on a pale, slim belly. Gordon's ribs stuck out. His arms were raised, hands behind head, revealing bushy underarms that he hoped stank. Not much in the balls department, hey, but nobody's perfect. Still, this kid was so damn near perfect that he wondered what he was going to do. If there was one thing the occasion didn't call for, it was seeming too vanilla for a yummy boy young enough to be his son — and then some.

"Yeah," Hal typed out. "I'm into all that stuff, too. And more."

"Cool. Can I phone you?" Gordon typed.

"Yeah. In five minutes, ok?" And Hal typed out his number, area code first.

"Kewl. Signing off. Bye."

Hal wasn't quite ready to finish the chat yet, but Gordon — geeky, beautiful, skinny, nearsighted, hopelessly twisted Gordon — was gone. He signed off and stood up from the office chair by his computer, pulling his shorts up from his ankles, over his hard dick. He looked down: tented. He shuffled off to the kitchen, poured himself a glass of cranberry juice over ice and splashed in some vodka, then a little more.

Back in the living room, he swept piles of tax returns off the sofa — he was an accountant, and it was late March. He turned off the overhead light and lit a little lamp in the corner. Fuck, he forgot lube; his dick was getting sore from using nothing but spit. He went off to the bathroom and came back with a pump bottle of moisturizing lotion and a box of Kleenex.

Daddy's Boyz

He took a swig of his drink — nice and strong — and stripped off all his clothes. Grabbing the cordless phone with one hand, he lay down on the couch and waited. For Gordon. For Gordon to call.

Lying there getting drunk, he looked down at his naked body. Nice blond pelt, good pecs, nipples. Not bad ... for someone his age. He spent a good deal of time at the gym, more than he enjoyed. Partly for reasons of his health, of course. But also, he had to confess, out of vanity. Had to keep himself in shape for the boys.

It had been eight and a half minutes already, and Gordon hadn't called. No surprise. As many times as he'd been chatted up by boys online, as often as one of those boys had seen his photo and typed out "handsome," he still couldn't understand why someone like Gordon would want to have sex with someone like him. This wasn't false modesty, nor was it self-pity. It was just a puzzle he couldn't figure out. He lay there for a minute, sipping his drink and looking at the ceiling, trying to imagine what emotions Gordon felt when he was with an older man, particularly an older man who did all those awful things to him. Or maybe Gordon was the one who did the awful things; that had never been established. And if something called "hangman" were involved, he'd rather not know. What would he have said to the kid if he had actually called? He would have bullshitted his way through, most likely. That's what men always did when it came to sex.

Just as he drained the glass, the phone rang. He jumped. It's not that Hal hadn't expected Gordon to call, it's just that ... well, Hal hadn't expected him to call. He grabbed for the phone, realized that the radio was playing classical music, which might be the wrong soundtrack for nasty talk, got up, turned the tuner off, punched the Talk button on the phone, and said, "Hello," as he was flopping back down on the couch.

"Hello? Daddy?" Gordon's voice wasn't what Hal had expected; it wasn't boyish or unusual. It was just a smooth, nondescript voice, a voice that seemed unworthy of such a perfect boy.

"Hey, Gordon?"

"Yeah?"

"Could we not do phone sex? I mean the conventional kind?" Hal asked.

"What do you want to talk about, then?" Gordon asked.

"Anything. Sex. You. Sex. Just not the 'now I'm sliding my dick into your hungry pussy' kind of script," Hal replied.

"Yeah, that's cool," Gordon said.

"So …" Hal was holding the phone in one hand, his dick in the other.

"So you're into twisted stuff, then?" There it was.

"Oh yeah, yeah," Hal said, trying to sound enthused.

"So you're into piss, huh?" Gordon asked.

"Oh yeah, big time." Well, it was true that Hal did piss, at least half a dozen times a day. He just had never pissed on anyone, much less in someone's mouth. And the idea of someone pissing on him always gave him the willies. Until now. Now he was lying there, jacking off his uncut cock, and thinking of cute, smooth-bodied Gordon standing over him, cock in hand, and soaking him down with a stream of hot pee. Where had that come from? And how come it seemed so exciting? Hal had to take his hand away to keep from cuming.

"Yeah, I'd like to piss all over you," Hal said, which was not exactly what he wanted, but since he was older, he figured he'd better be the top.

"Oh man, I'd like to piss on you, too," Gordon said.

"Really?" Hal asked.

"Yeah, of course. Why the fuck not? You're so fucking handsome, Daddy." Gordon had called him "handsome" online, too, something Hal couldn't see himself as. But he wasn't about to argue.

"You hard?" Hal asked.

"Yeah," Gordon answered.

"Stroking?" Hal asked.

"Leaking like a faucet. That's what some of my buds call me, 'The Faucet,'" Gordon said.

Cute, Hal thought, but he didn't say it. He pictured a perfect drop of fresh, young precum oozing from Gordon's slit, slithering over the swollen cockhead, down the boy's pretty shaft.

"Daddy?"

"Yes, son?" Hal put his hand back on his dick and squeezed.

Daddy's Boyz

"You're really into all that stuff you said you were, right? Because sometimes I've met men who'd lied to me just to get in my pants," Gordon said.

What the hell Hal thought, "Sure I am, son."

"Hangman?" Gordon asked.

"Oh yeah, sure," Hal's half-drunk mind was working overtime, inventing. "There was this boy I played with for five years, I used to wrap a rope around his neck and squeeze."

"Ohhh," Gordon cooed. It was something between an orgasmic moan and what Hal imagined would be the sound of Gordon getting choked. Hal found it scary, sobering, but disturbingly exciting. What was wrong with this kid? What was wrong with him?

"Gordon?"

"Yeah, Daddy?"

"Can I ask you a question? In all seriousness?" Hal wondered why he was doing this. He had a perfect, perfect 19-year-old on the phone and he was about to risk fucking that up? Christ!

"Shoot," Gordon said.

"Why ... um ... why are you into what you're into?" Hal asked.

"Kink, you mean?" Gordon asked.

"No. Older guys." There it was. The Big Question. Hal was uneasy about the reason he suspected: Gordon was into older guys because he was self-destructive. He could have boys his own age, hot boys, but he went after wrinkled old men instead. Gordon was punishing himself. For God knows what. The kink stuff merely provided additional evidence.

"Oh Daddy, it's because older men are so powerful and attractive," Gordon answered.

Hal could grudgingly accept the fact that some folks found him "attractive." But "powerful"? If there was one thing he didn't feel at the moment, it was powerful.

"And why," Gordon asked, "Are you into skinny, worthless boys like me?"

Hal had to jerk his hand away to prevent himself from cuming.

"Because ..." Hal began. Figuring out just what to say was tough. It seemed so natural that he, that any man like him, would want Gordon, inevitable as an earthquake. He knew, rationally, that not every middle-aged homo would agree, that plenty of them sought men their own age, or older men, or muscular men, or boys who didn't look like they'd just finished working on their science fair project.

But Hal knew he'd do anything, damn near anything, to make a boy like Gordon — to make Gordon — his. Even if that meant wrapping a rope around the boy's skinny neck? Pissing down his throat? Worshipping Satan?

Even if.

Hal shifted his bulk on the couch, knocking the glass to the floor. Ice skidded everywhere, melting fast.

"Oh fuck," Hal said into the phone.

"What, Daddy? What is it?"

Hal was suddenly drunk enough or sober enough to wonder what he was doing. Why he was playing into the semi-psychotic fantasies of some 19-year-old somewhere. At least, he hoped they were fantasies. If they were the truth, if the boy had actually done those things, such sick stuff, in his short life, then that made loving him even edgier. Yes, "loving." He'd let himself think the L-word, dangerous it might be, more dangerous than that earthquake.

If he was the Daddy, why did Hal feel so ridiculous, on his hands and knees, gathering up ice cubes from under the couch? If he was the nasty top, why was he so confused? Why did he suddenly feel so sad he thought that he might weep?

"Daddy? What's wrong?" The voice was thin and tinny, coming from the phone lying on the sofa. "Daddy?"

Hal rose to his knees, glass with rescued ice cubes in one hand, and, mostly hard dick protruding from beneath him, reached for the telephone. He clicked the Off button. Gordon was no more.

Time to go to bed. Past time. Hal would have to take care of his dick first, though, get off. He sat back down at the computer and opened Gordon's picture. Oh my God. He was so beautiful. Beautiful, beautiful, beautiful. If only he could touch the boy's smooth flesh, he would gladly worship Satan, sell his soul. Who knows, maybe he already had.

The phone hadn't rung. Gordon hadn't called back. Well, why should he? As far as the kid knew, Hal was just a fucking wanker, hanging up on him like that. How could the boy know the depth of an older man's feeling? Fuck, why had he hung up? Why hadn't he gotten Gordon's number? He reached for the phone, tried *69. That didn't work. Fuck. Fuck fuck fuck. So beautiful.

Hal got up, took the glass to the kitchen, rinsed out the ice and half-filled it with vodka, neat.

Back in the living room, he signed back online again. He brought up his Buddy List. No sign of Gordon. Maybe he should send e-mail? No, if he were Gordon, he'd just delete the mail unopened. The only way to explain was in real time, chatting, man-to-boy.

And so Harold Obermeyer sat there, lit by the glow of the computer screen, a naked man in his 40s, stroking his erection, sipping from his glass. Stroking.

Waiting for the boy.

Rampage
Jordan M. Coffey

He always wore his head shaved, only a fine stubble covering his skull. Not because he was going bald, he just liked the look. It went with the gray goatee and hard, gray eyes. He was big all over. Chest, arms, legs. All muscle. Not bodybuilding muscle, not that deliberate cut and perfect proportion, but 'living life' muscle. He worked out, all right, but it wasn't a thing with him. The bulge of his arm, the strength of his thigh, the ridge of his abs: I would have sworn it came from working, fucking, fighting.

He liked to fight. I always knew that. But it wasn't like he went around starting them, not really. More like he dared anyone to come do battle with him, hoping they would, knowing he'd kick their ass. I'd never known him to lose. Rumor was that he never had.

There were a lot of rumors about him. That he'd gotten so tough because of a harsh childhood back East, or that he had gotten tired of homophobic assholes terrorizing people, or that he was simply a hard-wired hard-ass who loved the rush.

I didn't know the truth of any of that, wasn't sure I cared. I only knew that he liked to fight and that just looking at him got my dick hard. Not that I was harboring any illusions. No way was I his type. I'd seen the guys he fucked around with. A certain crowd, a certain type, a certain age. Guys more like him. Guys other men would kill to fuck. Men who looked tough in leather, rough in denim. Broad shoulders and strong jaws. Attitude. Experience.

Not a young punk like me. I had never even seen him pay attention to any of the fine, young studs that were always checking him out. And me, I was just average height, average build, cute enough, I guess, but nobody was falling all over himself to get to me. No, I wasn't harboring any illusions, but I could dream.

I don't know how it all started. Just one night he walked into Rampage, already sweating and breathing hard. His white tee was plastered to his massive chest, and there was blood on his lip. He forced his way through the crowd straight back to the bathroom, and I followed.

Bob Condron

When I walked in, he was leaning on the sink, looking at himself in the mirror. His eyes slid to mine in the reflection, his fierce gaze like a punch to my gut, a fist on my cock. I had never spoken to him before, and my throat closed up around the words that I wanted to get out right then. To ask him something, offer him something. Instead, he spoke, his voice the low growl I imagined late at night.

"Come here."

Unlike my voice, my body had no problem responding. Legs automatically moving forward while my dick got a little harder. He turned to me then, and I wanted to touch him so badly, I could feel the ache of it in my balls, sharp and tight like the pain in my chest that was making it hard to breathe. When he turned away, going back to the last stall, I was on his heels.

He didn't close the door, just grabbed me with a fist to my crotch, gloriously intensifying the ache. My knees buckled, and I moaned, leaning toward him, held up solely by his grip. Two fingers, thick and callused, made their way into my mouth, and I sucked, putting the power of my passion into that act because my hands were scrabbling uselessly in the air.

A slight pressure had me on my knees, and I inhaled the ripe smell between his legs. His fingers invaded my mouth again for a minute, and then I was biting the head of his dick through his jeans, rubbing my face in the big wet spot I made.

I was pulled to my feet and looked at him. My eyes glazed over, while his were sharp and bright. I wanted to kiss him, taste the blood that had dried on his lips, lick him clean.

That train of thought was sidetracked by three fingers in my mouth and a hand roughly opening my pants. I slobbered as best I could, knowing what was coming, and groaned, my head lolling, at the irregular friction of spit-slick digits pushing into my tight hole. He fucked me fast, knuckles bruising my ass, strong arm holding me in place. My head dropped to his shoulder and my teeth sank into his flesh.

I barely had time to brace myself, both hands against the cold, gritty wall, as he turned me, bent me over and pushed more than his fingers inside. I saw red, imagined blood and fire, heard sounds of ecstasy and rage. Pain ripped through me, battling with pleasure in furious waves. Blinded by the sting of sweat and the force of fucking, I squeezed my eyes shut and held on.

I wanted to scream, but could only manage a wild, wheezing whimper, highlighted by his rumbling grunts. He fucked as I imagined he fought: hard and relentless, pounding my ass, making it last. The sensations peaked, and my head hit the wall as I came, my dick jerking spasmodically without me ever having a chance to touch it.

Powerful hands gripped my hips tighter, and I knew he was cuming too, emptying into me in rapid bursts like the pumping of a shotgun. When he pulled out, it hurt like hell, the pain punctuated by a sloppy slurping sound. I was in heaven.

I turned around, wanting one last look before he could disappear on me. He looked the same as he had when he'd first walked into the bar: sweaty tee shirt, lip smeared with blood, chest rising as he caught his breath. The only difference was his dick hanging out of the fly of his pants, flushed and slick, long even in its softening state. I took a deep breath, made a move before I could lose my nerve. Hobbling a few steps closer, I placed a hand on the swell of his pec and kissed him. More like licked him, really, tasting the metallic tang of blood, dipping my tongue inside his mouth for the hot warmth of his saliva. A shiver ran through me when his tongue met mine for a sweet, but brief, moment.

He pushed me back, tucked himself in and zipped up, his eyes burning into mine the whole time. Then, unexpectedly, he reached out and leisurely rearranged my clothes for me, pulling my pants up over my dripping cock and leaking ass.

"Want to go for a ride?" he asked, that sexy voice making my hole twitch in anticipation, sending more of his spunk trickling down my leg.

I nodded and once again followed him. Two guys were at the urinals, and one smirked at me as we left, but I didn't respond. In fact, I didn't pay attention to anything else until I was outside in the night air and it finally felt like I was breathing normally again.

He got into an old, beat-up black muscle car and leaned over, opening the passenger door. The engine revved as I got in, and, just like that, we were off.

We went on a road trip, of sorts — a cross-country trek through farmland and ranch country, stopping at bars in towns where he made no attempt to hide the fact that we weren't just two buddies. Practically itching for a reaction, and almost always getting one.

I was scared shitless a lot of the time, knowing that my fighting skills were nowhere near good enough to contribute if things got really ugly, afraid that one night, in that land of pickup trucks and rifles, things would zip past ugly straight into deadly. But, whenever men rose to his implied challenge, he would just focus on the leader. That was usually all it took. Then, we'd go somewhere, and he'd fuck me senseless — a cheap motel, a dark field on the edge of town, or even the battered, sticky leather of his back seat. I was only along for the ride, and a hell of a ride it was.

Scarred, bloody, bruised — it only made him hotter to me. And I had my own battle scars to prove it — teeth marks in places, bruises in the shape of his fingerprints all over, a sore and tender ass filled with his cum. I loved it all.

Then, it was over.

The return trip was very different, almost non-stop. He seemed to have expended that well of violent energy that had driven him to the road, gotten whatever it was out of his system. We had intermittent conversation where I actually learned a little about him, but he didn't offer any explanations. I probably talked too much, dreading our time coming to an end.

When we got back into town, he asked where I lived, and I felt my stomach drop, knowing he was done with me. But outside of my little apartment building he said, "Go get some clothes."

Heart racing, I dashed upstairs, threw some stuff into a bag, looking forward to whatever else was in store. Turned out, we went to his place, a huge two-bedroom in the warehouse district. I spent the next three days in his huge bed.

Eventually, life returned to normal. Well, almost normal. I moved in with him.

So far, he hasn't felt the need to go on another rampage. And I don't think he will. I know he still likes to fight, but we don't usually run into any trouble, though I can tell every now and then that he's gotten into it with someone. I used to worry that he would go back to the type of guy he used to fuck before me. Until I found the pictures. Him and a young man. Someone cute and slender and not me. Enough pictures to tell a story of life and love and loss.

Then, early one morning with me bent over the toilet, reminiscent of our first time, our gazes locked in the mirror as he plunged deep into my ass. The look he gave me made me shake. I recognized it, had seen that look on him in those pictures, but this time he was looking at me.

"I love you," I finally said.

He smiled and fucked me harder.

The Center of Gravity
Dale Chase

The cry invades my subconscious and is taken up as my own. I awaken with a jolt, disoriented. What in hell was that? I try to see inside the dream but, like always, the more I look, the faster it flees. And then, the cry again. Oh damn, someone's stuck in the elevator.

My apartment is next to the awful little thing, and when this happens, which is once or twice a year, I become a sort of default rescue party. The alarm bell is ringing, and I wonder why it didn't wake me but then it never does. Apparently, I've developed the ability to sleep through all but the human cry.

I pull on a robe, fetch the crowbar I keep for this purpose alone, and go out my door. Another wail, and I call out, knowing he probably can't hear me. I begin to pry at the door, which locks when the elevator is in use. Since I've done this before, I know how to pry it open without the damage inflicted on my first try when Lloyd, my partner, got trapped not long after we moved in. He was in full panic mode, which coupled with his heart condition, led me to nearly tear the door off its substantial hinges.

The elevator is consistent with its breakdown. It quits only when going up and always at the same spot a few feet short of my floor, which leaves enough space for the poor occupant to be pulled out. I recall doing that with Lloyd, seeing him red-faced, sweating profusely. For a second, it's him all over again, but another cry intrudes, and I'm back to now. And then the door pops open.

"It's OK, I can get you out," I call down. "You have to push open the gate and when I reach in, use it as footing to leverage yourself up."

"It won't budge," he hollers. I can tell he's young.

"Grab the handle, put your weight into it. Leverage is everything. I've done this before; trust me, it will work."

Grunts follow, a couple of oh shits, and then I see it open. Hands are raised as he braces against the gate. The opening is about two feet, but it's enough. I get down onto my knees, anchor myself as best I can and reach down. He grabs hold. As I pull him up, my back complains, reminding me I was 25 when I pulled Lloyd out.

The gate allows him a boost, and soon he's out and I'm falling back, out of breath. Only then do I realize my robe has come open. I've got nothing on underneath but at that moment am too tired to care. I note that even in his agitated state, the young man's gaze descends to my crotch.

"You OK?" he asks and I realize I probably look like Lloyd did, me now the graying 45-year-old. He helps me up, and as I rise, he crumples, falls into my arms. I smell alcohol. Suddenly he's shaking all over and losing his color. "You OK?" I now ask.

"I don't think so," His voice trembles. "That really got to me, ya know? I'm claustrophobic. If you hadn't pulled me out, I'd have gone nuts." He's leaning on me now, his body quivering in some kind of delayed reaction.

"Why don't you come inside for a minute. You're getting pale."

As he walks the few steps to my door, he says, "What's with that thing anyway?"

"Happens now and then. They can't find what's wrong. Just an old building quirk."

"How can you put up with it? It's insane!" he says.

"Kind of a trade off," I explain. 'Rent controlled apartment versus the occasional elevator mishap, easy choice."

"Well, they should warn people up front. For rent: studio apartment with man-eating elevator," the kid says.

Only after he's inside my apartment do I realize he has disarmed me, that I've become so caught up in his rescue, I've allowed him to breech the wall I put up after Lloyd's death. No one has gained entrance here for seven months. I see people but always elsewhere, and that alone has gotten me through this terrible time. Now a stranger has invaded this apartment that is my center of gravity, looking at the rooms where my life took place. Twenty years with Lloyd. I eye the stranger, wish now I'd left him in the hall.

"I'm going to throw up," he says.

I get him into the bathroom, leave him there. While he pukes, I make coffee, and as it brews I remind myself I don't want this. My life is empty for a reason. This intruder must go. Coffee to sober him up, then send him away.

"This is so embarrassing," he says when he comes into the kitchen. He's got a hand towel at his chin as if he might not be done. "I can usually hold my liquor," he offers. "That elevator freak-out did me in."

"Understandable. I often wonder what would happen if I was in it myself. Who would pull me out?" I ask.

"So it happens a lot?" he asks.

"Couple times a year. Mostly at night, which gives it a kind of personality, like it's waiting to trap somebody in the dark. I take the stairs a lot," I tell him.

"I'll remember that. Thanks for coming to the rescue. You sound like you've lived here awhile," he says.

"Twenty years. How about you?" I ask.

"Two weeks. My name's Kevin Burke. I'm in the studio down the hall, 406," he says.

"Skip Katzen."

As he sips his coffee, he starts to look around, and I want to stop him. He's running his eyes along Lloyd's stuff, and I don't like him touching it, but I can't say anything because I know how I come off to people. I've learned that these past months, been told enough times. Then out of nowhere he starts spilling his story.

"Did you ever have the rug pulled out from under you? Your lover tell you it's over, and he moves out and you can't afford the apartment alone, don't want to stay there anyway without him? That's why I got this place. That's why I go out drinking," he says.

"Where were you tonight?" I ask because his loss has scratched at something of mine.

"I went out to get laid and I did but, you know, well, you don't want to hear it. Life just sucks sometimes," he offers.

It's then that I realize I see some of me in him, some of what Lloyd must have noted when he picked me up out of circumstances not all that different. "How old are you?" I ask.

"Twenty-five." He lets out a long sigh, sips his coffee. "I thought it was real with Brian. You know how that is, you're done with all that out there, you've found your one and only, he tells you it's for keeps except he's screwing around and when you find out …"

Bob Condron

He trails off, looks into his cup, and I feel a surge that I haven't for some time. It's the pain of loss mixed with the need the absence has created, a need I have refused to fully address. It churns up through me like some inner storm, and I find I like the feeling. Beneath the robe, my dick hardens.

Kevin doesn't look his years. He is brown-haired and boyish, not quite filled out. His skin is fair, his eyes blue, and I wonder what lies beneath the faded jeans.

He finishes his coffee and looks at me and for the life of me I can't read him, but I plunge ahead because in my particular state I have nothing to lose.

"You gonna be OK on your own tonight?" I ask and before he can answer, I add, "Because if you're not, you're welcome to stay here."

As soon as I say it, I wish I hadn't because it means he'll be in Lloyd's bed with me, and I hate that, even as I desperately want it.

"Maybe I should," he says. "I'm still a little shaky."

I look at the kitchen clock. "It's after three. Why don't we get some sleep."

In the bedroom, he strips naked, as if we've been at this for years. I get a good look at his body before he slides beneath the covers and see that he is slight but well formed, smooth, a silky patch of hair surrounding a fine little cock that is halfway hard. It's then that I know for sure I'm going to fuck him.

I stand there in my robe, which had been securely retied and think about what is going to happen. And I think about Lloyd and all the times he took me to bed and how much I need to do it again. I pull off my robe, let it fall to the floor, and for a second I just stand there. Let the kid see what he's in for. My cock points at him.

When I get into bed, he rolls toward me, and we pass a few moments looking into each other's eyes. I have no idea how much real communication this is, if any. The only message I get is one of welcome.

I have not had this kind of sex since Lloyd died. I have gone to bars and back rooms and done some awful things, but I have not been in a bed with anyone. I have not allowed it. Now I run my hands down his smooth chest and get them onto his prick, handle his balls. He murmurs as I feel him, and his hands go to my tits where he plays in the fur. He finds my nubs and settles there, then leans in and starts to lick while I keep a hand on his cock.

I don't want to kiss him and get the idea it's mutual. I think we both need a long interlude, a quiet kind of fucking that is reassuring as well as satisfying. I get a finger back to his bunghole, and he gets eager as I push in. His muscle clamps down onto me, and this brings Lloyd to mind, which I both do and do not want. I think of the hours I would spend fucking Lloyd, whole afternoons given to our bodies. Even as he grew older, he kept me satisfied, but now it's a young bottom, and I am finally ready.

"I need to fuck you," I tell Kevin. I roll him onto his stomach, stop to get a condom and lube, and then I'm pushing into him. His ass swallows my prick, and I can't hold back. I want to make it last but there's too much backed up in me and I give him a rough ride, pound his sweet bottom until I unleash a load that seems truly a gusher. He, meanwhile, is creaming into the sheets and making it known.

When I finish and pull out, he rolls over. I look at his spent prick, the come in the bed. I savor that feeling of having just gotten off on a massive scale, sucking in long breaths. I look at him, run my hand onto a little pink tit and realize I want him all over again. Shit.

I'm sitting back on my haunches, playing with him and when he looks about to say something, I lean down and suck his cock. In seconds, it's up and I'm feasting, knowing I won't relent until I swallow his spunk.

I recall sucking Lloyd's dick, how often he'd present it to me and I'd gobble it up. Sometimes when I was reading or at the computer, he'd come up and get it out and I'd suck him dry. Of course, then I'd fuck him and wouldn't get back to work for hours.

Now it's a fresh cock I've got, and I concentrate on this fine young body. That's all I want just now. As I suck, I raise his legs, get a finger up him, prod until he cries out and starts to squirt. He's frantic with his little thrusts into my mouth, and his delivery is generous.

When I pull off, he grins. "That was so good," he offers, almost dreamily. I've still got his legs up and I withdraw the finger, look down at his pucker. I have to get into him again.

Bob Condron

When I've applied a rubber and lube, I push back in, and he lies there blissed out as I take my time. Setting up a steady stroke, I realize this is the best escape there is, a long slow fuck in my own bed. Maybe I'll have him over every few days to take the edge off. Maybe that wouldn't be so bad.

I add more lube and keep at him for what seems ages. He obviously likes getting speared and seems content to let me stay in him all night, which is just what I want to do. But after awhile a climax beckons, and I go for it. I push his legs back up around his ears and bore into him until he lets out a moan, and I fuck until I let go another good load. Kevin's prick is hard, but he hasn't touched it. This is about taking my cock, my cum. It feels like I'm filling him.

When I finally relent he grabs his prick and pumps the thing, delivering his third load. Cum shoots up onto his chest, he works his sausage dry, then closes his eyes. His hand falls away, like he's asleep. I'm still in him.

He is youth incarnate, this boy who sleeps so soundly. I withdraw from him, and he does not stir. As I clean up, I think I, too, will sleep soundly, but it doesn't go like that. When I return to the bedroom, I suffer yet another deja vu moment, see myself lying in a deep sleep, satiated, having finally worn myself out with Lloyd. It was he who often remained awake, or so he told me. Even though I'd fucked him for hours, he would still rise, put on his robe, make tea, sit and read. Or he might play his cello. He said it felt wonderful to take up the instrument he loved when he'd been calmed with sex.

Pushing aside these thoughts, I climb into bed and lie next to Kevin. We are under the covers, bedmates now rather than lovers. Awkwardness fills me. I sleep, but it is a restless kind.

At seven I awaken and as I pull back the covers to get out of bed, making every effort not to disturb my guest, I take a look at his morning erection. I allow that it is there for the taking and feel a familiar stir, but I cover him instead, dress, head for the kitchen.

Kevin emerges several hours later. I'm at the computer working. The day has turned warm, windows are thrown open, a soft breeze ruffling things, driving me to put paperweights onto manuscript pages.

Daddy's Boyz

Kevin wears only his Jockey shorts. I want to tell him to dress, that the night is past, but I remain silent because part of me wants him like this, wants to pull off his shorts and start in again. "There's coffee on the stove," I say, looking at my computer screen.

"Thanks. Maybe it will help. I feel like shit."

He comes back with a cup but doesn't settle. He looks over my shoulder for a second, then travels the room. From the corner of my eye, I watch, hands motionless on the keyboard. He looks out the window, at the shelves of books, at the cello in the corner. "You play?"

"No. It belonged to my partner. He was with the symphony."

"No kidding. So when you broke up, you got custody of the thing?" He grins, enjoying his little joke.

"He died seven months ago."

"Oh wow. Hey, man, I'm sorry. Really. That's too bad," he says.

I don't say anything more, and he gets the idea. "Guess I should go," he offers. He goes to the bedroom, dresses, comes back. "Thanks for last night. For all of it."

"My pleasure," I say.

"Maybe I'll see you again, hopefully not in a stuck elevator," he says.

"Right," I answer.

I know I'm being rude, but it's all I can muster. It feels as if I'm the one with the hangover. There is some kind of blame coming up in me that I don't understand. When he closes the door, I don't turn around.

My days are filled with my writing. Imagination has always been where I've lived, and I slip back into that world with ease, taking refuge in the lives of characters. I return to them now, setting my own indecipherable life aside. Two days later, I encounter Kevin on the stairs.

"Wise man," I say. We have stopped several steps apart and stand looking at one another. The attraction is immediate and once again unsettling. His hair is tousled, face flushed. He's been outdoors on this blustery day and has returned as if freshly scrubbed.

"You getting settled OK?" I ask, finding I want to keep him here.

"Sorta. You know how it is, there always seems to be another box of something to unpack," he says.

I want to tell him I don't know, that I have been rooted so long that moving boxes is foreign, but I go along and say, "Right. Maybe they multiply in the night." I never did ask him about himself, what he does, what he likes. All I got was the breakup. And his ass. Suddenly I want more of him. "You busy later?" I ask.

"Nope. How about you come over to my place this time. We can order a pizza, watch a movie," he says.

"You're on," I say.

"Seven?" he asks.

"Seven." I agree.

It is 2:00 p.m. when I reach my apartment, where I spend the next five hours in my own little self-inflicted maelstrom, one minute elated at connecting with this 25-year-old, the next hating the idea. In the bedroom, I pull out the photo album and turn the pages, watching myself age alongside Lloyd. I see us new, me the black haired young tough, he the graying man of grace, worldly, knowing, the big-hearted guy who took in the kid and made him into something. I see us at parties, on the beach, at Catalina, Carmel, Palm Springs. I see him onstage with his cello during a concert where I know he was happiest. I see myself beside him afterward, the adoring fan.

There is one photo that stops me. We are both in Speedos, his blue, mine white. Both tanned, in our respective primes. We stand with arms about each other. I recall the moment well as later on swimsuits were discarded, and we fucked not far from where the picture was taken. Even in middle age, Lloyd remained playful, adventurous, daring. We often had sex in public places, quick fucks under cover that thrilled us so much we would hurry home and do it again.

When Lloyd toured with the symphony, I often went along. As a writer I had a certain freedom and accompanied him to many cities. When my career blossomed, I sometimes stayed behind and prided myself on my loyalty to him. He would call, and we would jerk off via long distance while talking dirty, telling each other what we really wanted to do. I always marveled that the sophisticated gentlemen cellist was at heart such a raunchy dude.

I turn the later album pages faster, not wanting to linger on the last of us. Lloyd white haired at 62, weakening as his heart gradually wore out. The last shot taken at his 65th birthday party shows a valiant smile on a face drawn thin. Friends surround him while I take the picture, knowing it may be the last.

I close the album, set it aside. I'm in the big comfortable corner reading chair we both so enjoyed. I glance at the bed and think of Kevin, purposely recalling him naked, legs up, beckoning. Maybe there's a reason he's arrived on the scene. Maybe the elevator stopping was fate intervening to get me to move on. My cock stirs as I fix his image. I see him working his prick, watch it erupt, and I feel the want come up in me, make my dick start to fill. Maybe this is how it has to be, I tell myself, not knowing how it works with death and grief because it's all new to me. Maybe somebody has to barge into your life and push what you want to hold onto aside. Maybe there's a point at which you have to stop fighting it. I go out for a walk as I consider this. I kill time until seven, and when I knock at Kevin's door, I'm still not convinced.

He answers wearing an oversized white T-shirt and colorful boxers, the getup making him look about 16. He's full of energy, tells me he's already ordered the pizza because he hasn't eaten since noon. He's been out all day with friends. I don't ask for details.

His apartment is surprisingly well appointed, an eclectic mix of good color and great art. As I take it in my thoughts apparently register on my face because he laughs.

"You thought it would be bare walls, mattress in the corner, didn't you." he says.

It's not a question, and I get that he knows himself well, that there is more here than I thought.

"Have to admit," I say.

He tells me the drawings are his, and I take a second look. Large white squares with a few lines that weave into striking images, suggestive themes. I concentrate on a male figure twisting at the waist, enjoy the movement of the piece, note a cock defined by no more than a single line strategically placed.

Bob Condron

"Can you tell I'm a minimalist?" Kevin asks. "C'mon, the pizza's getting cold. You can view the gallery later."

He has a table at the bay window, and we take our meal there, San Francisco passing below. I get his story now, how he's been drawing since he discovered he could hold a pencil, how he retreats into that world when the larger one becomes more than he can handle.

"But not just then," he assures me. "I mean, I'll draw any time any place. I like to go walking around the city with my sketchpad, draw what I see. Other times, I just sit here and do it from my mind's eye."

"'Mind's eye,'" I repeat, savoring a phrase I seldom hear.

"Yeah, you know, imagination," he says.

"I know," I agree.

"So you're a writer, right?" he asks.

"Yes. A couple novels with good reviews and modest sales, short stories here and there, a bit of porn on the side," I tell him.

"No kidding!" he says with surprise.

At that moment I feel about a century removed from him, and I don't like it. I wish now I hadn't mentioned the porn. He's suddenly a kid, seizing on the dirty part when I had hopes that, as a mind's-eye kind of guy, he might not succumb. Still, maybe I ask too much. When I don't offer details, he presses, and I give him the condensed version.

"Short stories for magazines, anthologies; I'm still a novelist but I enjoy erotica, too," I tell him.

"That is so cool," he says.

"So what do you do?" I ask.

As he tells me about waiting tables, working in a hardware store, a bookstore, and a host of other places, I finish my last slice of pizza and start to tune out. He's going on about not wanting a career or some such thing, and I'm thinking I've heard enough, that maybe I don't want to know him after all, that maybe all we are is fucking. When he finally winds down, I get up from the table. When he follows, I take hold of him and don't let go.

I do him on the floor with an urgency that seems greater than our first time. I pull off his boxers and find he wears no underpants. I suck his dick, trying to swallow the thing, then push his legs up and get my tongue in his hole. Mouth plastered against his pristine bottom, I lick and poke while he carries on up top, talking and moaning, pulling on his dick now because I'm driving him crazy. Then I pull back, get a rubber from my pocket, a packet of lube. I strip naked while he lies there working himself and watching me. When I've got my cock sheathed and greased, I run a gob into him, and it makes him cum. I prod his hole while he squirts a good load up onto his chest, and then I get down on my knees, get my prick up him.

I fuck like the building is about to collapse, like the end of the world is minutes away, and I've got to get off before we're all obliterated. I bore down into him, and it's not pretty. I'm rough, spearing deep, reaming until he's grunting. My knees hurt against the hardwood floor, but who gives a shit. It's prick world, and I'm gonna cum in this little bastard. And then it's there, and it rolls through every inch of me, my balls drawing up and firing, sending jizz out of me in torrents. I let out a roar that doesn't stop until every drop is drained out of me, until the rubber is full to bursting.

When I stop shooting, I stay hard, stay inside him. He's looking at me with a kind of shock, a not unpleasant expression, but still one of awe. I'm thinking he's wondering what in hell is next. I'd like to tell him I have no idea, but I'm too out of breath to speak. Sweat drips off of me onto him.

As I settle, I take note of the feel of my prick inside him, me here on the floor with this kid, this gorgeous kid. I look down at his little pink tits, at his blue eyes, his pouty mouth, and I think I want to have the whole of him. For a long second, I consider a kiss, but it is this that causes me to withdraw, hurry to the bathroom. I close the door, toss the rubber, clean up, avoid the mirror.

I stay in there long enough to calm, but when I emerge the unsettledness returns. Kevin is lying on his sofa on his side, one leg up, bent at the knee. His prick lolls on his thigh. He offers a sweet smile that I find irresistible, and my turmoil shifts gears.

I want to carry him away though I don't know where, but I can feel the weight of him in my arms, surprisingly light. As he begins to play with his cock, I stand transfixed, the ache for him enormous.

My prick fills, and I allow that Kevin has brought me a familiar relentlessness in a new guise. Though I would get off with Lloyd in multiples, there still remained a sameness that has now disappeared. The hard-on is new.

At the sofa, I rearrange him so he lies against me and my hand assumes control of his dick. His breath is comforting, as is the feel of his cock in my palm. We say nothing as we slide into a languorous interlude that lasts for some time. My cock remains hard and after a time, I excuse myself to get a condom and lube from my jeans. Sheathed and greased, I again lie down under him, but this time I put him on my cock. As it slides up him, he settles against me, and we pick up where we left off, me playing with him only now we're fucking as well.

He begins to squirm after awhile, and I know it's time to get serious, to ram my sausage up his butt until he shoots. A thrill runs through me as I consider he is mine for as long as I want.

He adjusts his position until he's upright on me, squatting so I can see my prick up his hole. When he starts to bounce, it's a vigorous effort, and I push another pillow under my head to improve the view. He works me with his ass, gradually increasing speed as he pumps his prick. Frantic then, vocal, he's spraying cum. "Fuck yeah," he says over and over.

My climax is in the distance, and I'm in no particular hurry. When Kevin quiets, I lift him off, get up, and arrange us so he's lying over the sofa arm. I enjoy the tension in my calves and thighs as I get back into him and fuck him standing. He murmurs his approval, bunghole dripping now with liquefied lube. He's juicy, and the squishy thwack of a good reaming adds to the moment. The rise begins.

When the climax arrives all else disappears, firing dick the single constant. Nothing matters during a cum, not a goddamned thing, and I savor the oblivion as much as the getting off.

As I finish, Kevin starts to talk, which is the one thing I do not want. I pull out, drag him to the floor and lick the come off his cock head. I do not intend to surface. I am at him for hours, tongue, fingers and cock in and out of his ass until I lose count of his squirts. He finally lies limp, the valiant young prick as done in as mine, but still I lick him, sucking his sticky balls, fondling his soft little prick. I put a finger up him and lie in a kind of sexual stupor, done in but not done. I relent only when he says he has to pee.

Daddy's Boyz

On the floor on a small colorful rug, I await his return. He stands over me. "How about we get some sleep," he says.

I glance at the single bed tucked into an alcove, realizing we've fucked everywhere but there, find it amusing, but I don't give him an answer. I look up at his pink body and feel a craving even in my fatigue. He has washed his face, his hair is wet, and it gives him a freshness that comes off as a tease. When I reach for him, he darts away.

"I need sleep, man," he says. "C'mon."

He turns back the covers, and I am left to decide. I think of awakening to him in a few hours, fucking him as we lie spooned, but it is the interim that chases me off.

"I'd best get home," I tell him, rising slowly, exhaustion heavy now. He watches as I dress. At the door I turn. He's on his side, covers pulled up to his chest, and he looks sweet, delectable. I think he knows this, knows what it does to a middle-aged man, and it puts me off.

"I'll see you," I say and hurry down the hall.

The following day I go for a long walk then head home. When I open the elevator door, out steps Kevin. I push him back in, plaster him to the wall, grind against that sweet young body.

"Let's fuck," I growl.

"Here?" he asks.

My hands are on his butt and I'm ready to pull down his khakis and do him then and there but force myself to reason. He allows me to push the elevator button, and I keep at him until we reach our destination, which, mercifully, is at our floor. I pull him to my door, fumble with the lock, then push him inside. As the door slams, I tear at him.

I fuck him standing. I can barely get the rubber on, I'm so frantic, but then I'm in him, thrusting madly as he stands splayed against a wall. My balls are heavy, loaded with cum, and I am gonna give this kid a butt full. I push and grunt while keeping him pinned, and then it hits, and I'm shooting into him. It makes me yell and carry on, a freight train kind of climax that leaves me shaking when I'm done.

I pull out, wrap my arms around his waist, feel for his dick. It's gone soft. He must have shot his load. I ease him off the wall and see jizz dripping down the wallpaper.

"You fucked it outa me, man," he offers.

There's nothing I want to say. He lets me undress him and waits as I strip. I take him to bed and spend a long while with my face in his ass before I fuck him again.

Dusk is coming on when he says, "I'm supposed to be somewhere."

"You should have told me," I say.

I still have a hand on him. We lie side by side, and I wait for him to speak, knowing as the silence lengthens that he has no real commitment to be elsewhere, that whatever the plan was, a good fuck chased it off.

"Ah, never mind," he finally says. "How about we get some dinner?"

This is simplicity itself, the most common of comments, the logical progression of things, but it undoes me because it means walking out of here in his company, strolling to a cafe as a couple.

"Let's order in," I say. "I know a great Chinese place."

"I feel like going out. Maybe that diner up the block for a burger. C'mon, it will do you good," he says.

I want to slap him. How in hell does he know what will do me good. Fucking is what does me good. Beyond that, I don't go. I work to restrain the impulse, roll toward him, get playful.

"But we'd have to get dressed and besides, I'm not done with you," I say.

"There is after dinner," he says. "Don't you like going out when you know you're gonna come back and fuck your brains out?"

"I like staying in better," I say.

He issues a little laugh, sighs, sits up. "Is that all you and your partner did, stay in?"

"I don't want to talk about that. It's not easy," I say.

"No, probably not. I've never lost anyone that way, I'm green regarding death, but I can imagine it must be hell. How did he die?" he asks.

"Heart failure. A death sentence, a long battle, then the end," I tell him.

"He was kinda young for that, right?" he asks.

"No, he was twenty years older than I," I tell him.

"So you're, what?" he asks.

"Forty-five," I answer.

He takes this in, lies back down on his side turned toward me.

"And you were together what?"

"Twenty years," I recount.

"So he was 65 when he died," he says.

He goes quiet, and I start thinking for him, how with his youthful, untried perspective, he's calculating that I was 25 when I took up with the geezer, which makes the two of us a deja vu experience.

"And 45 when we met," I say to confirm things.

"I admire that," he offers as he starts rubbing my furry chest. He plays with a tit as he speaks. "I look forward to having that kind of relationship with someone, a solid commitment where you really know each other, a real couple. I bet it was something, the two of you."

"Yeah, it was and I'm not sure I'll ever get over it. Do you understand that?" I ask.

"Sure, of course. And hey, I don't mean to be pushy or anything, I just think we hit it off and age isn't a problem with me," he says.

What he does then is remarkable. He takes me. As I lie knowing where I've been but uncertain as to where I'm going or if I even want to go, he gets down between my legs and begins a two-handed exploration that is beyond anything I've ever known, even with Lloyd. He rubs my tits until the nubs are hard, he plays in my fur, licks me, kneads the flesh that has gathered with time. He works his way down my stomach, gets into the hair at my crotch, pets it, circling my stiff dick. He goes under to my balls, and I spread my legs to give him access. He eases down to get one then the other into his mouth, and he rolls them around on his tongue, sucks a bit. Then he surfaces and turns his attention to my prick.

It is the longest blowjob of my life, and the best. For a while he just sucks the knob until he's got me squirming. Slowly he descends, working me with what seems the master of all tongues. I watch his head begin to bob and thrill to both the feel and the sight and to the hint of climax. As I suck in a breath, he relents, and it does too. This is how he plays with me for hours.

Bob Condron

I am finally begging for release. My balls feel ready to explode, the load he has conjured is massive, and I'm going to choke him with jizz if he'd just stay on me. He lowers his head onto my prick again, and as he starts in, he works a finger back to my butt hole. I flinch, he murmurs that it's OK. He wets the finger, then returns it to my pucker, and I allow him to push in, to finger fuck me as I unleash a gusher into his mouth. I buck and squirt as he sucks and prods; I hear myself cry out as never before. It's a long one, an exquisite one, an amazing one since I'd already done so much earlier.

When I am empty, he is gentle, licking my spent cock as it softens, but I note the finger remains up my ass. He studies my expression, works me a bit. "How's it feel?" he asks.

"Not bad," I answer.

"Did your partner fuck you?" he asks.

"It wasn't his thing," I tell him.

"Is it yours?" he asks.

As he says this, his digit starts in and out, and I issue a little moan which makes him grin. "I take that as a yes," he says.

I don't know what to say. I haven't been fucked since I was twenty, it's not a priority for me, but not out of the question either, especially not now.

"Is that what you want?" I ask.

"What I want," Kevin says as he withdraws the finger and slides atop me, "is a two-way street. You have a body I want to get lost in and fucking is part of that. Let me do you."

Panic seizes me, or something akin to it, apprehension maybe, the idea of bottoming for him, for anyone. As I remain silent Kevin takes charge, gets rubber and lube, prepares himself, then crawls back down between my legs.

"Raise them, let me grease you," he says.

It hits then, what is happening, like I didn't know it was tied up with Lloyd, like he's come into the room, and we've never met before, never had a life together. He never fucked me, he never ate out my ass the way I did his, he never once got near my butt hole. It was his legs up as mine now are, his hole taking the gob of grease to ease the way, him in this vulnerable position. I think of him, try to catch hold, but it's an elusive thing, this panic kind of recall, a selective memory experience I wouldn't wish on anyone.

Kevin is in position now, pushing me back to get a good angle. I grab my legs, loop my arms behind my knees as Lloyd did, and bare my hole for the dick that will take it. As Kevin pushes in, I'm trying to feel the pleasure of so long ago, but in with it is the truth of what is taking place, that I am Lloyd, that Kevin is me. Scenes have been changed, a new cast of characters is onstage, and one of the leads has been reduced to a supporting role.

Kevin is now fucking me, and it feels good. He looks down at the connection as if he's never seen his prick up an ass. He smiles, and it's adorable, like he's some untried kid with a new toy. Look Daddy, I can fuck. He's good at it; he pumps a bit, then starts grinding into me, and I marvel how much he gets out of that little prick of his.

And as he does me, the weight of the changes taking place in me begins to shift, and I want to laugh and cry at the same time. I want to hold on and let go; I want to scream and remain silent. But mostly, I finally discover, I want to take what this man gives me for he is, indeed, a man. Not a boy as I first thought but a man who knows his way around another man, who is not only caring but complete, who will give and receive, who will extend himself with all the care his young years can muster to help the old guy move on.

I gaze up at him as he drives his prick up my chute, as his face tightens with an impending climax, and I say the words that, to me, seal the bond, "Fuck me."

As Good As It Reads
Thom Wolf

I was ten minutes late arriving at the November meeting. My mother was delayed at work, which meant dinner was late. That, in turn, meant that I missed my bus and had to run all the way into town, resulting in an agonizing pain in my side. I stumbled down the steps of the hall and burst through the doors in time to hear Mrs. Aileen talking dispassionately about the tragedy of Bridget Jones.

The Durham reading group met on the first Wednesday of each month, assembling in a plain room in the basement of the town hall. There were eight members of the group, including me. At 19, I was the youngest — by centuries. The ratio of women to men was six to two. Each month, we would discuss a book proposed at the previous session by one of the members. Though I had nothing in common with the other attendees beyond an interest in literature, I looked forward to our meetings. It was a great opportunity to absorb a selection of books that I ordinarily would not read. So far we'd read and dissected *The Hours*, *Winnie The Pooh*, *The Alchemist* and the *Wasp Factory*.

Tonight, however, Mrs. Aileen had the floor, and I knew, in all likelihood, she would go on forever. I nodded breathlessly at my companions, mouthed an apology to the coordinator, Mr. Rice, who gave me a filthy look in return, and I sank into a chair at the back of the class, feeling like a scolded kid in a school English lesson. I tried to remove my coat and scarf without making too much noise. Mr. Rice shook his head and tutted — miserable bastard.

There was a new face in the hall that evening, and one I found myself drawn to. Sitting three rows in front, he turned around as I wrestled with my coat, smiled briefly and nodded before turning back to face Mrs. Aileen. I didn't listen to a word she said; I was too intent on studying the newcomer. He sat at an angle, and I watched him in profile. It was a strong profile with a high forehead, a boxer's nose and a square jaw. He had mellow blond hair, which was cut extremely short, there was practically nothing left on top. His skin was tanned and deeply lined. Mrs. Aileen made some supposedly funny comment on the book, and he laughed politely, increasing the depth and scope of the lines around his mouth and eyes. Oh God, I thought, even his crows feet turn me on.

I've always liked older men. The new man was definitely older — maybe mid-forties — I didn't know, I have never been very good at guessing ages. He had the appearance of a mature man; the thick build, thinning hair line, weathered skin, serious expression — beautiful imperfections that I loved so much.

I could not stop looking at him. I didn't give a shit about the discussion going on down the front or any of the other members, I just wanted to know who he was and what he was doing here. Would he be coming again? I wondered how best to find out. Should I ask Mrs. Aileen? I was too intimidated by his looks to speak to him myself. I hate that about myself, I've never had the confidence to speak to the men I find attractive. Why would they be interested in me anyway; skinny, pale, immature, lacking the qualities I find so attractive in others.

His name was Lawrence. I got the information in the coffee break from Jenny, a middle-aged social worker who had a habit of pestering me to read Jane Austin books. She told me that, as was the custom, Lawrence had introduced himself at the start of the session. Had said he worked in the alcohol dependency unit of the local hospital and didn't know anyone else at the group. He had seen the tiny advertisement in the free paper and rang Mr. Rice a week ago to ask which book we were reading this month. Wow, I thought, *Bridget Jones's Diary* and he still came.

The really big news about Lawrence was that he had published a book of his own, a novel called *Soul on Fire*. At the end of the session, Jenny proposed we read his book for the next meeting. Lawrence smiled, a little nervously, and insisted we study something else. Mr. Rice said that as the new comer, Lawrence could suggest the next book for discussion. He tried gamely to get out of it, but the old bods were quite insistent. Lawrence relented and said, "If you haven't already considered it, *Animal Farm* is a very good book."

I'd already read the George Orwell classic, once at school and once for pleasure, and was infinitely more interested in *Soul on*

Fire. At the end of the meeting, I hung around and made a show of apologizing for my lateness. I wasn't that sorry at all, just hoping to spend a few moments in Lawrence's presence. Ultimately, I didn't get to speak to him that night, Mrs. Aileen kept me talking at the front, going on about some nephew of hers, whom I couldn't remember from school, while Lawrence left. I was sure, almost certain, that as Mrs. Aileen bored me rigid, I caught Lawrence at the corner of my vision, throwing me a look before he left.

That night when I got home, I logged online and went straight to Amazon to execute a search for *Soul on Fire*. I found the book in minutes, a novel by Lawrence Harley. The customer comments were good, averaging four out of five. Scrawling down the page, I gasped as I read the blurb and learned his book was "one memorable year in the life of a man discovering who he is." It was a queer book. Lawrence had written a queer book. Lawrence was queer.

I can't remember sleeping that night. I lay in bed and touched myself. I stuffed a pillow between my thighs, squeezing tight and riding it, thinking about him. I rubbed my hands all over my body, feeling what Lawrence would feel; flat stomach, under-developed chest, slender legs, my big balls. My cock, which was almost always hard, was raging hard now at the thought of his hands upon me. I lay on my front and rose up on my knees, spreading my legs wide, so I could touch my ass, feeling the night air on my hole, needing it too cool down. The tiny little opening was like a ring of fire. It burned with an ache that no amount of spit and fingering could soothe. I'd been fucked before, of course, and I loved it. I was 19, not naïve. I wanted Lawrence to fuck me. That's all I thought about all night; riding him, kissing, loving him.

His book arrived two days later, and I read it in a single sitting. It was the story of a man, coming to terms with his sexuality late in life. I couldn't help but think of Lawrence as I read; something about the story and the way he told it rang true. It had to be autobiographical. It just had to be.

I was inspired by his writing to create a story of my own. I have always dabbled with fiction as a means of expressing myself, purely for my own relief and not for public consumption. Over the next three nights, I wrote a ten page story called "Body Language" about a young man who was my perfect alter ego; fit, good-

Bob Condron

looking, confident, and the affair he has with an older man, who looked exactly like Lawrence. The story was sex intensive with the two men doing it at every opportunity. The sex scenes in Lawrence's own book were nearly pornographic, and I took them as the inspiration for my story. My mind was full of ideas, but getting them onto the page was not so easy when I was raging with such excitement. I stroked my dick the entire time that I was writing and had to stop two or three times each session to blow a load over my belly.

I made sure to arrive early for the next reading group meeting and chose a seat at the side of the room that would give me a great view of Lawrence wherever he sat. When all the regular attendees had arrived and he still wasn't there, I began to worry.

He arrived just before 7.30. When he sat in the chair beside me I could barely breathe. "Hi," I managed to gasp, in response to his greeting, feeling a redness spreading over my face. I contributed little to the discussion that night, not trusting myself to speak.

Instead, I focused on Lawrence, consolidating the image of him in my mind, ready to be drawn upon the stories I planned to write about him — about us — over the next month. I studied his hands, which were large with long fingers. The back was brown and weathered and covered in honey brown hair. His forearms looked more than twice the thickness of my own, and his thighs, which threatened to spit the fabric of his trousers, were massive, like a rugby player. I wondered if he played the sport, he had the perfect build for it. I was electrified by each movement that he made; the crossing of an ankle over his knee, the scratch of an itch on the back of his hand. When he cleared his throat to speak I thought about the sound he would make just before he came.

"I read your book," I said hurriedly at the end of the meeting, as he fastened his coat to go. I felt that if I did not get the words out of my mouth quickly enough I would never say them at all.

Lawrence stopped, the zipper on his jacket half fastened, and looked straight at me.

I felt myself blush again and wanted to run for the door. But I didn't. It had cost me a lot to overcome my natural reserve and get this far. No turning back. "It's really good."

"Thank you," he said, and smiled.

Daddy's Boyz

I babbled on, "In fact, you inspired me to write a story of my own. I'd love for you to read it — give me your opinion."

"Really?" He seemed genuinely flattered.

"Yeah," I looked around the room. "Only ... not here."

We were in his living room, together on the sofa, close, very close — kissing. It was two hours and two bottles of beer later. I had made the first move, running a finger over his thigh as he read my story. The beer and the tent in his jeans had given me courage.

"We don't have to do this," he said. "I don't want to take advantage."

"You're not. I want this."

The pages of the manuscript fluttered to the floor as I launched myself at him, throwing myself over him. His body felt huge beneath my own, a mountain of muscle and flesh. I squirmed against his chest, crushing my dick against his stomach and buried my tongue.

"I want this too, I really want it," he said. The sweet, helpless tone of his voice made me want him more. "But I'm much older than you. It doesn't seem right."

"That doesn't matter," I nibbled his bottom lip.

"I think it does. How old is your dad?"

"Forty something," I gasped, groping the hardness at the front of his jeans. "Forty six, I think."

He gripped my wrists just as I was about to open his fly and said, "I'm forty eight."

"So?"

"So, don't you think I'm too old for you?" he asked.

"No. Am I too young for you?" I asked.

He groaned, "You could get a man arrested."

"It's all legal," I assured him.

It seemed to me that if Lawrence was reluctant to take advantage of a younger man, then it was up to me to get what I wanted. I eased myself back, sitting right across his lap, and pulled my T-shirt over my head. I took his hands and guided then over my body, around my hips, across the curve of my lower spine, down to my ass. The look on Lawrence's face was enough to say he wanted me, but I could see there was still some quandary in his eyes. I rocked my hips a little, feeling the hardness of his cock somewhere between my ass and balls. I bore down, applying pressure to the mound in his jeans. He gasped and suddenly his hands began to take over, cupping my ass cheeks, squeezing through my pants. I gripped his shoulders and kissed him again, more passionately, bruising my lips against his mouth. His tongue came into my mouth, and he made it his own.

We stayed like that for ages, kissing, rubbing against each other. I sensed that he was still nervous, afraid to push me. I had to take charge. I slithered down onto the floor and bent over his crotch.

"Oh," he sighed as I worked at the fastening of his clothes, hitching his ass, so I could tug his jeans down his thighs. He wore white cotton briefs, bulging with meat. I could feel the heat of his groin before I even got close. I reached inside the waist band and uncovered my prize, which was harder and thicker than even in my fantasies. I gripped the base and covered my mouth over it, pushing back the skin with my lips. Lawrence groaned and shifted his pelvis, leaning into my mouth. I gave his balls a tug, and when his dick responded favorably, I got to work on his hairy sack, tugging and twisting with wanton enthusiasm.

I glanced at his stomach as I sucked. At the thick expanse of his waist, at the dark trail of hair that widened beneath his navel into a dense bush of honey colored curls. His belly rose and fell, juddering with tension when my tongue caressed him in an extra special place. I'm a boy who knows how to suck and who enjoys it. Despite the girth, it was not long before I had the whole of his cock crammed into my mouth, deeply inhaling the funky sweat of his pubes.

He gave good warning when he was about to cum, but I ignored it, holding him at the back of my mouth, gobbling hard until his jizz began to shoot. I swallowed the lot, licking his cock clean before sitting back proudly.

His bedroom was cozy, plainly decorated with just a double bed, a chest of drawers and a small television. He turned on a lamp and undressed me slowly, kissing me everywhere. It seemed like forever before I was finally naked, lying on his bed. Lawrence lay on top of me, kissing me on the lips again, his cock pressing hard between my thighs, nudging my balls.

"What do you like?" he asked, flicking his tongue over my top lip. "What's your favorite thing to do?"

Daddy's Boyz

I slipped a hand between our bodies and held his cock, giving it a good squeeze. "Lick my ass," I said, "then ride me."

Lawrence wriggled down the bed as I raised my knees. He got to work on my hole with his tongue, making me moan and squirm. Nothing gets me more excited than a tongue in my ass. I shuddered with little paroxysms of pleasure. His hands held my ass, and he rocked his face back and forth in the crack, pausing to whisper how sweet my hole tasted. My body felt like liquid, melting from the ass inwards.

"Fuck me now," I groaned.

Lawrence grinned, getting off the bed to fetch lube, rubbers and a towel from the bathroom. I held the back of my knees, watching as he covered his cock in rubber, anticipating that he would soon be inside me. He got back onto the bed and down between my legs, pushing a lube-loaded finger into my hole. The gel was cold, and I gasped as he wriggled his way inside.

"Need any more?" he asked, pushing into the knuckle.

"A little," I said. I was hot and ready, but his cock was bigger than what I had been used to. My ass gratefully ate the extra finger of lube.

Lawrence lay across me, missionary style, holding his weight. He guided his cock to my hole, hesitated for a moment's assurance before pushing in. With his big meat bound into my ass, he started kissing me again I was completely destroyed. I wrapped my arms and legs around him, locking on, and swung my hips from the bed, grinding his dick deeper and deeper into my body. Soon we were dripping with the heat we generated.

He pulled out, leaving me wanting for a precious few seconds, before turning me over and re-entering me from behind. This position was even better. He dug his fingers into my hips and hauled me onto all fours, driving his dick into my chute. I felt the tremendous power of his hips impacting with my ass, a loud crack reverberated through the room with every thrust. I loved the sounds he made as he fucked, groaning like an animal; one moment he was all powerful, another helpless and lost. I was lost entirely; lost to my ass and lost to Lawrence.

"Oh God," he groaned, shooting, riding through me, tearing up my asshole. I got a hand on my dick and finished myself off quickly. With Lawrence still firing away, I began to cum, blowing a soppy white load all over the covers.

Lawrence's bathtub was just about big enough for the two of us. He took the end nearest to the tap. The water, infused with lemon grass and mandarin oil, came precariously close to the brim, and had spilled onto the floor more than once. Lawrence didn't seem to mind. Below the surface our bodies touched, our ankles lying easily over each others hips. A soul CD played in the bedroom, and the sound drifted through the steamy milieu. It was three days since the night we first slept together.

"I've been looking at your book again," I told him.

Lawrence looked at me with heavy eyes, smiling softly, a little embarrassed. "You must know that story better than I do," he said.

"How much of it is true?" I asked. "How much of that story is your own?"

He shrugged, "What does it mater?"

"It matters to me. I want to know who you are," I said.

He sighed and dipped his broad shoulders below the surface. "It's true," he said, "the book; most of it anyway, all the important parts."

"So you were married ... until you were forty?" I asked.

"Actually I was 39. I rounded it up," he said.

"And you have kids?"

"Two daughters," he said. "Both at school. The eldest isn't much younger than you. She's about to take her exams."

"Does it bother you? That I am so much younger than you?" I asked.

He shrugged, "A little bit. I'm more concerned about what people will think. I don't want my girls distressed by gossip."

"It doesn't matter to me," I said.

He stroked my calf beneath the water, "That's because you're only 19. Nothing is a problem at 19."

"That's not true," I said, a little upset that he could underestimate the strength of my feelings.

"Before you met me, how many boyfriends did you have?" he asked.

"Not many. A couple." I answered.

"A couple? What about casual sex?" he asked.

Now it was my turn to feel embarrassed. "A couple," I said shyly, "... of dozen."

His eyes widened, "I haven't had that many men in the last five years."

"Then you need to get out more," I teased.

Lawrence offered me the benefit of his experience in more ways than one. It was his suggestion that we write a story together. He had been reading a collection of stories by a writer in San Francisco and several of the stories had been written in collaboration with other writers. He thought it was something we could try for ourselves.

"What should we write about?" I asked. We were in his study, looking at the computer screen, cursor blinking on a blank page. Lawrence was sitting in his chair, while I sat across his lap, my small butt pressing against his groin, his hands holding my waist, keeping me in place. We were wearing T-shirts and nothing else. My ass was warm and wet from the fuck he'd recently given me.

"Let's write about us," he said. "That way we can both contribute."

I went first, placing my hands upon the keyboard. I started typing, not really thinking, just letting the words splatter from my mind onto the page. I wrote a sex scene, a depiction of the afternoons and early evenings I had spent in Lawrence's bedroom; fucking, drinking beer and wine, eating chocolate, sucking cock. Sometimes for fun, Lawrence would spank me; I hadn't been into it to begin with, but now, with his hand upon my ass, he couldn't hit me hard enough. "I am always the bottom," my story began.

Lawrence's chin rested on my shoulder as he watched my words filling the flickering monitor. "Do you want to change?" he asked, his fingers played just beneath my T-shirt, trekking around my navel. "Do you want to fuck me?"

"No," I said, quite determinedly. "I don't want to fuck you." To prove my point, I squirmed a little in the seat of his lap, rubbing my butt crack against his groin. He chuckled and moved his right hand to my cock, using his thumb to spread precum across the head.

Now that he had me hot, there would be no more writing — not for a while at least. I shuffled forward on his knee, getting my feet back on the floor. I stood up, leaning across the desk, shoving my ass back for Lawrence to appreciate. He pushed back his chair and opened my ass wider with his hands, breathing softly on my hot, sticky little pucker.

"It's like a little candy heart," he said, kissing my rim. "It tastes better than chocolate, better than strawberries." His tongue played around the opening, poking softly into the interior. "I can taste my cock on your ass. I can taste where I've been and where I'm going."

I wriggled, leaning forward on the desk, giving my ass in supplication, wanting only one thing.

Once his tongue had tasted enough, he replaced it with his finger — going further, deeper. Then his hands grasped my ass, pushing my cheeks together, wrenching them apart. "Tell me want you want, son."

"I want your cock, Dad. I want you to fuck me, Dad." This was part of the game now. I found it embarrassing, but I went along with it. It made Lawrence happy and that made me happy. No complaints, especially not once he started to fuck. Lubed and rubbered, when his cock was in my ass, that's where he was and where he belonged. He held me, digging his fingers into my cheeks, and ground my ass with his meat. I listened for the sounds my ass makes when he rode it — deep and wet — sweeter than music when he pulled all the way out, squelching shut before his cock opened me up again.

I held back until Lawrence started to cum. The throb of him inside was always enough to trigger my own reaction; a pulse deep inside my ass, electric oscillations through my balls, and then spunk bursting out my cock in high, white arches that splattered the keyboard and the oak wood desk.

Lawrence pulled out, sitting back in the chair. As I rested forward, supporting myself on the desk in front of me, he prized my ass cheeks apart with both hands and pressed his face into the crack, inhaling and tasting the ambrosia of my freshly fucked hole. I reached for the mouse control and clicked the save button on the menu bar, saving my story for a later date. There was so much more for me to experience with Lawrence before the story could continue. Maybe one day, if we kept up the work, we'd have enough material for a novel of our very own.

The Big Dog
Tulsa Brown

Damn, I hurt. I hunched on the locker room bench and unlaced my skates, tired fingers fumbling with the knots. The muscles in my legs howled, and thin welts burned up between my shoulder blades. Even the arches of my feet ached. And this was called the fun league.

The loss sat on my shoulders like bricks. Nobody wins — or loses — a hockey game by himself, but in the low rumble of my teammates around me I imagined I heard my name, and worse.

"Fast as frozen fucking molasses. What is he, anyway?"

"Gotta be 40 this year. That's old-timer league, for sure."

"Hey, Doze!" I looked. Andy, our center, was already in his jacket, duffle in one hand, "You coming for a beer?"

"Sure, aw ... shit. I don't know. It's an early morning," I said.

"Come on. We can win this thing in three," Andy said.

He meant pints. The Raiders re-played every game in the bar. We were the best table-top team in the league.

Andy leaned in and thumped me on the shoulder, "Don't let the asswipes get you down, Doze. They got in a few lucky shots."

"Yeah — about five to one," I said. We laughed, and my spirits lifted an inch "OK. The usual place? Save me a chair."

Andy glanced over his shoulder at the men milling about. Our locker room was separated from the Visitors' by a single hallway. "I'll wait for you. You got in some pretty fine shots yourself," Andy said.

He was right. I was a defenseman, and what I lacked in speed I made up in bulk — and intent. Fighting was an instant suspension in our league, but I wasn't afraid to nail a guy legally. My full nickname was Bulldoze, and I lived up to it: 230 pounds that felt like more if it caught you against the boards. One little shit had goaded me all night, darted needlessly in and out of my zone; I swear he called me "Pops." I'd caught him twice with hard, clean, wind-sucking checks that made him kiss the ice. But it was only fair. They'd nailed our guys with some cheap shots, too.

Bob Condron

I grinned at Andy's worry, "They already got the win. They're not going to risk a default by beating the crap out of me."

I finally convinced him to go on ahead. By the time I'd peeled off my pads, the locker room was deserted, and I decided to treat my aching muscles to an after-game shower.

It was a rare luxury. I'd been boyfriend-less for almost a year except for an occasional lucky one-nighter. I didn't trust myself, even with my team mates — their long, powerful backs, hairy thighs and tight, tough little asses. I wouldn't just raise a flag of interest, I'd be waving it. My friends were easy-going enough to rib me: Hey, Doze, go bat your eyelashes at the ref. He's murdering us! But there was a tacit agreement — they never saw the real thing.

I could have been more militant, maybe. But I loved this game, and I was one of the "six pack," original members who'd been the core of the Raiders since we began seven years ago. I'd worked hard to be one of the guys, not the queer guy.

So how do you know when it was time to hang up your skates? I wondered. When your body paid two days for your hour on the ice — or when the whole team began to pay for it? And would anyone have the guts to tell me to my face?

A shower is short work for me. I'd shaved my whole head down to auburn stubble, to beat my retreating hairline at its own game. Still I lingered under the warm stream even after the soap was gone, soaking the parts I knew would hurt tomorrow. Finally, I turned off the water and stood, waiting to stop dripping.

"Do they call you Doze because you can sleep on skates?"

The voice was young, unfamiliar — trouble. The "Pops" guy? Needles of alarm sped through my veins. I should have listened to Andy!

Without turning, I reached for my towel and began to wipe off with calculated ease, buying time while my mind raced. Had he brought friends? How many was I up against? Well, I wasn't going down without a fight.

Heart thumping, I tied the towel around my waist and finally turned. Only one man leaned against the end of the lockers, a long stretch of denim and black leather, topped by a rowdy thatch of dishwater blonde hair. The moment cracked, then split. He was one of ours.

Daddy's Boyz

Shaun was barely 20, a smart-ass college rat, who'd played forward in the Raiders' last three games. He missed practices and had a mouth as reckless as a high stick. Everyone grumbled but not loudly. Shaun was fast, and we needed him.

Now, he smirked, chuffing his hockey stick against the black sponge floor, and looked me up and down. In a gay bar I would have been flattered — the kid was a flare. But we were a long way from that territory, and he'd given me a jolt along with the snide remark. Adrenaline still burned under my skin.

"You say something, Shaun?" I asked.

"You're in pretty good shape," Shaun said.

He didn't add "for an old man," but I heard it anyway, tasted it like an oily film.

Walk, I told myself. I strode past with determination, and the next words landed on my back.

"Must be all the beauty rest you get — hiding behind the net." The blade of his stick prodded my ass.

I wheeled around, seized the wood and yanked hard. He couldn't let go fast enough and stumbled forward, landing on his hands and knees with an ungainly thump. When he looked up, surprise had wiped the arrogance off his long cherub's face.

"That sleepy enough for you, Shaun?" I tossed the stick and it clattered on the shower tiles.

I turned the corner to my locker, still vibrating. I pulled on my clothes like an automaton, listening intently, muscles coiled for the moment he came around, swinging.

Instead, I heard him get up and leave, a blustery stomp punctuated by the squawk of the door hinges. My heart rate slowed, and I wilted, then sat down. The first blaze had burned off, leaving the blackened, bitter stubble of regret. Disgust.

Dammit, Roy. What's the matter with you? You let a kid get to you? What the hell was that?

But I knew its twisted face: Envy. I might have mistaken Shaun's voice, but his body had seared me these past three games. Watching him strip down and suit up had been a sweet kind of agony, his lean, healthy frame was a distant memory to even the fittest among us. Our bodies were condensing, settling; at our very best we were broadswords on the ice, burnished but unwieldy. Shaun was a rapier, resilient, flashing.

And to see him go! His skates dug at the ice in jagged strides when he hurtled toward the puck, a wild clawing for speed. My own lungs burned to watch him. He didn't bother to pace himself because the well of energy was bottomless. A geyser. And each time he rushed, I remembered it, felt the magic like a ghost in my own body: Indestructible.

Then the next moment I awoke in clay and resentment. And today I'd dumped that bitterness all over him, the price of a harmless joke. It wasn't just stupid it was shameful, and there was nothing I could do about it now.

I finished dressing and packed my gear. At the end of the arena's long hallway, I pushed open the last door with my shoulder. The December night smacked me awake, a hard, bright bitterness against my face, cold fingers clutching into my jacket. I hunched down and started toward my car.

The parking lot was nearly empty, the towering light standards drawing stark circles on the snow. It crunched like Styrofoam under my feet and gleamed with slicks of ice. I kept my gaze in front of me, so I wouldn't wind up on my ass. That's how I almost missed him.

Shaun was standing under the lamp post closest to the street. Hands deep in his pockets, jaw tucked into the collar, he was a sapling in black leather, swaying aimlessly in a private wind. His breath rose in delicate puffs, gathered in a halo of steam around his silky hair. Forgotten angel.

I felt the sudden burn of my regret again, and more. Studying him closely, I could see his whole body trembling — that stylish jacket was paper thin. The kid was freezing.

"Hey, Shaun. You got a ride?" I asked.

He turned and his gaze glittered, holding me at bay. A little boy's wounded pride had been poured into the long pitcher of a man's body.

"I'm supposed to be getting one," he said.

But the street was empty. That bit of truth rang loudly in the lonely lot.

"You want to phone? I've got my cell in the car," I jerked my head toward the Passat.

He hesitated, still glaring, then bent down to pluck his bag and stick out of the snow.

"Fuck," he muttered under his breath, yet he trotted along obediently to the car. Inside the close darkness, I fired the ignition and leaned over to click a gauge on his side, then one on my own. "The seats will be warm in a minute."

He snorted, "Heated leather. Is that for your old arthritic bones?"

"It's for my cold Canadian ass," I said.

Shaun grinned in spite of himself, surprised, and the sudden sparkle lifted me under the ribs. Damn, did he know how devastating that smile was?

"The phone's in the glovebox," I said.

The engine was a quiet purr. I couldn't miss the faint ramble of the wiseass recording against his ear, some young buck bragging he was too busy getting laid to answer the phone.

"Yeah, well I hope he's hot," Shaun blustered into the mouthpiece. "I hope he burns your nuts right off. It's ten-fucking-thirty, Brandon! You let me down again. And guess what — I'm done. No more chances. We're through, asshole. Yeah, you say 'it's so right, it's so right,' then you can't even …" His voice broke, then tumbled to a whisper, "It's not like I ever asked you to come watch."

Beep. End call.

Shaun lowered the little silver module, clutched it tightly against his thigh, and leaned his forehead into his other hand.

Waves of revelation rolled over me, but one thought struck like an arrow and stayed, quivering in my psyche. That had been his lover.

I started to drive. I had no destination, but Shaun needed to move out of that moment, and I was determined to take him. The air in the car seemed raw, like a scrape. I ached with my own memories, men who demanded everything in bed, yet never came to a single game. It ignited a fierce, protective flare. I would have liked to meet Brandon — introduce him to my shoulder and the arena boards.

But I had my own garbage to deal with.

"I know you're having a shitty day, Shaun, and I sure didn't help," I took a breath. "I was a jerk, back at the rink. I'm sorry."

Long, agonizing seconds. It was hard to keep my eyes on the road.

"I just wanted a chance," he said to the window. "The six of you — it's like you're welded together. Out on the ice you're always watching their backs. Somebody nails Andy and bam! You're right there. The enforcer."

I winced. It was true. The guys in the "six pack" looked out for each other.

"Even afterwards, somebody's always around you. Paul, Mike, Kevin. I never get a chance," he said.

That word again. "Chance for what?"

His voice softened, suddenly shy, "To ask you out."

I was stunned. He'd been cruising me — poking me with his stick? Impossible, yet I had a painful flash. I remembered being 20, wanting someone and not knowing how to start. Doing it wrong, playing it badly. You remember how agile your game used to be, I thought, and forget how clumsy the rest of your life was. And underneath the miracle blazed in a thousand-volt burn: This gorgeous kid was interested? My heart was pounding. I had two hands on the wheel, trying not to crash, trying to play it cool. "All you had to say was, 'Hey, Roy. Want to go for a beer?'"

"Your name's Roy?" Shaun asked.

"Last time I checked the roster."

In the corner of my eye I saw him staring, boldness crystallizing his watery surface. His eyes were hazel, his chin an abrupt turn, a playful curve at the bottom of the straight, handsome planes.

"Hey, Roy," he said.

"The answer's, Yes," I said.

Pressure on my thigh, sudden, firm lips on my cheek. The blunt force of his kiss astonished me, electric and smooth. Jesus, did he even shave? The thought licked up my balls. I veered over the line, then pulled the car back.

He was enjoying my distraction, "So, still want that beer?"

No. I wanted him to kiss my ice — lay him out spread-eagled on the white sheets of my bed, ass up. But something occurred to me, and I explained my promise to Andy. If I didn't call and cancel, the guys would worry, suspecting the worst. "Hand me the phone," I said.

"No, let's go meet them," he blurted. "They've never asked me and ... I want to go."

Daddy's Boyz

I felt a clutch. The six pack had known me for seven years. They'd look at my face and see it — slobbering lust. The old guy. The old queer guy, a fool or worse. And then there was the unspoken agreement: ours was a closed circle, a private club whenever we met. Like a clearing hacked into the forest, it was a haven where we could be ourselves, howl at the moon if we had to.

I glanced at Shaun. His chin tilted up bravely, but his eyes were wet stones. Hungry. He wanted to be at that table with the big boys. And I wanted him. Goddamn it. When did I get to howl at the moon?

"Then let's go get a beer," I said.

A cheer went up from a corner table in the crowded little pub when I walked in, another wash of noise over the din. It faded away to a prickly silence as Shaun edged up beside me. I could feel his tight, tense body at my elbow, his rapid breath. The audacity he showed on the ice had vanished; this was a different arena.

Five wary men gazed up at us. These were my friends, but I'd caught them by surprise, and resentment glimmered in their faces before they could hide it: If we wanted the mouthy pup, we would have invited him.

Well, I just did. I seized a couple of chairs from another table and brandished them boldly.

"Got room for two?" It wasn't a question. Chairs scraped, and Shaun and I squeezed in. For an uncomfortable moment the conversation hovered, no one sure how to start up again. I glanced across at Andy, and he raised an eyebrow, the devil twinkling in his familiar eyes: My slobbering lust was loud and clear. Suddenly he leaned over the table toward Shaun.

"Jesus, kid, it's about time you showed up," he announced. "I was starting to think: Yeah, he can skate, but can he drink?"

Poker faces grinned at last. The ice didn't break, but it cracked, voices rumbled to life again, and my guts began to unwind. It wasn't long before we were re-hashing the game, reveling in the finer moments of sportsmanship.

"You know, Roy, we ought to change your name. You weren't a bulldozer tonight, you were a fucking animal. A bulldog."

"The big dog!" Andy chortled.

"Yeah, well, I wish I would have bit them on the ass instead of pissing on their leg," I said, and the table rang with laughter.

I felt drunk on a single beer, my shoulders wide across the back of the chair. Shaun's knee connected with mine under the table, an insistent press of desire and gratitude. He was happy to be here.

I scoured him surreptitiously from the corner of my eye, savoring his long thighs and the alluring bulge in his jeans, just above the inside seam. When I dared to glance at his face, the combination of softness and masculinity gripped me between the legs. His bones were still growing and remnants of prettiness clung to the emerging man: his Cupid's bow mouth, the silky skin. At the same time, there was a gangly eagerness to him — he was the first to laugh, or knock something off the table. Away from the ice, he was a long-legged puppy.

And mine. He was only here because I'd made a place for him. That thought wrapped an exciting coil around me, different strands that twisted into a thick rope of desire.

I stood up, "Well, it's an early morning ..."

"And a school night," Andy waggled a finger at me, eyes glinting. "That boy should be in bed already."

I laughed — wicked son of a bitch! I caught his eye as I pulled on my jacket and winked.

Farewells from the table followed us out the door, warm and easy now, and I walked into the parking lot a taller man. I had better friends than I knew.

"They're good guys," Shaun said, a note of wonder rising up with the vapor of his breath.

"Sure, as long as you behave yourself," I said.

"And if I don't, then what?" he asked.

It was a tease, a nip at the big dog's tail, but loaded with a dare that sent a scalding wave from my balls to my belly. He wanted to play?

"Guess," I said.

I drove to my apartment without asking him. Inside the door, he grabbed me, arms around my neck, long, light body grinding against me. My kisses bit and gouged; I knew my stubble burned his milky smooth skin. Yet wordless instinct urged me to mark him, even with razor burn. I groped under his jacket in a blind, unthinking way, hungry for the feel of his body. When his hands dropped to fumble with my belt buckle, I caught him by the wrists.

"Not so fast, little man," I said.

He pulled back, panting lightly through succulent parted lips, heavy-lidded hazel eyes turned to smoke. Two fantasies had intersected, wires sparking.

"Go into the living room and strip. Not too fast," I said. I'd had enough stolen glimpses in the locker room; this time I wanted the whole show.

"Yes, Roy," he said. There was an obedient clip to the words. He made my name sound like a title, or rank. I liked that.

I shrugged off my own jacket, then sauntered in to lean against my living room wall, fully dressed. My hard-on threatened to tear the teeth of my zipper, but I savored the thrilling discomfort, feeling more powerful because of it. I was almost 40 — I reveled in my stamina and patience.

In the center of the room, Shaun began to peel off his clothes, littering the carpet with a teenager's disregard, and for long seconds I was enraptured. Lean, tight, his chest was hairless and smooth, pecs firm but not too pronounced, nipples budding in a surprising shade of pink. His arms had the swooping curves of muscle still gathering, corded with veins, far more sinew than bulk. He was too young to fight. Nature had built him to run.

When he unzipped his jeans, my mouth watered. A thin stripe of dark brown hair rode down his abdomen into his underwear, but it was a signpost I didn't need. My gaze was riveted on his white briefs and the hard jut in the pouch, the fabric so taut I could have traced the ridge of his cock head with my tongue.

He let his pants fall and tramped them down, then slipped his thumbs into his waistband and played there, teasing. For the first time, I realized he was smirking at me; he knew the effect he was having. Cheeky little god, I thought.

"Pick up your clothes and fold them," I ordered. "Or do you need to be taught manners?"

Shaun inhaled sharply, a sound that said more than words. We were both deep in the same intoxicating dream. I unzipped, easing the pressure on my swollen, bent cock. In two steps I was beside him, his hair a handful of silk in my grasp.

"This is my house you're in. You're not going to forget that," I said.

"No, Roy," he was breathless.

"And here's to make sure," I turned him sideways in front of me, my left arm on his naked chest to steady him. He clutched my solid forearm, hanging on. I yanked down his shorts to mid-thigh and gazed at the saucy globes of his buttocks — mouthwatering.

And then I saw it — the wide, tilted crescent of angry red on his back, already turning purple, one of the worst cheap shots our team had taken in a long time. I remembered seeing that check, a dirty, expert elbow under the pads that had slammed Shaun into the boards and sent him down. I'd winced for him at the time, then immediately forgot it. That was the game.

Now a new sensation went through me, a leap of paternal outrage. I wanted to protect him – after I made him mine.

I brought the flat of my hand down once, twice on the curve of his ass, ringing smacks that made him quiver, gasping. My balls seethed and my hand hummed with heat. I tore my T-shirt up and off, and turned him to face me.

Shaun moaned softly at the sight of my naked chest then melted into it, rubbing his face across the wiry hair of my broad pecs, into the valley of my breastbone. He stroked one cheek then the other in a dreamy, nuzzling trance. Animal worship. I held him with one arm and reached down with my other hand to unbuckle my belt, just as his mouth closed on my nipple.

Lightning. He tugged on me in swift, savage pulls that sent claws of lust deep into my body. My newly-released cock twitched, pugnacious and famished, nudging his naked skin. I closed my hand around us both, squeezed the broadsword and the rapier together as two throbbing lengths. Forget stamina and patience, if I didn't mount this man soon, I'd shoot all over his legs.

"Bed," I said tersely.

This was going to be a two-cock-ring event. Shaun sat on his haunches, rapt, as I secured one rubber circlet at the base of my shaft, the other around my balls, drawing them into a tight, swollen peach. My member surged before my eyes, thick veins and satiny mushroom cap oozing precum. It felt like a thick arm swaying between my legs, fist clenched.

Daddy's Boyz

"Holy shit," Shaun whispered. He moved to fall on me, devour me, but I caught his pretty face in my hands.

"Uh uh. In Roy's house we play safe," But I let him crouch on his knees and lick my balls, tugging up my cock, so he could reach the sensitive underside. His wet lapping and eager little grunts were almost unbearable. I stepped back and raised him to his feet, enveloped him in an embrace as I spoke against his ear.

"Tell me what you want, Shaun."

He hesitated, breathing rapidly, excited and frightened, "Take me, Roy. Lay me out and fuck me hard."

The wallop of lust made me reel, then reality shouldered in: Go slow or you'll tear him apart. On the bed I straddled him, oiling his back, buttocks and thighs in sinuous circles, carefully avoiding the deepening bruise. But the sight of it was a cinder in my eye.

I brought him up on his hands and knees and lubed his crevice, entered him gently with a thick finger, then two. I tugged lightly on his cock until he was rocking back against my hand, impaling himself on it, his guttural grunts rolling through my urgent murmur.

"That's it, that's a good boy. You can take it. Come on, little man, fuck my hand."

Ready. I thought I'd split the condom when I rolled it on; my engorged cock looked huge even to my own eyes. But the moment I pressed past his tight rosebud I was beyond all caring. The hot squeeze was sweetness itself; a gravelly groan unfurled from my belly. As if from a distance I heard Shaun's voice, not a cry but a bare animal call of being opened, overwhelmed, bested. I began to buck slowly, my buttocks twitching with unstoppable instinct. I reached between his legs, gripped his greased hard-on and let my thrusts power his.

Each stroke sent unearthly pleasure cascading down my shaft, goaded me to the next. Faster. My cock was a carnal beast, plowing heedlessly into its own craving. My churning balls soon contracted, irresistibly rising, and at last I shot in wave after wave of scalding bliss. Emptying. I clutched Shaun as release thundered through my body, tolled in slow, exquisite reverberations through every muscle. Glory.

Cuming like that leaves you wordless. For long moments, we simply lay together, breathing. I felt weightless in the ebbing tide, light and strong. Pleasure had made me new again. Indestructible. When I finally stretched out under the covers, Shaun nestled into the crook of my big arm. I was amazed that his long-legged puppy frame fit against me so neatly.

"I was going to quit, you know," he said quietly.

Leaden alarm. "Not the team. You're the fastest thing we've got," I said.

He nodded against my chest. "I love this game but ... I was so lonely. Nobody seemed to give a shit. And it wasn't just all of you guys going out together. On the ice ... well, nobody gave a damn there, either," he said.

I felt the pang again, but this time regret hardened into resolve.

I kissed the top of his silky head, "You know what, little man? I'm not going to hang up my skates any time soon. And the next guy who comes after you looking to score a cheap shot, well, he'd better be ready to meet the big dog."

Eating Fugu

Marcel K. Bromius.

"Professor?"

Armand glanced up from the book he was reading. He didn't recognize the man before him, and raised an eyebrow at him in questioning.

"Professor Lehrer?"

"I'm sorry I can't place you, and it has been a few years since I was a professor," Armand frowned; he did not normally forget a face.

"My gods, it is you!" The man said smiling as he sat down on a wire mesh chair, across from Armand at the outdoor café, his books falling from his arms onto the small, glass tabletop. "I never imagined I would see you here of all places!"

Armand looked amused as he watched the man unload his belongings while trying to get comfortable. He didn't say a word the entire time while he waited for an answer to his question.

"Oh yes! I'm sorry!" The man glanced at his silent amusement. "It's me, Jordan — Jordan Mcbride. I took two of your classes on molecular genetics, and then you helped me with my thesis."

Armand smiled slightly, remembering Jordan five years ago, as a young student with shoulder-length brown hair, a thin wiry build, and always dressing in three piece suits; he still looked the same. "I recall."

"So what are you doing here?" Jordan grinned.

"I'm retired and living here," Armand smiled. "Would you like some coffee or something to drink?"

Jordan shook his head no, "You haven't changed. I mean …well, I recognized you."

"What are you doing in San Francisco?" Armand's eyes mischievously twinkled as he watched Jordan's nervousness.

"Oh, I'm here for a conference," Jordan stared at Armand. He tried to figure out how old he was, and how the five years seemed so long ago since he last saw him. He couldn't believe the man was in shape at his age, with a full head of blond hair and goatee.

Only wrinkles had proclaimed the passage of time on his face with small frown lines around his eyes and on his cheeks.

"What type of work are you doing?" Armand summoned the waiter and ordered another Café Latte. At the last moment, Jordan ordered a black coffee.

"I'm a senior protein biochemist for Stellar Biotechnologies," Jordan responded. "I work with production of marine derived compounds for the pharmaceutical industry." He shifted nervously in his chair before blurting, "The conference I'm attending is about experimental biology and translating the Genome. Do you mind if I smoke?"

"Of course not," Armand chuckled.

Jordan pulled out a pack of Marlboro cigarettes and lit one as he glanced around the busy wharf, his eyes centering on the distant view of Alcatraz. The prison sat alone on top of an island in the bay surrounded by smog. He wetted his lips before his eyes moved back to Armand, "So are you here with anyone?"

"No."

Jordan nodded, finding himself at a loss for words.

Armand watched him for awhile, relishing in his discomfort, "Do I make you nervous?"

Jordan inhaled deeply on his cigarette before responding, "Actually professor you've always made me nervous."

"Please don't call me professor," Armand laughed. "I've been retired for about three years. You can call me Armand."

Jordan nodded before looking away from his piercing stare.

"Why do I make you so nervous? I don't bite unless you ask me to," Armand said.

Jordan didn't respond nor look at Armand's eyes, but shifted uncomfortably.

Amused, Armand watched as this young man nervously tapped his foot on the cobblestones, and remembered when he used to do it in his lab.

The coffees were brought to their table and set down, and Jordan immediately began adding sugar to his and stirring it, while Armand thanked the waitress.

"Married? Children?" Armand asked.

"No to both questions," Jordan kept his eyes lowered and stared at his coffee. Finally, as if throwing caution to the wind, he said, "I'm gay ... And I had a crush on you back in college, professor ... err ... I mean Armand."

Jordan peeked up through long eyelashes at Armand to see how he would respond to the confession, and was surprised to see his professor still unruffled by the proclamation.

"Well you've come to the right place," Armand grinned, his lips curling up in amusement. "They don't call this the gay capital for no reason. So, do you still have a crush on me?"

Jordan squirmed in his seat, "Ah ... Well ... That was a long time ago."

"You still don't like answering my questions directly," Armand chuckled. "Remember when you didn't know the answer in class and you used to do that? You would try to answer it with another question or make reference to something else."

"That's not true!" Jordan quipped, "I normally knew the answers!"

"Hmm, funny how we remember it differently," Armand said.

"So, why did you decide to retire here, in San Francisco?" Jordan asked.

"Apparently we have some things in common," Armand nonchalantly replied.

I knew he was gay! Jordan thought. He had always fantasized about him, but he never believed he would actually find out the truth. Perplexed, he wasn't sure what to say next, and shifted uncomfortably to relieve his hardening cock.

"I guess that would explain why you never married," Jordan confessed, "Most of the kids used to say you were such a bad ass that no woman would be able to deal with you."

"Why am I not surprised?" Armand chuckled, "I've heard worse over the years."

"They weren't all bad. You were a great inspiration to me," Jordan said.

"I hope you don't mean that in the way of your sexuality?" Armand asked.

"No, of course not," Jordan quickly responded and then realized Armand was joking. He smiled at the remark, and looked at his watch frowning at the time. "I'm sorry but I need to get going or I'll miss the next lecture."

"Well, it was wonderful seeing you again after all this time!" Armand said.

Jordan gulped the last of his coffee, and crushed his cigarette before gathering his books and standing. He pulled at his baggy pants to hide his erection, but not before Armand's eyes dropped to his crotch assessing the situation. Nothing ever escaped Armand's attention, not even now, Jordan cursed under his breath.

Armand stood and held out his hand.

"Perhaps we could get together later and talk or something after my conference is over?" Jordan shook Armand's hand while balancing his books in his other arm.

"I'm sure we can work something out," Armand said.

"The answer is yes," Jordan blurted while staring at his professor's angular face. "Yes, I still have a crush on you."

"Are you making a pass at me?" Armand raised an eyebrow, and smiled.

"Christ! Why do you make me feel like I'm a child again?" Jordan shook his head in disbelief, "I suppose I am."

"You flatter me, but I fear my tastes run more extreme or kinkier than what you might get into," Armand said.

Jordan's heart sped up and he felt the blood rushing to his cheeks. His eyes dropped to the ground again before he spoke, "You might be surprised."

"Well, I won't keep you," Armand pulled out his wallet and handed Jordan one of his cards, "Call me and we'll talk some more."

Jordan's conference lasted until Friday, and that same evening he found himself standing in the upscale area around Golden Gate Park, in front of a row of townhouses.

He breathed deeply standing out front of Armand's house, willing himself to knock on the door. He didn't understand how the man aroused him with just a look.

They had spoken on the telephone the previous evening, and he discovered Armand was into the leather scene. Somehow, he wasn't surprised because of the authority that oozed freely from his persona.

He had similar fantasies but never the courage to get involved, instead remaining in secure vanilla relationships. He didn't tell

Daddy's Boyz

Armand he was already involved, and his lover, Rich, waited for him at home; he figured that information best kept secret.

No older man should look so good, Jordan decided when Armand answered the door in a pair of boots, leather pants, and a black muscled T-shirt. He looked comfortable, and it was obvious the pants were well worn.

Armand invited him in and showed him briefly around the first level.

"Would you like a drink?" Armand asked.

"A rum and coke would be fine," Jordan replied. He became fascinated with the large aquarium on the side of the wall, and bent down to look at the fish swimming inside.

Several fat puffer fish swam to the front of the glass, their fins moving faster than the eye could see as they buzzed around the tank, looking back at Jordan. Their large blue eyes reminded him of puppies with their sappy look. He placed a finger against the glass and one of the puffers drew back its lips, revealing its sharp teeth before it turned its back and swam away.

"Don't let them fool you," Armand chuckled, handing Jordan a drink. "They've already eaten this evening even though they're acting hungry."

"I didn't know you kept puffer fish," Jordan said.

"I find them fascinating," Armand replied. "I have some freshwater ones from South America upstairs, and a brackish tank with green spotted ones in my den. This is my marine tank, which houses the common puffer most people associate with, the porcupine fish."

"I believe we might be doing lab experiments with their Tetrodoxin poison," Jordan said.

"I wouldn't be surprised. Their poison is more potent than cyanide. When I was in Japan I actually ate some Fugu," Armand said.

"I don't think I would have the guts to do that," Jordan shuddered and took a sip of his drink. "They don't have an antidote for the poison."

"True," Armand replied, his eyes twinkling at the memory. "Interesting thing about eating Fugu, you actually get a little high. I honestly believe that is one of the reasons people take their chances."

"Or high off the fear," Jordan said.

"Ah we humans thrive on taking risks. Isn't that why you're here this evening?" Armand cocked his head, "Taking a chance?"

Immediately, Jordan dropped his gaze before the intense stare of his old professor. His heart thudded loudly up in his chest and his cock immediately swelled, but not knowing what to say, he remained quiet.

An uneasy silence seemed to fill the room, and when he glanced at Armand, the man looked to be in his element, his stance was at ease, but he watched him intently. Waiting.

Finally, Jordan sat down on the couch and set his drink on a coaster on the table before him. The table was a lacquered piece of driftwood, and it went nicely with the oak décor, and homey feeling Armand's house radiated. He ran a hand through his long-brown hair and realized he was sweating a little.

"I want you to do something for me," Armand said. "In my bathroom is a butt plug and harness. I want you to put it on, put your pants back on, and then come out here when you're done."

Jordan squirmed to relieve his arousal that pressed against his pants. His mind went blank, and without a word he nodded, stood up, and went to the bathroom. He found the butt plug and leather harness lying on the basin with some lubrication and condom. The plug was made out of jelly, and it wasn't very large, only about four inches with a tapered tip.

Breathing deeply, Jordan stared in the mirror at his shocked expression before he dropped his pants and underwear.

He mechanically went through the motions of lubricating his ass, putting a condom on the plug, then attaching it inside the harness, and stepping in. When he had brought the harness up to his body, he slowly worked the plug into his ass, squirming as the thicker part entered, and adjusted it securely inside.

His cock became instantly erect and pressed against his stomach with precum leaking from the slit while his hand itched to stroke it. However, he refrained, and finished dressing, making sure to place his cock in an upward position before securing his pants.

He sat down on the closed toilet seat for a moment to regain his composure, and felt the plug inside his ass, pressing against his

Daddy's Boyz

prostate. The feeling was exquisitely delicious. He wasn't used to feeling something in his ass, spreading his hole.

Why hadn't I bought toys before to play with Rich? He wondered, and found himself mentally excited to a degree he had never felt before. We have the occasional dildo, but seldom use it. I suspect Rich, uses it more when he's alone.

Finally, he worked up the courage to return to the outer room. Walking with the plug proved a different situation, it felt awkward, but the harness kept it in place. He tried to walk normally but found his gait a bit off, with the feeling of something shoved inside his ass, and his hard-on in the front. He tried to appear nonchalant about the whole situation, but he was already feeling embarrassed, like a child caught doing something wrong in front of his parents or teacher.

The conflicting emotions inside of Jordan made him uneasy, since he wasn't used to them nor knew how to handle them. Part of him was terribly excited beyond anything he had experienced before, and the other part was scared, not sure what would happen next, but unwilling to stop once the events were already in motion.

Jordan returned to his seat on the couch, acting as if nothing had changed; when in actuality everything was different.

The positions were very clear on who was in charge but had that ever changed? Jordan thought.

He finished his drink in several gulps, the alcohol warming his stomach and helping him to relax a little bit.

He finally and just briefly met Armand's eyes, and then quickly looked back at the fish tank. The puffers swam sporadically up and down the sides like caged tigers.

"How does it feel?" Armand asked.

"Fine."

"How do you feel?" Armand asked.

"Fine."

"Good," Armand chuckled.

More silence passed, and Jordan tried not to squirm because now his sitting position only pressed the plug deeper and harder against his pleasure zones.

He saw Armand had placed some items on the table while he was gone; a wooden paddle, some condoms, more lubricant, and a strange leather contraption with which he was not familiar. The knowledge of their impending union only heightened his already honed excitement.

"Tell me," Armand said, as he sat casually in an over-sized stuffed chair, "Exactly how does the plug feel in your ass?"

His mind swimming, Jordan's mouth dropped open for a few seconds before he closed it. The question made him extremely embarrassed, not being used to talking so blatantly about sex. The words, "what do you think" sat heavily upon his lips, but he dared not say such a thing because it was only an attack at something he didn't want to talk about, and he knew it.

"I'm not comfortable answering that," Jordan said.

"Ok."

Armand stood up and pushed the table away from Jordan. He moved in front of Jordan and stood regally in front of him with his legs spread in a conqueror's stance. The pants and shirt hugged his body like a second skin and defined his toned form, while his neatly trimmed goatee and blond hair were starkly pronounced against his black clad body.

"Take off your shirt," Armand ordered.

Jordan's eyes slowly moved up Armand's physique until he stared at his blue eyes glaring back at him. His heart beat so loudly in his chest he believed Armand could hear it.

Slowly, he unbuttoned his plaid shirt and slid it off his arms, placing it on the couch. Curly brownish dark hairs twirled thickly around his nipples and over his chest before they trailed down his stomach and disappeared into his pants.

Damn I need a cigarette! He thought, but dared not ask for one.

"You know I have a confession, too," Armand ran a hand over Jordan's face, stroking his cheek and lips. "I knew how you looked at me in class, and I would go home to beat off, thinking about fucking your tight ass."

Jordan gulped and thought he would swoon.

"You were always trying to impress me with your intelligence and knowledge," Armand bent slightly so he could play with Jordan's nipples. "I must confess it worked. I'm also glad to see one of my students has excelled so well in life."

"Some how I don't believe our roles have changed much," Jordan gasped, pushing his glasses back up his nose. "You're still teaching me."

Daddy's Boyz

Armand twisted Jordan's nipples gently at first before he pinched harder. He pulled both nipples upward, pulling against resistance until Jordan didn't have a choice but to follow. Jordan found himself standing so close to Armand he could smell his musky cologne.

Reaching around Jordan's body, Armand's hand slid between Jordan's ass cheeks, applying pressure to the plug, pushing it deeper into Jordan before his hand moved up Jordan's backside to rest behind Jordan's neck.

Armand held Jordan's head, kissing him deeply, his moustache whiskers tickling him, and crushing his lips with passion. Continuing to hold his head, he forced Jordan's mouth open, and pushed his tongue inside.

Jordan melted against Armand and feverishly returned his kisses until Armand pulled away a little breathless himself. Jordan smiled at his response.

"Take your pants off," Armand ordered.

Jordan sat back down to undo his docker shoes, before he undid his khaki-green pants and slipped them off, placing them on the couch with his shirt. He stood in his briefs, but Armand indicated they needed to come off as well; he took them off slower with more trepidation.

Before long, Jordan stood naked, with his erect cock displayed for them both to see. Blush flooded his cheeks. He glanced at Armand's pants and was secretly delighted to see his hard cock outlined against the tight-skinned pants.

Armand reached down to the table and picked up the leather contraption; it was a cock and ball harness. He gracefully dropped to a squat position in front of Jordan, and expertly wrapped the leather strap around his balls, pulling them down and separating them before snapping the second piece of leather around the base of his cock.

Careful not to adjust it too tightly, Armand checked the straps, making sure it was snug but not too taut. Once done, his fingers stroked Jordan's arousal, causing his dick to jump from his touch. He stood back up, his hand lingering in Jordan's crotch as he pulled playfully with his balls.

"Feel ok?" Armand asked.

"Yes," Jordan said.

"Let me know if otherwise," Armand said.

Jordan nodded his head and tried not to squirm too much. His balls felt heavy and the feeling slightly uncomfortable, yet arousing to him.

Armand's fingers traced around Jordan's nipples, and he began to play with them again, this time pulling and twisting more harshly than before. He leaned into Jordan's ear saying, "Just say when, if you want me to stop."

Jordan clenched his jaw determined to handle whatever Armand would do to him. He breathed deeply, while the intoxicating pain shifted through his body, his arousal weighed heavily in his crotch, and the plug titillated his anus. With all the contraptions on his body confining him, he stood bound and ready for more.

"If you get close to cuming I want you to tell me first," Armand said.

"It won't take much to get me off," Jordan panted, his hair plastered to his forehead and the back of his neck.

Armand looked thoughtful as he unzipped his pants.

Immediately Jordan's eyes dropped to the sound as he hungrily stared, watching Armand reach in and proudly brandished his erect cock.

Armand wore a thin leather band around the base of his cock, which had produced the swelling in his pants. His dick was long and hard, the foreskin rolled back, revealing the glistening head. While he stroked his dick with one hand, his other hand grabbed the lower part of Jordan's jaw, and he directed him down onto his knees and level with Armand's cock.

"I know you're hungry for this," Armand said.

Jordan licked his lips in anticipation, as Armand played his wet cock-head over Jordan's lips, not allowing him to take it into his mouth, pulling it away whenever he tried, and stroking it over his cheek. Jordan reached up to grab the base of Armand's cock, and Armand smacked his hand away.

"No. I don't want to feel your hands on my cock. Use them to play with yourself," Armand said.

Armand placed the head of his cock into Jordan's mouth. He grabbed his hair, and controlled the on and off motion, over and over, until his dick slid smoothly down Jordon's throat, and Jordan swallowed the whole length, only breathing when he came off of him.

"Suck it," Armand commanded.

Jordan complied, sucking his cock with great relish; he inhaled his dick, licking and swallowing it, and worshipping it as it was given to him.

Time telescoped and Jordan's life narrowly evolved around this dick, the center of his universe. I now understand why most cultures worship the phallus. His hand absentmindedly stroked his own arousal, speeding up unconsciously, when without warning he exploded in a lightning orgasm, hips thrusting into the air, shooting onto the wooden floor, and come all over his hand. His body wracked in spasms, and he gagged on Armand's cock before the cock was withdrawn from his mouth.

"Fuck!" Jordan said and mumbled an apology. He dared not look at Armand, afraid of seeing any anger, but when he finally glanced up, amusement graced Armand's face.

"Forget something?" Armand asked.

"Sorry," Jordan said sheepishly, "It sort of surprised me."

"Get on your hands and knees," Armand said.

Jordan dropped to all fours trying to regain his breathing. He felt his semi-hard cock dangling beneath him.

Armand picked up the paddle. Dropping to one knee, he positioned himself so he could strike the full roundness of Jordan's ass cheeks.

The first blow landed on Jordan's left cheek, and it was carefully positioned to the side to avoid the plug in his ass. The next blow landed on the opposite side.

"This is for not asking permission," Armand said.

The blows came faster and harder after that, each one alternating sides so neither would get use to the paddling.

"And these are for me," Armand said, "I love to fuck a hot ass."

Armand soon found his rhythm, with each strike landing hard and fast before the next, and Jordan lurched with each one.

The blood flowed into Jordan's engorged dick, until he had a full erection bouncing off his belly with each paddling he received. The pain was quick and intense, but afterwards a surge of pleasure coursed through his body, and he looked forward to the next strike, even moving into each blow.

The blows rained down upon Jordan's flesh until his ass shined red from the beatings. His skin became sensitive and heated until he cried out. He found himself solely focused on Armand's actions and caught up in the pain and pleasure that nothing else mattered except getting release again.

Finally, Armand stopped and lightly stroked Jordan's enflamed skin. Even the gentle caresses brought pained cries to Jordan's lips.

Armand dropped the paddle and grabbed a condom. He opened it, rolled it down his erect shaft, and then added lubrication. He undid the harness, and slowly pulled the plug out of Jordan's ass. Jordan cried out with the withdrawal, and suddenly felt exposed. Armand lubricated his inner walls some more.

"Ready for me?" Armand pressed the tip of his cock against Jordan's back opening.

"Hell yes!" Jordan was beyond thinking, and all he wanted was to be impaled upon Armand's cock, to be the center of pleasure for this man; nothing else existed in this world, but to pleasure this teacher of his.

I want to give you everything, Jordan thought. Nothing else matters, but the here and now. Life is meaningless except for the pleasure of this man.

Armand teased his cock in and out of Jordan, slowly inching it in, before pulling it back out of Jordan's heated ass. Jordan cried out from the penetration and withdrawal.

Finally, Armand pushed the full length all the way in, until balls touched balls, spearing Jordan's ass with its thickness. Powerfully, he began fucking him while gripping his hips with both hands, he expertly worked his cock in and out, slamming his dick fully in, before pulling out and doing it over and over again.

"Take it," Armand growled, "Take it all."

Spurred by Armand's words, Jordan thrust back to meet him, until the two became a synchronized machine, pleasuring the sensitive zones, both searching for the ultimate release. Riding high, they fucked harder and faster, flesh meeting flesh as they pounded together.

Daddy's Boyz

"I'm getting close!" Jordan moaned, feeling his balls constrict and the overwhelming urge coming on.

"Cum for me," Armand growled, and began slamming Jordan in fast, quick strokes.

Armand hammered his ass hard, and Jordan knew every time he would sit down, he would think of him.

Jordan cried out as his balls contracted, and his orgasm raced up his swollen shaft, globs of hot come spurted all over the floor and his belly.

His ass contracted around Armand's shaft, squeezing him hard. The pressure of Armand's nails bit into Jordan's flesh, as he rode him hard, cuming deep in his bowels.

They both collapsed onto the floor, sweaty flesh sticking together, and Armand wrapped his arms around Jordan. Both their bodies shuddered from the aftershocks and overly sensitive skin.

They silently lay in each other's arms for several minutes before Armand whispered, "Did you like the plug in your ass earlier? Did you like feeling filled by it?"

"Yes," Jordan said. I can't believe how filthy my professor's mouth is, but damn it arouses me! He found himself getting aroused just hearing his deep, baritone voice. I would never get tired of hearing it.

"Maybe I should send you back to your hotel with it," Armand said, "Make you keep it in until tomorrow at which point you'll have to return to get it taken out."

"Anything you desire," Jordan shuddered at the thought of seeing Armand again.

"Don't say anything," Armand replied, "I told you I get into hard sex. Probably more than you can handle. This is only child's play compared to what I do."

Jordan glanced at the puffer fish swimming in their marine environment and recalled what Armand had said to him about taking risks. I don't need to eat Fugu to get high. He thought. Armand can take me there all by himself, and the risk is worth it.

Getting the Message
Louis Gerard

He said he had an average build, except for his dick. Uncut and thick. The image stayed with me.

"Yeah," he'd said. "It's really thick. And about eight inches long."

"Pretty impressive."

"Hey, what can I say. I come from Brazil. Land of the king-sized condom," he told me. And the laughter bubbled up in his throat.

Sexy, with a sense of humor. He sounded hot as hell. I told him that. I told him with a dick that size he could do some damage.

I was not wrong.

I met him online, swapped numbers, and for the next couple of weeks, he remained just a husky voice on the other end of the phone. We'd spoken almost every night since he'd first messaged me. Hearing his voice night after late-night grew strangely comforting. I was relieved that he didn't press for a meeting. I liked what was developing. It was something I'd never expected — a genuine dialogue.

He said his name was Jesus. At 42, he was almost twice my age — and 100% top. That suited me just fine. But only looking for friends, he said, and tired of fucking around. It didn't seem to impact on our sex chat. It didn't seem to impact at all.

I told him I liked older men. That I didn't know why, exactly, but they did it for me. I liked to please them. I liked to look in their eyes when they fucked me missionary style. A young buck is OK, I told him, but an older guy just works you better. Has the experience to know what he wants. Has the sexual confidence to be relentless and caring and sincere.

Jesus seemed to like that, though he claimed he was still uncomfortable about our age difference.

"You're still young," he said. "My god, at 23, you must have more in common with guys your own age."

"Not really," I said. "They can't hold a conversation. Not like you."

Bob Condron

"You're sweet ..."

My turn to laugh, "No, just horny."

Saturday afternoon in the park. A public place No pressure. You don't like what you see, you just turn and walk away, he'd said. But I did like what I saw. I liked it a lot. He was a tad shorter than I was. His black hair was cut short. He was cute, with brown eyes, and an olive complexion. He had fairly big hands — strong hands. He was athletic, though not overly muscular. He wore black sweatpants that day and — yes — his king-sized cock swung like a hammer underneath the loose-fitting material of his pants as he jogged towards me.

Charged by all the telephone foreplay, I wanted to grab a hold and kiss him right there and then. I wanted to grab a hold of his cock. I wanted to pull him into the bushes and have him fuck me while the world passed us by — literally.

But he had other ideas. He was a perfect gentleman throughout. He bought me a hot dog and walked me down by the lake. When, eventually, we said our goodbyes, he shook my hand. It left a lasting impression. When I stroked my cock that night it was with his hand — his big, strong hand with its iron grip pumping me to ball-bursting climax.

I read somewhere that butterflies in the stomach are the body's way of preparing us for action. Taking blood from where it's not needed and channeling it to where it does — the phallus. And I was proof positive. Every time I talked to him I'd get the all too familiar tingling sensation in the pit of my stomach even as my cock grew hard. We could talk about jack shit and the blood would pump. It was something in his voice that pushed my buttons. A deep, manly baritone. His exotic accent. The way he breathed into the phone and said, "Oh, you ..." when I said something funny. The way he told me he missed me when we hadn't spoken for a couple of days. The way that he wished me Happy Valentine on Feb. 14.

But despite our regular phone contact, Jesus always found some excuse why we couldn't meet again in person. When I told him my hole was about to heal over — that I couldn't hold out much longer — he just laughed and told me to start dating. So I did. A guy named Daniel — another guy I met online. But unlike

Daddy's Boyz

Jesus, Daniel came straight over and did the business. Jesus seemed content to share in every detail.

Daniel was beautiful. A muscular, black stud in his mid-twenties. Bisexual — or so he claimed, and something of a triumph of form over content. For, whilst I was fully attracted to him physically, there was something in his personality that irked me. Overbearing. Like I would be sucking his dick and he'd demand that I suck harder. Not a request but an order.

"Don't just lick that dick — suck it!"

If I had been sucking any harder I'd have turned into a fucking blowfish. "I've never had complaints before," I said mid-suck. "You want me to stop?"

His swollen, spit-soaked manhood was now twitching only centimeters from my face. "No, baby, it feels good. Don't stop ... Just suck it hard. Really hard."

I didn't suck any harder and Daniel came anyway. He told me he wanted to fuck me that night. I was a bit annoyed, so I made him wait a full 24-hours.

Jesus thought that was funny. He told me he'd never complain about a blowjob, especially if someone with lips as beautiful as mine was devouring his length.

Instant hard on. I fed him his line. "Oh, you ..." I squeezed my dick through my jeans. "Can I tell you something?"

"Shoot. Tell me anything," he said.

"I like you, Jesus."

Silence.

I rushed to fill the empty space. "I mean, I'd like to suck your dick."

"I kinda figured that much," he said.

"You did?"

"Yes. I could sort of tell," he laughed.

"So what do you think of that?" I asked.

"I think that's nice."

Not quite the reaction I'd hoped for.

"But it'll have to wait," he added. "I'm kinda busy. Work. You know how it is?"

This last remark threw me. No, I didn't know what he meant. Me? I would have made time. But I told him I understood. Resigned myself to some future date.

I made the mistake of mentioning Jesus to Daniel. My timing could've been better. We were lying naked in each other's arms at the time. I was tired that afternoon, wasn't really in the mood, but had stripped down for him anyway. We hadn't yet gone much beyond kissing and tugging. I could tell he wanted more. His swollen cock was digging into my inner thigh. He didn't register my physical discomfort.

"What are you thinking about?"

I shrugged.

"Tell me. Talk to me," He fingered my ass. No subtlety. Daniel and I didn't talk much. Our bodies did it for us usually, but not today.

"What do we have?" I asked.

He sighed, irritated at the prospect of a conversation that stretched beyond: "Stick it in."

"I don't know," he replied. "I know I like you. I know that I love fucking you."

"Is that dating? Are we lovers?" I asked.

He cleared his throat. "I don't really use those words when I think about what we have. I know I like having fun with you."

"Are you even gay?" I was only half joking. Daniel never used that word to describe himself. Gay men were flamboyant, he'd say. Maybe it was some fucked up idea of guilt by word association. But this day he didn't protest. "You got me lying here, dick hard and everything, and you need to ask me that?"

"It's just, I was talking to my friend Jesus ..." I said.

"Who's that?" he asked.

"Jesus, my friend. I talk to him sometimes ..."

"Oh, no," He rolled away from me, sat up on the edge of the bed. "Don't get all religious on me!"

"Not that Jesus. Just a regular guy," I said.

"Oh, a guy," he said as he lit a cigarette, narrowed his eyes. "Latino? Must be with a name like that. You talk to him about me?"

"Brazilian. But there's some Portuguese in there. And, yes, I talk about you," I said.

"No personal details I hope." He blew smoke out of the side of his mouth. "Sounds cute. What, you're fucking him too?"

I wish, I thought. But said simply, "No."

Jesus didn't call that night. Or the next. I rang him.

"Sorry about that," he didn't sound sorry. "I met this guy in real time. It wasn't anything serious. I don't really have expectations — as you know. But it was fun," he said.

"Really, that sounds cool," I lied. I wanted to sound upbeat though, honestly, I was upset. I didn't understand why Jesus would have had this other guy when he could've had me.

"He was maybe your age," Jesus continued. "Maybe a bit young for me. Asian mixed with something. I didn't ask him. Actually, we didn't talk much. A mouth that talented would've been wasted on talking. The only thing was, he couldn't take my dick up his ass. Said it would split him in two."

Painful for me too. Painful on the ear. If he'd given me the chance, I would have taken Jesus willingly. I would have suffered the initial pain to feel him deep inside of me.

"Maybe you should have tried a different position," I said.

"Nah, he was really tight. I told him to sit on it, but he didn't want to. I even had him lie flat on his stomach. He said it hurt too much." He laughed, "Oh well. Maybe I should just stay celibate. It's easier. You young guys! I get my hopes up and the chicken chickens out."

My cock was swollen so hard it hurt.

"You're quiet, what's wrong with you?" he asked.

"Nothing's wrong. I think I might stop seeing Daniel."

"Oh, baby. What happened?" he asked.

"He got mad when I mentioned you. He thinks you and I are fucking," I said.

"Ah, baby. I'm sorry. Maybe he's just insecure," he said.

"I don't know why he's worried. Doesn't seem like you and I will ever get it together, does it?" I asked.

Silence.

Panic set in. Quick change of subject.

"Did I tell you he digs it when I lick his hole?" I said.

A pause before the familiar throaty chuckle.

"He likes to get rimmed? My kind of guy!" Jesus said.

"Yeah, smooth bubble-butt — shaved smooth. You'd probably like it," I said.

"And this guy says he isn't gay? How many straight guys do you think shave their hole?!" Jesus confirmed.

"It's a really nice ass," I stated.

"If only you were a top," he sighed " I could live vicariously through you. You should have stuffed his shaved ass full with your cock," he said.

"That's what you would do?" I asked.

"Oh yeah. I would impale him on my thick, long tool," Jesus said.

"Jesus, you shouldn't talk like that," I said.

"Why?"

"Well, now I have to take care of this boner that you caused," I said.

"You're so sweet," he said.

"No, I'm serious. You've got me so fucking horned, I really need to beat off," I said.

"Don't mind me. Go ahead," Jesus assured.

"What? You're going to listen?" I asked.

"Why not?" he asked.

And while he whispered sweet words of encouragement, I honored him with a king-sized wad of my own.

Every time I spoke with Jesus, my desire for him grew that much stronger — and struck me as increasingly pointless. When Daniel found himself a girlfriend and dumped me, I made the decision to leave L.A. Too much of a country boy at heart. I'd never really settled. There was nothing to keep me there. I hated my job, secured a new gig closer to home and felt justified in doing so. Fucked off with being fucked around. Jesus failed to make his move. Time to move on. No surprises there — until Jesus suggested we meet for a second and last time to say our farewells with a night on the town.

We hit the bars before making our way to Club Ghetto, his choice of venue and a surprising one located in a seedier part of town. Not what I'd expected or was used to. An after-hours club but one focused squarely on sex and full of macho Latino men — rough neck, gangster types. Some twinks here and there, a handful of transsexuals in glamour-drag, but mostly macho men in baggy jeans and bandannas dancing to hip hop and reggae. I followed Jesus to a table. There, we took our first round of drinks, before stepping onto the dance floor.

Daddy's Boyz

Holding me at my waist, he began to move with the music. I followed. His pelvis was glued to mine. It felt like heaven, that dance. It was the closest I'd ever been to him. The closest I suspected I'd ever be. I knew he could feel my pulsating tool against his groin. How could he not. And I felt his. I felt it grow. I felt the heat of it against my thigh. I felt it strain against his zipper with every swirl of his hips.

One song flowed seamlessly into the next as a man, much bigger than the both of us, came up behind me. He reached around, put his hand on my stomach and pulled me back towards him, his crotch pressed up snugly against my ass. Jesus smiled and stepped back. I made to grab out for his hand, but he danced just out of reach.

"Why should your friend have all the fun?" the unknown guy whispered in my ear. His hand dropped to cup my aching bulge.

Jesus smiled at me, smiled at the big guy over my shoulder. "Have fun." And with that he backed up to the edge of the dance floor. The big guy turned me around, pressed his hard body against mine, and we fell into step. For the first time I got to take a look at him. He was pretty tough looking, older than I, older than Jesus and maybe in his late forties. Thick black hair flecked with gray. He had a goatee and wore a plaid shirt and baggy jeans. Rolled up sleeves exposed the tattoos that covered his muscular arms.

Jesus's eyes were watching me — were watching us. Smiling and nodding his encouragement from the sidelines. Was this what he wanted? Was this how he got off? Vicariously, like he'd suggested? OK if that was what he wanted, I'd give it to him — and then some. I didn't wait for the music to play itself out but took hold of Big Daddy by the belt and led him into the darkroom.

It wasn't completely dark in there. A faint light from a red bulb prevented us from tripping over or bumping into the scrum of heaving bodies. I found space by the far wall and positioned myself as close to the light as possible, certain that Jesus wouldn't be far behind. He didn't disappoint. Moments after we took up our position the curtains parted and he entered.

Nothing quite like being swept up in a big, strong pair of arms. It was like being enveloped in a cloud of pure testosterone. Big Daddy ground his hard tool against me, buried his face in my neck. Jesus edged in closer, continued to watch. I couldn't see his eyes, but I could feel them, boring into us, caught up in the moment, sharing the intimacy. Big Daddy peeled off my top shirt, lifted my T-shirt up over my head and within moments he was feverishly kissing me — my face, my neck, my chest.

I popped the buttons on his shirt and felt his sweat-soaked torso press against mine. He undid my jeans, unzipped his own. Suddenly, I felt the exquisite sensation of my hard, exposed phallus pressing up against his. Felt the warmth of his flesh. Precum oozing from my piss slit and from his, too. His rough fingers spread the goo over our twin shafts before he clamped his fist around them both. Squeezing our slick dicks together, he fell into his stroke with a slow, practiced hand.

High on the moment, I raised up on my toes to meet his mouth. His free hand grasped the back of my head and crushed my mouth to his. A kiss so electric, my body seemed to convulse almost immediately. The rhythm of his fist increased, and with it, his hunger, his desperation for release. His mouth was sucking on mine, my tongue, my lips — threatening to consume me, until I could do nothing to stop the raging torrent in my balls from erupting. Nowhere to run, even if I'd wanted to. My back pressed up against the wall. And, as I shot my steaming load, so did my tormentor. Shuddering. Growling. Groaning.

He held me then. Covered me until we had caught our breath. Held me until Jesus appeared directly at his shoulder. Jesus handed Big Daddy a cloth and he, in turn, wiped the cum from my stomach and his hands. The cloth turned out to be my T-shirt. He handed it over to Jesus — who held it like a trophy. Big Daddy handed me my top shirt and buttoned himself up.

"You're hot," Big Daddy said and kissed me one last time — long and deep. "I'm Hector. What's your name beautiful?" he whispered.

"I'm Lou," I said. "And this is my friend ..." But when I turned my head, Jesus was gone.

"Yes, I know," he replied with a wink. "He works in mysterious ways." And tucking the tail of his shirt into his pants, he turned and walked away.

One last phone call.

"What's with the vanishing act?!" I blurted it out as soon as he picked up the receiver."

The all too familiar chuckle rumbled down the line. He said nothing.

"You we're playing with me! All along. It was just a game, wasn't it?

No reply.

"Wasn't it?!"

"It was fun. You had fun, didn't you?" he asked.

"Fun while it lasted, you mean? Here is the news: I can get fun anytime I want, Jesus," I said angrily.

"Don't tell me you expected more?" he asked.

"Why not? What if I did?" I asked.

"Because a relationship built on telephone sex isn't about more. It's about the moment. It's about the here and now," he said.

"You promised more," I said.

"I didn't promise you anything," he said.

"Silly me," I said.

Dead air.

"Is that it then? Is that all you have to say?" I asked.

"Ah, baby. Put it down to experience. When you get to my age maybe you'll know better," he answered.

No answer to that. No words came. Just a click, followed by the dial tone buzzing in my ear.

Politics Unusual
Ian Hawke

Standing at the window, he idly runs his hand around the tumbler, rubbing off the condensation. He wonders why anyone would locate the nation's capital in the middle of a God forsaken southern swamp. In a few days, the House will go on summer recess, and he can return to the air conditioning of his restored southern plantation where he can relax in comfort. He brings the iced tea to his lips and enjoys the chill going down his throat. It would be nicer if there were a hint of brandy to spice things up, but while his constituents would wink and nod at the hint of alcohol on his breath, the committee chairman from Utah would frown upon such behavior. Damn those Mormons and the sanctimoniousness, he thinks.

The Representative looks at the road construction going on below his window. Those poor souls must be dying in this heat. Even though the air conditioning in the building was losing the battle against the heat; at least it stirred the humid air. Those men and women outside had no respite from the oppressive blanket of moist air that cursed the city for going on two weeks. But those workers were toiling for a good cause. They were installing some Homeland Security facilities, and he smiled as he thought of the tax dollars provided by industrious Americans, some of them from his very own district, to make the capital safe so democracy could forever shine.

As he takes another sip of the iced tea, he continues to watch the laborers, hard working men and women, each and every one of them. The women are stripped almost to the point of indecency. Their tanned arms and midriffs rippling with muscles developed from honest labor. Some of the women are even so brazen as to wear bikini tops, although that is perfectly respectable these days. Not like some of those string bikinis people wear on the mall. Clothing that revealed more than it hid. He shakes his head at the loose morals of today's youth.

Working besides the women are men cut straight from a Marlboro ad. The work has toned their muscles and stripped away fat. Most of the men have stripped their shirts and are wearing only day glow orange safety vests. The vests hang open revealing washboard stomachs, well-defined pectorals and bulging biceps. The Representative takes another sip to replenish the moisture that has suddenly disappeared from his mouth.

There he is. The Representative's eyes find the mouth watering physical specimen. His eyes roam over the muscles rippling under the perfectly golden tanned skin. The Representative's tongue moistens his lips as he watches the vest fall open to reveal a dark nipple. The worker's chest is smooth and hairless. His body glistens with sweat. Sweat must have trickled into his eyes because he takes off his hardhat and rubs a hand across his brow. The worker takes a moment to squint into the sun. The Representative feels his heart trip in his chest. Something about the damp dark locks falling casually around the worker's face strikes deep into his heart. The curly hair and strong features are perfect. The Representative closes his eyes and can almost imagine the worker dressed as a gladiator, holding a sword as he prepares to do battle in the Coliseum.

He can see as the iron gate opens and the roar of a lion rings out of the inky blackness of the tunnel. The crowd roars back its approval. The gladiator has established himself in the hearts of the Romans. The scars across his chest attest to the many battles he has survived. His eyes focus on the dark tunnel, waiting for the beast to appear. The lion comes bounding out of the tunnel, its mane pulsating with each leap. The gladiator crouches, holding his sword at the ready. There is no fear as the lion closes the distance. The animal springs and the gladiator kneels, raising his sword to open the cat as it passes overhead. The beast crashes behind the gladiator and struggles to its feet, getting entangled in the viscera released by the gladiator's blade.

The gladiator spins to face the mortally wounded creature. As he pirouettes, his leather skirt flares up, revealing the gladiator's genitals and ass. The crowd roars as they take in his size. It is like a wooden peg hanging between his legs. As he spins, the muscles in his ass ripple. Women swoon and men of both persuasions look with jealous envy. The gladiator is a statue come to life.

The Representative feels a pleasant tingling in his groin as the gladiator image plays in his mind. He spins the gladiator again, causing the leather skirt to rise once more, exposing the massive shaft of manhood. The gladiator steps forward and plunges his blade deep into the beast's body. With a meek quiver, the animal gives up its life. The Romans roar of approval shakes the very stones of the Coliseum. The gladiator bows for his adoring fans. As he bends forwards, the leather rises, once again revealing his muscled ass. The Representative feels the pleasant tingling increase to a dull throbbing.

As the fantasy ends, he opens his eyes to find the worker. His heart skips a beat as he sees the worker looking up, almost as if he has felt the hungry eyes from the anonymous third floor window. The Representative's cheeks color in embarrassment. Could he have been caught? The worker turns away and the Representative sighs in relief. It must have been a coincidence. He feels a weightiness in his groin, and he is surprised to find he has an erection. When was the last time that happened without Viagra, he wonders. That train of thought is interrupted by a knock.

The door opens and his staffer pokes his head in. "Mr. Jenkins, the kids from Altmont High are here. And your wife called to remind you about dinner at five."

"Give me a minute and then send them in. And call my wife. Tell her I'll pick her up on time." Lord, how he detests high school visits. They are almost as bad as church groups. But their parents vote, and it is free publicity for him when they go home and speak of how nice the good Mr. Jenkins was, always so caring about the people of his district.

He raises his glass and toasts the Adonis working below. He drinks the last dregs of iced tea and sits behind his desk, hoping his erection will disappear before the kids show up. Getting a stiffy in front of the pride of Altmont High School would definitely start a rumor better left unstated.

Dennis Jenkins settles into the leather chair in his home office. It has been a long day, and the sun is sinking into the horizon like a ball of molten lead. He is exhausted after having spent hours shaking hands and making idle conversation with donors to his reelection campaign. His wife was her usual charming self, but now she is upstairs, watching television. What has become of their marriage? When it started, it was flames and sparks and thunder and lightning. The romance was tender and the sex blistering.

Now, what were they? The best that could be said was they were roommates who were too old to change. Settling in with a thick cigar, he thinks at least she is good at fundraisers. He wonders if she has a lover.

The thought fades from his mind as he opens the folder on his lap. The bulk of the folder deals with some dry Congressional issue. But in the back he has hidden something that would definitely cause him to lose reelection if it ever came out. He kept this little secret to himself knowing that any secret shared between two people would be leaked to the insatiable press. He rationalized that everyone had their fantasies and he had no intention of acting on his although this fantasy was getting more powerful.

He flips through the file to the flimsy magazine. The cover of the magazine leaves almost nothing to the imagination. The title "Beefcake" is in brilliant yellow and was what captured his attention. The half dozen men on the cover are dressed in string and scraps of fabric. Their smooth, muscular bodies seem to leap off the cover. Bulging pecs, washboard abs, oiled biceps. It was a feast of flesh. The mouth-watering aspect of the cover was the bulging g-strings, which barely contained the hunks of meat. It was obvious that all the men were massive in size and this was when they were flaccid. Surely, they would be awe-inspiring when erect.

Guilty pleasure tingles through his brain as his fingers reach for the dog-eared corner of the cover. His tongue moistens his dry lips as he opens the magazine. He quickly flips past the beginning of the magazine to get to the juicy part. As the glossy pages fall open, he feels a warm tingling in his crotch. Oh yes, he thinks, come to daddy.

The first few pictures are teasers. As Dennis turns the pages, the model is wearing progressively less. Then there it is. Perfection. The oiled body. The firm muscles. The flawless skin. The cocky smile. The model knows exactly what his purpose is and his smile is an offer. Dennis's hand drops to his crotch and feels the swelling of his cock. At this moment, he is thankful for the heat of the summer. It allows him to wear thin slacks, and he can easily massage himself.

He flips to the next page and feels a quivering in his stomach. It's the same model but with an erection. Even though he has seen

Daddy's Boyz

the picture many times, Dennis's breath catches in his throat. The model is massive, larger than should be humanly possible. The man must be on the verge of fainting because there must a couple of quarts of blood in that shaft to keep it hard.

As he flips to the next page and sees the black model, Dennis feels the heat building in his groin. His hand massages his swelling cock with more need. He is a superb physical specimen, almost as good as the previous model. Instead of a knowing smile, this model has a scowl, almost a look of condescension.

Dennis finds himself hesitating before he turns the page. The glossy paper is well worn, and he is fully aware of what lies on the next page. His mouth has gone dry in anticipation, and he knows he should close the file and go up to bed but the pull is irresistible. The paper curls under his fingers and begins to fold the page back on itself. Dennis feels his heart fluttering and the throbbing in his crotch growing more insistent. A smile teases his lips as he thinks of the embarrassment his wife would face if he were to have a coronary while flipping through a gay magazine.

As the page falls open, there it is. The model is hung like a bull. Dennis's eyes bulge as he looks at the half erect shaft. If the model lost a leg, he would have no need for an artificial one. Dennis's hand becomes more insistent on his crotch.

He closes the file and leans back. His eyelids fall and he imagines the feel of the model's massive cock in his hand. He can feel the oiled skin, the pulse throbbing in the base, and the ridge around the head. He imagines looking into the model's eyes and seeing the contempt. The model knows what this white boy needs, and he knows just how to give it to him. Dennis watches as the black hands, hardened from working in the fields, reach up and grab his shoulders.

Shaking his head to clear the image, Dennis opens his eyes. Enough of this. He rises from the chair, letting his hand fall from his throbbing erection. Looking down, he sees his cock poking against the thin fabric. There is an uncomfortable throbbing, and he is glad he stopped. Any further and he would have soiled himself, which would have been interesting to try explaining.

He slides the file back into his safe. As he closes the door to the safe, he thinks of the other classified material inside. He knows much of it will appear on the front page of the Washington Post. A muffled laugh escapes from his lips as he thinks of the fall out if his little secret were to appear in the Post. A quiet prayer of thanks slips through his mind because the safe gives him a place to hide things from the prying eyes of his wife. Not that he has any evidence of her prying eyes, but he has a sneaking suspicion.

As he drove through the dark streets, he was thankful Congress was finally in recess. The blanket of humidity had grown thicker over the city, and the smothering air led to an increase in crime. In addition to the riff raff causing their usual problems, tempers in the House were growing dangerously short. Several members had already exchanged words that could never be taken back and would find pork projects for their districts reduced in the next budget cycle.

While he was spending the final hours on the floor, trying to get some last minute business finished, his wife had been busy getting their house ready for their departure. Fortunately, the house was in a gated community, so security through the summer months was not a concern. Nothing in the house was irreplaceable anyway, and his secret file was sitting safely in his briefcase in the trunk. That would most definitely have to come back with him, but everything else could be left behind.

As he cruised the darkened streets, the neighborhoods were getting seedier. He was not sure exactly where he was going, but he knew the general area. D.C. was not that big a city, but he was unfamiliar with this particular part of town. Upstanding members of Congress did not cruise these neighborhoods. At least if they did, it was not common knowledge.

The area shifted from residential to commercial. The lighting became slightly better and the traffic increased. He knew he was close. In the next two blocks, the number of working girls skyrocketed. They were dressed like walking billboards, advertising their sex. Many of them barely looked old enough for braces let alone sex.

His gaze swept over the working girls. This was not the flavor he was looking for although some of them did look delectable. No, he was in search of more exotic fare for this evening's pleasure. As he cruised the street, he was not even sure he was in the right area. Did the two groups work together?

Daddy's Boyz

Pulling over next to a worn out hooker, he rolled down the window. The sticky air filled the car, and Dennis felt the sweat beading in his armpits. The woman sauntered over and leaned through the window. The reek of cheap perfume and cheaper tobacco rolled off her. Underlying the powerful aromas was the dank smell of used sex.

"You looking to party, sugah?" the woman asked.

Dennis almost laughed. He was not expecting the line. He had heard it so often in movies that surely it could not be real. But, she had said it. "Yeah. I am. But something a little different."

"Something different eh?" she asked while cracking her gum between her teeth. "Different costs more."

"No, not that kind of different. Different as in something along the other side."

She cocked an eyebrow, "The other side. Are we talking the other side with a dick?"

He winced as the crudeness of her truth hit home, "Yeah. Something along those lines."

"Well sugah, you in the wrong part of town. You familiar with D.C.?"

He nodded and listened to her directions for where he could fulfill his particular need. It was not far, and he could be there in an easy ten minutes. When she was finished, he pulled out five dollars and held it out. "Thanks for your help."

She plucked the money from his fingers and tucked it somewhere he did not want to think about. "You have fun now, sugah."

Following her directions, he noticed she had guided him around the endless road construction that plagued every metropolitan area. It took him less than ten minutes to find the dimly lit neighborhood. The traffic was sparser, but the pattern similar. Cars and trucks cruised the street, much like shopping carts trolling through a supermarket. He watched the action. A car would slow and someone would walk out of the shadows. If an agreement was reached, the man or boy would climb into the car, and they would move off. He could handle this. No problem.

Putting the car in gear, he entered the school of sharks on the prowl. As he pulled onto the strip, his stomach tightened. The anticipation was delicious. He had not committed to anything. He was still window-shopping. Women did it all the time. It did not mean he was buying. He was just checking out the merchandise, and surely they was no harm in that.

As he drove the street, he peered into the darkened doorways. Most of the men were boys — young, emaciated, desperate. This was not what he was looking for, and he knew he made a mistake. He needed the anonymity of a prostitute, but a prostitute was unlikely to fulfill his fantasy.

He sighed and turned the corner at the end of the block, ready to go home, disappointed. But a flickering glare caught his attention. As he turned toward the light, he saw someone lighting a cigarette. The man stood in a doorway and was wearing a loose fitting leather vest and skintight jeans. His hair was long and clean, unlike the dank locks of the other men. As Dennis drove by, the man glanced up. His expression was one of indifference, just like the black man in the magazine. Dennis felt his insides quiver. This was the one.

Pulling towards the curb, Dennis looked in the rearview mirror. The man stepped from the doorway and walked towards the car. No, he did not walk. He sauntered like a cowboy. Or at least the way Dennis thought a cowboy should move.

As he came to the window, Dennis pushed the button and let in the moist night air. The man leaned against the door and looked in the car, blatantly ignoring Dennis. After he had inspected the car's interior, he met Dennis's eyes. "Nice ride."

Dennis opened his mouth and no words came out. Licking his lips, he tried again, "Thanks."

"Let's see it," the man said.

For a moment, Dennis was lost. What exactly was the man asking? Thinking it had to be one of two things, Dennis reached into his pocket and took out a wad of bills. He fanned out the cash, showing off $500.

The man's eyes squinted as he looked at the wad. "What do you want?"

Dennis's mind whirled. His mouth moved, but again words refused to come. Moistened his lips, he tried again, finally managed to squeak, "You."

The man nodded and he looked back at Dennis, "So let's see it."

This time Dennis knew what the man wanted. He fumbled with his zipper and dropped his pants, exposing his limp penis. The man's eyes dropped to inspect the organ for just a moment, before he went back to looking at the street.

"Does it work?" the man asked.

Dennis swallowed a few times, "It won't matter."

The man's eyes snapped back to Dennis's, his surprise obvious. "Ahhh," the man said.

Dennis could only nod in silence.

The man took a drag off his cigarette and blew the smoke over the car, "So this door unlocked?"

Searching along the console, Dennis found the button and clicked open the door.

The man nodded and opened the door, climbing inside, "Go down two blocks and then pull into the alley on the right."

Dennis followed the directions while his insides quivered. He could not believe he was doing this. His tongue worked around his mouth, desperately trying to get some moisture to his parched lips. Thankfully, the drive was short and conversation was not needed.

"In there," the prostitute directed towards an alley.

The alley was dark, and a finger of fear traced its way down Dennis's spine. Maybe this was not a good idea. Was it possible to back out?

"Pull into the middle. No one will see us."

It was pitch black in the middle of the alley. The light from the street seemed reluctant to penetrate the darkness. His headlights illuminated a strip of asphalt littered with debris from an adjacent restaurant. Dennis had to navigate around pallets and dumpsters, and he realized he was probably going to die here.

"Stop here."

Dennis put the car in park. The man had not looked at him since he got in the car. What now, Dennis wondered.

The man opened his door and looked at Dennis in overhead light. "Get out and go to the front of the car."

As the man closed the door, Dennis knew this would be his only chance to run. Yet, he found his hand on the door handle. As if he was under hypnotic suggestion, his feet walked through the debris of the alley and he stepped between the headlights. The stench was incredible. The smell of rotting food was enough to turn his stomach. But there were other things on his mind besides the stench.

"Put your hands on the hood," the man commanded.

Dennis complied and heard the man step behind him. He felt the man's hand slide into his pocket. Leaning in close, the man whispered, "I'll just take this first," as his fingers pulled out the wad of bills.

A moment later, Dennis felt the prostitute's hands at his belt. With smooth efficiency, the man undid the belt and yanked down Dennis's slacks. The oppressive air of the evening felt cool on his legs and a shiver went through his body. Was it anticipation? Maybe a touch of fear? A moment later, he felt his boxers pulled down where they joined his slacks bundled around his knees. The man's hand pressed between Dennis's shoulders and pushed him onto the warm hood of the car.

Dennis felt the breath choke in his throat. The only man to ever see him this way was his proctologist and that was once a year and coldly clinical. He could feel the prostitute's eyes inspecting his ass and Dennis felt a blush of shame on his cheeks. He became brutally conscious of the fact that he was overweight. He knew his ass must be a terrifying sight.

A distinctive snap sounded. Dennis knew the man had pulled on a latex glove. He felt the man's weight on his back and heard a whispered "Let's see what we have here."

Suddenly a white-hot explosion seared through his anus. Squeezing his eyes shut against the pain, Dennis felt the breath hiss from his lungs as his body tensed. He felt the man's fingers deep inside him, digging with a brutal intensity. The pain was excruciating, and Dennis almost felt a plea for mercy escape his lips. The only thing that stayed his tongue was the fringe of exquisite pleasure dancing on the edges of the pain. As Dennis's body grew acclimated to the intrusion, the fringe of pleasure grew larger, slowly blotting out the pain. As the last vestiges of pain retreated, Dennis relaxed.

All too soon, the man's fingers pulled away and a sigh of discontent escaped Dennis's lips. Upon hearing Dennis's frustration, the man whispered, "Don't worry, it ain't over yet."

There was a rustle of clothing and the tearing of cellophane followed by the sound of the man spitting. With a cocky voice, the man said, "Safety is rule one on this job."

The man grabbed one of Dennis's meaty hips. Suddenly, Dennis felt a slick pressure against his ass. It was unlike anything he had ever imagined. He squeezed his eyes shut and relaxed his body. The latex covered shaft slipped between his cheeks and came to rest on his puckered anus. Dennis tensed and then forced himself to relax.

With a sharp thrust, the man rammed himself forward, driving his cock all the way inside. As he felt his anus brutalized, Dennis's eyes squeezed out a few tears and a pitiful moan escaped from his lips. His fingers curled, trying to dig into the hood. He felt like he was being torn in half. But again, dancing on the edge of the agony was the smallest glimmer of pleasure. It was that glimmer that stilled the scream in his throat.

As the man began to move his hips backwards and forwards, Dennis felt the glimmer of pleasure grow like the rising sun. His fingers uncurled and his body relaxed. This was better than his wildest fantasies. The feeling of the man's cock was exquisite, and mews of pleasure began to escape from Dennis's lips.

Dennis jumped as he felt a hand wrap around his cock. He had not realized he was erect. The man began to stroke his shaft. The pleasure was divine and Dennis felt the throbbing at the base of his cock. He could not believe how close he was to orgasm. The last time he was with his wife it had taken forever for him to cum. Now he was within a hair's breadth of losing it and it had only been moments. God, he felt like a teenager again.

Then it happened. He felt the trembling in his balls as his climax came. He held his breath as the first thick gobs of cum splashed out. He heard the sticky goo splattering against his car grill and was distracted between bursts wondering if there was a local all night car wash. That thought was dispersed by another thick explosion.

As Dennis felt the final trickles dripping out, he felt the throbbing of the man's cock in his ass. The tight bundle of nerves in his anus felt the swelling as the bubble of cum worked upwards along the man's shaft. With an animalistic grunt, the man drove his cock deeper inside, and the pleasure was indescribable. Dennis held his breath as the condom swelled with each explosion.

Too soon, it was over and Dennis felt the man withdraw. A contented sigh escaped from Dennis's lips, and he crumpled in bliss. The warmth from the engine was a pleasant embrace, and he felt the desire to sleep right there.

He was startled from his torpor by the snapping of latex. He realized the man was stripping of his condom. Dennis heard the squishy slap as the used condom and glove was discarded with indifference on the cracked pavement of the alley. The man's clothing rustled, and then he was sauntering back down the alley, towards the street.

Dennis was stunned. His fantasies had always ended at the moment of climax. The sight of the man's back as he walked down the alley was almost a slap. Shame burned through the remnants of pleasure, and Dennis quickly pulled up his slacks. He tucked everything back in, not caring about how he looked. He got in the car and felt an uncomfortable burning in his ass. He wondered if he had torn anything and hoped he did not bleed onto his underwear.

Georgia was full of brilliant colors in the summer. He was glad to be out of Washington and back on his home turf. The slow pace was something that always took him a couple of days to get used too. However, a few days of relaxing on his porch with a mint julep was just the medication he needed to unwind.

Even the shame of his last night in D.C. had burned away, leaving the comforting glow of the fantasy memory. The pain of the initial intrusion was forgotten, burned away by the exquisite memory of the pleasure.

He lay back in the wicker chair and let the warm rays of the sun scorch his skin. The small smile on his lips hinted at the memories in his head. However, the swelling in his groin told the story clearly.

The phone was a distant buzzing, which was cut off in mid ring. Shifting position to get more comfortable, he was glad his wife was home from her garden club. He was too content to rise and get the call for himself.

The sharp clacking of his wife's high heels sounded across the cobblestones. "It's for you," she said.

Daddy's Boyz

He opened his eyes and saw her standing there, holding out the phone. As he reached for the phone, he asked "How about we go to the General's tonight?"

Her eyes glittered. He knew she loved the lobster, and he could use a thick steak. "I'd love to," she said.

"I'll make reservations as soon as I take care of this," he said, holding up the phone.

He watched his wife as she went back into the air-conditioned house. Georgia was good for her, he thought as he ogled her perky butt. As she disappeared into the darkness of the house, he lifted the phone. "Hello."

A familiar voice responded "Representative Jenkins?"

"Speaking."

"Mr. Jenkins, this is John. From Washington."

Dennis's mind clicked through the names and voices he could recall like a computer. But this voice and name did not have a face. "I'm sorry John, but I can't seem to place the voice."

"We met last week … in the alley."

The air seemed to go wintry cold. Now the voice was familiar. It was the Marlboro man. This could not be happening. He could think of nothing to say, and the silence on the phone grew.

"Mr. Jenkins, are you still there?"

Dennis moistened his lips and whispered, "Yes."

"Mr. Jenkins, you have a reputation for being a conservative. What I want is for you to begin a slow move towards the center."

"And if I don't?" The mettle in his voice was betrayed by the fear, which caused his words to crack.

"Pictures, Mr. Jenkins. Pictures."

Dennis sagged in the chair. He had built up tremendous power in D.C., and now he could see the first cracks in the foundation of his empire. He thought he had been so safe and with one moment of passion, the bedrock under his empire had turned to sand. He began to utter a prayer but stopped when he realized the God he had worshipped for all his life would never accept his sin. He was lost — totally and completely lost.

He wondered if it was a fair exchange. As he thought of the exquisite feel of the man's cock in his ass, the scales tilt towards the pleasure and a smile crept to his lips. Yes, he knew it was more than a fair exchange.

Victim of Pleasure
Bob Condron

Sammy could not get laid to save his life.

Coming out had been painful enough — but this? This wasn't just painful, it was agony. To have gone through the whole process of disaffected childhood, miserable adolescence and the soul-searching of his early twenties; to finally accept the truth; to tell family and friends, his boss and work colleagues; to have weathered the storm, only to find himself unwanted and unloved? He took another slug of tequila, but it failed to numb the hurting part of him.

The bar was half empty. No surprise, it was a Tuesday night after all. Sammy lifted his eyes from his empty glass and allowed them to flicker furtively in the direction of the well-built barman. Sven was from Scandinavia, this much was obvious from his Swedish Chef accent, albeit peppered with the Chelsea twang. Thick blonde hair and translucent blue eyes were also a dead give-away. He looked like he could have stepped straight from the pages of *Tom of Finland*. His black leather waistcoat flattered his massive, gym-built upper-torso; leather chaps framed his firm, fuzzy peach of a bare ass. A tribal tattoo, wrapped around one bulging bicep, tightened as he flexed, opening yet another bottle with practiced ease. Under cover of the night and this candle-lit dungeon of a bar, Sven looked almost too perfect. What I wouldn't give for a piece of that, thought Sammy. But even as he thought it he knew it was hopeless. Any confidence he might have once had, had been knocked out of him by his brief exposure to the New York gay bar scene.

Sammy cast his eyes once more around the room. Over by the corner of the bar was a big ol' Papa Bear, maybe 45, stocky and tall. His plaid, flannel shirt was open to reveal a forest of chest hair as he puffed deliberately on a huge cigar. "Maybe?" thought Sammy. He waited for what seemed like an inordinately long length of time until he caught the big guy's eye and Sammy smiled. Papa Bear looked straight through him. Sammy's smile did not even register on Papa Bear's impassive face. Fuck! thought

Bob Condron

Sammy, dropping his eyes to his glass, watching his fist curl around it. Fuuuck!

He drained the invisible dregs and held the glass in the air towards Sven. "Gimmie another double," his voice slurred.

Sven crossed to the bar directly in front of Sammy and raised a quizzical eyebrow. "Don't you think you oughta take it easy, Loretta?" he said in his peculiar accent.

"Just this one and I'll go," Sammy said.

Sven hesitated a moment, then finally acquiesced. "OK." He turned to pour the drink, and when he returned with the double shot of Tequila he said simply. "It's on the house. Should I call you a cab?"

Sammy shook his head and looked away. Sven raised his eyes to heaven then turned and busied himself polishing the bar. Sammy's eyes fixed once more on Papa Bear. Papa Bear now had a little bear cub suckling on his pierced nipple. Papa Bear's shirt had burst open like an over-stuffed mattress, and Baby Bear was feasting enthusiastically, first on one hairy mound then the other, seemingly desperate to garner a reaction — any reaction. Papa Bear's face remained impassive. He simply sucked on his cigar and exhaled a steam of smoke like a big ol' automaton.

Oh, my God! Sammy closed his eyes and, throwing back his head, downed the drink in one. When he opened his eyes again, Sven was standing directly in front of him, waiting expectantly for his departure. Sammy wiped his mouth on his sleeve. "What am I doing wrong?" he asked, his eyes meeting Sven's. Sammy's eyes were pleading.

Sven looked over his shoulder. For the moment, there were no customers waiting. "You really wanna know, girlfriend?" he said.

"Sure."

"Men like these don't want men like you. They want what they are. You wanna get laid, you gotta wear the uniform, you gotta make an effort," Sven said.

"Help me?"

Sven reached for a serviette and a pen. "Let's make a check list, OK? First, despite the prevailing wisdom, men do not make passes at guys in glasses. So get rid of those bottle bottoms and invest in contacts."

Sammy listened intensely, as if he was hearing the secrets of the Sphinx.

"Second," Sven continued, "You come to a Leather/Levi bar you wear the regulation gear. No one is gonna look twice at a dweeb in a suit and tie." Sven shook his head, "If it wasn't a Tuesday, you would never have got past the doorman."

Sammy nodded, furiously.

"Third, you're going to have to work out, princess. You're way too skinny for these guys. They're into muscle and bulk just like you are, right?"

Again Sammy nodded furiously.

"Hell, it's not all bad news." Sven grinned. "You got a full head of hair — even if it is in need of a serious restyle. Facial hair wouldn't go amiss either. But you got nice teeth, nice bone structure. And there's still time ... you're only, what, 35?"

"Twenty-five," Sammy said, almost apologetically.

Sven pursed his lips, "You do need to do some serious work, girlfriend. You want cock and muscle, you gotta pay in sweat." He handed the serviette to Sammy, who clutched it to his chest like a map of buried treasure.

"And if you had one single piece of advice for me?" Sammy asked, his bottom lip quivering.

"You got your plan of action right there," Sven jabbed a finger towards the serviette. "But one thing more ..." Sven looked left and right to check that no one was listening, "One extra piece of advice? Even membership to a top class gym won't get you the results ...without a course of Big Daddy Allsorts' Magical Muscle Beans."

"Big Daddy Allsorts' Magical Muscle Beans?" Sammy said as he was at something of a loss to understand.

Sven reached into his pocket and pulled out a handful of what looked like common or garden jelly beans, "Hey presto! The very things."

"Are they like ... like ...?" Sammy asked.

Sven cocked an immaculate eyebrow, "Like what, dearie?"

"Like steroids?"

Sven snorted, "Better than steroids, honey. Any gains you make, you keep. So you better work your butt off to maximize the results." He ran a hand over his own rock solid pecs. "Couldn't have got these beauties without good old Daddy Allsorts."

Sammy was too stoned to ask if they were for real or not — neither the tits nor the tabs. "And how many do I need," he drooled.

Sven smirked. Sammy was hooked. "A twelve-week course should do you. But it'll cost," Sven said.

"Do you take credit cards?" Sammy asked, reaching to his back pocket for his black, leather wallet. Taking it out, he flipped it open.

Sven plucked the card from Sammy's trembling fingers and swaggered off to process the order. He returned with a plastic bag bursting with multi-colored beans and a wafer thin, yellow receipt. Sammy didn't dare look at the latter as Sven discreetly handed both over while returning his card. Sammy tucked everything safely away.

"Now, quit wasting my time, and go home. Don't come back till you've done the business. You'll only set yourself up for a fall," Sven said with a finality that was punctuated by an index finger that stabbed into Sammy's chest.

Sammy reached out with both hands and gripped Sven's. He thought about kissing it, then thought better of it. "Thank you," he said simply — and fell off his bar stool.

The transformation took no more than the prescribed twelve weeks. And given the degree of transformation, it could not be considered long by anyone's estimation. But all credit to Sammy, he had worked like a man possessed. He took to the task of recreating himself with all the manic zeal of Dr Frankenstein working on his beloved monster.

Well, maybe not all credit to Sammy — Big Daddy Allsorts' Magical Muscle Beans did appear to make a significant contribution. From the initial dose, taken after the first training session, his muscles quickly responded to the demands of his gym routine. Fueled, no doubt, by the miraculous jelly beans he had secured from the delectable Sven, his muscles had begun to pump full of life blood. Sammy had felt it, the pump pump pump. His face had begun to burn, his muscles began to twitch. Something was happening — something extraordinary. Whenever his energy levels threatened to flag, he would conjure up the image of countless rejections. The corresponding rage he felt had enabled him always to push through the pain barrier and one rep beyond.

And something else was happening. As his muscles bulked up, his lank, greasy hair began to thicken. The fluff on his top lip and chin began to transform into a shadow that needed to be shaved twice a day, The two hairs on his chest bone bloomed into a swirling mass of fur. Hair sprouted from his shoulders. Sammy was maturing, metamorphosing, into a hunk to die for.

Certainly, it was not the first transformation he had performed in his young life, though the other had proved effortless in comparison. He had gone from computer nerd to computer whiz-kid in a matter of months. His flair for technology had brought with it significant wealth, and it now allowed him the opportunity to indulge his new found obsession.

Thank fuck for the Internet. That was where he found his exercise routine along with all one might want to know about bodybuilding but be too afraid to ask — face to face. This way he could be reborn and nobody would disturb his empty grave.

Late evenings were spent equally productively, reading up on the leather lifestyle. *Ask Barry: The Leatherman's DIY Guide* became his bible; an invaluable fund of information. If this was what these guys wanted he would give it to them. Oh, yes. He would be more than happy to fulfill their requirements.

Three short months and Sammy was a new man. No longer Sammy boy, but Sam the Man.

Another Tuesday night. Sven hated working Tuesday nights. Tips were as thin on the ground as were customers. But what the hell, working the bar was better than "resting." An out of work actor with time on his hands was always at risk of despair. He did better to occupy himself in whatever manner, sure in the knowledge that it was only a matter of time before he got his big break. He stifled a yawn as he polished a glass. Just then the door opened.

Filling the doorway was the great, dark man. Sven's jaw dropped open, and he almost dropped the glass. Dressed from head to toe in leather — from peaked cap to biker boots — the handsome stranger waited until all eyes had turned in his direction.

Bob Condron

Then, with an almost imperceptible sneer of triumph hidden beneath his walrus moustache, he made his way over to the bar.

"Tequila."

Sven dropped his voice an octave, "Coming right up ... Sir!"

The stranger cast an eye around the room. Over by the corner of the bar was a big ol' Papa Bear. Papa Bear waited until he caught the stranger's eye and smiled. The stranger looked through him, Papa Bear's smile didn't even register on the stranger's impassive face. "Fuck!" thought Papa Bear, sucking on his cigar, like a baby looking for the comfort of his mother's nipple. Fuuuck!

"Did anyone ever tell you, you look just like Glenn Hughes?" It was Sven. He placed the drink in front of the welcome customer.

The stranger sipped some of the clear liquid, rolled it around on his tongue, "Glenn who?"

"Glenn Hughes. The leatherman from the Village People?"

"Never heard of them," the stranger said.

"Oh you must have! You know ..." Sven began to sing. "Y.M.C.A. It's fun to stay at the ..."

"No. Never heard of them," the stranger didn't so much as blink.

Sven suddenly felt embarrassed and wished he hadn't done all the hand gestures that accompany the tune. He blushed and added. "They were a big hit in Sweden. My old Swedish mammy says I was singing that song in my cot."

The stranger grinned. He had beautiful teeth.

Sven felt himself go weak at the knees. "Well, you do look like him. Just like him." Again he blushed. "But even more handsome, if that's possible."

The stranger's eyes took on a new intensity, "Do you want me to fuck you?"

"Well, there's nothing wrong with the direct approach, I always say ..." Sven answered.

"I've got a big cock," the stranger declared.

Sven trembled uncontrollably. "I get off in an hour. Can you wait?"

Again that grin, that glorious grin. "That depends on whether you can follow instructions." And, snapping his head back, the stranger downed his drink in one.

Daddy's Boyz

"Yes, Sir! Absolutely, Sir!" Sven said.

The stranger pulled a fifty dollar bill from his inside pocket, and folding it down the center, he held it towards Sven.

"What's this for?" Sven asked.

"Cab fare. Now, you got something I can write on, boy?" the stranger asked.

Sven handed him a serviette and a pen.

Work over, Sven took a cab from the West to the East Village. Now he stood before the old brownstone building and looked up. Second floor, the stranger had written. Buzz to get in. Sven climbed the front steps and did as he was told. From the hall, he skipped up the stairs, two at a time. The door to the apartment was unlocked just as the stranger had said it would be. Once inside, Sven threw the bolt and began to strip, folding his clothes in a neat little pile by the door, again as directed. The leather jock strap and blindfold awaited him on the hall table just as the stranger had said they would. He slipped them both on before calling out. "Master! I'm here, Master. Ready to do your will."

Wait. He knew he had to wait but how long? Silence. Minutes ticked past. Still no sound. He shivered in the darkness. A trickle of cold sweat ran from his brow down the side of his face. "Master? Are you there, M ..." Suddenly, he felt a gloved hand clamp over his mouth. His master's voice hissed in his ear.

"You only speak when you are spoken to. Got it, boy?"

Sven held still.

"I said, got it, boy?!"

Sven nodded furiously.

"Good."

The hand dropped from Sven's mouth and busied itself behind his back. Then came the unmistakable crick of handcuffs being tightened around his wrists. The stranger gripped Sven's shoulders and manhandled him forward, maneuvering him down a long corridor, and through a doorway. The pungent smells of leather and incense hit Sven like a slap in the face, threatened to overwhelm him. He heard the door slam behind his back, heard a series of bolts being thrown and locks being turned and then silence once again. No going back now. Minutes passed before he felt his master's breath on his face.

"Kneel, boy. Kneel before your, Master."

The pressure of firm hands pressing down on his shoulders forced Sven to his knees. He didn't resist but complied willingly. Suddenly, the blindfold was yanked from his bowed head.

"Welcome, my little lamb. Welcome to the Temple of Ultimate Sacrifice."

Sven blinked, his eyes slowly growing accustomed to the light. His master sat on a medieval throne atop a raised platform, looking down at him; stroking his moustache leisurely with a leather gloved hand. Ornate candelabras were positioned to his left and to his right, casting a warm glow over the otherwise austere surroundings. The room had a theatrical feel — part prison cell, part ivory tower. The walls were clad in stone. Manacles hung from them. An elaborate sling hung down from the ceiling. Over to one side was the metal frame of a bed, the foot and the head took the form of prison bars, a thick rubber mattress lay across it.

"Look at me!" His master demanded his attention. Sven snapped his head around. "You like what you see?"

"Yes, Master." Sure, Sven liked what he saw. This master was second to none. The brim of his cap shaded his eyes, his thick moustache shaded his mouth; but his body was revealed in all its oiled glory, the body of a muscle god, thickly coated with brown fur, adorned by only a pair of boots, a studded cod-piece and dog collar.

"Am I not beautiful?"

"Yes, Master. You're beautiful. Very beautiful."

"And you want only to worship me?"

Sven licked his parched lips, "Yes, to worship you, Master."

"But are you worthy?"

"No, Master. I'm worthless," Sven dropped his chin to his chest and hid a secret smile. He liked this game.

"That's right. You're a worthless piece of shit. What are you?"

"A worthless piece of shit, Master."

The Master bared his teeth in a smile, or was it a sneer? He stood majestically, towering above Sven as he looked down from his platform. Breathing deep, his rib cage swelled to capacity. Sven's eyes were filled with wonder. Candlelight flickered over every curve and groove, caressing the contours of his Master's awesome body. Sven watched him flex as he stepped down from his dais and crossed the space between them to stand before him.

Sven's eyes now focused on his Master's bulging basket, and his mouth began to water. His Master smiled down, benignly, and began to tug the fingers of his leather glove free from his right hand. Sven smiled up at him, awaiting his Master's permission — permission to let him bury his mouth on his plump, swollen mound. He was unprepared for the thwack of the open-handed slap that struck him hard across his face. It was just hard enough to be threatening.

"You belong to me now. I can and I will do anything I want with you. And do you know why?" He gripped Sven's hair and yanked his head back so that his teary eyes were lifted to meet his own. Eyes like burning coals. Sven shook his head, blinking away the tears, his bottom lip trembling. "When you entered my world you left your own world behind ... and there is no going back." His Master's face took on a sinister cast; a cruel twist to the mouth, his nostrils flared. "You can beg for mercy, but no one will hear you. You have entered into a contract that is iron-clad."

Just another Tuesday night. On first appearance, nothing in the bar had changed. Nothing save for the advent of Sam the Man. As if on cue, as the door closed shut behind him, Madonna's "Beautiful Stranger" erupted through the sound system. All eyes turned, however subtly, to feast on fresh meat.

As he strode towards the bar, Sam basked in this new found adoration. It was only when the barman turned around that he was caught short. This wasn't Sven! Where was Sven? After all his hard work, was he to be robbed of his moment of glory?!

"You look disappointed," The big, beefy barman gave Sam a winning smile. "Expecting to see Sven?"

"That obvious, huh?" Sam asked.

"Just guessing. You're not the only one. That guy sure is a hard act to follow. Get you a drink?"

"Tequila," Sam answered.

The barman poured.

"Many people asking after him?" Sam asked.

"One or two. My boss would sure as hell like to know where he's gone. Just disappeared into thin air — a week ago tonight, in fact. Not a word since," the barman said.

Sam toyed with his glass.

The barman watched him intently and asked, "You a friend of his or something?"

"Not exactly," Sam said.

"No. The way I understand it, the guy didn't have friends. Only admirers," the barman said.

"Guess that's got me pegged," Sam said.

"Oh, no, handsome. I would have pegged it the other way around." The barman turned away reluctantly to serve another customer, adding, "Don't you go away now."

As Sam took his seat at the bar he was aware of a presence alongside him. Turning his head, he came face to face with Papa Bear.

"Anyone ever tell you, you look just like Tom Selleck?"

"As a matter of fact ..." Sam turned back to his drink.

Papa Bear leaned into Sam's ear, "I love Tom Selleck."

Sam didn't know how to reply to that one.

Papa Bear plucked two fat cigars from his breast pocket. "Join me?" he asked.

"No, thanks," Sam answered.

"Haven't seen you in here before ..." Papa Bear said.

Yes, you have, thought Sam.

Papa Bear lit up, "You from out of town?"

"Nope," Sam said.

"Waitin' on a friend?"

"Not, exactly. I came in to see, Sven. You don't happen to know where I might find him?" Sam asked.

"You tried his place?" Papa Bear asked.

"Lost the address," Sam lied.

"I could maybe let you have it. I got it somewhere," Papa Bear offered.

"That would be great," Sam said.

"Yeah, only I don't have it with me," Papa Bear said.

"Really?" Sam asked.

"It's back at my place," Papa Bear declared.

"You want to take me home?" Sam asked.

"It isn't far," Papa Bear said.

"Lead the way," Sam said.

True to his word, ten minutes later they were entering Papa Bear's darkened loft. Sam closed the door behind him. Instantly,

Daddy's Boyz

he felt the grip of Papa Bear's paw on his arm as it swung him around. Hands pushed against his chest, hurling him back into the wall.

"Ain't no one ever telled you it ain't safe to go home with strangers?"

Sammy's hands were now pinned at shoulder height. The full weight of Papa Bear pressed up against him, his face within inches of his own.

"Answer me, boy?"

Sam blinked but didn't reply. He could feel Papa Bear's hot breath on his face, was held in place by his heaving chest. Flattened against the wall, Sam suddenly felt like a seven stone weakling, felt puny, felt like Sammy all over again. He braced himself for the worst.

With a low growl, Papa Bear crushed his mouth down on Sam's. A furious, slobbering, tongue-bath of a kiss. Sam's response was immediate, hard in seconds and fit to burst. As if he had sensed it, Papa Bear began to grind his hips against Sam's own. Sam stopped resisting. Papa Bear let go of one wrist and let his hand fall to cup Sam's buttock, using the leverage to press Sam's swollen mound directly up against his own. Sam let his free hand slip around Papa Bear and clutch his back. Enjoying the ride, he clung on for dear life.

Sven lay back on the thin mattress covering his hard, metal cot, an arm thrown across his eyes to protect them from the glare of the single naked bulb illuminating his windowless cell. One, solitary army blanket was tossed aside, too coarse for Sven's naked skin. He was exhausted, disorientated and thoroughly fucked on every level.

Time had lost its meaning. He did not know if it was night or day, and he surely did not know how long he had been kept prisoner. There were no certainties in this dark world, save for the predictability of his Master's visits. Visits during which he would be stuffed full of that monstrous cock and fucked until he cried out for mercy, cried until he wet the mattress with his tears. No. One thing was certain. His master did not know the meaning of mercy.

His thoughts were interrupted by the unmistakable clatter from afar. A ghostly echo. Keys being turned in a lock. Like Pavlov's dogs, Sven's response was reflexive. Blood began to pump, and his cock twitched into life. He knew exactly what was coming. Tears sprang into his eyes. He was a prisoner, a victim of his Master's pleasure. And the worst thing about it was that he did not know if he ever wanted to be free.

He heard the footsteps, at a distance. Drawing closer, ever closer — and the trembling began. Cold sweat. Bathed in a cold sweat. Awaiting the inevitable. His imagination tried to reach beyond the door, to see. No picture came to mind beyond his Master's boots striding purposefully towards him. His Master's footsteps resounding in his ears. Coming closer. Inexorably. Coming closer. Nothing lay beyond the door except his Master's boots.

Footsteps, growing louder, growing louder till they filled his ears like a flood, like a tidal wave threatening to drown him in its deafening roar. His hands flew up to cover his ears. No more! Please, no more!

The footsteps stopped. And the key turned in the lock.

Sven buried his face in his horse hair pillow … and grinned.

Sam was awakened by the sound of chanting. Where the hell was he? He felt like he had been hit by a truck. Not altogether inappropriately. Papa Bear had slammed into him pretty hard.

The smell of incense wafted under his nose. Patchouli. He struggled to open sleep-encrusted eyes. Morning light filtered through curtains the color of a violet sky, transforming Papa Bear's lair from a cave to a glade. It was quite probably the most bizarre living space Sam had ever seen. Decked out in greens and browns and fur and wood. A tree, with love-birds on the branches. A fucking tree in the middle of a loft! And over in the far corner of the room, a naked Papa Bear knelt before an elaborate altar, his furry ass resting on his ankles, raising his hands to the abstract figurines that were carefully arranged before him. He was gone. Lost in his own little world.

Ritual over, Papa Bear stood, bowed and drew a curtain across the sacred space. He turned and saw that Sam was both stunned and awake.

"You must be hungry," Papa Bear said with a smile. "I'll make you breakfast."

Daddy's Boyz

It was with some trepidation that Sam entered the kitchen shortly after. A bed sheet tied around his waist and trailing behind him. Papa Bear's solid, hairy ass hung out the back of his apron. An appetizer?

"Omelet and toast OK?"

"Maybe I should just be going," Sam said.

"I took the precaution of locking the door. You ain't going nowhere without my say so, boy."

"But I need to go find Sven," Sam said.

"He ain't going nowhere for the moment. And neither are you. So just sit yourself down and relax. Believe me, you won't be disappointed. I'm quite a cook."

Forever after, Sam would never understand why he did not cause a fuss, but he didn't. Instead, he sat compliantly at the breakfast bar and waited for the mystery to unravel. Sat with difficulty, that is. His ass still smarting from the night before.

Silence reigned until after they had eaten

Papa Bear wiped his mouth on the back of his hand. "You're probably wondering what the hell is going on?"

"Something like that," Sam said.

He took a slurp from his coffee cup. "Maybe I should begin by introducing myself. My name is Wayne, Wayne O'Grady. I'm a research scientist. Develop new drugs," Papa Bear told him.

"I'm Sam. I work in computers. Nice to meet you," Sam replied with more than a touch of sarcasm.

Wayne let it pass, "I should qualify that. In the eyes of the world, I'm Wayne O'Grady, research ..."

"No, let me guess. But in reality you are Fergie, Duchess of York?"

"To a select few, I am also known as Big Daddy Allsorts," Papa Bear said.

That caught Sam off guard, "Of Magical Muscle Beans fame?"

"The very same," Papa Bear said.

So this ..." Sam ran a hand over his six-pack, "Is all thanks to you?"

Papa Bear shook his head. "No," he replied, matter of factly. Standing up, he carried the dirty plates over to the dishwasher and stacked them inside. "Wish I could take the credit. But, no." He closed the washer door with a clunk and a click. "Sven has been a real bad boy. Made the mistake of passing off standard jelly beans as my muscle beans. Supplemented his income by taking advantage of the likes of you. Didn't know I had my eye on him, was checking him out. He'd no idea who I was."

"But ..." Sam tried his best to sound coherent. "These muscle beans ... they worked."

"Placebo effect."

"How ...?" Sam asked.

Papa Bear's voice took on a new edge of authority as he crossed the room towards him. "The man you are, Sammy boy, is the man you always had the potential to be. You just needed that special ingredient: Belief in yourself." He sat on the stool beside Sam, reached out his hairy mitt and ruffled Sam's hair.

Surprised by the tenderness of the gesture, Sam relaxed his neck and shoulders. Up until this point he had not recognized the tension he harbored there. All at once the tension was gone. He dropped his head to one side. "And Sven? Where is he now?"

"Ah ..." Papa Bear smiled. "There's the rub."

"Eh?" Sam was suddenly alert. "You didn't ..."

"Didn't what?"

Sammy gulped. "You didn't make him disappear?"

"Me? Naw," Papa Bear plucked a cigar from his apron pocket and considered it. "I understand he's currently being held captive by an Off-Broadway producer who has a unique method of auditioning his new leading men." He lit his cigar and puffed out a cloud of smoke. "Let's call it a novel twist on the casting couch principal. Whatever." He plucked a fleck of tobacco from the tip of his tongue. "He's somebody else's problem now. And no longer mine."

"So, Pops ... now the mystery is solved ... should I be going?" Sam asked.

Papa Bear lifted the front of his apron. "Suck that first."

And Sam the Man did as he was told.

The Kid from Left Field
Dale Chase

When they brought up the kid, I knew my days were numbered. I'd owned left field for 15 years, won three Gold Gloves and carried a lifetime 310 batting average, but I'd made the mistake of aging along the way. At 38, my numbers had begun to slip, which rendered me expendable. Forget home runs, forget what I'd contributed to the team, it was the beginning of the end. The kid was younger, faster, stronger, newer.

I was initially blindsided by the sense of loss he brought with him because I believed I could hold off the inevitable. When my production faltered I worked harder, took more batting practice, and honestly thought I had it beat. Then the kid arrived, was dropped into the lineup and that was that. I was told nothing. These things weren't done with ease or consideration, no matter how long you'd been with the team. Nobody sat you down to explain how it was. It was a business after all.

He was twenty. I tried to go back for my own twenty but all I got was a blur of minor league bus rides, nowhere ballparks, and an ache for the bigs. Unlike this guy, I'd had to wait to a ripe old 23 to be called up, but once I arrived on the scene, I'd blown them away. Now none of that mattered. He had left field and I had the bench.

His name was Harrell Wade, and I knew it was going to be one to remember. He was southern and therefore polite, deferred to me in a way that made things worse. I had to stop him calling me sir. "Just Ray," I told him.

"Yes, sir."

Sometimes it was like watching myself out there, and it stirred memories of years when everything was ahead of me and endings didn't exist. When the kid dove for a fly ball my muscles tensed. I felt my body parallel to the ground, airborne those few seconds, glove outstretched. I felt the ball hit the pocket, heard the crowd roar and this always brought me back to the present.

I could not deny his talent and now and then actually let myself enjoy it as he leaped high against the wall to rob the opposition of

Bob Condron

a home run. His powerful arm cut triples to doubles, doubles to singles; his speed seemed effortless, his skills second nature, everything about him inborn. Concentrating on his talent helped me not think about my loss for awhile and in looking at him I couldn't help but take note of his other attributes. He had a good body, six feet tall with the promise of filling out into a fine man. Blond, ruddy, handsome, he was the classic farm boy come in out of the sun.

In my off-balance state, I sometimes tried to hate him but found it beyond me to do such a thing because he was innocent, because he was young, because I had once been like that, and because I was starting to care.

In the clubhouse, he good naturedly went along with the pranks every rookie endures. Me, he avoided. I glanced his way in the showers because I did this with every attractive guy on the team. I had, over the years, become expert at checking them out without appearing to notice. I'd scoped countless dicks and asses, but this one got to me like no other.

His butt was a round little number, but it was that rope of cock that turned more heads than would ever be admitted. He was immediately nicknamed horse and put up with torments about what he could do with that thing. This brought on a blush that, for me, heightened his appeal. Beyond deflecting the hazing, he didn't talk much. When he did, he kept it mostly to baseball.

He was awkward off the field and more so around me. This brought out the daddy in me, something I had never before experienced and which I did my best to hold back. On one hand it felt natural, mentor the kid, enjoy his presence. On the other it was encouraging the enemy, not to mention officially kicking off my old age.

I resisted the attraction for over a month, and this was probably the easiest part because I knew all about containment. Sex was not an option with the ball club, and knowledge of outside activities could mean the end of a career. I'd had a few relationships — all outside the game — and frequented certain bars in certain cities, but was careful with all of it. So now I did what I always did, simply enjoyed being around him. It confounded me like nothing ever had though, the push and pull, but then I'd never been facing the end.

Daddy's Boyz

I got to know Harrell when the guys got him drunk one night after a 12-4 loss in Cincinnati. Hearing a commotion in the hotel hallway, I went out to see what was up and found the kid in bad shape. As the others weren't much better, I sent them on their way and took him into my room. He fell onto the bed and passed out.

Since he reeked of booze, I stripped him and will confess to doing it slowly. I got in beside him, hoping he wouldn't freak in the morning but hey, I'd rescued him and all I had was one bed.

He woke before dawn, stumbled around trying to find the bathroom. "Shit," he cried when he bumped into the dresser. I turned on the light and he froze.

"You were drunk, ready to pass out, and your buddies were in no shape to get you to your room, so I took you in."

When he stared at me, I realized it was because he'd thrown back the covers and exposed my erect cock. His eyes fixed on it, then did a slow climb to my face.

"Yeah, OK, thanks," he said. "I need to pee."

He didn't shut the door, and I listened to his stream, then water at the basin. He emerged with a towel at his face.

"I should not drink," he offered in that sweet southern drawl. "I am no good at it. Don't even remember where they took me."

He came back to bed, hesitated, then lay down atop the covers. I feasted on the sight of that long prick lolling on his thigh. It took great restraint not to make a move.

"So this is kinda awkward," he said as he lay looking at the ceiling.

"In what way?" I managed, panic rising.

"Well, me in left field when you've sorta owned it."

Relief washed over me. He meant baseball. At that moment I would have given a lot more than left field for him to stay put.

"Things change," I offered. "I accept that."

"So will you stay with the team? There's talk you might retire."

"It's a big decision, and I'll probably make it after the season ends," I said.

"Must be tough," he offered.

"Sometimes, yeah," I said.

A long silence came up between us, and I could feel him working his way toward something or maybe away from it. "You could have put me in my room last night," he finally said.

"I thought you needed looking after."

More silence. We were going to take this in stages, and I left it to him because I was coming to realize we might, as I hoped, have more in common than left field.

"You're not married," he said after a bit.

"Nope."

"Why's that?" he asked.

"Just is," I said.

He nodded. I noted his cock had stirred. He ran a hand down onto his thigh but left the blossoming boner alone.

"So what do you do?" he asked.

"About what?" I asked.

He looked at my cock, "About that."

"Same as most guys. If I find someone to fuck, great, if not a hand job," I told him.

He smiled, sighed, and wrapped a hand around his prick. "Me too," he said, tugging on the thing. "I come from farm country and you know how that is, livestock breeding all over the place. You turn around one's fucking another and you get to thinking why can't it be like that with people, your dick gets hard you just stick it in somebody close by, never mind all the rules and stuff. I'd watch a stallion fuck a mare and it would get me hard and I'd go out behind the barn and jerk off. The animals have it made, fuck any time they want."

"But they'll never know the thrill of hitting a home run," I offered.

He laughed, "Guess not."

"You're right about the freedom, though. Hard cock equals fuck," I said.

It would have been easy to take him at that point. His dick was up, he was obviously in need, hadn't panicked about being in the room with my woody and sounded like he was trying to talk himself into doing something but I held back. What I did do was wrap a hand around my dick and work it a bit. He watched, then said, "Are we talking horses?"

"We don't have to," I said.

"No rules, then?" he asked.

"None in here," and with that I reached over and took his prick in hand. The flinch was obviously a pleasurable one.

Daddy's Boyz

"Oh, God, yeah," he said as I worked him.

"So do you fuck?" I asked as the barriers crumbled. "Did you get up to things down on the farm?"

"I got up to things but mostly it was in Triple A with a shortstop from New York. We clicked right off, not a word about it, you know how that is? You just feel this heat. Soon as we were alone we were all over each other. Couldn't get enough."

"You gonna let me fuck you?" I asked.

"You let me do you first and you can fuck me 'til the cows come home," he said.

I hadn't taken a cock in awhile. Never a priority but not out of the question, I'd always concentrated on getting into the other guy. When Harrell saw my hesitation, he grew concerned, "You won't let me?"

I looked down at the long prick in my hand, thought of how it would feel going up my chute.

"Do it," I said and I hopped out of bed to dig in my bag for lube and condoms. Crawling back to him, I took a gob of grease, then handed the tube and rubber to him. As I greased my hole, he pulled the sheath over his prick and slathered on the lube.

I lay on my stomach, knees up under me, and felt him get in behind. Hands on my butt cheeks, he pulled them open and paused. I had to wonder if he'd ever seen a hairy butt crack, but soon his cock head was poking around. And then he hit the center.

As his knob popped in, I took a deep breath.

"Oh, man," Harrell said.

I tried to echo the sentiment, but he was pushing the whole piece of meat into me and speech became impossible.

"Danny Martin, he was the shortstop," Harrell said. I couldn't believe he was talking. "First one to call me horse dick. He's still down in Shreveport."

I had no reply. Sweat had broken out across my forehead, my breathing was labored all because I had a mile of cock up my ass. And then he started to thrust. I let out a groan, but he didn't stop, probably couldn't. No chatter now. He drove in and out for just a few seconds before flattening me and unloading. Long grunts came with each squirt and when he had quieted, he stayed put. "I like it up there," he whispered in my ear, "but I know it's a butt full so ..." He then pulled out.

Bob Condron

He rolled onto his back as if we were done. I gave him a few minutes, then told him to go wash.

"Your turn now," he said, and I nodded.

When he returned to bed, he simply stood, long prick now at rest but still impressive.

"You gonna fuck me?" he said with a grin.

"Oh, yeah. C'mon down here," I said.

Unlike his effort, mine was a slow and thorough performance in which I devoured the whole of him. I licked his every inch, put a finger up his butt while I sucked his balls. He agonized with the attention, prick up again. He held it as I played with him, sucking his pink little tits until he begged me to fuck him. I then pushed his legs up around his ears and made him stay that way while I put on a rubber, added some lube. And then I had my cock aimed and I took a second to look at what he had to offer, a fine pink pucker just waiting to be used. I put my cock head up to it and pushed in.

He took me without any indication of pain, and I wondered just how much he and that shortstop had gotten up to. He held his cock as I fucked him, and I took my time. Settling into an easy stroke, I purposely called to mind the fact of us — two left fielders getting it on. I saw us out there together and wished it could be that way — that I was twenty again and we were platooning in the outfield. I refused, at least while I had my dick in him, to address reality.

When a climax beckoned, I picked up speed and Harrell got verbal, telling me how much he liked getting done which got me going even more. He pulled on his dick as I thrust for all I was worth and as I began to shoot, so did he. For a few glorious seconds, the world and all its circumstances disappeared.

Afterward, I told him he'd best get to his own room and to be careful about being seen.

"Can we get together again tonight?" he asked.

"We're gonna have to be real careful but yeah, we can definitely get together. Maybe we can go somewhere else. Let me think on it."

I didn't play at all that day. Opportunities for a pinch hitter were limited so once again I rode the bench, restless as hell. Time weighed on me, innings ticking by. Concentrating on Harrell was all I had so I pictured him not in left field but naked, on his back, legs up, taking my dick. When he hit a home run with runners on first and second, I was well along into my fantasy world where he bared his butt and gave me what I wanted. He came into the dugout all hyped from the homer and after a high five and all that crap, I couldn't stand to be near him. I headed for the clubhouse where I jerked off in a bathroom stall.

That night Harrell begged off dinner with his teammates, saying he wanted to call home, have a quiet night. Me, I had no problem with cover. I was known as the independent sort, not a man to be tampered with. So I told Harrell where to meet me, then took him to a seedy motel and fucked the night away.

He was agitated from the game, talked about it on the way to our room and didn't stop until I put my cock up him. I did him rough the first time, partly to shut him up but mostly to erase the facts of us. I wanted no more than here and now, screwing in a lowlife room, which added distance to our reality.

I wore myself out with him that night and realized there was some good in the situation. I didn't have to worry about being game ready the next day, I could use it all up in bed, then drag myself to the bench for a rest. Harrell had to face the game, but he had youth in his corner. He'd be up for it with no problem, just as he was up for a night in the sack.

Of course I let him fuck me that night. There was no getting around his two-way street thing, and I had to admit I was getting to like having that snake up my butt. He did me standing so he could watch in the mirror and I looked back over my shoulder to see him nailing my ass. I found I liked the image.

Our management was fortunately not into bed checks so there was no problem in us not getting to the team hotel until the wee hours. We had used each other so thoroughly and yet in the elevator I still wanted to get a hand on him. I held off though and, being the mature one, offered counsel instead.

"Getaway day," I said. "We can sit together on the plane if you want. It's OK for us to play out the rookie-veteran mentor scene, but be sure to kid around with the others. Don't make me a favorite."

"When can we fuck?" he asked.

"We're going to have to hold off a bit being headed home, but once we're there we can pretty much do as we want. Where are you staying?"

"At a hotel right now," he said.

"I have an apartment. You can visit anytime. How about we connect after we land. It will be late, though," I said.

"Who cares," he said as we reached our floor. "I won't be able to sleep if I don't fuck."

It was then that I did the unthinkable. I kissed him. I moved in and planted one and he responded fully, tongue and all. When I pulled back, my arms around him, I told him he was the best thing that had ever happened to me. Before he could reply, the doors opened and with that, conversation ended. We hurried to our rooms, nobody the wiser.

So that was the start, that fateful early season road trip when he arrived to claim what had always been mine. On the plane home he did well, keeping things very vet-rookie-mentor while making an effort with the others. I sat in a kind of calm I never would have imagined possible for a guy who has met his fate. Of course fucking fate did soften the blow.

The team manager, Danny Fitzgerald, a man not yet 50 whose face was so lined from the sun that he looked 60, sat down next to me and began a folksy sort of talk that was well meant and predictable.

"I see you and the kid are getting along real good. We appreciate that, Ray, you being big enough to accept him the way you have. He's a fine person and a great ball player. Who knows how much he can do, but we think it's a lot. Your influence right now is important."

I took this in, thinking back to fucking the kid and the irony of the person who was to replace me bringing so much into my life.

"Have you given any thought to the future?" Danny asked with a somber tone appropriate to my waning career.

"I'll decide after the season. Right now I just want to help the team any way I can."

"Good man."

That night back in our home town, I took Harrell to my apartment, covering our departure together by a last minute, "Need a ride?" We'd barely gotten out of the parking lot when he got out his dick.

"Christ, kid, we'll be there in fifteen minutes," I said.

He didn't say anything, just tugged at himself. As I pulled up to my building he said, "I had to jerk off in the airplane bathroom. I was hard half the flight, and I really need to fuck."

"Well tuck it in, and we'll do something about that once we're upstairs."

Inside my apartment, Harrell threw his bag down and began to undress.

"I need me some ass," he said and, as I savored his urgency, I also felt an uneasiness. "C'mon," he said, holding himself how. "Get 'em off."

He fucked me standing. I leaned against a chair as he went at me from behind and for the first time the fact of us, the greater fact, began to intrude. He was fucking me all right in more ways than one.

When he came, which was quickly, he let out a yelp. He then pulled out and gave a long sigh. Relieved, he settled while I simply stood and turned. My prick had responded to him initially, but that dose of reality had done me in and I now hung limp. Harrell ignored this, starting looking around the place. I scooped up my clothes, took them and my bag to the bedroom. Before I could get there, the kid raced past, jumped onto the bed and lay smiling at me, cock in hand. "You gonna suck my dick?" he asked.

"Give me a minute, will you?"

I unpacked for no reason, put stuff away, threw dirty clothes into the hamper, all the while something building inside me until I was finally ready.

"All done," Harrell declared as I approached.

"Not quite," I said.

I wanted to do him in the worst way, to fuck him so hard it would permanently wipe away that grin, kill off his aw shucks country boy front, reduce him to a piece of meat. I wanted to spear him, make him choke on my cock as I rammed it up his ass.

"Turn over," I commanded, my dick starting to fill. "Spread 'em."

He fixed on my eyes for a second, then did as told. Butt thrust up, he pulled open his cheeks. I stared at his pink little hole, thinking about getting into it and staying put, but instead I climbed onto the bed and got my nose down there, then my mouth. He moaned as I licked, then grabbed his cock. When I put my tongue into him, he began to work himself.

"Oh, man," he squealed as I fed at his dirty little place, eating ass until I knew I'd cum in the sheets if I didn't fuck. So I pulled back, put on a rubber and stuck my prick up him, began to ride full out.

This wasn't like the other times. We'd graduated to something else and I didn't know if it was more or less, if something had been gained or lost. I only knew I wanted a long hard fuck, one that would leave him red, raw, and spent. As I pounded his ass, he went silent.

Sweat ran down me and onto him. He moaned once and I didn't think it was with pleasure. Nothing mattered now but my dick. When the rise began, I slowed, thought about the game, batting averages, schedules, pumping easier until the climax retreated. I kept at him that way for a good long time.

"Please," he finally said.

It wasn't the same now, but I couldn't tell if it was him or me. I only heard a kid sounding like he thought I'd never let go. Grinding my cock into him, I let him know I was in charge, and with this, I finally allowed myself to cum. Afterward, as we lay side by side, I didn't want to think about what was happening.

Harrell got up after a bit, went to the bathroom. The water ran for some time and when he returned he had a wet cloth in hand. "You fucked me raw," he said, rubbing his butt.

"You wanted it," I said.

He studied me, shook his head, "Something else going on."

For a kid he was pretty bright.

"Come down here," I said and he crawled onto the bed. He allowed himself into my arms and as I held him I felt whatever it was that had gotten into me retreat for the moment. He nuzzled against me which led me to kiss him. We spent a few blissful minutes doing nothing more than that.

"We're fine," I assured him when he looked into my eyes. "You're the best thing that ever happened to me."

"Or the worst," he said.

It was a surprisingly perceptive statement, dead on it turned out. He, in his youth, with everything ahead of him, could face facts while I wanted to fuck them away. Being in the winning spot

Daddy's Boyz

in left field, he had no trouble maintaining a balance between us that left me to deal head on with the gain-loss scenario.

As the season progressed, the team got stuck in second place, knowing a wild card slot was our best bet. A playoff spirit was with us and Harrell became a key element. He gradually became a hero to the fans, and when a sportswriter dubbed him the kid from left field, everyone seized on it. He was batting 345 and covering the outfield like nobody ever had. Through it all he and I kept going strong.

Riding the bench became no easier for me, and there were times when resentment surfaced. It was usually over some petty thing and more than once Danny Fitzgerald sauntered over after the game to give me one of his casually supportive talks.

"The kid's doing it all, ain't he, and the fans love it. You're a big part of that, Ray. I know you and him have gotten close and a kid like that needs a veteran to help him along. You're much admired to not let your own situation get in the way."

I almost laughed because I'd just kicked the shit out of the water cooler when I couldn't find my favorite bat, not that there was any need of one. I just nodded and Danny moved on.

Harrell knew I was fighting a battle, but young as he was, I don't think he knew how to approach it any way but with his dick. So the sex kept on, and I tried to make it take away the pain, even though I knew it was a losing game. The season was getting away, we were into September, and my future was an unknown. I would not have a job in October, and it was his fault.

When I sometimes now begged off, he didn't understand. He said he did but it was with that little-kid look of disappointment, like he was being punished for something he didn't do. I would assure him we were fine, then hole up in my hotel room buried in a kind of anguish I'd never known before.

Life had always been the game. There had been no other plan, no consideration that one day it would be stolen from me. As I lay in my solitude, trying not to blame Harrell, I still wondered what would have happened if he hadn't come onto the scene. Maybe they would have kept me out there a few more years. Guys were playing into their forties now, conditioning could do that, but the phenom had arrived and it was over.

Bob Condron

Sometimes the solitude worked against me, became unbearable, and it was then I would call up the kid and have him come over. His dick would be hard when he arrived and there would be a quick and urgent fuck, followed by what I needed — the whole of him. It was on one of these nights that I allowed that I was falling in love with him, that I wanted him part of my life.

He told me around this time that he had never kissed another man. "It was always just the sex, ya know? Like me and the shortstop, just get it on. Nobody's ever done me like you."

I didn't comment. His presence eased my torment, and I kissed him again. He had such an untried quality, never mind his experience, and I couldn't get enough of it.

In time he grew confident enough to talk about our situation. It was a topic I avoided because there was no answer. He was in, I was out, end of story. But he went ahead, reverting to that aw shucks manner that would probably remain with him forever.

"How ya doin' on the bench?" he asked as he lay in my arms one night. We were home, had won that afternoon in a 4-3 cliffhanger. "I know it must be tough," he added. "Ya know when I'm out there I'm thinking about you."

"I appreciate that and I'm doing fine on the bench. It's not where I want to be but hey, I've had my time. It's yours now," I told him.

"I want to say I'm sorry but that doesn't sound right. There's no good way to tell you how I feel, guilty a little, I guess. And wishing we could play side by side," he said.

"Never happen. The most they're going to let me do is pinch hit now and then. I think the writing is on the wall."

"You'll retire?" he asked.

"Not much else to do," I said.

He went silent and I was glad because I didn't want to get started on what that would mean. He settled against me and I shut my eyes, forgot everything but him.

"Are we in love?" he said after awhile.

"I can only speak for myself," I said.

"OK, what do you say?" he asked.

"I'm in love with you, have been for some time," I said.

He raised up onto his elbows, looked down at me, grinned. "Well I'm sure as hell in love with you. I've never felt like this before, ya know? I mean there's been crushes and stuff but never like this. You're so ... much, I guess. You give me everything I could ever want," he said.

It almost made me cry. Instead I held onto him and we spent some time kissing in a non-sexual way that truly felt like we were sealing the bond. "I love you," I said.

"And I love you," he said.

I thought it would make things better but it turned out it got worse. Loving each other just deepened the pit inside me. At times I could barely eat and my stomach began to complain, but I wasn't about to tell the team doctor anything was wrong. I'd have to drop over before that. But I spent time in all kinds of pain and finally a kind of exhaustion set in. When we blew five games in a row, even with Harrell and all his talent, we dropped out of the wild card race. The season was nearly over.

The day we sank to third, everything changed. The loss was no longer just mine, the whole team was reeling, and I sat in a clubhouse where everyone's days were numbered. Nine games remained, but we had been mathematically eliminated. We would play the final dates, but none of it mattered. Ironically, I would now see some playing time.

Harrell was crushed by all this. We were in San Diego, and he came to my room that night, breaking one of our rules. "I don't give a fuck who sees," he said when I opened the door. He was near tears and I took him into my arms.

"Goddamned fucking game," he cried.

We sat for some time talking about baseball, and I heard myself playing mentor again, reminding him how many seasons lay ahead, that he had to learn to lose gracefully. All the clichés I'd heard from the coaches my first year, I now trotted out for him and found, much to my surprise, that I liked sharing them. Gradually, he righted himself, allowing promise of the future to soften the immediate disappointment.

"You've got a long career ahead," I assured him. "Maybe twenty years. Look at the start you've gotten. Most guys never manage half that. I know it's a sad time, but you've got to look at the positives, move on. Talk about next year, be upbeat in the clubhouse. Don't let it sink you."

The sex that night was a kind of consolation. Harrell wanted me to get inside him and stay there and I did just that. It was one of the best ever. The next day I found myself in the starting lineup.

Nothing was said, but just before I took the field, Harrell slapped me on the butt.

"Beat hell out of 'em, Ray," he said.

I hit no home runs, made no spectacular plays. I played journeyman left field and hit a single that drove in a run. We won 3-2, and Danny Fitzgerald slapped me on the back afterward.

"Hell of a good game, Ray."

I knew it was more solace than anything, but I was grateful.

When we were down to a single remaining game, I found myself unable to bear the thought of the post-season because a decision would have to be made. It was a given that my contract wouldn't be renewed. I could try to get picked up by another team, but 38-year-olds on the way down aren't in much demand and there was no way I'd sign a minor league contract, embarrass myself like that. And in with my decision process lay the Harrell Wade factor. He would continue with the team while I would not, and the thought of this was more than I could handle. I had been spoiled by what the game had given us and had no idea how to let go.

And then an opportunity presented itself. On the final day of the season after a 10-2 blowout that meant not a damned thing, Hitting Coach Jack Riley announced his retirement. Harrell said he thought I'd be perfect for the job.

"I never considered coaching," I said.

"But you're a natural. You're good at more than just hitting, you can talk to the fellas, get 'em to see the bigger game like you did me. Talk to Danny. Go on," Harrell said.

I hated the idea. I still wanted to be on the field, so I spoke to no one, but Harrell apparently did because Danny called me the next day, asked me to see him when I came to the ballpark to clean out my locker.

"What are you plans, Ray?" he asked when I sat across from his desk. "You know we're not going to offer you a new contract."

"I pretty much figured that. I'll retire. There's no point in trying to catch on with another team."

Daddy's Boyz

"Have you considered maybe coaching? You know Jack Riley is leaving. I think you'd be an asset to the team as hitting coach. You're a good presence in the clubhouse, you've got lots of knowledge, good people skills. Just the person we need."

I shook my head, not in refusal of the job but in frustration. Danny knew what I meant.

"I know, it's not what you want, but there comes a time for all of us when we have to face facts. I did it twelve years ago when the Mets didn't want a 36-year-old left-hander anymore. They had better fish to fry. Went into coaching and look where I am now. Still in the game, Ray. Still in the game. Maybe not like you want, but it's a good life and you can have a lot of impact on the team, sometimes more than when you played. Give it some thought."

I didn't go home after that. I went down the street to a sports bar and got drunk. Harrell hadn't been in the clubhouse, had yet to clean out his locker, and it was just as well. He was the last person I wanted to see. It was time to have my cry if that's what this was, to grieve or mourn or some damned thing. Beer and bourbon and God knows what else until I didn't care any more. I lay sprawled in a booth, nobody bothering me because they all knew which made it worse. And then Harrell was there, pulling me up, helping me to his car.

I woke up in my bed the next morning sick as hell, the kid snoring beside me. After heaving my guts out, I crawled back to him. He slid an arm around me.

"Welcome to the post season," he said.

"Fuck you," I replied.

He laughed. "You sure tied one on. Danny says he offered you Riley's job, that you said you'd think about it. That how you do your thinking?"

"I don't want to think. I don't want to do a goddamned thing but sleep. Let me alone, OK?" I said.

He got out of bed and I drifted back to sleep, waking hours later, my stomach somewhere near calm. My head still ached but that I could tolerate. A shower, medication, and I emerged at last. Harrell was watching cartoons. I fell onto the couch beside him, shut my eyes, heard Daffy Duck going off on Bugs Bunny. It somehow seemed appropriate and I began to laugh which got Harrell into a playful mood.

"You over it now, coach?" he said, tickling me.
"Stop it and don't call me coach."
"OK. How about retiree? That's got a nice porch swing kinda sound."
"Don't make me laugh," I pleaded as I did just that. "My head is still pounding."
He snuggled up next to me, began to nuzzle. "How about Dr. Wade's miraculous cure all," he whispered.
"And what would that be?" I asked.
"Well, you have to undress and lay on your stomach and we run this hose up your butt. Makes things happen, ya know?"
"I am too hung over to fuck," I said.
"Nobody is too anything to fuck," he countered, opening my robe to get at my cock which was, damn it, getting hard. "Looks like your dick's into it."
As he began to work me he attempted to soothe and that was a turning point of sorts. Holding my cock, gently stroking, he told me how life would be.
"You'll be my coach, officially. You'll coach the other guys, too, but you'll really be teaching me, and I know there's still lots to learn. You won't have to retire and sit on the porch, you'll be with the team. You'll be with me."
"Coach," I said, trying it on.
"Coach Ray McCullough," Harrell added, "Veteran slugger responsible for the amazing rise in team batting averages."
"Yeah, we'll see."
"I can't bear to lose you, Ray," he said, tugging at me now. "Let's get back in bed."
As we walked to the bedroom, my hand in his, I asked him if he'd tipped Danny about me coaching.
"Nope. It was him asked me," he said.
As I threw off my robe and settled into bed, Harrell stripped and as he did so, offered more.
"I think Danny's got an idea about us. He's real soft spoken, like he's kinda going around the edge which I guess he'd have to, but I think he knows we're happy together. So this is his way."
"You don't know that," I said.
"I suppose not but I do pick up on things. I'm not just some kid, ya know."

As he climbed on top of me, settled his body against mine, I had to agree.

Love in the Arms of an Older Man

Louis Charles DePasquale

    Timmy Harvey pushed open the unmarked door and walked into the building. He looked behind himself furtively worried that someone he knew might have seen him enter. This was his first time here, a few of the guys he had tricked with mentioned it, but he had never been here before. He walked up to the counter and handed the attendant three one dollar bills and got a handful of tokens back. As he walked through the archway, Timmy was nervous, he knew why he had come but still wasn't sure what it said about him.

    As he entered the back room, he thought he had walked into one of Dante's levels of hell. The room was rectangular; in the center of the room was a second rectangle with doors spaced about every two feet around the inner rectangle. The only light in the room were naked light bulbs painted red between each door giving the room a dark reddish glow of unreality. Standing up against the walls of the outer rectangle were about twenty men. Some were standing by themselves others in small groups, but they were all standing against the walls clearly watching and waiting for something or someone.

    Timmy not sure what he should be doing copied the others. He found a spot on the wall in a corner facing a dark open doorway. How long he stood there Timmy wasn't sure. It felt like hours but was probably only minutes. Through the dark haze of cigarette smoke and reddish light he saw someone walking toward him. Initially all he saw was a large bulky dark shape. It took him a second or two to in the dark to realize that the guy was wearing a black leather jacket. As the man closed in on him, Timmy realized that under the jacket he was wearing a white wife beater, a pair of greasy blue jeans and a pair of motorcycle boots. He also noticed the man had a full beard, not the neatly trimmed beards some of his friends wore but a thick bushy salt and pepper mass of facial hair that made a serious statement about its wearer's lack of concern about appearance.

The guy stopped in front of Timmy, looked him up and down from the top of his head to the toes of his sneakers, and smiled at him. The guy stepped through the doorway in front of Timmy leaving the door slightly ajar. He could hear the sounds of coins dropping from inside the doorway, and he could see a light come on in the booth as the movie started to play. He wasn't sure what he should do so he stayed against the wall. After a few seconds had passed, the guy pulled the door open, looked at Tim, and waved at him to come into the booth. Timmy was a little bit scared, but this was what he had came for, so clutching his bravery around himself like a shield, he entered the booth as the guy closed the door behind him.

The booth wasn't very large, just enough room that the two of them could stand comfortably without being pressed against each other. Against the back of his legs, Timmy could feel a low bench, and in front of him on the wall a guy was being fucked hard and fast by a big masculine guy. The movie playing in front of him only added to his feeling of discomfort. As he looked up at the guy in the booth with him, he started worry. What if they guy were a serial killer or wanted to hurt him?

Unconsciously, he tried to step backward only to find the bench blocked his movement. He almost lost his balance and started to fall backward, but the guys caught his arm and helped steady him.

The guy smiled at him and said, "Don't worry. Everything's going to be alright. What's your name?"

Nervously with a catch in his voice, he said "Umm Tim — Timmy."

"Hi Timmy, why don't you have a seat and get comfortable. We can just watch the movie for a few minutes." The man had a strong and powerful voice, but it was obvious that he was trying to sound reassuring to calm Tim down. As he sat down, the guy reached across and put a few more coins in the slot, and turned sideways standing against the door, his eyes darting back and forth between the movie and Tim's face.

As he watched the movie, he couldn't stop himself from glancing at the man in the booth with him. He was at least three or four inches taller and twenty years older than Tim. He was really

Daddy's Boyz

cute even with the bushy beard, which seemed to give his face a sense of character. This guy was certainly different than any of the other men that he had been with.

After a few minutes of silence, the guy looked at him and asked, "Are you feeling better?"

Still a little afraid of the guy, he just nodded his head yes.

"Why don't you take my dick out?" The man asked him.

Because of the way the guy was standing Timmy had to get off the bench and hunch down in front of him. He pulled down the zipper and saw that the guy had gone commando. He reached in and pulled out a semi hard cut dick. Rather than let go of it, he continued to hold it once it was out of the man's pants.

"Go ahead and play with it some," said a voice above him.

As he started running it though his hand he could see it getting harder and stretching out. Rather than wait to be asked, Tim leaned forward and put the dick in his mouth. As he moved up and down on it, he could feel it getting harder in his mouth. He could take it all the way down to the base on the first few passes, but then it grew too hard to comfortably swallow. As he kept making passes up and down while swirling his tongue around the head, he started to feel himself getting excited. He could feel his own dick lengthening down his leg. After a few passes, he realized that it wasn't just sucking dick that was getting him so excited, it was the forbidden nature of the encounter. He was on his knees in a porno booth sucking off a complete stranger. He could smell the tang of cum and sex in the air, and under his knees he could feel the floor sticky with the cum of who knew how many men.

He tried to deep throat again, but couldn't quite get the whole thing down and started to choke a little.

The guy pulled his dick back a little bit and said, "Don't go too fast just relax."

He slowed down his approach some using more tongue action trying to get a little more in his mouth with each down stroke. He could feel the guy's hands holding onto his ears and feel the dick starting to thrust into his mouth as the man moved his hips in a fucking motion. All of a sudden the lights in the booth turned on, and the movie stopped playing on the screen, Tim was startled like a deer caught in the headlights.

The guy pulled his dick out with a pop and pulled Tim up off the floor. He smiled and said, "Why don't we get out of here. We can go outside and talk for a minute."

Unsure of himself, Tim just nodded and followed the guy's lead as they walked past the attendant and out into the afternoon sunlight.

He led Tim over to a motorcycle parked up against the side of the building. The bike was a Harley Davidson Sportster painted black with a flame design on the tank and front fender. The bike was in great shape, and Tim couldn't take his eyes off it. He loved bikes. He'd never had the courage to ride one, but he loved to look at them. At home, he had a dozen plastic models of bikes he had built as a kid, and bike magazines cluttered his living room tables.

The man smiled at Tim's interest in his bike, held out his hand, "My name is Alex by the way."

Without taking his eyes off the bike, Tim reached out and shook the man's hand only half noticing how strong and firm the grip was.

"I can see you like my bike; ever ridden on one?"

Tim looked away from the bike and up into Alex's big blue eyes and said, "No."

"Why don't you get on, we can ride over to my place and pick up where we left off?"

Tim nodded, but wasn't quire sure how he should mount the bike. Alex realizing his dilemma reached over and gave him a hand.

As he got on the bike in front of Tim, Alex turned around and said "Hold on to me tight."

As he kick started the bike, Alex waited until he felt the arms encircle his waist tightly before pulling out of the parking lot and driving onto the street.

For the boy, it was pure heaven. His senses were alive with the new experience. He could feel the engine rumbling beneath him, causing his dick and balls to vibrate with a very pleasant feeling as his dick hardened down his leg. With his arms wrapped around the biker, Tim's face was pressed against the leather jacket Alex was wearing. The smell of the leather was intoxicating. It smelled of smoke and sweat and real manliness. The wind rushing through his hair and against his face gave him a sense of freedom he had never known before. It was like he was flying through the clouds with the earth beneath him free from all cares and worries. He laid his head down against the shoulders in front of him with his eyes closed overwhelmed by everything he was experiencing.

All too soon, the ride came to and end. As he opened his eyes he saw that they were parked in front of a small rancher. The lawn was neat and trim, the house painted a bright blue, and another Harley was parked next to a Suzuki in front of the garage. As Alex helped him off the bike, he smiled and said, "Home sweet home, at least for now anyway." As they walked through the front door, he could see that the décor in the living room could only be described as minimalist. A couch, two chairs, a couple of end tables, and a carburetor in pieces on some newspaper in the corner were the only pieces of furniture in the room.

"Have a seat? Can I get you a drink? I should probably have asked you this earlier but how old are you, cause you look like you're 16?"

Timmy grimaced as he sat down on the not so comfortable sofa, "I get that all the time. I'm 22."

When Alex re-entered the room, he sat down next to Tim and handed him a beer. As they sat sipping their beers the silence grew uncomfortable. Neither of them knowing what to say next, they started to talk at the same time.

"You first," Alex said with a grin.

"I was just going to say that I really enjoyed the ride on your bike. I have always wanted to ride a motorcycle but never had the chance before."

"Do you prefer Tim or Timmy?"

"Everyone I know calls me Timmy but I feel like I am getting too old for that Y on the end of my name."

"Then Tim it is," Alex said.

Not quite sure what to talk about Alex brought up their only common frame of reference, "Sorry I stopped you back there," Alex said, a little sheepishly, "But I really don't like those places too much. I usually just go into to jerk off when I am horny, but you just looked so cute standing against that wall I wanted to talk, to meet you."

"I've never been to a place like that before," Tim said quickly. "I couldn't believe it when a friend told me about the place, so I wanted to check it out for myself."

Alex just smiled as he leaned in and pressed his lips against Tim's. As he felt the tongue licking his lips Tim opened his mouth and let it in. His taste buds caught a hint of cinnamon as his head started to swim. Alex hadn't taken his jacket off yet and Tim could smell the leather near his face. The aroma seemed to intensify everything he was experiencing.

As their tongues dueled in Tim's mouth Alex moved himself on top of him his arms going around and rubbing his back and shoulder blades.

Alex pulled back and with a smile asked, "Is that a tongue ring I was playing with, I've never kissed anyone wearing one before?"

"Yeah," he said with a grin, "I've had it for like a year and sometimes forget it's there. Want me to take it out?"

"Nah I kind of liked it. You OK?" Alex asked. "You seemed uncomfortable when we first got here."

"I was kind of nervous, but I'm OK now," Tim said to Alex's back as the other man walked back into the kitchen.

"Cool." He walked out with two more beers. Handing one to Tim, he said, "Why don't we get a little more comfortable."

He took off the jacket and threw it casually across the armchair next to the couch. As he started to pull the wife beater over his head he glanced down at Tim, "Go ahead take your shirt off or something." As the shirt cleared his head, the first thing Tim saw was hair. Alex was covered with it. He compared that to the two or three hairs clumped in the middle of his chest and felt less than attractive. As he was pulled to his feet, Alex's nipples were at his eye level. They looked like two hills lost in a forest of trees.

Feeling a hand lifting his chin up, Tim looked deep into Alex's eyes for the first time and marveled at just how blue they were. When the eyes were coming toward him, they looked large enough to swallow him whole, he felt arms encircling him, and lips descending on his, opening his mouth, he was lost in the moment. The kiss felt like it went on forever. He felt an arm under his knees as he was picked up off the ground and carried out of the room. All that mattered to him were the lips, the tongue, the sensation everything else faded into nothingness.

Daddy's Boyz

He could feel the mattress under his back and the weight of another person on the bed with him. Tim wrapped his arms around the person lying next to him and just kept kissing back. He felt a hand fumbling with his belt; reached down and undid the loop himself. He kept on kissing. He pulled his mouth away just long enough to feed his air-starved lungs and then reconnected with the lips in front of him. His pants undone and zipper down, he felt a hand on his stomach and a finger playing with the ring in his belly button and still he kept on kissing.

Tim felt a void, as if a part of him was missing, and then he realized that Alex had stopped kissing him. He looked up into those blue eyes without saying a word and reached to pull Alex back down to him.

"Stop for a second I just want to look at you," Alex said.

"Why? My body sucks. I have no definition and no matter how hard I try I can't seem to gain any muscle."

"I think your body is beautiful. You still have the build of a teenager but are developing the curves of a man," Alex said.

While he was talking Alex's finger was running up and down Tim's chest and stomach and every where it touched Tim felt fire running up his nerve endings.

"My God your beautiful," Alex said as he rolled over on top of Tim.

Alex was all tongue and teeth and Tim was lost in abandon under their guidance. Every inch of his body was licked, nipped, and sucked. He was so lost in the moment that Tim wasn't even aware of time passing just a haze of incredible sensations. He felt a finger trying to enter him and spread his legs wider giving it easy access. New sensations were added to the ones he was already experiencing. He was barley aware that his ass was pushing back against the finger trying to pull more of it in. He felt two then eventually three fingers pushing in and opening him up. Each time the momentary sensation of pain was replaced with pleasure increasing the depths of his lust.

Alex's tongue licking his ear, a voice deep with desire said, "I need you, to be inside you."

Tim just spread his legs even further and answered, "God yes."

He felt his legs being lifted toward his head, his ass rotating upward, fumbling, penetration, pain, and pleasure which sensation was which he wasn't sure as they all seemed to blend together. Teeth were biting at his neck, his mind was lost in a sexual haze, and he realized for the first time that this must be what people mean when they describe heaven. Not the sex, no that was wonderful, but the sense of being secure. He felt safe and secure with those hairy arms wrapped around his body. Nothing could ever hurt him as long as he was in these arms. He had never felt this way with any of the other men he had been with.

They pushed against each other again and again dancing to some primeval beat. Tim felt Alex quickening, felt him reaching orgasm inside him. The sensations were so incredible it only took him a few more minutes to reach that point himself. They rolled apart slowly still facing each other Tim lying on top of Alex's arm. They looked into each other's eyes as their breathing returned to normal. They reached in to kiss each other, but the kissing was tentative with little of the passion they experienced a few minutes ago.

They pulled apart not sure now what to do. Desperate to cut the silence Tim looked at the clock and said "I really need to get going. I have to be at work early in the morning."

Alex just nodded and turned his head a crestfallen look crossed his face. "Should I drop you at the bookstore or take you home?"

"The bookstore is fine that's where my car is. Where's your bathroom?" Tim asked.

"It's the open door next to the closet."

They dressed in silence neither one sure what to say. When they walked out the door toward the bike, the air was cold on their exposed skin. Helping Tim on the bike Alex put his leather jacket around Tim's shoulders. He wrapped his arms around the man in front of him leaning his head against the plaid shirt Alex had put on over top of the wife beater.

On the ride back to the bookstore, each man wondered what he had done wrong. The sex had been great but the after was awkward. For Tim it was like a blindfold had been lifted off his eyes. He now realized why all of his partners had seemed inadequate. Not one of them had given him the feeling of strength and security that Alex had. Even now after the sex was over, he still felt it with his arms wrapped around Alex. He realized that he would never again be content with any man who didn't give him that same feeling of security. He also knew why it had been awkward. Alex was a man, and he really wasn't. It didn't matter what his biologic age was compared to Alex, he might as well have been twelve. The vibrations from the bike helped him relive the ecstasy he had felt earlier. He could still feel the fullness of Alex deep inside himself. He could still feel Alex fucking him as the bike vibrated beneath his ass. He never wanted that sensation to come to an end.

As the bike came to a halt in the parking lot, Tim got off the back end. They looked at each other with an awkward silence neither one knowing what to say to the other. They kissed briefly, and Alex started to move the bike backward.

Making a quick decision Tim moved over and tapped Alex on the shoulder. "Can you wait a minute?" He ran over and unlocked the door to his car. Rustling around the front seat, he found a scrap of paper and pen and wrote down his name and phone number. "Call me some time if you want."

Alex just nodded and drove off.

Not sure what he should do, he drove home, fixed himself a snack and went to bed. When his alarm went off, his belly was sticky, and he knew that he had been dreaming about Alex. He got up, showered, dressed, and headed to work. He ran through the routine of his day forcing himself to not think about Alex while he worked. All he accomplished was shuffling a lot of paper on his desk while thinking about the copy machine. The girls stopped by to ask him to join them for lunch, but he begged off saying he had a lot of work to do and was going to eat at his desk. Knowing full well that he was going to run home and check his answering machine.

As he drove home, he tried to think of anything accept his answering machine. He had to just accept the fact that Alex wasn't going to call and that he would have to move on. He was still disappointed when he got home and the light wasn't blinking on the machine. The rest of the day at work he kept thinking about the copier and shuffling papers on his desk. He left for the day realizing that he had accomplished nothing all day. As he walked through the front door, he forced himself to not glance at the traitorous answering machine with its non-blinking indicator light.

Bob Condron

After dinner, he sat down to ignore some TV as he wondered if he would ever find anyone who could make him feel the way Alex did? Tim was so lost in his own thoughts that he almost didn't hear the phone ring. "Hello?"

"Tim?"

The voice on the other end of the line answered with a bit of hesitancy. "Yeah, who is this?"

"It's … um … Alex. I probably shouldn't have called, but I had such a good time yesterday that I wanted to see you again. I'm sorry I was such a shit to you when I dropped you off at the bookstore. You're probably busy, but I was going to go out riding and was wondering if you wanted to come. But if you're too busy or don't want to see me again I understand." The words all came out in a rush and it took Tim a moment to decipher them.

His heart took a jump up into his throat and he managed to reply "No, I have nothing planned."

"Cool where should I pick you up?" Alex asked.

"I guess my place is fine."

After directions were given, Tim raced to his bedroom — thinking to himself: "Oh my God I have nothing to wear." After tearing through half his wardrobe, he settled on a tight white tee shirt, jeans, and sneakers. While putting gel into his hair he heard the bike on the street outside his window. Racing out the front door, he saw Alex getting off his bike. Alex said, "Hey," as Tim stepped up on his tiptoes to give him a quick furtive kiss. As Tim got on the back of the bike, wrapped his arms around the man in front of him, and buried his face in the leather jacket, he realized he had no idea where they are going. In a way it didn't matter, he just hoped they would be going there together.

Boy in the Pool
Jay Starre

All of Clark's friends were dubious, if not outright disapproving. Jordan was too young for him. Jordan must be using him. Over twenty years separated them — but their bodies did not care about that. It was the boy in the pool Clark fell for, and it was that boy's carefree lust that turned all doubts aside in the end.

It was a brilliant summer day at the outdoor pool when Clark first noticed Jordan lounging on a towel in a skimpy swimsuit. Jordan had a sweet look about him, with dark brown hair and eyes and small features on a slim, yet fit body. He looked young enough to be a college student. Clark was in his late 40s and not at all interested in chasing younger men, but there was something about Jordan that attracted him.

Clark was a classic silver fox; tall, muscular and with short grey hair. He was a stunning man. In his racing trunks, Clark's big thighs and smoothly powerful chest were boldly displayed. Jordan's eyes seemed to wander in his direction every few minutes.

It was when they were both in the pool swimming laps that Jordan introduced himself. At the end of the pool, while both were resting, Jordan reached over the lane rope and shook Clark's hand. His quiet smile turned something over in Clark's heart. He wanted to know this young man, even if it had nothing to do with sex. During their conversation, neither mentioned being gay, or asked about it. Clark didn't really care, he was merely enjoying the afternoon and the young guy's smile and unassuming chatter.

"Can I walk with you?" Jordan asked half an hour later when Clark was gathering up his things to leave the pool.

"Sure. It's a beautiful day for a walk. My place isn't far from the beach," Clark answered.

Clark and Jordan talked easily as they strolled along the beach walking path. It was a gorgeous summer afternoon with the hot sun softened by an ocean breeze. When they left the water and went into the city streets Jordan continued on with Clark. Finally Clark was at his corner.

"See you around. It was nice to talk with you," Clark smiled.

"OK," Jordan answered, his eyes on Clark's. Jordan reached forward and shook Clark's hand. Their palms locked firmly for a moment, then Jordan leaned forward and kissed Clark on the cheek.

It was so simple and so unexpected, Clark just laughed. But then Jordan did not let go of his hand.

"Do you want to see my place? I have a great view of the beach," Clark found himself saying.

Once inside, Clark and Jordan wandered around the tidy apartment talking and laughing. Clark was very much at ease and not expecting anything to happen, even though there was that unexpected kiss to consider. Jordan was just too young to be interested sexually in him, he assumed. Clark had never slept with anyone that much younger than he was. He had just assumed guys that age were only interested in each other.

They sat on Clark's couch gazing out the window at the ocean and sky. Both were wearing shorts and tank tops. When Jordan's hand came over to Clark's thigh, it rested on bare flesh.

They turned to each other. For one moment there was utter silence, then their faces came together and they kissed. Jordan's hand slid into Clark's crotch and began massaging his stiffening cock as their tongues slipped between each other's lips. The kiss was wet and deep as they both began to explore each other's semi-naked bodies. Hands roamed over backs and thighs and into crotches. Clark found a surprisingly fat cock in Jordan's lap, rising up hard and throbbing.

"You are such a hot stud! I'm all yours if you want me," Jordan murmured as soon as their kiss broke.

Clark was surprised and a little shocked by Jordan's breathless confession. Was it real, or just the heat of the moment? He found himself not caring, just feeling. "I want you. Let's get naked," he grinned.

Clark hadn't realized how excited he was until they were naked and writhing on the couch together. Jordan's cock was big, juicy and uncut, which was another surprise. His balls were smallish and silky smooth. He was also practically hairless, with a short silken mat around his cock and little hair anywhere else. Their bodies slid

Daddy's Boyz

over each other in a hot embrace as they rubbed their hard cocks together and continued kissing.

Clark's hand was down between their bodies pumping Jordan's big tool and feeling the slippery hood when Jordan pulled his thighs back and up. There was no mistaking the signal. Clark's hand moved down into the open crack. Satin-hot flesh welcomed him. A small butthole pouted and clamped as Clark's fingers trailed over it.

"It's all yours. Do what you want with it," Jordan sighed into Clark's face.

Their breath mingled as they stared into each other's eyes. Clark's vivid blue orbs blinked a few times as he wordlessly accepted the offer. He smiled and slid his body down Jordan's.

His lips and tongue traced their way over Jordan's compact chest and to his stomach. He tickled the navel a moment, then with his fingers stroking around Jordan's hairless pucker-hole, he engulfed the hard cock with his mouth. He sucked the hood up and then pushed it down to tickle the exposed cap with his tongue. Jordan writhed upwards into Clark's mouth and fingers.

Clark sucked the fat torpedo with loud slurps as his fingers continued to tease and explore Jordan's ass slot. The hole spasmed continually, gaping open and clamping then pouting open again. Clark tickled the rim and the distended center but did not push beyond just yet. He had other plans.

Suddenly he rose up from Jordan's cock. He pressed Jordan's slim, tanned thighs back toward his chest. Their eyes met briefly before Clark buried his face in Jordan's crack. His tongue snaked along the hairless crevice, up and down in long swipes. Jordan's body shivered and pressed back against the wet mouth. Clark settled on the pouting hole. He used his tongue to lick and moisten it before sucking gently to open it up.

Jordan was moaning non-stop, and his body was shaking. He pulled his own thighs farther back, and his asshole blossomed open to Clark's probing tongue. Clark planted a pair of fingers against Jordan's sphincter, then slid them into the wet maw of Jordan's hole.

It was tight, but accommodated the fingers as they slipped deep into the heated interior. Jordan was squirming around them and gasping, but made no protest. In fact, he seemed to be fucking himself over them with all his wriggling. Clark smiled around the asshole he continued to lick and suck.

Clark worked the pair of fingers around inside Jordan's hole, twisting and searching and stretching. He made his next move. Sliding upwards over Jordan's bent-backwards body, Clark pressed his hard meat into the open crack. His fingers slid out of wet hole and were replaced by the throbbing head of his cock. With a slow prod, he sank his shaft into the pit of Jordan's asshole. Clamping lips and walls encased it, then opened up to accept it. Clark stared down at Jordan's dreamy brown eyes and smiled.

He fucked Jordan like that. Driving in and out in a steadily increasing pump, Clark fucked deep and hard until finally his balls pulled up and his cock erupted. He pulled out just in time to spray Jordan's sweaty ass crack with a load of goo.

Jordan had been grunting and moaning wordlessly, but now he spoke out. "Yeah, spray me with your Daddy-cum! Fuck your boy good!"

Clark was shaking with his orgasm and grinning down at Jordan's laughing face. Then Jordan was whacking his own stiff cock, rubbing the hood back and forth over the head until only moments later he too shot a sticky load.

They didn't bother to clean up but instead lay on the couch together and talked for hours. "I guess you've figured out I like older guys," Jordan told Clark.

"I'm not really into young guys, but I don't limit myself," Clark admitted.

And that seemed to be the definition of their new relationship. Jordan liked older guys, and Clark filled the bill. They were now a Daddy and his boy. After Jordan left that first evening for his job as a security guard at a mall, Clark contemplated the enjoyable encounter. He wasn't sure if anything more would happen. The sex had been awesome, and yet there was more to it than that. Jordan was very loveable.

Amazingly enough, Jordan called him the very next day. They spent the rest of the summer meeting at the pool on warm afternoons and fucking the nights away. Clark's friends were mostly closer to his age, and were not very encouraging. They called him a chicken-lover and warned him that Jordan was probably going to take advantage of him. Jordan was over 20 years

Daddy's Boyz

younger than Clark, and that was just not a workable situation according to them.

Clark enjoyed Jordan's carefree company at first and didn't think much about where it was going. He didn't worry about what people thought, being gay itself was not something everyone approved of anyway. But Clark did wonder if their age difference was an obstacle to more than just a summer of good sex. As a lawyer, Clark did not worry about money, he was well-off. Jordan was not going to rob him. Whatever else developed was for the future.

Jordan exhibited no qualms. He offered himself shamelessly. He got on his hands and knees and waved his rounded, dimpled butt and told Clark to take his hole and make it his. He laughed when he rode Clark's cock and told him to stuff it up his boy hole. One of his favorite things was to have sex in the shower.

Jordan would lean against the front of the stall with his legs spread and his hands on the tiled wall. "Play with your boy's hole, Daddy," Jordan urged Clark.

Clark soaped Jordan's lush butt. He dug his fingers around in the deep crack and massaged the pouting butt hole. Foamy fingers pushed into the tight orifice and twisted deep. Jordan moaned and squatted backwards to take as much of those rough fingers as he could.

"Yeah, Daddy. Shove those fingers up my tight ass. It's all yours. That hole belongs to you, Daddy!"

The softly spoken words were full of passion. Jordan seemed totally uninhibited. "Pinch my nipples. Tug on them good," Jordan begged.

Clark had discovered Jordan loved that. Jordan's nipples were both sensitive and able to take a lot of punishment. Clark worked one hand around in Jordan's soapy crack while he wrapped a muscular arm around Jordan's compact torso and pinched his nipples. He could squeeze the small nubs mercilessly, and it only made Jordan more excited.

With Jordan's body squirming in Clark's arms, Clark fingered his ass and tortured his nipples. Clark rubbed his own hard shank against Jordan's smooth ass cheeks while digging deep into his hole with his fingers. He felt the tight channel work open as foam eased the way until Jordan was taking a third finger and practically sitting on Clark's hand. Clark rubbed his cock in the foamy crack alongside his fingers and tweaked Jordan's nipples harshly. Finally Clark's cock stiffened and spurted, shooting a load all over Jordan's wet ass and thighs. Then he turned Jordan around and sucked his fat cock while continuing to tear at his nipples until Jordan thrust forward and cried out.

"Suck the jizz out of me, Daddy! Suck your boy dry!"

Jordan spewed down Clark's throat. Clark drank Jordan's cum, reveling in the total release he felt in Jordan's trembling thighs. At those moments, Clark experienced no qualms, only raunchy lust for the young flesh he gave pleasure to and took from. His boy was hot!

Jordan met Clark at his office on a Wednesday afternoon. Dressed in shorts and tank top, with a football in his hand, he grinned at Clark in suit and tie. "Wanna toss around the ball for a while? It's nice out."

Clark ignored his secretary's wide eyes and his fellow lawyer's glances. They may have wondered if Jordan was his nephew or something, most did not imagine they were butt-buddies.

That night Jordan ran a bath in Clark's tub. He lit candles and soaked in the water by himself until he called in Clark to join him. Rolling over on his hands and knees, he grinned at the older lawyer.

"Rub some baby oil on my ass. I like it nice and smooth."

That ass rose from the water, hairless and lush. Jordan writhed it in circles as Clark squirted the baby oil all over it. Clark slowly massaged the oil all over Jordan's ass while Jordan tensed and relaxed his ass cheeks and then spread his thighs. Clark knelt by the tub while he played with Jordan's oiled butt, his cock stiff and drooling.

Clark began to finger the crack while Jordan moaned. He found the puckered hole and slid oiled fingers past the rim. The hole opened obligingly while Jordan continued to squirm around in the water. Clark worked his fingers in and out of the hole while running his other hand all over the mounds of Jordan's ass.

"It's your ass. It's yours whenever you want it, Daddy," Jordan murmured.

Clark grabbed his aching cock and whipped at it with an oiled palm. His fingers dug deep between Jordan's writhing ass cheeks into the crack and hole and guts. He dug and twisted and explored, whipping his hand faster and faster.

"Yeah, Daddy! Jerk off over my hot ass! Yeah, come for your boy!"

Clark spewed all over the side of the tub with his fingers deep in Jordan's oiled anus.

Afterwards Jordan kissed Clark and laughed off his raunchy talk in the bath. "I like to add a little spice to the sex. It's OK, isn't it, Clark? All this Daddy and Boy stuff is a turn-on, but we're real people, you know. Am I making sense?"

"Perfect nonsense," Clark laughed back. He was well-aware of all the little tricks it took to get off. Sex was both complicated and simple. That's what made is so interesting.

One night toward the end of the summer, Jordan was at Clark's apartment. He was sprawled on the carpet in front of the television naked. Clark found himself unable to take his eyes off that well-formed, shaved ass. When Jordan noticed Clark watching, he pretended he was watching the television and wiggled his butt and spread his legs enticingly as if merely readjusting his position on the floor.

Clark pounced, dropping down to squat naked over Jordan's thighs and take those luscious mounds in his hands and spread them apart.

"Jerk off on my ass, Daddy! Mark me with your cum!"

Clark's cock was so hard he knew it wouldn't take more than a pump or two. Instead he massaged and squeezed those pliant cheeks and watched the hole between pulse and quiver as his hands spread it open. Jordan arched his back and exposed his hole, laughing as he did.

"Do you like that little hole? It's all for you. Lick it, Daddy."

Clark bent over and crammed his face in Jordan's crack. He pulled the cheeks open and clamped his mouth over the quivering hole, sucking like a crazed man. His cock was hard and dripping as he fucked Jordan's hole with his tongue.

Clark was obsessed with that ass and that welcoming, hungry hole. He was obsessed with Jordan, there was no longer any point in denying it. With his tongue reaming out that pulsing maw, he reached down to pump on his aching cock. Clark mewled around asshole and jerked furiously over his stiff boner.

"Yeah. You love that hole, don't you, Daddy? You can't get enough of it. You'll never get enough of it! Oh yeah ... yeah ... eat it up!"

Jordan's urging voice sent Clark over the edge. With his tongue buried in Jordan's sweet slot, he creamed himself. His body rocked and shivered and finally collapsed on the warm mattress of Jordan's naked flesh.

It was true. He would never get enough of Jordan's ass. Clark chuckled as he crawled up to lay beside Jordan and cradle him in his arms. It didn't matter. It only mattered to Jordan and to Clark, and no one else.

Clark ran his fingers into Jordan's smooth crack and toyed with the spit-slick butt lips. Jordan writhed against the fingers slowly.

"Are we going to live together? I love you, Clark."

Jordan's muttered confession rocked Clark. It took a moment for him to wrestle with his emotions. He knew what he felt, it was just that he questioned it. But wouldn't that be truly getting old? Being afraid was getting old. Not surrendering to your true feelings was getting old. Clark was not old.

"I love you too, baby."

They huddled together naked on the floor, hands roaming, eyes locked. "Boyfriends?" Clark whispered the question.

"Boyfriends," Jordan sighed back.

Encore

John McFarland

Coming to town on my free Fridays was always a pleasure, even after the routine started to seem fairly predictable. From the train, I'd head to the design office where my old college roommate Erik worked. Once the receptionist announced me and asked me to wait, Erik would race out from the back, claim he had to pick up some custom paper stock, and off we'd go on an afternoon jaunt around the city. This Friday was different. First, the receptionist told me to proceed to Erik's cubicle, and then other surprises kept coming.

When I knocked at his cubicle entrance, Erik stood up and grabbed a cane. He hopped backwards from his desk on his good foot and waited for me to say something — anything. He had a walking cast on his other foot.

"What did you do to yourself now?" I asked.

He scowled at me. "That's right, blame the victim first and then maybe at some later date say that you hope I'll recover nicely. Or, you could ask if at least the sex was great."

I laughed.

"Oh, yes, and laughing makes it even better!" He limped toward his coat tree. "I can only leave for an hour, so we're going to a gallery nearby. Don't worry, though, I prepared a complete itinerary and instructions for the rest of your day."

I gave him a thorough once-over as he struggled into his cashmere topcoat. "You know, the effect suits you ... you look fabulous. If you were fifteen or twenty years older with that extra ripeness of experience, I wouldn't be able to resist you."

"Stop right there," Erik said, "I don't want to hear another word about your sordid preferences. We are now beginning a serious journey to teach our eyes something we don't already know."

The gallery Erik had chosen was showing black-and-white photographs of men with handicaps — or maybe the men had lost limbs in accidents and wars, or maybe the photos had been digitally altered to achieve the same haunting effect.

Bob Condron

"Can you fake an amputation that authentically?" I asked Erik since he would know. He was humming merrily as we circulated around the room.

"Let's get down to brass tacks: Can you fake a boner like that?" Erik asked and pointed his cane at a shot of a man with one normal-sized leg, with his other one a stump and his dick worked up to more or less the length of the stump. He started humming again.

"You don't really need that cane, do you?" I asked.

Erik stopped humming. He turned and glared at me.

"I'll have you know that I could be asked to pose by this brilliant artist, that's how seriously damaged I am. And I'd be a knock-out, too, equal to any of them."

"Some day God will strike you down if you keep over dramatizing," I said.

Leaning toward me, Erik said, "This exhibit is about to make me cum in my pants. Is that over dramatizing? And we'll see who God strikes down first, won't we?"

At that moment, a gentleman in the gallery with us bumped into Erik. More off balance than usual, Erik came flying at me. An act of God or divine intervention? I grabbed him under the arms and kept him from falling. His cane clattered to the floor.

As I restored Erik to a free-standing upright position, the man who had collided with him was showering us with apologies and explanations about not having seen Erik, about being a little distracted that morning. He held out the cane as an embarrassed offering.

Erik spun around deftly on his walking cast while I steadied him under one arm. Ballet dancers could learn from him. He licked his lips and opened his mouth the better to deliver what I expected would be a blistering verbal attack on the unfortunate man. Never give Erik an opening or an advantage, that's my philosophy, and this was an opportunity if I ever saw one. I prepared myself for the worst.

But the expected didn't happen. Erik's eyes opened wider than I had ever seen them, and he actually smiled. That disarming smile has no doubt sold many, many accounts for the design shop, and every dancer taking a bow could envy its naturalness.

The man stood stock-still and held the cane out further.

Erik said, "Why, thank you!"

The man started in again with a slew of apologies about not having seen Erik. "I was too enchanted by the art, you must forgive me," he said.

He was very sweet. His eyes showed how genuinely sorry he was. They were almond-shaped eyes Matisse would draw, heavy-lidded and strikingly blue.

Mercifully, Erik did not point to the wall and say, "Well, with a boner like that staring you in the face, I can understand that collisions will happen." Instead he said simply, "No problem."

He hopped to the side on his good foot and blocked my formerly clear view of the man. I had to scoot to the right to keep an eye on the perp who was getting off so easily. Erik was pouring on the charm like there was no tomorrow. Yes, the man was attractive, but older than Erik usually goes for, more my type.

"We should go," I said to Erik. "You have to get back to work." And I hustled Erik away before he recovered enough to start sniping at the poor man.

On our way down the stairs, Erik said, "You do realize who that was, don't you?"

"No, who?"

"You joke, of course," he said.

"I told you I don't have a clue."

"That ..." Erik said, pointing his cane at my crotch from two steps down the stairway as he held on to the banister, "... was Joel Winwood, your supreme hero in the world of rich and famous kiddies-lit authors and illustrators."

"Get out, no way. Why would he be at that exhibition? It has zero kid-appeal, as you so vividly pointed out."

Narrowing his eyes, Erik shot me a withering look. "And you may have noticed he's no kid either."

"That man who looks like the better-looking of the Smith Brothers on the old cough-drop package? That is the creator of *The Day the Stairs Stepped Out*?"

"Trust me," Erik said. "And we're going back so you can meet him under conditions when he has to be nice to us and we have him at our mercy."

When we reentered the gallery, Erik exaggerated his limp almost as much as he turned up the wattage on his smile. I trundled along behind and hoped I wouldn't be too grossed-out by Erik fawning like some sex-crazed groupie.

"Mr. Winwood," Erik said ever so tentatively, an approach that must be considered winning in some circles. "We thought we recognized you, but only as we were about out the door did we decide that we had to come back and say a real hello. That kind of collision is no accident, I'm sure you agree."

Joel Winwood bowed and kept his hands safely in his pockets. He admitted nothing.

"Jimmy," Erik declared, indicating me, "is one of your biggest fans."

"Metaphorically speaking," I said, but not tentatively.

Joel chuckled and said nothing else. He was shy even though he was rich and famous. Nothing could be more enchanting to me.

"Isn't the show fabulous?" Erik probed.

"It's strong," Joel replied.

"Very," I added. Nobody mentioned the undeniable allure of gorgeous naked men, aroused, commanding and fully available for our viewing.

"When Jimmy comes to town, I drag him here first. It's the one gallery you can rely on to have used their brain."

"Their eye," Joel said.

"Yes," I said. "The eye has to be served before the brain. With photography."

Joel looked at me closely as if he were examining me for some special thing he was desperately in search of. I could feel my ears burning and turned to wait for Erik to lay his next sure-fire line on us.

"If you're walking out now, let's go together," Joel proposed. He motioned toward the staircase.

We tottered down the steep stairs again. Going for broke, Erik waved his cane around dramatically and held fast to the handrail for dear life. I pretended to keep a watchful eye on him, but I felt drawn to Joel as if he needed more help — his combo of awkwardness and authority is a killer for me.

On the sidewalk in front of the gallery, Erik said he had to be off. He embraced me warmly, using the closeness to whisper, "He's all yours! I can tell he likes you — when was I ever wrong about this? Just don't blow it." He then told Joel that they'd meet again soon. "I'm sure of it, I feel it deep, deep down in my gut," Erik responded after Joel had said, "Perhaps."

"He's certain of so much," I told Joel once Erik was inside a cab and heading safely down the street.

"Ones like him are often right when their intuition is untrammeled," Joel said, but then immediately seemed to want to take back his statement.

I tilted my head to consider what he had said. His beautiful world-weary eyes shifted to follow mine.

"Do you know The Inn of the Three Wives?" I asked.

"Yes," he said. He forced a wan smile. He was trying to make the most of it, but it was up to me to keep the ball rolling by being extra-on.

"I've never been, and Erik said I had to go there today or else he was never giving me another piece of advice. Would you like to join me for lunch?"

"Would that be advisable?" he asked. I would have thought he was teasing me if he hadn't broken eye contact out of nervousness.

"Yes, of course, I'd love you to come." Thank God, he wasn't looking at me when I could feel myself turning scarlet.

"Well, yes, why not?" he said, and we began the trek through the lunch traffic.

"Erik insisted I have the chicken pot pie," I said as I scanned the menu in the cozy confines of the restaurant. Joel managed to give a grunt of approval, but I could tell he was tiring of any reference to Erik. Since most people want more and more and then more again of Erik, he was obviously different from most people.

"What looks good to you?" I asked, stumbling into another double-entendre as I attempted to counteract Joel's shyness.

"The cod," he said. "They have marvelous French fries here, as you've probably been informed."

"How about the mashed potatoes?" I asked. "I have this thing about mashed potatoes."

"They're very creamy here, but with a pot pie?" he said.

Since I saw his cheeks flush as soon as the word "creamy" passed his lips, I decided to let my full devil out to see if that could possibly kick us into something like a comfortable connection. "Will they make a stink if I order them together?" I asked.

"By no means," he said. "This is not France, after all."

I threw back my head and laughed. "And we can certainly be thankful of that," I said. "What a wonderful place."

Joel kept his eyes trained on the table's wooden planks. They were painted dark green, a forest green mixed with black and gray pigments. Maybe he didn't like laughers.

"It's really old, isn't it?" I remarked when I saw him start withdrawing even further.

"Yes."

As if he'd run out of verbal energy, Joel stared blankly at me, his eye taking in the particulars. If he was waiting to recharge, I filled in the silences with aplomb with my story of starting out as a musician.

"A violist," I said. "But I have to teach because, really, despite the prodigy impression from way back I just plain and simple suck." I didn't even blush; it was now too late for that.

Joel smiled politely, once more with great effort. He surely understood exactly what I meant, but he reacted as if he didn't approve of my terms, as if he were thinking, "So much is going to the dogs, why does language have to be collapsed into four concepts, all of which allude to either sexual acts or bodily expulsions?"

I have to give him credit: he didn't object, he simply changed the subject. He asked if I had ever danced. I didn't know exactly what he was driving at and evidently showed it.

"You know ..." he prodded, "... in a troupe."

"Oh," I said, "No, I never have. Why?"

"Something about the way you hold your head when you listen, I think," he said. "Like a dancer." He went silent.

I turned a blue packet of artificial sweetener between my thumb and forefinger and watched its slow rotation. The stop and start of our conversation had made me ravenous. I really needed the food to be there now.

"Would it be better if I were?" I asked.

Joel squirmed under my steady gaze and had to look down again at the pitted surface of the table's planks. He adjusted his place mat without even seeing it.

"No, not at all," he said. "But, you see, I am famous for a very limited repertoire."

I smiled warmly. "Like a prodigy who refuses to go along with the plans of others?" I asked.

"Probably," he said.

Finally, our food arrived, and we had a delightful meal. Joel seemed to relax a little once I gave the charm campaign a rest and just went for being selfish. I'd never had lunch alone with a famous person, much less one I had idolized for years, and I didn't want it to end. I asked every question I could think of: where he was born; where he went to school; what his favorite book was; what his favorite of his books was; whether he preferred living in the city to living out. To most of my questions, Joel gave one-word answers. He would never be an easy interview, but I wasn't about to capitulate. I'm used to getting my way. Even while his eyes, ripe with experience, ate me up, I could tell that this particular flirtation was going to remain its fitful self and go no further. It was far from unpleasant, but there was so much room for improvement I could hear echoes.

There came a time, though, when he looked at his watch and said, "Oh, my God, I'm terribly late. Is it really two-thirty?"

I grabbed the bill. "My turn this time," I said. "Next time, you can get it."

From the alarmed look on his face, I suspected that Joel thought there'd never be a next time, but then I've learned that sometimes guilt can work for you in ways that good manners won't.

Once we were on the street, I kept up my barrage of questions, now about geography and where Broadway was in relation to where we stood, while I consulted the itinerary Erik had prepared for me. Joel wasn't wild about being made even later than he already was, but I got the distinct feeling that he thought I was really lost and he worried that I'd fall into the wrong hands. One wrong turn in that neighborhood, you know, and you can end up with your heart on a spike and your liver sold to the highest bidder. I'd read the stories and so had he. Headlines like, "MAN SET ON FIRE AFTER ORGY" grew out of scenes one block west of us. Everybody knew.

As he waved his arms and pointed mostly east and mostly uptown, a handsome man walking an enormous Irish Wolfhound came along. He cried, "Joel, let me guess, you're a ... windmill!"

Joel jumped a mile in the air.

"Charles, you scared the living daylights out of me," he said.

"And what do you suppose that little display of yours did to me?" the man replied, smoothing his graying sideburns. He glanced over at me, smiled and then quickly returned full attention to Joel. "Have you had a chance to get somebody to look at those royalty statements yet?"

If he had appeared nervous or shy before, Joel now started to stammer and look everywhere else but at either one of us. Was it Charles's extraordinary good looks that made him so jumpy? Or were the two of them possessors of a common history that Joel would rather keep in the past? At any rate, he was more of a wreck than ever. At last he said, "I'm sorry, Charles, I'm an hour late. I've really got to go." Before he rushed off, he said, "Thank you for the delightful lunch," and touched the shoulder of my overcoat.

Joel's friend, the dog and I stood on the sidewalk and watched him disappear down the street.

"Was it something I said?" the man asked. He waited until I laughed to laugh himself.

"I'm Charles Loesser," he said and extended his hand.

I took the hand that seemed more accustomed to being bowed over and kissed than taken and shaken. I pumped it vigorously. It was a strong hand and stood up to the test of my grip. "Jimmy Holden," I said.

"Are you over 18?" Charles asked next.

When I said I was, he advised me to call myself James.

"Jimmy is my given name, not James," I told him.

"Well, then, you are forever young," he winked and smiled. The corners of his mouth curled up like crisp bacon. I could feel the electricity.

"What's your dog's name?" I asked.

"Odette," he said. "Because of her past."

"A big dog for a female," I said.

"Do you think so?" he asked.

To be asked a question after almost two solid hours of asking one after another myself was a tremendous shock. I stood there with my mouth wide open and stared at him. Comfortable with being looked at during the lull, he calmly turned his head from side to side and smiled as he looked down the avenue. The electricity was growing into pure heat.

"Has Joel been that exhausting?" he asked.

He was watching my every move. I reached down to pet the dog. Her fur was unpleasant to the touch, like dirty split ends.

"No," I said, "but I had to ask so many questions to keep the conversation going, I forgot that I'd ever get to answer one myself again."

"Here's an easy one," he said while he trained an appraising eye on me. "Do you have time to come up to my place?"

Once we were inside his apartment, Charles let Odette go and was all over me. The dog wandered off, dragging her leash behind her. His tongue was so far down my throat that I thought I was going to have to vomit it up just to get some air. This man was hungry. I like that in my tricks.

The clothes came off in the entry hall, and we got a good gander at one another. Charles, tall and proud, reminded me of those Greek fishermen back from a successful day's haul with an unexpected catch. Since I didn't think he was going to sell me, gut me or fry me, I didn't hesitate to follow him into the bedroom. In front of the mirrored doors of a wall of closets, we rolled around on the floor's thick cocoa carpeting. It felt great. Whatever he uses on the rug might be worth a try on the dog's coat too.

Erik has cautioned me time and again about older men, "They either know what they want, and it's so limited that you practically don't have to be there, or they've forgotten entirely what it is they like." What did Erik really know? Charles may have been slightly older than I was accustomed to, but he had it all under control and would have given Erik a run for his money. He was a man who knew how to kiss and use his hands. This scene was very hot even before it got to the stage where pillows arrived from somewhere and the propping up happened as if choreographed by a master. There was quite a bit of enthusiastic switching around before the mutual fireworks went off.

"God," I said, lying on the floor and swinging a pillow under my head. "That was great."

"Umm," Charles said, "Umm."

We snuggled together and drifted off.

Bob Condron

You go to a gallery at eleven in the morning with your old college roommate and you end up fucking a very sexy man who turns out to be a major literary light on his floor by three in the afternoon. Disregard all other claims, this is the real reason people come to the city.

An alarm somewhere in the room startled me awake. My stomach was sort of stuck to Charles, hair and cum being what they are, and we had to gently pull ourselves apart before we could sit up.

"I liked that," Charles said. "Very much."

"Me too," I said. "You're ..."

"Shhhhhhhh," he said and kissed me to prevent another word from coming out.

When I finally pulled away, he stared at me in an endearingly bewildered way. "Your pecker's scrumptious," he said and reached down to hold it. "It's beautiful." His touch was enough. There it was growing hard in his hand.

"Oh," he said, "So sensitive."

He gripped it tightly and it went on about its business. "Youth!" he said. "It's a wonderful thing, Jimmy. Don't waste it."

"I'm not wasting it here, let me tell you," I said. I leaned over and put a lip-lock on him and we were at it again. He was up for it in no time, too, whether he could claim an age-advantage or not.

After that round, he switched to singing the praises of my ass, which I don't get to see objectively enough to have an opinion on. I guess it's fine. I've never had any complaints.

"Ever danced?" he asked at last.

"No," I said, "but your friend asked me that too."

"He would," Charles said. "He has a very limited repertoire."

"He mentioned that."

"Yes, it's one of his few complete sentences. And a true one."

He ran his fingers down my spine and just barely grazed the hair on my buns. A shock went all the way up to my head. Pleasure. He did it again.

"Every cell is alive," he said.

"For those with the touch," I added. I rolled against him and threw my arms over his shoulders. I pushed up against him. I was getting ready again.

"Tell me," he said, "did you just get out of prison?"

I used his same trick on him. I stopped him from saying one more word by thrusting my tongue down his throat. He didn't say no. He didn't have to say yes. This time was less frantic. His repertoire was anything but limited.

When we were lying glued together once again, he said, "If you'd like to come to the ballet tonight ... I could get you a ticket."

He seemed almost shy as if I might say no or drag out some excuse that amounted to the same thing. I think some people get so used to tricks as a way of life that nobody expects anybody to want to do anything together besides crossing pork-swords.

"What time?" I asked.

"Do you have to go home?" he asked.

"I'm not dressed up," I said.

"You can wear what you had on. You looked perfectly presentable."

"Thank you," I said and laughed. "Although I'd like to stay here like this and see what number we can get up to."

"You know, I hate to bring this up, but some of us are no longer twenty-three with raging hormones. Some of us need a break, or have to have one. Sometimes."

I rolled over against him and proved him wrong again. He was loving it, there was no denying. Then we got cleaned up and took a cab to the theater. We sat down just as the curtain was going up. I grabbed his hand and held it tightly until we had to applaud at the end of the first piece on the program. I had had such a fabulous day so far that I felt I was clapping for myself.

Elegant
Daniel Ritter

Elegant. That was my first thought. The man was elegant. He was in his fifties, maybe even sixties, trim, fit and elegant, with steel-gray hair and the lines of decades marking his face. He wore a coral pink polo and spotless white trousers, confident, expensive, even a little arrogant. Even in this enclave of the rich and powerful, this was someone who mattered. I took a deep breath and went over to his table.

"What can I get for you today?" The waiter's ritual.

The man's eyes flickered up and down my body — assessing? Or was that just wishful thinking? "I'll have a Manhattan, please. As far as lunch is concerned, what would you recommend?"

"Do you like fish?" I asked.

"Yes."

"We have fresh lake trout today. Everyone's been raving about it. It's served with an assortment of steamed fresh vegetables and rice pilaf with almonds."

"Sounds good," he said, then he peered at my nametag. "Patrick. A man who dislikes nicknames."

"Yes, sir." I'd never liked being called Pat.

"What's your last name, Patrick?"

"Aubry."

"Patrick Aubry," he said, rolling it over his tongue. "Very well then, Patrick Aubry, I'll take a Manhattan and the lake trout."

"Thank you, sir," I said. I was two steps away from his table before I remembered to breathe.

I worked summers at the country club attached to Harbor Point, a small spit of land closed off to motor vehicles, locals and other riff-raff. The club was so exclusive that local kids weren't allowed to work there, not in visible positions anyway. My family was from Grosse Pointe Farms, and we had summered in Harbor Springs since B.C., which meant that my pedigree was impeccable. It was a small town, very quaint, with a population that tripled after the prep schools closed. It wasn't the most cosmopolitan place on the planet. Entertainment consisted of various forms of hanging out, whether it was at the beach or at a party or on a friend's boat getting drunk, or maybe in one of several restaurants, some of them very good. There was barely any life at all, much less gay life. It was one of those heterosexual anti-fairylands where homosexuality doesn't exist, but if you knew where to look, you could scare something up as long as you were discreet. I knew where to look. I'd spent the summer before trading blowjobs with a local, half Native American, sleek and brooding.

And now I was getting all breathless over this man who was old enough to be my father. Hell, my grandfather! But there was nothing sad about him, nothing elderly in the usual sense. For that matter, I wasn't even sure he was gay. It might have been wishful thinking. It would take extraordinary balls for a gay man to wear pink in that town.

My hands were shaking when I brought him his drink, and I had to take a few deep breaths before I dared to handle his plate. "Here you are, sir," I said.

He inhaled slowly, sensually, then took a bite and smiled. "Excellent choice. Thank you, Patrick Aubry."

"You're welcome."

I watched him, trying to figure him out, trying to figure myself out. This wasn't age like my father, who was growing fat and complacent, or a panicky age that fought to look young. This was something almost mythical in its power. He sat alone, looking neither pathetic nor self-conscious, as if a wife or a "niece" might even cheapen him. It drew me, and I went past his table more often than I needed to.

When he caught my eye, I came to a sudden halt, and he reached out, touched my elbow, steadying me. "I'd like another drink," he said.

"Yes, sir."

I took his glass and brought him a second Manhattan, setting it down in front of him. He looked up at me. "You have a good memory, Patrick Aubry."

"Thank you, sir." I was proud of my memory. I could handle six full tables without once referring to my checks.

"Where do you go to school?" Not if I was going to school. If I was working at the club, I was in college somewhere.

"Cornell," I said.

He nodded. "Very good. What are you studying?"

"Economics," I said.

"Economics …" he mused. "Am I correct in presuming there's a family business somewhere?"

"Yes, sir." As the only son, my trajectory had never been in doubt.

"Where are you staying this summer, Patrick Aubry?"

"On The Point with my parents," I said.

"Does your family come here every year?" he asked.

"Just about," I said.

"Do you like it?" he asked.

"It's OK," I said.

"Rather dull for young people, I've always thought." Then he grinned at me. "Us old fogies can always find ways to amuse ourselves."

My heart raced for my throat, pounding madly. Did that mean what I thought it did? "Yes, sir," I said.

He glanced around the room. The club was filling up "I'd better not keep you from your work any longer," he said. "Thank you very much, Patrick Aubry." He raised his glass and met my eyes.

"You're welcome, sir." I guessed that was that. He tipped well, though, generous without overdoing it.

It was my day off before I saw him again. I was taking an afternoon run around The Point, careful to avoid the horse turds, when a voice called out, "Patrick Aubry!"

Even my mother never called me by my full name and anyway, that voice was unmistakable. I looked up and to my right, saw him on the other side of a gate. I stopped, panting. "Hi," I said.

"What a surprise," he said, his voice dripping with delicious irony.

I crossed to the gate, gasping a little. "Yes. How are you?"

"I'm fine." He held out his hand; his grip was firm. "My name is Ben Lourdes."

"Nice to meet you."

"You look like you could use a drink."

"Yes," I said. I was dying for water.

That was what I got. Nothing alcoholic, just a tall glass of ice water that I downed in one gulp. I looked around as he refilled it. Like many of the houses on Harbor Point, it was furnished carelessly, a summer cottage in spite of having six bedrooms. "Is this your place?" I asked.

He laughed. "No. It belongs to a friend. I'm staying here for a few months."

How good of a friend? I wondered. "Where do you live?" I asked.

"I split my time between New York and Berlin."

"What do you do?" I asked, then kicked myself. Idiot! I thought. He was probably retired.

"I consult here and there, assisting companies that are trying to do business in another country. I used to be in intelligence, trying to keep an eye on the East Germans. Now my capitalism is more personal and less ideological." His smile was a bit self-mocking. This was a man who did nothing without thinking it through from all sides.

I wanted to be him. I wanted to be elegant and powerful. I wanted to speak more than one language. I wanted to be someone that other people looked to, whose opinion mattered. I wondered if I touched him, would I be able to absorb some of it? If I stayed near him, would he teach me his secrets? I wanted to sit at his feet as if he were Socrates; I would do anything for him if he would share the tiniest bits of his wisdom. I wasn't in love, but it was a longing that matched it in intensity and scope.

"So, Patrick Aubry," he said, "is anyone waiting for you right now?"

"No," I said. "I stay with my parents, but they don't ask questions."

He smiled wickedly. "They're accepting that their child has grown into a man."

Actually, if my parents had had a clue of some of the things I'd done, they would have kept me in the basement under lock and key. "More or less," I said. "My mother worries."

"They always do," he said. "My own mother died at the age of eighty-seven, and she never stopped worrying. Come, Patrick Aubry. There's something I'd like to show you."

I set my glass down and followed him up the stairs. He took me to a largish room furnished in the wicker that was almost mandatory on Harbor Point. There were books on the shelves in English, German and even French, and a travel alarm on the table that set itself periodically to the atomic clock. I knew because I recognized the brand. I'd wanted one for years. The curtains were open and the sunlight streamed in. "Take a look," he said.

Out of his window was a view of the bay and the town of Harbor Springs. It was a beautiful place. The water was calm and blue and full of boats, and the town itself nestled like a sleeping child in the arms of the bluff. He stood a bit too close behind me, and I wanted to lean back into him, but I didn't dare. "Have you ever been here in the winter?" he asked softly.

"No," I said.

"It's quite different, barren, but very beautiful. It's down to the locals and a few skiers. The Point is closed off, of course, and so are parts of Wequetonsing, but you can ski across the bay to Petoskey. It's a paradise for anyone who likes snow. Do you ski, Patrick?"

It was the first time he had called me only by my first name. "No," I said, terrified that I would disappoint him.

"You should," he said. "It's exhilarating. A difficult run takes every ounce of courage and every muscle in your body and the finish is a burst of triumph and delight. Much like sex. I assume you have some experience with sex?" His mouth was a bare inch from my ear, and I could hear his smile in his voice.

"Yes," I breathed, fighting to keep the tremor out of my own voice. Who was I trying to fool? He was over twice, possibly three times my age and ten times more sophisticated.

"Ever slept with a woman?"

"Once," I said, thinking with mixed feelings of a college friendship that had gotten out of hand for a while.

"Did you enjoy it?"

"It was OK." Which was hardly fair to her. She had, surprisingly, given excellent head, but she hadn't thrilled me.

"And men?" His hands settled on my shoulders, and I felt his breath on my neck. "Do you like men better?"

"Much better." My cock, restrained by my jock strap, was nonetheless making a conspicuous bulge in my shorts. Just talking to him about sex made me crazy.

"Good, though, that you were willing to experiment a bit," he said, running his hands up and down my arms, caressing. "It broadens the mind and that never hurts. Turn around, Patrick."

I turned obediently, unquestioningly. We were nose to nose, he was barely taller than I was, and his eyes were a startling cornflower blue. He put one hand to my face and brought his mouth down on mine.

Up close I could feel the fragility in his bones and skin, but while he was no slob, he had not grown scrawny, either. I could believe he still skied. Under his tanned skin, the muscle and sinew were still strong, there was still power in his body as well as in his mind. Under a musky, unfamiliar cologne were the smells of soap and age, a scent I remembered from when my grandfather would dandle me in his knee, disturbing, dangerous. Someday it would be my own. With Ben's hands lighting fires under my skin, the idea didn't seem so bad.

He broke the kiss and took me to bed, and I stripped my T-shirt off as I went. It was too warm in that room, even with the air conditioning on. He took off my shorts and reached under my jock, sighing as I thrust into his touch. Underneath his clothes he was heavy and thick but not really hard, and it confused me. He showed no sign of surprise or shame, though, and he took my hand and guided it to his crotch. At my touch, he rose to life, swelling and filling to a very acceptable heft. Viagra? No. Just Ben. That was just how he was.

He wasn't an athletic lover unless this was an endurance race, his preferred pace was more tortoise than hare. His mouth and hands worked my nipples, my cock, my balls and my ass, but lingered in other places, too. He ran delicate fingers over the crests of my hipbones and licked the sweat from under my arms. He tickled the soles of my feet with his teeth, biting into the arch and making me writhe.

I could do anything to him. When I went down and kissed him, he reached for his bedside table and fished out a condom. I was hit by jealousy, the worst I'd ever felt. I did not want him prepared for sex this way. I did not want to share him. Still, I sucked him in and found his less than iron rigidity comfortable in my mouth, I played him with my tongue, but he didn't cum. I eased a finger into his ass and discovered that he had no prostate gland, which hurt. I did not want him to be mortal. Even so, the penetration made him groan, made his balls pull up, and I thought I had him, but I didn't, just a bit of precum glistening at the tip of his cock, and he sighed with pleasure when I rubbed it into the head through the latex.

I should have come more than once, but he always held me back, stopping just before I couldn't have stopped myself. He had years of experience, years of men, and I envied every one of them. I wanted to be them all. He could be gentle and teasing, his lips barely brushing until my cock sat up and begged; he could bruise when he wanted to, those cornflower eyes boring into mine, daring me to scream. He stroked me slowly right to the edge then squeezed the head of my cock, choking off my orgasm so it almost hurt. I started to lose my erection, started to panic, but he kissed me quiet and kept going, his fingertips dancing just behind my balls until I hardened fully again. I could feel his silent chuckle; he had done something to me that nobody had but myself, but he could do everything he wanted.

Everything. There came a time for it, and he said nothing, only smiled as he put the condom on and reached for a tube of thick lubricant. I lay on my back, knees pulled to my chest, watching.

He took his time, but when he went into me, it was clear that this was the homestretch at last. He fucked me steadily, firmly, let the heat and friction build and build until it alone might have saved me, but he waited until that moment had passed before he greased his hand and wrapped it around my cock. He watched me intently as he slowly jacked me off and this time, I knew he'd let me go, all the way, into that incredible blue yonder. My balls were alive inside, churning, I could feel it building, and it terrified me. I looked at him, begging without words for mercy, and he gave me none, only stroked me smoothly and firmly until I snapped, hitting myself in the face with it, babbling through clenched teeth as light exploded behind my eyes. It was what he needed, and as I came down from it, his stroke quickened, his eyes squeezed tight shut, and he sighed blissfully as his cock pulsed deep inside me.

Afterward, I could barely stay awake. It was three in the afternoon; it felt like three in the morning. I'd been running earlier. That couldn't have helped. Ben lay beside me, wiping my face with a warm cloth. Now I worshipped him and loved him, and could only hope that I meant something in return, anything at all.

"Stay here," he said, kissing my ear. "I'll be back."

But when I woke up an hour later, he was gone. I put my shorts back on and went down the stairs, rubbing sleep out of my eyes. The sun was low, and I was hungry.

I heard voices from somewhere and followed them. One was unmistakably Ben's. The other was male, also familiar, but I couldn't place it just then. I went through the living room and found the patio doors.

I froze. Of course I knew the other man, he was a neighbor on The Point who sometimes played tennis with my father. I'd known him since I was a boy, when he'd helped me with my grip and my backhand. I had no idea what to do. I was there in nothing but my running shorts, probably looking as fucked as I felt. I was turning away, thinking of sneaking out the front door, when Ben caught sight of me.

"Patrick," he called through the screen. "There you are. Come on out. Do you know Mark James?"

"Of course I know Patrick," Mark's voice boomed cheerfully as he rose, and he offered me a hand. "Good to see you, son. How's your mother doing? I haven't seen her yet this summer."

"She's fine," I said, the manners the aforementioned lady had instilled in me from birth kicking in just in time. "She's been busy. One of her friends has a new grandchild, and she's been helping out until they can find someone."

"Ah yes, the Saiges' little girl. Everyone was very pleased to hear about that," he said.

"Patrick, are you thirsty?" Ben asked, his eyes sparkling with mischief. He didn't wait for a reply. "What's your pleasure?" he asked.

In my mind's eye, I saw that drop of precum I had worked out of him. "Gin and tonic," I said.

Mark and I made the usual small talk, as if it was perfectly normal for him to find me in dishabille alone with another man. Then again, whether Mark was or wasn't, knew or guessed, he would say nothing. Ben would see to that, and the idea gave me a deeply naughty thrill.

Ben rejoined us and handed me a glass, letting his fingers brush mine. I shivered, not just from the cool June air. I felt both grown-up and school-boy daring, standing in the doorway of another world, and as Ben sat down in the chair beside mine, I stayed put but what I really wanted to do was curl up at his feet with my head on his elegant knee.

A Man of Taste
Michael Stamp

"You can't stick your monster dick up my ass, Mr. Weston," Jake says anxiously as he lies down on my bed. "You'll rip me open!"

"I'd never hurt you, Jacob," I answer as my hands urge him over onto his stomach.

I'm flattered by his exaggeration. My cock isn't the foot-long weapon sported by the studs in every one-hander I'd ever read, but it's a good eight inches when I'm hard. And I've never been harder as I look down at Jake.

His delicate profile is displayed dramatically on my pillow. My eyes linger on it before traveling down to the other parts of his alluring young body: the smoothly muscled shoulders, the unblemished back, the slim hips. One bent elbow protrudes out from under the pillow, the other stretches up over it. My eyes are drawn to the richly curved buttocks, pale against my dark green sheets, and stark white in contract to the rest of his sun-bronzed body. The legs, spread wide, allow an unobstructed view of the small, puckered pink hole, and below the pale globes, the small ball sack and long, slender cock.

I climb onto the bed and straddle his thighs "You said you wanted me to teach you everything, didn't you?" I ask in my best schoolmaster voice.

Jake looks at me over his shoulder. Limpid blue eyes seek mine. "I trust you, Mr. Weston," he manages, his voice trembling slightly as he prepares for his first lesson in the mysteries of sex.

"Of course you do, Jacob," I tell him. "Don't worry, I'll be gentle, and if it hurts too much, I'll stop." I reach down to ruffle his unruly mop of blond hair. "I promise."

It's all such nonsense I can barely get the words out without laughing. Jake is anything but a novice where sex is concerned. Our very first time together, he took my entire eight inches quickly, and without so much as a whimper. He just enjoys playing games when we fuck, and this particular scenario is one of his favorites: the pure young boy and the lecherous old man about to steal his innocence. It's harmless fun, just Jake's way of chiding me about the difference in our ages.

He knows the subject still concerns me. I think about it often, but it has been weighing especially heavy on my mind all evening. We had dinner at La Luna tonight to celebrate my birthday. Jake doesn't care much for the restaurant; the place is far too fancy for his tastes. He dislikes the ornate decor, the stuffy maitre d' who checks our reservation, the fact that he has to wear a suit and tie, three of the many things I find most appealing about dining there. His dislike of the restaurant is just one more thing that emphasizes the difference in our ages and backgrounds, and drives home a reality I have been doing my best to ignore. At 24, Jake is half my age.

To the heterosexual couples that were dining at surrounding tables, Jake and I could easily have passed for father and son, but I could tell from the looks that passed between the male couples around us that they knew I was more "Daddy" than Dad.

"Who cares what they think, Eddie?" Jake said much too loudly. "They're just jealous that none of them will be getting the fine piece of ass that you will tonight."

Even though Jake tried his best to put me at ease, the knowing glances of those men had made me feel awkward and uncomfortable, feelings I couldn't shake until we left the restaurant. But once we got back to the apartment, it was a totally different story.

It's always the same. Whenever Jake and I cum together on my king-size bed, all my doubts and concerns disappear, replaced by the communication of skin on skin, and the extraordinary feel of my hard flesh rooted in Jake's warmth. Such pleasures can make me forget anything, even the nagging fear that I'm just an old fool making a spectacle of himself over a beautiful young man.

My insecurities aren't totally groundless. Getting dumped can do serious damage to a middle-aged man's ego. When Kevin left me for a man five years younger and with a heftier bank account, I was stunned. I never saw it coming. And I handled it the way I'd always handled rejection. I hid.

For months, I buried myself in my work, staying at the office until seven or eight each night, then coming home to nuke my dinner and eat it in front of the television set. Half the time I'd fall asleep before whatever program I was watching was over, and if I did manage to stay awake, I couldn't remember what I'd seen. It wasn't a life. It was barely an existence, but it was the only way I had been able to cope.

If it hadn't been for my well-meaning friends, I would have continued to stay away from my old haunts, but they had been hounding me, telling me it was time I got out of the house again. What they really meant was that it was time I got laid again, but while they were thinking it, they didn't put it into words. They knew better. "It's too soon," I'd have told them. "I'm not ready." But despite my insistence that I needed more time, I wondered if I ever would be.

I knew my friends had my best interests at heart, so I decided to take their advice and went out for a drink one night after work. It couldn't hurt, I told myself, even if it only served to remind me that there was still a world out there, one beyond the one in which I was living.

The moment I walked into The Cockpit, I remembered why I'd stayed away for so long. I was suffering a bad case of deja vu. Everything was the same as it had been the last time I'd been there. The noise. The smoke. The wall of lonely men looking to connect with someone — anyone — just so they won't have to spend another night alone. I recognized their desperation only too well. I had been one of them — until I met Kevin. I took a seat at the bar, determined to have one drink and leave, but luck wasn't with me.

"Edmund? Is that you?"

I looked up to see a familiar face. "How have you been, John?" I asked without much enthusiasm.

"Great." John leaned over and grasped my hand firmly. "It's good to see you, Edmund." He stepped aside so I could see the man who had accompanied him to the bar. "You remember Hank, don't you?"

I didn't, but then it wasn't surprising. When I'd still been a regular here, John had come in nightly, but never with the same man. His companions had been a specific type: tall, dark-haired, mustached, between 30 and 35, but each with a subtle difference. An inch taller or shorter, brown hair instead of black, but otherwise, they all fit the mold. I remembered wondering if John had managed to perfect cloning before that English scientist had reproduced Dolly, thereby ensuring himself an endless supply of his favorite man. I nodded in Hank's direction, non-committal.

"Where's Kevin?" John asked.

"I'm alone tonight," I said because it was easier.

"That's the spirit, Edmund," he said. "You can still browse, even if you aren't looking to buy."

"I'm not even window shopping tonight," I said. "I just stopped in for a quick drink on my way home." I drained the last drop of Scotch from my glass and pushed back my chair. "It was nice to see you, John," I told him.

"Same here."

I made my escape, getting as far as the front door before I felt a pair of arms slide around my waist and suddenly found my mouth being explored by a strange tongue. Though it was anything but unpleasant, I pulled away in surprise. "What the hell …" I began, but my words were cut off by another kiss.

"It's about time you got here!" the young blond who held me said loud enough for the whole room to hear, then just for my ears, added, "Play along, will you? There's a guy over there that's been hitting on me all night. I told him I was waiting for someone, but he won't leave me alone unless I prove it."

I nodded dumbly, and with the blond hanging all over me, we left the bar. Once we were outside, he untangled himself from me, and I told him, "Even though I know that wasn't for real, I still enjoyed it."

"Me, too," he grinned, extending his hand. "I'm Jake."

I was surprised by the introduction, having anticipated his quick getaway once we got outside. "I'm Edmund," I said, shaking his hand. When he continued to stand there, looking at me expectantly, I asked, "Is there something else I can do for you?"

"Yeah. You can take me home with you. I told that guy I was going home with my lover. You're not going to make a liar out of me, are you?" Jake asked.

It's against my nature to do anything without considering the consequences, and looking back on it now, I can't believe I actually did it, but that night, I threw caution to the wind and brought a perfect stranger home with me.

I don't know what I expected when I took Jake into my bed, but what I got was a night of unbridled passion the likes of which I had never known before. When I woke up the next morning, exhausted but totally satisfied, I expected to find it had all been a dream. Or if it had been real, that my enthusiastic young lover had left while I was still sleeping, taking with him my wallet, my watch, and anything else of value he could carry.

What I found instead was Jake, snuggled up against me under the covers. We got up and ate an enormous breakfast together, after which Jake gave me a blow job that sent me to work with a smile so wide I'm sure it kept my colleagues wondering all day just what I'd been up to.

To my great surprise, Jake returned that night, the next night and every night after that, and for reasons I still can't fathom, he shows no sign of ever planning to stop. Everything may change tomorrow, but until it does, I'm relishing our time together. For the first time in my life, I'm enjoying living for the moment.

Especially for moments like this.

I work my way inside Jake, my pulse racing as I feel his muscles yield to admit me. It happens every time my cockhead passes through that tight ring of muscle, the entrance to the place I desire most in the world. Whenever I fuck Jake, even though a thin layer of latex separates us, I always feel as if my whole being is flowing into him, and in return, I'm drawing out of him his strength, his vitality, his very youth. Driven by desire, I often have the endurance of a teenager, but tonight, my body fueled by lust, I know our coupling will be hard and fast. I drive my cock deeper and begin to thrust.

"Do it, Eddie!" Jake cries, all his schoolboy pretenses gone. "Fuck me hard!" His need as urgent as mine, he raises his ass higher and pushes back against me, trying to impale himself on my cock. Urged on by his excitement, my thrusting becomes primal, the frenzy of my fucking forcing Jake back down onto the bed. He retaliates by clenching his sphincter muscles around my cock, making each one of my strokes exquisite torture.

I don't last long. There's a roaring in my ears and a churning in my balls as I near my climax. When I cum, I don't just ejaculate — I erupt, pumping wave after wave of semen into the condom that encases my cock. Under me, I feel Jake's hips jerk convulsively. When my spasms finally subside, I collapse onto my back. I am bathed in sweat, my heart is beating a jungle rhythm inside my heaving chest, and my head is throbbing. I've never felt more alive.

Jake rolls over, exhaling loudly. He swirls a finger through the semen on his belly like a child creating a masterpiece with a set of finger paints, then leans over and plants a kiss on my lips, declaring, "Happy Birthday, Mr. Weston!"

"Thank you," I reply. "That was the best birthday present I've ever gotten."

"Me, too," Jake grins. "And it wasn't even my birthday!"

"Well if you're a really good boy," I tell him, giving him a kiss of my own, "when it's your birthday, I might just give you the same present."

Totally spent, I'm now ready for sleep. What I love even more than sex with Jake is the cuddling that comes after. I love falling asleep with my cock nestled in the crack of his ass, so I turn on my side, expecting him to settle back against my chest. Instead, he sits up and announces, "I'm starved!"

"After the meal we had tonight?" I marvel. "That's impossible."

Jake feigns innocence. "It's your fault, Eddie. Getting fucked by you always gives me an appetite."

It's true. While I always feel totally satisfied and want nothing more than to sleep, Jake always needs refueling immediately after our sex. I've gotten used to his post-coital munchies, but tonight I don't want him to leave our bed. It's my birthday, after all.

"Don't go," I whine like a petulant child. "Stay here, and I promise I'll make you a huge breakfast tomorrow morning. Eggs, pancakes, anything you want."

"I want pizza from Natoli's!" Jake trumpets, pulling out of my arms despite my protests.

Knowing I can't talk him out of the pizza, I try for a compromise. "Call somebody that delivers."

"No way. After a great fuck, it's got to be Natoli's."

Jake pulls on a pair of jeans, and I sigh as I watched the blue denim cover the beautiful young ass I possessed so completely only moments before. "At least take the car," I tell him.

"It's only a block away, Eddie."

"I'll be asleep when you get back," I threaten.

Dodging my attempts to grab him and pull him back down onto the bed, Jake slips into a shirt, pulls on sneakers, and bounds through the bedroom door. Seconds later I hear the apartment door slam. I shake my head, amazed as always by the stamina of youth.

Preparing to make good use of the time Jake is away, I go out to the living room and get my laptop. Within minutes my bed resembles an extension of my desk rather than the site of one of our most intense sexual unions. I get through only half a column of monthly projection figures before the numbers begin to swim before my eyes. I take off my glasses and lay back against the pillows, planning only to rest my eyes for a few minutes before going back to work.

The next thing I know, Jake is on top of me, munching on my nipples between bites of a huge slice of pizza. "I'm tired, Jake," I tell him, trying to turn over. "Let me sleep."

Jake wraps his fist around the base of my cock and squeezes. My reaction shows I'm not quite as tired as I profess to be. "Get it up, old man," he says lewdly, "and keep it there. I expect you to fuck me again once I'm finished eating."

More awake now, I see that my laptop has disappeared, replaced by the box containing the steaming pizza. Stretching out beside me, Jake reaches in for his second slice, then lies back to enjoy it. Knowing I'll regret it in the morning, I take a slice for myself, then another, and between the two of us, we finish the whole pie.

Once again, Jake has forgotten that I prefer sausage on my pizza. I try to appease my craving for meat by taking Jake's cock in my mouth, but it doesn't work. The nap and the food have revitalized me, and just tasting him like this won't be enough to satisfy me now, so I kneel between Jake's thighs and hook his legs over my shoulders.

As I slide my amazingly hard cock into his always welcoming asshole, I warn him, "Now you're really in for it. You should never have gotten me started again, kiddo."

"Do your worst, Eddie," Jake dares me, his eyes bright with anticipation. "Natoli's stays open until 2:00 am!"

Trey
Jordan M. Coffey

"You're the only one that I trust with this, Dixon. Consider my son your personal responsibility now."

Those words, spoken years ago, haunted Dixon Blackwell. Some had considered him too young when he'd been promoted to head of security for PowersTech Corporation, but he had earned the position through hard work and dedication. He had eagerly applied that same level of commitment not just to the security of the company, but to the protection of Max Powers and his son.

Powers' wife and daughter had been killed in a car accident years earlier, and subsequently Powers had become obsessed about the safety of his remaining child, Christopher Maxwell Powers III, known to everyone as Trey. Because of his wealth, not to mention his own ruthless business practices in the always changing, fiercely competitive world of technology, Powers grew concerned about the possibility of attempts to get to him through Trey. With his promotion, watching over Trey had become Dixon's sometimes difficult job.

Trey Powers was beautiful, taking his looks more from his South American Indian mother than his WASP father. Curly black hair and large, dark eyes, and a lean, muscular build suited to the sport of swimming at which he excelled. A beautiful boy, who had grown into an even more beautiful young man, something that Dixon Blackwell had always been able to view with the detached eye of a proud "uncle."

As the child grew, he became more rebellious, mostly aimed at getting his busy father's attention. Dixon learned to handle Trey's willfulness, but lost count of the number of times that staff assigned to keep an eye on Trey had been outwitted by youngster's antics. Trey always promised to behave better in the future, and each time, Dixon would stay a little closer to the boy, watching him under the cover of outings and activities the two could share. Though Dixon wasn't Trey's personal bodyguard, he had, over the years, been the closest person to him — a friend, often a surrogate father — and had grown to care for him a great deal. The problem was that he had gotten too close.

When Trey turned sixteen, Dixon noticed something significant in Trey's behavior: that the boy's head didn't seem to be turned by the many pretty young girls that were always trying to get his attention. Instead, Dixon saw and recognized the wistful glances directed towards other young men. Eventually, he noticed a certain cocky awareness on Trey's part and assumed that at least some of Trey's attentions had been returned. He had thought that like most everything else, when ready, Trey would talk to him about it, but Trey never had.

For his part, Dixon made sure that he got detailed, private reports, and let Trey feel his own way, wanting Trey to date and experiment without shame. During Trey's freshman year in college, Dixon got word that Trey had gotten very close to a senior soccer player named Jack Winger. Without interfering, he had the student thoroughly checked out, and steadfastly refused to acknowledge as jealousy those stabbing pains he felt deep in his gut.

Dixon let out an agitated sigh, leaning back at his desk and ignoring the panel of monitors that took up one wall of his office. He was a formidable figure, large and imposing even in a suit, his expression almost never betraying his emotions, except to show that he meant business — tall, chocolate brown, with eyes to match, a goatee just starting to show gray. His strong hands rubbed tiredly over his smooth scalp, and he closed his eyes.

The summer before Trey went off to the university, Dixon had been troubled to find that he was no longer seeing Trey with a purely platonic eye. He wasn't sure how it had happened, but he made sure to keep it hidden. Younger men had never been his thing, but then he had never adhered to any particular type. He reasoned that he'd just been alone too long, spent too much time with too little social interaction, and his affection for Trey was getting twisted up with his loneliness. Throughout those hot months, he tried to convince himself that he wasn't attracted to the young man that he saw almost daily, that he didn't care for Trey any differently than before, but that didn't stop the vivid fantasies that plagued his waking hours, or the sensual dreams that infiltrated his sleep. And for the first time in years, he found himself thinking about sharing his life with someone. There were so many reasons why that was not possible, that he was actually relieved when Trey finally left for school.

Dixon had never made a secret of his sexual orientation, and, in fact, had been up-front with Powers about it when he'd been offered his current position. Powers had raised an eyebrow at the disclosure, but said simply that his only concern was that Dixon do the job for which he was paid so handsomely. Dixon had accepted that as truth since Powers had entrusted his son to him. A trust that he felt he had as good as broken.

There had always been a line he had sworn he would never cross. Until late one night while he was sitting up reading reports in a hotel on a business trip with Max Powers and his cell phone rang. The voice responding to his terse greeting actually scared him.

Trey hadn't sounded so young and unsure in years.

"Sorry, Dixon, you sound busy."

"What's wrong, Christopher?"

"Nothing. I just ..."

"Where are you?"

"I'm in my apartment," Trey answered, speaking of the large two-bedroom unit in a secure building where he lived off campus courtesy of his father.

"OK. Now, tell me what's happened," Dixon asked.

"It's nothing, Dixon. I'm sorry I bothered you," Trey said.

The connection was broken, and Dixon closed his phone, a frown deeply etched on his face. He made a few quick calls, checking on the team currently assigned to Trey, only to find that they had lost him for most of the evening. Without a second thought, he made the arrangements necessary to use the company plane, thankful that Powers trusted him enough to take his vague but urgent request at face value.

He used his key to let himself into Trey's apartment and walked through the quiet darkness to the bedroom, focusing on the shape of a body in the bed. Moving closer, he could see Trey's face, peaceful in repose, and breathed a sigh of relief, feeling slightly foolish for having flown all the way for nothing. But after turning on a side lamp, he froze at the sight of stark bruises on Trey's wrist where an arm rested on top of the covers. Stripping back the sheet, his blood chilled at other signs of physical force marking Trey's body.

"Christopher!"

Trey opened bloodshot eyes, starting at the figure leaning over him until he recognized Dixon.

"Dixon?" Trey sat up, covering himself as Dixon sat down. "What are you doing here? I told you I was fine."

"You're not fine," Dixon answered, his face even more grim than usual. "Who did this to you? Was it that boy, Jack Winger?"

A look of surprise flashed across Trey's face and anger showed clearly in his quiet words. "So, you knew about that? What, now I'm the little fag who got what he deserved, right?"

Dixon drew back as if he'd been slapped. "Of course not, and you should know better than to think that's how I'd feel."

Slumping back on the bed, Trey closed his eyes. "Sorry, I didn't mean it. And, I would have told you about me ... and Jack ... and everything ... someday."

"Christopher, let me take a look at your injuries."

Sighing, Trey said, "I wish you'd call me Trey like everyone else does."

"Trey," Dixon said deliberately, "how badly are you hurt, and how the hell did this happen?"

"It wasn't Jack," Trey said. "We ... we aren't seeing each other anymore. Didn't the crack team you have tailing me inform you of the big break-up last month?"

"If you'd stop trying to evade them every chance you get ..." Dixon said.

Trey sighed again. "Dixon, I'm old enough to live my own life."

"Your father ..."

"Yeah, my father, my father. Why does everything always have to be about my father?"

"Your father knows nothing about this. I'm here ... for you. Now, will you let me see?"

"It's just some bruises, Dixon. I can take care of myself. You taught me, remember?" But, he submitted to Dixon's scrutiny, and averting his eyes, admitted, "I went to a bar. I thought maybe I should broaden my horizons beyond campus, but I guess I picked up the wrong guy."

Daddy's Boyz

"That was very dangerous, little boy," Dixon said, concerned about the evidence of an obvious struggle, but satisfied that Trey wasn't badly hurt.

"I'm 18. I'm not a little boy!" Trey spat out, covering himself again.

"Well, then, maybe you should stop acting like one and realize that the people I assign to you are there for your protection, not your aggravation."

"Yeah, yeah," Trey said.

"I'm serious. Things could have turned out very differently tonight, and that would have meant a report to your father," Dixon said.

"Does he know about ... you know?" Trey asked.

"No, not from me, anyway," Dixon answered.

"And you don't ... it doesn't bother you?"

Dixon was tempted to reveal his own truth, that he himself had been with only men since just a little older than Trey, but he only said, "No, not at all."

"Do you have to leave right away?" Trey asked.

"I don't need to be back until tomorrow afternoon." He took Trey's hand in his, the pale slender one a visible contrast to his own large dark one, even in the dim light. "I can stay if you'd like."

"Yes, please," Trey mumbled drowsily. "I've missed you," he added a second later.

Dixon squeezed the fingers in his. "I've missed you, too, Christopher."

"You promise you won't leave before I wake up?" Trey asked.

"I promise," Dixon answered, settling a little more comfortably, planning to go doze on the couch as soon as Trey was asleep. His mind went over how to handle the bodyguards who had lost Trey with such unacceptable results, vowing to himself that it would never happen again. Before long, his eyes closed, and he lost his own fight against sleep.

Trey woke to a heavy pressure holding him down and almost panicked until Dixon's face came into view resting near his own. God, how he loved that man. He'd wanted him for so long that it was almost like a living thing. Nobody he had ever fooled around with had been able to make him forget Dixon Blackwell.

When he had met Jack at school, he thought he had finally found that somebody, until he realized that Jack didn't love him, just the Powers' name and money. The ensuing depression had eventually chased him out to a bar, where he had foolishly fixed his attention on someone who had reminded him a lot of Dixon. He had been too embarrassed to mention that little detail to Dixon, especially since, despite appearances, the man had turned out to be nothing like Dixon at all. The whole incident had only left him more frustrated than before.

At least Dixon still cared about him, even if it was as a kid and not a lover. Over the years, he'd come to think of Dixon as his best friend, but in his fantasies they had been much more. And having the man actually in bed with him was like a dream come true.

Wincing a little at some residual pain, Trey moved a little closer. One hand ghosted over Dixon's bare scalp, while his eyes traveled over Dixon's face coming to rest on the full lips. "Just one," he thought, wondering did he really dare, knowing that Dixon would never hurt him, no matter how angry, and then he'd have the memory of a kiss to give a touch of reality to his dreams.

A tilt of his head and they were lip to lip, his tongue darting out eagerly. He swallowed a groan, grabbing Dixon's arm as his tongue tried to probe further, his cock instantly hard and raring to go. A rumbling sound from Dixon fueled his blood, and he grew bolder, deepening the kiss, pressing his body close, gasping at the thick, rigid length he found himself rubbing against. For long, sweet moments, he wasn't just kissing; he was being held and kissed in return, that simple reciprocation enough to take him to the edge of climax.

"Christopher," he heard, as his hips jerked, involuntarily seeking more contact. It took him a few moments more to realize that his name hadn't been growled in passion, but in warning.

Crushed, he fell back, eyes closed, shaking as he tried to catch his breath and ignore the hard-on throbbing angrily in his underwear.

He heard his name again, and a gentle touch moved across his chin. His eyes opened and he was embarrassed to find them blurry with unshed tears.

"I'm sorry," he whispered, "but I can't help it. I love you, Dixon, and I want you so bad. I've tried to get over it, really I have, but I can't."

"Listen, Christopher ..." Dixon started.

"You just don't understand. You don't know what it's like to ... to want another guy ... want to be with another guy."

Trey was surprised when Dixon said, "Yes, I do. Believe it or not, I'm not straight. But, you're too young," Dixon went on. Stopping a protest with a finger to Trey's lips, he amended, "OK, then, I'm too old ... twenty years older than you. I work for your father, and by extension, for you as well. It wouldn't be appropriate." Dixon got up, rearranging his clothes.

Angrily, Trey sat up. "So, I'm just a job to you, then? I thought we were supposed to be friends."

"We are friends, and we don't want to ruin that, do we?" Dixon asked.

"I want you to love me back," Trey said, watching Dixon's face.

"I do ... maybe more than I should," Dixon admitted, "but we can't do this." His voice was quiet, and very, very serious.

But Trey already felt his spirits lifting. Somehow, he just had to convince Dixon that it could work. "Let's have breakfast," he said, pulling a pair of sweats from the pile of clothes near his bed. "You'll have to get back to my father soon."

Later, when Dixon was on the jet headed back to D.C., Trey took a walk in the park across the street from his building, ignoring the bodyguards following him. His hopes were high; he didn't care about two guys just trying to do their job. School was almost over for the year, and he'd be back at home, close to Dixon. All he had to do was plan his next move.

Trey soon realized that making a move on Dixon wasn't going to be easy. He had to at least be in the same room with the man, and he couldn't even get Dixon on the telephone. Finally, he decided a direct confrontation was the only way to force Dixon's hand. He woke up early one morning, dressed to impress, jumped in his sports car, and sped to his father's corporate headquarters, feeling desperate enough to smile his way past Dixon's assistant, Jayne, and walk unannounced into Dixon's office, desperate enough to ignore the look on Dixon's face at the intrusion.

"What do you think you're doing, Christopher?"

"No, what do you think you're doing? Avoiding me so that you can pretend you don't feel anything for me?"

"Lower your voice," Dixon said in a tone that Trey hadn't heard since he was eight years old.

Automatically, he spoke more quietly, his voice soft, but urgent. "Dixon, we can be good together. Just give me a chance."

"We are not going to have this discussion," Dixon said.

"Dixon, please," Trey said, feeling his moment slipping away in the face of Dixon's stony resistance. "Just one chance. I love you and you can't deny that you love me. You told me. How can you just turn your back on that?"

"I explained why the situation is impossible, Christopher," Dixon said.

"And that's that? You just say 'no' and I have to live with it? You're wrong to do this Dixon, you are so wrong. Come on, let me show you."

"It's out of the question. In the first place, your father …" Dixon said.

"Right. My father. See, it is always about my father. Well, what would my father think about you coming to my apartment in the middle of the night, using your key and getting into bed with me? I wonder what he'd think about that?" Trey asked.

Instantly, Trey knew that he'd gone too far. Dixon's face went ashen and took on a tangled expression of anger and pain.

"I'm sorry, Dixon. I didn't mean …" Trey said.

"You will leave my office, right now."

"I'm just trying to …" Trey began.

"Now, Christopher," Dixon demanded.

Trey turned and practically ran out the door, ignoring everyone who spoke to him as he made his way out to his car. He felt sick to his stomach. He had never screwed up anything so badly in his life. And no matter how much he wanted to be with Dixon, it was more important not to lose him completely.

It took him a whole week to get up the nerve to return to Dixon's office, only to find that Dixon had resigned his position. Either no one (including his father) knew where Dixon had gone, or they just weren't telling him. He had done little since seeing Dixon last, except think about what to say to make it right, but evidently he had missed his chance. Unable to believe that Dixon had simply disappeared without saying goodbye, Trey left PowersTech and drove home, feeling totally alone for the first time in his life.

Dixon put his feet up on the porch railing, sighing with contentment as he closed his eyes, a book lying open on his chest. Though sometimes his was a lonely existence, more often the sense of peace was very satisfying. Not being responsible for the lives of others had eased a weight from his own life. And when he craved companionship, there was a sizable city not too far away, home to more than one bar where he could find quick, rough encounters to sate his urges and quench his thirst for contact. He only picked up brawny hard-asses like himself, staying far away from beautiful, lean boys for reasons that were too obvious, and still too painful, even though four years had passed.

In the beginning, he hadn't planned on staying up in the mountains very long, thinking that even for him the solitude would quickly get old, but he had enough money to pay for whatever amenities he wanted, and had settled in with little difficulty. His satellite and high speed internet connections kept him from feeling cut off, and eventually he had started a small consulting business, something with little need for travel. Something that didn't stop him from fishing or hiking the trails, or just sitting on his porch reading. He told himself he didn't need anything more in his life.

The scuff of gravel and the low rumble of an engine reached him long before he saw the approaching vehicle, and instantly he was on alert, feet swinging to the floor, wedging the book beside him on the chair. He wasn't expecting anyone, and in fact, except for delivery or repairmen, no one ever visited, which meant it was probably either trouble or bad news. When he finally caught sight of the car, sleek and red, he had the feeling that it would be trouble. Then the car stopped, and Trey Powers stepped out, blinking against the sun as he looked up in Dixon's direction.

Trey was several inches taller since Dixon had seen him last. His hair was shorter, still wildly curled on top, but cut close and neat on the sides, setting off his big, black eyes. Definitely trouble, Dixon thought, sitting perfectly still, watching and waiting.

After Trey had thundered into his office, Dixon realized that he might always be perceived as having taken advantage of someone much younger who had been entrusted to his care. Despite it all, Dixon had had stray thoughts of being with Trey one day, and had decided that removing himself was the only way to allow things between them to naturally fade away.

Time and distance, however, hadn't seemed to make much difference because Dixon's heart beat faster at the sight of Trey climbing his stairs, though he hid it behind the stony façade that had served him well over the years. When Trey reached the top, they stared at one another for a few tense beats, until Dixon finally broke the silence.

"A bit out of your way, isn't it?" Dixon asked.

"A bit out of everyone's way," Trey quipped. "I would have called, but ... you know."

"It's good to see you, Christopher," Dixon said, wondering what he would have done if Trey had called up asking to visit.

Trey smiled rather hesitantly. "Good to see you, too."

"Congratulations on your graduation. Well done," Dixon said.

"Thanks. I would have invited you, but ..." again, Trey trailed off, and Dixon was reminded of how their last encounter had ended. "Anyway, I wish you had been there."

"I'm sure your father is proud of you and eager for you to join the company. When do you start business school, or are you going to work at PowersTech for a while first?" Dixon asked.

"Actually, I'm not going to work there at all. I, um, start architecture school in the fall," Trey said.

Dixon couldn't hide his look of surprise, and Trey smiled.

"Dad wasn't too pleased, but he couldn't very well bitch about me doing something constructive. I think he was expecting me to make a less industrious announcement. Not that I blame him. You of all people can testify that I've been known to act rashly," Trey said.

Dixon let that remark slide. "So, what brings you here?"

Trey shuffled his feet, looking down at them and swallowing visibly. After a moment, he said, "I ... I owe you an apology. The last time I saw you ..."

"There's really no need for that."

"Yes, there is, Dixon. I acted like a spoiled brat, and I'm sorry for making you feel you had to rearrange your life the way you did. And, I appreciate you not telling my father about my part in it. And, you were right ... it wouldn't have worked out. I couldn't expect you to take me seriously and not treat me like a child when I consistently acted like one."

"The past is past," Dixon said, not sure what else to say.

"Yeah, well ... I was hoping we could talk about ... the future."

"Oh?" Dixon asked.

"Yeah. Are you happy here? All by yourself?" For a second, Trey looked startled, glancing quickly around. "I mean, are you by yourself?"

"Yes, I'm alone, and I'd say I'm happy," Dixon said.

"I thought ... I um ... well, to be honest, I still have feelings for you and I was hoping ... well, wondering how you felt. I thought I could stay here a while ... maybe for the summer ... and we could try getting to know one another again ... or better ... and see what happens," Trey said.

Surprised that Trey hadn't grown out of his old crush, Dixon was caught totally off guard by that little speech.

"Or," Trey said, when Dixon only stared, "I could go find someplace to stay near here, and whenever you felt like it, we could get together or something, spend some time with each other."

"OK," he said, finally, when there was still no response, "or I guess I could go back home." With a shrug of his shoulders, he added, "I hope you'll accept my apology." Then, he turned to go.

"Christopher."

Trey turned back around, but didn't meet Dixon's gaze.

"You don't have to go. You can stay for a while if you want," Dixon said.

"Really?" Trey's smile was instantaneous. "That's great. But, on one condition ..."

Dixon raised an eyebrow and waited.

"You have got to call me Trey. When you call me Christopher, it's a lot like talking to Dad," Trey said.

"Fair enough, and I have a few conditions of my own."

"Figures," Trey said, rolling his eyes.

"You have to stay in the spare room, and I don't want you to have any preconceived expectations."

"OK," Trey said, shaking his head, smiling again, "it's a deal. But, Dixon, you have to learn to lighten up. So, are hugs allowed?"

When Dixon nodded, Trey gave him a tight embrace, mumbling, "I told myself I wouldn't be a baby about this," in a shaky voice.

Dixon eased them apart, lifting Trey's face with a finger under the chin. "There's nothing wrong with showing emotion, Trey."

"You don't," Trey said with a dismissive snort, but pleased that Dixon had remembered about his name.

"Right, well, everyone can't be like me. You have to be your own man," Dixon said.

"OK, just remember you said that the next time we have a difference of opinion," Trey said cheekily, before running down the stairs to his car. Opening his trunk, he pulled out several pieces of luggage, carrying them back up to the porch.

"Pretty sure of yourself, weren't you?" Dixon rumbled.

"No, not at all. But, it pays to be prepared."

The two went in, spending the next bit of time setting Trey up in the second bedroom. Dixon couldn't help thinking that in reality he was setting himself up for trouble — with a capital "T." Maybe one summer together would work out, but Trey was young and spirited, and wouldn't want to stay isolated up in the mountains for long. Plus, by the time Trey had to leave for school, the thrill of finally having gotten to Dixon would have worn off.

"Dixon?" Trey's voice broke into his thoughts, and he turned to see the young man staring. "Everything all right?"

"Yes, fine," Dixon said, dropping clean towels on the bench at the foot of the bed. "One more thing, though. Don't try to use being here as an excuse not to go to school as you've planned."

"Yes, Dad," Trey joked, tossing a pillow at Dixon's head.

"And, speaking of your father ..." Dixon said, replacing the pillow on the bed.

"No, he doesn't know where I am. Well ... I didn't tell him, but as you know, he has eyes everywhere. And, in case you're also wondering, yes, he does know that his son is a practicing homosexual. I'm still not sure how he feels really, but he's never

Daddy's Boyz

given me a hard time about it. Actually, he keeps giving me boxes of condoms."

Trey laughed, a sexy, infectious sound, and Dixon briefly laughed along with him before saying goodnight and going to his own room. In bed, Dixon wondered if Trey had been using up the condoms supplied by his father, wondered what he liked, how he liked it. It was all too easy to imagine himself in the scenarios, naked and hard and sweaty. A tangle of limbs, a chorus of grunts, the heady scent of male musk. In the end, he had to jerk off in the bathroom, water running to muffle the sound, in order to get to sleep.

Obviously, Dixon had meant it when he'd said "no expectations." Any time that things started to get interesting, he would back off. It wasn't that Trey only wanted a sexual relationship, but he had assumed once he got in the door, he would get past Dixon's defenses and a physical development would naturally follow. But Dixon never made a move and ignored all of Trey's hints. To have Dixon right there within reach, but keeping so distant was rapidly exhausting Trey's patience.

After one too many mornings waking up alone with Dixon only a room away, Trey determined that something had to be done. He wanted to just go jump in bed with the man, but remembered that last time the direct approach hadn't turned out very well. So, he searched his brain trying to come up something a bit more subtle.

"I have some errands to run later. You going to be OK here?" Dixon asked.

Trey looked up to see Dixon standing in the doorway to his room. "Why don't I just come with you?" Trey asked.

"No, it's some ... business, and I'm not sure how long I'll be."

"OK," Trey said, shrugging. "I'm sure I can keep myself busy."

"Fine, then I'll leave after lunch," Dixon said.

The morning was spent with Dixon working on his computer while Trey flipped through the hundreds of available cable channels, his mind on the night ahead and an emerging plan to seduce Dixon, rationalizing that an orgasm or two would get Dixon to abandon his "no expectations" attitude.

Though he wasn't much of a cook, Trey wanted to start with a good meal. So, with Dixon gone, he found a place on the Internet where he could generate recipes from ingredients that he had on hand. He picked one that seemed quick and easy, and when it was ready, he showered, dressed in a tight tee-shirt and tighter jeans, and sat down to wait. And waited. After it got dark, he ate some of the dinner and waited some more. When Dixon finally came back, Trey could tell that Dixon was surprised to find him still awake.

A little worried and a lot annoyed, Trey stood up. "Are you OK?"

"Yes, sorry. You didn't have to wait up," Dixon said.

"Now I know how you must have felt when I used to give the guys the slip all the time," Trey said as he walked over trying to shake his irritation and gather the remnants of his plan together. Leaning in for a kiss, he was overwhelmed by the scent of smoke and alcohol and sweat. Surprised and angry, he met Dixon's eyes, growing even angrier when Dixon looked away. "My coming here was a mistake, wasn't it? Fine, you win. I finally get it now. You and me will never happen. Don't worry, I'll be out of here in the morning." Turning, he stormed down to his room, hastily packing his clothes, then stripped down and got into bed.

He hadn't quite calmed down when Dixon walked into the room and sat on the bed next to him, smelling clean and fresh and familiar. Trey squeezed his eyes shut against the pain.

"I'm sorry," he heard Dixon say, but it didn't help.

"Don't be. You can fuck whomever you want. Tomorrow, I'll be out of your way for good."

"Christopher ..."

Enraged, Trey faced Dixon head on. "That's it, isn't it? To you, I'll never be Trey Powers, a goddamn grown man who wants to be an architect and to be with you. I'll always be little Christopher, the boss's kid that you have to baby-sit!"

"That's not true. And I didn't ... well, despite my intentions, I didn't end up with anybody," Dixon said as he touched Trey's face, but Trey moved away, and Dixon settled for trailing a finger along the back of one of Trey's hands. "Don't think that I don't love or want you. I do, very much. You are ... beautiful, and I'm incredibly proud of the man that you've grown into. I've just always wanted to do the right thing by you. I didn't want to push you into a situation you weren't ready for, or hold you back from other experiences you might want to have."

Daddy's Boyz

"You think that because I'm young I don't know what I want," Trey said, petulantly.

"No, but at my age, I've learned that you can't always have what you want," Dixon said.

"Yeah, well, I've learned that at my age, too," Trey retorted.

"But, then there are the other times ..." Dixon said, leaning over and kissing Trey.

Trey threw his arms around Dixon, kissing him back, trying not to yell when Dixon pulled away. "If you stop now, Dixon," he groaned, "I swear I'll do my best to kick your ass."

"I'm not going to stop, but I do want to slow it down ... take my time ... enjoy you ... savor you ..." Dixon said.

Dixon lowered Trey to the bed, punctuating his words with kisses that traveled down Trey's body, sucking and biting until he got to Trey's groin, where he sniffed appreciatively, nuzzling as Trey squirmed. He spread Trey's legs apart nibbling along Trey's inner thigh, ignoring Trey's darkening erection, opting instead to probe between the cheeks of Trey's ass with teasing licks. Trey was swearing, muttering curses under his breath as he tried to rock his body to meet the thrusts of Dixon's tongue. Dixon held Trey's hips in a firm grip, and Trey had to settle for grabbing Dixon's head with tense fingers. When Dixon finally moved to Trey's cock, Trey cried out, hips surging upwards, breaking Dixon's hold. That motion coupled with Dixon's suction caused his dick to slip practically all the way down Dixon's throat, and he climaxed almost immediately, moaning incoherently, the only recognizable word being Dixon's name as he slumped back onto the bed.

"Dixon, just fuck me now," Trey whispered, after a minute's rest.

"Are you sure?"

Trey answered by reaching out, getting the appropriate supplies from a drawer, and turning over onto his belly.

With slick fingers, Dixon slipped inside of Trey's body, trying desperately to maintain his control. He sought out Trey's prostate, rubbing it until Trey started making whimpering sounds and grew hard once again. As he slipped off his shorts, Dixon felt afraid. He was about to cross one more line with this boy that he'd known since a child, but he wanted it so much that he could feel the burn of it sizzling every nerve in his body as he prepared himself with condom and lube. As slowly as possible, he pushed into the tight entrance to Trey's ass, trembling with the effort of restraint.

"Go ahead ... it's OK ... I'm not a virgin, you know," Trey said.

Those weren't exactly the words Dixon wanted to hear. Though he had no right to be jealous of the men Trey had been with before, he was almost embarrassed at the satisfaction he felt when he thrust in a little deeper and heard Trey moan his name, wanting to finally claim that place as his own. It was hard to believe that he was there, making love to that beautiful body, but the friction as he eased in and out was incredibly real. He kept up a slow pace until Trey began to rock back against him, heightening his pleasure, taking the rhythm up a notch higher. With one hand he reached around, fisting Trey's cock, pumping it with a deliberately irregular stroke in counterpoint to their fucking, hoping to make Trey lose control. But instead, pleasure seized him by the balls like hot, sweet fire licking up his spine, and he groaned low and deep as his dick pulsed in release, grateful that seconds later Trey also came, coating his hand with slick warmth.

Pulling out, he drew Trey down with him to the bed, scattering kisses on Trey's sweaty skin, resting contentedly for a moment, before getting up for a warm cloth to clean them both.

"Is it all right if I stay in here with you?" Dixon asked, putting the washcloth aside.

"Of course," Trey answered, already sounding half asleep, but snuggling closer when Dixon spooned up behind him.

They both had the hint of a smile on their faces when sleep overtook them.

When Dixon woke up, he was alone in bed, but he heard noises coming from the kitchen and hastily pulled on his shorts, thinking of coffee and kisses and cuming hard. In the front room, he found Trey fully dressed, looking out the window with his bags by the door.

"Trey, what's going on?" he asked.

"I'm going back home until time for school to start," Trey answered without turning around.

"But, I thought last night ..."

"Last night was great," Trey said, finally facing him. "Beyond great even. But, I shouldn't be here. I came because I knew where to find what I was looking for, but just yesterday you were still out looking for something else. The sex was unbelievable, but I need you to want this the way that I want this, and I can't force that on you. You know how to find me, so you can call me whenever you want." Trey smiled, but in a way that pained Dixon inside. "And, I'm really glad I got the chance to be with you for a while."

Trey moved to leave, but Dixon was right behind him, one strong hand reaching over and holding the door closed.

"I want you to stay. I meant every word I said last night. You're right, I've tried to fight my feelings, but I am in love with you. Stay and let me prove it." Trey didn't answer, didn't move. "Stay," Dixon repeated, wanting it to sound assertive, but hearing a plea.

Slowly, Trey turned around, eyes shining as he looked into Dixon's face as if gauging what he saw there. "OK," Trey said, finally. "But this time, I set the rules. From now on, we share a bedroom, and you have to start thinking of us as a couple and give it a fair chance. And, in case the obvious needs to be stated, there'll be no more little trips for you like you took last night. And, when I leave to go to school ..."

Dixon laughed, cutting him off with a kiss. "You're getting awful bossy, little boy," he whispered against Trey's lips.

Emotion flashed like dark fire in Trey's eyes. "Let's get that straight, too," he said, jabbing Dixon in the chest with his finger. "I am not your 'little boy'!"

"No, you're not," Dixon said. "But you are mine," he added to himself as he moved back and picked up Trey's bags carrying them to their bedroom.

"And don't you forget it," Trey said following him.

"I think you need to learn to lighten up, Trey. Come here," Dixon said, pulling his lover into the room to start the day off right.

Learning the Ropes
Jay Starre

Blake stripped off his tight T-shirt and tossed it onto the porch swing. Mopping his lined forehead with a kerchief, he pushed his cowboy hat back to reveal a short mop of white-blond hair. He was sweating, pearly drops collecting on the thatch of blond curls across his broad chest.

Gavin hovered on the porch steps, half in the shade and half under the bright burn of Colorado's afternoon sun. He stared at Blake, naked from the waist up, muscles bulging across his torso. The ranch foreman was a real man. Gavin's breathing grew faster, his heart pounding in his chest. He couldn't take his eyes off of the burly, older foreman. A sudden boner chafed against the rough material of his jeans. The 19-year-old cowboy wanted sex. He wanted that sex to be with Blake, even though he was more than twice Gavin's age.

Gavin bit his lip and gawked at Blake's semi-nude body as the foreman plopped down in the rickety porch swing and spread his beefy arms across the back of it. Gavin suddenly thought of his father, who would be close to Blake's age. Gavin's dad had been a miserable drunk, who abandoned his family when Gavin was only 12. Gavin had longed for a father figure in his life, and the moment he met Blake, he realized this was it. But it hadn't taken long for his adoration to turn sexual. Now it controlled him.

"Come on over and rest your feet a spell, Gavin. It ain't gonna hurt you to waste a few minutes doing fuck-all."

The sound of Blake's gravelly drawl sent a shiver through Gavin's young body. Those soft grey eyes on him, looking him up and down so keenly sent another shudder through his long limbs. His cock jerked in his jeans. His mouth was dry.

"Uh, OK, boss," he managed to blurt out as he rushed up the steps to join the foreman.

Blake hadn't missed the puppy-dog looks and eager smiles Gavin had showered on him lately. For the past two months, since Gavin had been hired on at River Wide Ranch, Gavin had followed Blake around at every opportunity, watching and learning everything the older foreman offered to teach him. Blake knew the young cowboy idolized him. But that afternoon when he looked over and saw the shining glow in Gavin's bright blue eyes, for the first time Blake saw the lust.

He stared back at Gavin, noting the wide shoulders and thick forearms, the muscular thighs and full package. Gavin was young, but he was a man and old enough to decide what he wanted for himself. From the swelling bulge in his jeans, he apparently wanted Blake.

"Maybe we should go out to the northeast pasture this afternoon. There's some fence I want to check. How about it?" Blake asked with a smile. He watched Gavin stumble closer, the young cowboy's eyes never leaving Blake's torso.

"That sounds exciting, Blake," Gavin mumbled, aching to touch the dark brown nipples poking out of Blake's curling chest hair. The man had a massive chest.

"Exciting, ain't the word I'd use for an afternoon mending fences," Blake chuckled, pulling Gavin down to sit beside him on the bench. He turned his head and smiled into Gavin's eyes. "But maybe we can make it exciting."

Gavin was breathless. His thigh was actually touching the foreman's beefy leg. His body quivered like a roped calf. He smiled back at Blake, but otherwise couldn't speak. For one frightening, and thrilling moment, Gavin believed Blake was suggesting something sexual. But then he dismissed the idea, believing it was just his own desire causing him to think that way.

They rocked silently in the porch swing for a few minutes, taking in the cool breeze that wafted up from the river below the bunkhouse. Gavin was acutely aware of Blake's naked chest so close, and the foreman's long arm stretched across the back of the swing grazing his own shoulders. He could smell Blake — the musky odor of hard labor, unmasked by cologne or deodorant. Gavin's stiff cock drooled in his underwear.

"I guess we should skedaddle. Why don't you fetch the fence-mending gear, cowboy," Blake said.

Gavin leapt to his feet, eager to obey Blake's every command. Blake almost laughed, but didn't want to embarrass the big cowboy. "We'll meet at the coral," he called to Gavin's disappearing back.

Rather than taking the ranch pick-up, they chose a pair of geldings and rode out under warm summer skies. Along the river where icy-cold mountain water sparkled in the sunlight, they picked their way over a rough trail. They reached the rolling northeast pasture and followed the fence line on horseback, Blake leading.

Gavin eyed Blake as much as the fence line he was supposedly inspecting. Gavin gawked at Blake's arms and back; the foreman had tucked his shirt in a saddle-bag and rode half-naked under the warm sunshine. Blake had swirling blond fur that covered his arms, and that thick almost white thatch on his head under the cowboy hat. Gavin loved Blake's eyes, soft grey under thick eyebrows, pale as straw. Gavin was fascinated by Blake's hands, big and calloused, and so competent. Everything about the foreman was raw and rough and untamed, except the deliberate way he moved, walked and rode his horse. Blake's body was utterly under his own iron control.

Gavin longed to be under Blake's iron control. Gavin fantasized bending over and spreading his own ass cheeks, then taking Blake's dick up the ass, those beefy hands on his body, Blake's furry thighs against his naked legs.

Blake turned to catch Gavin staring at him. The big blue eyes were fixed on Blake's naked upper body, and when Gavin realized Blake was looking at him, the young cowboy flushed and grinned. Gavin had a sweet smile, straight teeth between plump lips. The obvious worship in Gavin's look made Blake grin back.

Blake had to admit he enjoyed Gavin's hero-worship. He had a good idea of his own worth, proud of his competence, which he'd earned through diligence and hard work. But pride didn't get the job done, and he didn't think he was any better than others just because he was a first-rate cowboy. Still, Gavin idolized Blake, and Blake liked it. He also liked the hungry look lurking under Gavin's sky-blue eyes as he feasted on Blake's masculine figure.

Blake reigned in his mount, turning on a dime to face Gavin. With a wink and a grin, he nodded to the wooden gate a few yards away. "Looks like that old gate could use some fresh nails. Should we do some nailing?"

Gavin flushed the moment Blake turned and caught him staring. His face still burned pink. With wavy black hair, Gavin's pale coloring and blue eyes stood out. Gavin's pink cheeks were an obvious give-away when he was either embarrassed or feeling lusty. He was feeling both.

"Sure, Boss. I'll get right to it."

Both cowboys dismounted with an easy swing, leading their horses to a nearby cottonwood to tether them while they worked. Gavin quickly pulled out a pair of hammers and a handful of nails from his saddlebags. He tried not to look at Blake, still embarrassed at being caught ogling the foreman. He hurried over to the wooden gate, tools in hand, intent on work. As he examined the rickety wooden rails, he sensed Blake watching him. An erection strained against his fly.

Blake was watching Gavin. Almost as tall and well-built as the foreman, Gavin was eager and uncertain, naive and innocent, and sexy as hell. Blake rubbed his crotch, feeling his pecker swell to a nice stiffness as his eyes roamed over Gavin's sturdy body. The cowboy had big legs and a chunky, rounded butt. Riding horses since his childhood, his legs were slightly bowed, leaving an emptiness between them only accentuated by the deep crack of his ass barely concealed by his tight, work-stained jeans. Blake stared at Gavin's ass, suddenly imagining it naked, and spreading for his hands, and his hard cock. Blake made his move, confident as ever.

Gavin was bent over the fence, searching for loose rails and shaking with the sensation of his boss watching his every movement. Suddenly, a pair of hands cupped his ass cheeks from behind. For one terrifying moment, Gavin froze, feeling those big palms cupping his ass and lightly squeezing. There was absolutely no mistaking Blake's actions.

In a blur of fierce desire, Gavin rose and whirled around. He threw himself into Blake's arms and planted his mouth over the foreman's in a desperate embrace and lip-lock.

They slammed together like a thunderclap. Big chests banged against each other, muscular arms wrapped around powerful bodies. Blake was astonished by Gavin's intensity. Blake had been entranced by the young cowboy's innocent sweetness. Blake was just as thrilled as that innocence became raging lust. Their tongues stabbed into each other's mouths.

Gavin felt Blake's nude torso pressing against his, inhaled Blake's masculine scent and sucked his fat tongue deep into his mouth in a rapture of liberated passion. Blake was not pulling away, his arms were pulling Gavin closer, his hands were down on Gavin's ass again, cupping and fondling the young cowboy's cheeks. Gavin vibrated from head to toe, snorting for breath, mewling around Blake's tongue as he thrust his hard cock into Blake's crotch.

Blake realize he had a wildcat on his hands. It was time to establish some authority. He kissed Gavin deeply, swapping spit and smacking his lips loudly as he massaged Gavin's tongue, lips and throat. It was a hot kiss, and Gavin's butt cheeks felt pliable and eager in his groping hands. He was going to fuck the hot young cowboy. Then and there. Right now.

The foreman pulled his mouth off Gavin's with a slurp. He stared into Gavin's baby blues and grinned. "I'm gong to bend you over that wooden gate and fuck your ass with my fat pecker."

Gavin moaned. "Sure, Boss — please. Blake, fuck me!"

Blake chuckled and winked, before spinning Gavin around as if he was a leaf in a windstorm. Gavin gasped, shaking all over as Blake's competent hands reached around his waist and tore open his buckle and the buttons of his fly. Gavin attempted to help, but Blake was too quick, yanking down on the waistband of Gavin's jeans. Suddenly Gavin's pants were around his ankles and Blake was shoving him forward. Gavin stumbled and fell over the top rail of the gate, his pants in a tangle around his cowboy boots.

Gavin's butt cheeks swelled the tight pair of cotton skivvies the cowboy wore. Blake had bent over to pull down Gavin's jeans and was face-to-face with that butt. He grinned as he opened his mouth and bit at the tight underwear, taking a mouthful of firm butt cheek along with it. Gavin yelped and jerked. Blake rose, grinning at the sight of the cowboy bent over the gate in his underwear and trembling violently. Gavin's innocent lust was more exciting than anything Blake had yet experienced. He slapped Gavin's butt and laughed.

"Pull down your underwear. I want to see your ass before I fuck it good."

Gavin's face flamed pink as he obeyed. His fingers shook as he hooked them in the waistband of his underwear and pulled down on them. He was stripping himself in front of Blake, bent over and waiting for the big foreman to fuck him up the ass. It was a dream come true. As he felt air on his naked butt, the big cheeks twitched and he spread his feet as far apart as he could, without consciously deciding to. His pants restricted him from opening up too far, but he could feel air on his ass crack, and bent over, he was acutely aware that his asshole might be visible. Blake could look at it, and see how excited Gavin was by the way it quivered and gaped with desire for cock, Blake's cock. Gavin was almost delirious with the intensity of that moment.

Blake watched Gavin pull down his underwear, his eyes going wide as he inspected the quaking butt cheeks revealed. That cowboy can was totally hairless, pale as fresh milk, and with a deep crack that promised sweaty pleasures Blake's cock longed to taste. Blake unbuckled his belt and unsnapped his fly, shoving down his pants and underwear to let out his aching hard-on as he watched Gavin's naked butt shiver and spread apart.

He got just a glimpse of Gavin's puckered hole deep in the recess of that butt valley. Blake grabbed hold of Gavin's ass cheeks, feeling the satiny-hot flesh for the first time. Firm muscle and chunky padding quivered under his fingertips. He pulled the cheeks open, peering down for a better look at the open crack.

"Sweet," Blake murmured.

Gavin heard the lust in that gravelly voice. He felt the foreman's calloused hands splitting open his ass cheeks. He felt Blake's eyes boring into him from behind. The burly cowboy was staring at Gavin's ass. He was inspecting him and finding him desirable. Gavin had never felt so naked and so vulnerable. He wanted to shout out loud — fuck me Blake, God fuck me hard!

The crack Blake scrutinized was as hairless as the cheeks, but there was a wispy swirl of dark hair ringing the crinkled lips of Gavin's asshole. The hole twitched, clamping then pushing outwards nervously. Blake's cock leaped at the sight. He shoved his big member into Gavin's parted crack and rubbed the gooey head all over it. Gavin moaned and wiggled his ass seductively against the hot pole. Blake loved that. The young cowboy was eager, now that he was admitting to what he craved. Cock up the ass — that was what they both wanted.

Blake rubbed the blunt head of his cock over Gavin's hole, teasing it with little thrusts, feeling the silken lips squeeze and gape excitedly. He rubbed his cock shaft up and down and pressed it between the cheeks of Gavin's butt, imagining that fat shank disappearing up inside the young cowboy's snapping anus and filling his warm guts. A trail of sticky precum mingled with Gavin's sweat, creating a slippery lube, but Blake knew it wasn't enough.

While Gavin mewled and squirmed against the foreman's prodding cock, Blake leaned down and hawked into the crack, gobbing on his cock head where it pressed against the pink folds of Gavin's hole. He rubbed the slick goo into that pulsing entrance with his purple knob, aching to shove hard but holding back.

"Fuck me, Boss! Stick that fat poker up my ass," Gavin bleated. He was insane with lust. The feel of Blake hard pole rubbing along his crack and prodding his asshole was maddening. He had never wanted anything so much as for Blake to shove that cock up his ass.

"Eager for cock, pup, aren't you? Don't complain when my fat pecker is stretching you every which way," Blake laughed breathlessly.

The foreman was heated up beyond his own control. He spit down into Gavin's crack again, watching the string of sticky goo land on his cock head. He planted the knob against Gavin's quaking ass lips and began to push. He spit again, and again as he exerted steady pressure against the resisting ring of anus muscle.

Gavin moaned as he stopped his wriggling. He held himself still as he felt the blunt heat of Blake's cock head pressing against his ass lips. His body trembled, but he managed to bite his lip and wait it out, attempting to will his asshole open, open for cock.

Saliva and sweat eased the way. The tapered head began to disappear, then the broad flange. Ass lips parted and stretched to both the cowboys' groans. All at once, cock head slipped past butt lips. The clinging sphincter wrapped tightly around Blake's advancing cock. He gasped and kept on shoving, loving the snug heat enveloping his dick. Gavin was groaning in a low rumble, his head down and his ass quaking violently.

"Are you feeling that cowboy? Are you feeling my big, fat dick up your ass? Do you like it, Gavin? Do you?" Blake growled huskily as he continued to push farther inside Gavin's heated butt oven.

Gavin could not speak. His asshole was on fire. His butt lips stretched painfully around the fattest thing ever up his ass. But the pain was nothing compared to the sensation of solid heat filling him from behind. It was his foreman fucking him up the ass, Blake who was so incredible. Gavin moaned and wiggled his butt, suddenly feeling his sphincter relax and inches of steamy cock slither deeper into his guts. Pain disappeared in a rush of hot pleasure.

Gavin raised his head and hollered, "FUCK ME, BOSS!"

Blake laughed with shaking delight. The tight hole had opened up, and he drove his cock into it, squeezing Gavin's lush butt cheeks with both hands. The tender young cowboy was crying out for cock! Gavin's hero-worship was finding fulfillment in that rough thrust of cock up the ass. Blake loved the realization as much as he loved the feel of Gavin's ass. He thrust half-way into Gavin's steamy hole and then pulled almost all the way out, pausing just for a moment to stare down at his purple shaft all slick with spit and goo and Gavin's pale butt cheeks flushed and sweaty. He slammed deep, feeling Gavin's body jerk and quiver, hearing Gavin's startled shout. He pulled out and then thrust even deeper. Out and in, deeper every time until his purple pole was entirely buried up Gavin's asshole, and his hairy balls slapped against Gavin's dangling nads.

Gavin rode the powerful fuck like he would the wildest of broncos. He had tamed more than a few recalcitrant horses, and he sensed that the best way to endure that awesome fuck was to ride it out, let Blake do the fucking and take whatever the burly foreman offered. He took every fat inch as Blake ploughed his ass like a fresh spring furrow. Gavin felt his asshole heat up, grow slack and welcoming, and his own cock grow harder as it banged against the fence rail in front of it. Blake's furry blond thighs pressed into his from behind. Blake's big hands squeezed and fondled his naked ass cheeks. It was heaven.

Blake pummeled Gavin's sweet butt. He slammed in and out in a furious rush to orgasm. The willing acceptance of the cowboy's body, bent over and wide open, his mewls and grunts, and his warm hole called to Blake. He wanted to master the younger man, fuck him with all his might, and spew a gallon of cum up his sweet ass. Gavin's asshole was a fiery channel, his cheeks heated mounds of welcoming flesh. Gavin's crack was split wide, Blake's stiff prong sliding in and out of it with piston-like rapidity.

The afternoon sun beat down on them. The cottonwoods swayed in the breeze. Blue sky domed overhead. Blake slammed into Gavin and shot his load. He threw his head back and howled as he creamed the young cowboy's sweet hole. A river of jizz pulsed up his stiff cock and flooded Gavin's asshole.

Gavin felt Blake blowing. It was too much for him. He was taking Blake's load up his butt! He rammed his ass back against the erupting tool and fucked himself into an orgasm of his own. His cock swelled, and then disgorged sticky spurts all over the fence and the grass at their feet.

The cowboys spilled their seed under the Colorado afternoon, gasping together in breathless, heart-pounding release. Blake felt Gavin's orgasm as the cowboy's asshole snapped and milked at his spurting pecker. He pulled out and let his cock dribble over Gavin's hefty, white ass cheeks.

"We got work to do, Gavin. Let's finish up our chores and head back to the ranch."

Blake's order returned some sense to the young cowboy. He rose on shaky legs and turned to meet Blake's eyes. Gavin was embarrassed at his own lusty performance, but Blake smiled and nodded, pulling up his pants and buttoning them without making any comment. Gavin still blushed as he bent over to pull up his own jeans and underwear. He couldn't help wondering if that was it, if Blake was going to fuck him once and never again.

Blake's hand slid around Gavin's waist as he pulled him close and kissed the surprised cowboy. That hand probed brazenly up into Gavin's sweat butt crack. As they kissed, Blake fingered Gavin's scummed asshole. Gavin moaned around tongue and a pair of fingers tickling just inside his fucked hole. He shook from head to toe.

"Come on, cowboy. Let's get to work."

Blake stepped back and nodded, his smile becoming firmer. He was in command, and Gavin jumped to obey. Out of the corner of his eyes, Gavin gasped to see Blake lick his own fingers, fingers that had just been up Gavin's ass. He blushed at the nasty feelings rekindled by that action. That wonderful fuck, as awesome as it had been, would just never be enough for Gavin. He was more infatuated with the older foreman than ever.

After that afternoon fuck, they went on as before. Blake had no problem being himself, confident and commanding. Gavin was adoring and obedient. But there was the unspoken chain of desire between them now, and Gavin longed for it to pull him back into Blake's burly arms.

Everything about the ranch felt sexual to the young cowboy after that. Ropes, leather, chaps, jeans, horses, fences, everything seemed to stimulate Gavin's sexual feelings. Blake's hands fascinated him, the way he held his reins, a branding iron, a rope, his fork and knife at dinner. Gavin feasted on Blake's big body, especially when they stripped down to bunk at night.

They shared the bunkhouse with half a dozen other cowboys, and privacy just wasn't an option. But after a week had passed, and the weekend approached, Blake made an announcement that had Gavin quivering with anticipation.

"You dudes go to town this weekend for the supplies without me. I know you're hankering for some fun. I'll just slow you down. Gavin can stay here with me and help out with the chores."

With that, the other hands fled, happy to be off on an adventure without any supervision. Gavin was on fire with nervous anticipation. His cock oozed a steady flow of precum in his underwear as he worked beside Blake the remainder of the afternoon. The young cowboy never knew if or when something might happen. His skin burned with the sensation of imminent stroking or probing by the foreman's strong hands. Night fell without any incident. Gavin was only more excited. What would happen once they were alone in the bunkhouse?

"Get in my bunk, naked, cowboy. Time for some fun."

Blake's drawled order after dinner hit Gavin like a blow to the stomach. He was trembling as he leaped to obey. Tossing aside his clothes, his boots and his cowboy hat, the dark-haired young hunk jumped on top of Blake's small bunk and dropped face down with his legs spread.

"Are you gonna fuck me up the ass again, Boss?" Gavin blurted out.

Blake laughed, stripping languidly as his grey eyes roamed over Gavin's sturdy young body sprawled naked across his bunk.

The cowboy was shaking like a leaf. Blake's desire flamed to a torch in his gut. His cock rose up stiff and twitching. But he intended on more than just a slam-fuck that night. It was time to teach the young cowboy about sex.

"There's more to sex than just fucking. Roll over onto your back."

Gavin immediately complied, rolling over and spreading his big thighs and beefy arms. His cock lurched up from his belly like a pink fence post. He gasped at the sight of the foreman, totally naked and approaching. Blake was tall, all muscle and all man. His shoulders bulged. His thighs bulged with blond fur. His chest was tanned dark, while his lower body was paler, with a thatch of straw-blond at his crotch surrounding his rearing boner.

Gavin's mouth dropped open, and he moaned as Blake climbed up on the bunk and lifted his beefy thighs to straddle Gavin's head, facing the young cowboy's feet. Blake's big pecker pointed down toward Gavin's face. Blake's massive, muscled ass cheeks dropped down over Gavin as his leaking cock head began to rub and stroke his face.

"Eat some cock, cowboy."

Gavin opened wide, capturing Blake's hot shank with his lips and tongue as it thrust into his mouth. He moaned around pumping male meat, amazed that he was finally slurping on the foreman's huge pecker. It was unbelievable. But the next sensation was even more surprising, and pleasurable.

Gavin felt his thighs being lifted and pulled back. Air on his spread crack tickled his asshole. Blake's grizzled cheeks suddenly pressed into Gavin's tender butt flesh. A mouth was on his crack. Then a tongue swiped up and down it. Suddenly lips and tongue were stroking his asshole! Blake was kissing Gavin's ass.

Gavin's thighs fell wide open as tongue penetrated his aching butt slot. He gobbled half of Blake's steamy tool in a fierce passion that transformed the sturdy young cowboy into a pair of holes, open to whatever his older, more experienced boss deemed appropriate. Cock-sucking and ass-eating just became part of the Gavin's new repertoire.

Blake slobbered over Gavin's tasty young hole, fucking the cowboy's sweet mouth while he ate his ass. Gavin's cock thrust up into Blake's hard, furry belly, stiff as a board. Blake had the young cowboy just where he wanted him.

Gavin creamed himself with a tongue up the ass and a cock deep down his throat. He was in heaven. Blake felt the young cowboy cuming, and stabbed his tongue deeper. Blake had his boy-cowboy. Gavin had his Daddy-cowboy. It was a perfect match.

Me, Daddy — You, Cub
Tom Lever

A bar in Madrid. Appropriately called HOT! One of those Bear bars that are popping up all across Europe at the moment. Or at least it seems like it. Anyway, there I was: fresh in the city.

I'd arrived late, but after greeting the doorman, I made my way through the crowd. And, then I saw him. He was hanging out with a couple of friends of his. It was a Saturday night. The bar was full. Our eyes connected. Get the picture? Aha, thought you did. Well, nothing happened. He was shy. I was tired. And so the "eyes meeting across a crowded room" shit, remained just that. I went home to bed — alone. No worries. Provided he wasn't a tourist, I was bound to see him again.

I was taking some time out — sort of a sabbatical from my job up north — and I was spending six months in Madrid. It was an opportunity to brush up on my Spanish, to spend some more time with my friends in the city, and to enjoy life. Plus it made a change from the cold climes of Northern Europe where I'd spent much of my life. And it gave me an opportunity to relax — both mentally and physically. At 45, I was tired of work and career and wanted to live some. And Madrid seemed like a good place to do it. I had friends there. I liked the city. I liked the language. It was a fun place to be — relaxed and uncomplicated. And, Spanish men are hot. Fucking hot. And passionate. Forget the clichés, I hear you say, but they're true. Latin men are fucking hot. Hot, hot, hot. Believe me.

Saturday night came around, and I debated whether or not to go to the bar, but after about five minutes of wavering, I got dressed and headed out. My luck was in; he was there. His eyes lit up when I walked through the door. Keen, I thought, well, let him wait. I drank one beer, then another. By the third, he could not keep his eyes off me. Blue eyes. Unusual for a Spaniard. I played with him — winking, letting him know that I was interested — but kept him at bay. Eventually, he came over and said hello.

"Hola! Que tal?"

"Bien. Y tu?"

Bob Condron

A standard exchange. Then our names — Tom and Juan. Easy to remember. We got talking. I was taking in the information he was offering, all the while drinking him in. He was about 180 cm, so a good head shorter than I. Hairy. Shaved head and close-cropped beard. And a cute way of leaning his head to one side when he talked. Jeans and a T-shirt completed the picture. He was working for Telecom, but planning to move to another city in Spain. He was tired of Madrid. Having lived there his whole life, he was ready for something new. He was just coming up to 30 and eager for new experiences (his emphasis, not mine). In saying this, he lowered his voice and looked directly into my eyes. Begging? Or was I just imagining it? A hot young guy like this, lusting after me? Well maybe. I had been getting used to younger guys coming on to me in the last couple of years. Getting off on my age and experience? Whatever, I wasn't about to complain. This guy was definitely on for it. And I for him, but something about him was different.

He was giving off something else. A longing. A hunger for experience. A thirst. He was needy. Wounded, somehow. He reminded me of myself when I was his age — oh how I'd wanted someone to come along and take charge, to overtake me. It had never happened. But now, here was an opportunity to make this little cub's dream come true. And he was excited about all the right things — like my age, my salt-and-pepper beard, my shaved head, my height and how it made him feel so small, so like a little boy as if he wanted to cuddle up to me, wanted me to put my arms around him and make everything better. Fuck, if I was reading the signals right, he was on for it, and in a big, bad way. It was time to put him out of his misery.

I took a slug from my beer and, leaning over, pressed my lips against his. He opened his mouth and I fed the beer to him. The beer trickled from my mouth into his. He drank it down, his eyes telling me wanting more. I did it again. His breathing got heavy. His eyes began to take on that scared sort of look. You know, the one that happens when you're on the threshold of something you've always dreamed of, always wanted, and now here it is, staring you in the face. It's like a reality check. Can dreams come true? I smiled down at him. A smile that reassured him it was OK

Daddy's Boyz

to be anxious. Tense even. But that he had no need to be scared. Not with me. That I was going to be his fantasy.

"I'm booked into a hotel room close by ... wanna come back?"

"For more beer?" he asked.

"That, too, my friend, that, too," I said.

That was all it took.

Fifteen minutes later we were back in my hotel room, kissing, our tongues merged into a muscular mass of spit and sweat. Licking around his beard, his eyes, sticking my tongue up his nose, in his ears. Nibbling on his neck, the back of his shaved head. Getting sweaty. Peeling off his T-shirt and licking his armpits. Then I stood back.

"Take off your clothes," I said.

"What? All of them?" he asked.

"Yeah", I replied. "All of them."

I was gonna enjoy this. Me, fully clothed — him, naked. Enjoying his not knowing what was gonna happen next. Enjoying the power. Me Daddy! You Cub!

I watched as he slowly stripped down — shucking off his T-shirt, his jeans, his boxers, his boots and socks, until he was standing buck-naked before me. He was as handsome naked as he was clothed. Not just a pretty face, this guy. Nicely muscled in a natural sort of way. Tanned skin. Hair that ran from his balls up his chest and over onto his shoulders and upper back. Then there was a gap and it started again at his lower back and ran in between his legs. Nice cock. Nice ass. My idea of a Latin lover. (Though don't call me shallow or anything!)

I leaned over and sucked on his dick briefly — just enough to get the blood flowing. Meanwhile, I reached down into the satchel I kept beside the bed and produced a series of thick white lengths of cord.

Then, looking him in the eyes, I said, "Hands behind your back." And with that, I began to tie him. First blindfolding his eyes, then binding his hands, and then — after laying him on his belly on the bed — his legs, spread-eagled.

I looked down at my handiwork. Juan's face was turned towards the wall, eyes unseeing. His mouth, yeah, his mouth. He didn't seem to know what to do. Breathing heavily. His tension was palpable; it was exciting, watching him. Watching his body vibrate with desire. His hairy ass. His slack, heavy balls exposed between his thighs. Waiting for me. Aching for me. It was hard to know where to begin, which part of him was ripe for the taking. I leaned over and licked his shoulders. Kissed them. Nibbled the skin on the back of his neck. His body arched beneath me. I allowed my cock to rub against his ass, eased it between his ass cheeks. His ass rose to meet me. I licked some spit on my hand and lowered it to lubricate my cock head, and then moved it rhythmically between his crack, pressing it against his rosebud. I felt his body shudder. Fuck yeah. Juan was gonna have a good night. And so was I. Time to up the ante.

I sat down on the end of the bed and began to rub the tip of my index finger against his asshole. Teasing it. Massaging it. Pressing it in slightly. His hungry ass pushed back, begged for more. Well let him have it! Finger inserted, fucking his hole, slipping it in and out. Loosening up his asshole, feeling his muscles relax as my finger eased in and out. Then two fingers — holding his hole open, feeling his pulse. He was moaning at this stage, grinding his ass upwards to meet me.

I reached underneath and pulled his cock back. Licking the length of the shaft from cockhead to balls, then up to his shaved asshole — a trinity of pleasure. Juan was moaning. Long, low moans of pleasure. His ass rising up to greet me. Not knowing where to begin, where to end. His ass thrusting back to meet my tongue. It was time to fuck him.

Cockhead against rosebud. Pressing against it. Rubbing against it. Feeling it relax. Feeling his muscles open. I slipped inside. Slowly at first. Bit by bit. Fucking him slowly. Getting into a rhythm. His whole body focused on the contact between us. My cock. His ass.

And then I began to release him, my cock deep inside him. I untied his hands, removed the blindfold. His eyes blinked in the candlelight. His arms reaching back to grip my ass. Pulling me tighter to him. Drawing me deeper into him. His every thrust urging me to cum.

Fucking him. Increasing the pace. Feeling my balls slap against his ass. Feeling the cum building inside my balls. Aching for release. Racing towards the inevitable. Fuck!!! Fuck!!!! Fuck!!!!!

Wave upon wave of cum shooting out of my cock and into the depths of him.

But it wasn't finished yet. Juan still had to cum. One last treat for this cub of mine. I stayed inside him as I eased us over onto our sides. I licked the back of his neck, nibbling the tender skin, as he reached down to wrap his fist around his straining tool. I felt his body tense up again — his energy focused on his cock. His hand was moving faster now. I reached around and pinched his nipples between my fingers and worked them. Teased them. Tugged them. He began to whimper. And then it came: stream after stream of white cum spurting out of his cock. His mouth wide open in a silent scream. His ring pulsing around my dick with each and every spurt.

We lay cuddling then. Me behind him, my arms reaching around to hold him close. Nuzzling my face into his hair, feeling his body close to mine, how he pressed his back into my chest and belly. Curling up while I surrounded him. Feeling his breathing return to normal. Coming back from fuck-heaven where we'd been.

This young man — a reminder of the young man I once was. A young man who, many years ago, would have given his eyeteeth for such an experience. Well, maybe not that much, but you know what I mean. When you are young and horny, all you want is for a Daddy to come along and make everything OK. A Daddy who can do things to you to make your whole body electric. A Daddy who will cuddle you at night, make you feel warm, keep you safe. A Daddy to last your whole life long. I could feel the responsibility of what I had just done with Juan. Feel his reliance. His trust. And now, here he was, lying within my arms, sleeping like a baby. My baby.

Sleep now. Daddy's here.

Even Daddies Need Daddies

Simon Sheppard

When I first met him, I figured he wasn't my type. Too old, way too old.

"I wouldn't want to be your boy," he said sometime later, after we'd gotten down to the subject of sex. "Just your slave."

Even that didn't much appeal to me. I glanced around the bar, looking for a route of more-or-less polite escape.

Then he said something so true, so needy, so, well, beautiful that I looked at him again. He said, "I need to be touched." Not "I want to be touched" or "I need to get fucked." Need. Touched. And then: "To be held."

I was in his bed within the hour. Yes, I'm awfully softhearted for a sadistic Daddy top, and no, at this point in my life, I don't give a shit who knows it.

But he was my age — well, two years younger. And though I do play with men my age sometimes, I generally prefer firmer, much younger flesh. Not "smoother" than his, though: His body might have been out of shape, but his flesh was almost unnaturally pale and soft. My body, in any case, was very much to his liking.

"You're perfect," he said. Then, when I made a face. "Well, at least, you're just my type."

And then he said it, "Daddy." He called me "Daddy." We agreed you wouldn't do that, I wanted to say. But he had such an eager expression on his face that I just kept quiet.

We had been messing around, the way that guys who don't know each other and are starting to have sex for the first time sometimes do. I'd started out by biting his nipples, big ones on a chest that was so soft and generous it might almost have been a girl's. When I bit down harder, so hard I was afraid I'd maybe draw blood, he acted like it was Christmas and I was Santa Claus. Only every time I looked down, his dick — a big, almost floppy piece of meat — was still soft.

Bob Condron

"It almost never gets real hard," he said, noticing my repeated glances, and I decided to believe it, instead of giving in to insecurity. "Anyway, except for the head, I don't really have too much feeling in my dick. Not like my ass."

I reached down and patted his butt.

"Oh, yeah," he said. I slapped his ass harder, and a big smile lit up his face. He was looking handsomer by the minute. He kept on liking me, too. He drew back, looked me over from head to foot, and said, "Yeah, just my type."

I smiled.

"Slap me some more. Please, Daddy."

I did, ramping up pretty quickly until I was waling away on his ass, hitting hard. His soft ass. My boy's soft, reddening, beautiful ass. I looked into his eyes. He still, oddly, had his glasses on. Behind the lenses, it looked like he might cry.

This wasn't where I'd hoped the scene would go. At least, not so soon. I backed off, stopped slapping, stroked his face. The glasses got in the way. I lifted them off, put them on the bedside table.

"Daddy?" he said. He was going to keep calling me "Daddy," and there was nothing I could do about it. There was nothing I wanted to do about it, actually. He might not be the boy of my dreams. He wasn't the boy of my dreams, not even close. But he was my boy, my son, and my dick was hard, and for the moment, that was enough. More than enough.

"Yes?" I said, my hand on his big tit, squeezing his nipple.

"Oh God," he murmured.

I squeezed harder. He squirmed. A fervent gasp, "Oh yes, Daddy."

As I squeezed, I saw, or thought I saw — which is to all intents and purposes the same thing — his face change, become younger, more filled with wonder, with need. I took him to what I imagined was his limit, then pulled my fingers from his nipple.

"Thank you, Daddy. Thank you so much."

"You're welcome, son." Suddenly, calling this balding, graying man "Son" didn't seem an improbable thing to do. It seemed like the most natural thing in the world.

"Dad?"

"Yes?"

Daddy's Boyz

"Would it be all right for me to lay my head on your hairy chest?"

"Of course, son."

He rolled on his side, threw an arm around me, and gently laid his cheek on me. I felt stiffness against my thigh; for the first time, his dick was rock hard.

"God, Daddy. I needed this so badly." He moved his hand down my flank, over my hip, onto my cock. He stroked lightly, barely touching the sensitive flesh. "Thank you, Daddy."

As I lay there, I remembered playing with Karl the week before. Karl was such a good boy, a hot boy: cute face, damn near perfect body, and a thoroughly edible asshole that wouldn't take no for an answer. And Karl was in his early twenties, half my age. But Karl, despite his sweetness, his intense desirability, didn't bring forth the feelings that this new "boy" did. Odd. But my new son's hand felt great on my cock, and his head was just where it belonged.

"You OK?" he asked.

"Sure, fine."

"It's just that you haven't said anything for a while," he said.

"I'm sorry," I said, "but I forgot your name." Actually, I wasn't all that sure I ever knew it.

"Bert."

I told him my name.

"I know," Bert said.

"Bert, suck your father's dick."

"Yes, Daddy."

His hand still gently grasping my hard-on, he moved his face down to my crotch. His tongue, just the tip of his tongue, flicked against my dickhead. I shivered with genuine pleasure. Often when I end up with guys my own age, I have to use a bit of mental gymnastics to stay fully hard — I think of younger guys I've fucked. Boys like Karl. Karl, who'd slung himself over the edge of my bed and presented his perfect ass to me, whose hole had felt so welcoming as I stroked the smooth young flesh of his back. Karl.

But with Bert, I was discovering, I didn't have to think of boys like Karl to stay hard. Because, by some strange alchemy, some slip in the time/space continuum, Bert was no older than Karl. No, in fact he was younger. And getting still younger all the time, so fast it was almost scary.

The boy's mouth had closed around my dickhead, was nursing on it like a baby at a tit. Great, it felt absolutely great. Might as well let him know it. "Feels wonderful, son." His mouth sucked harder as he slid his lips down, down over Daddy's hard flesh. I felt my cock head hitting the back of his throat. I reached down and pressed the back of my boy's balding head. He made swallowing motions with his throat. God, his cocksucking technique was great. God, I was close, getting close. God. I moved my hand, pulled his head away. Close call.

"Did I do something wrong, Daddy?"

I could feel a bit of errant cum oozing from my slit. "Nothing wrong at all."

"Dad, I'm glad. It's a boy's mission to give his father pleasure, to make his daddy proud."

I looked at his face. He was my own age again. I stroked his wrinkled cheek.

"Bert, can we break scene for a minute? I want to tell you something."

"Sure." Just one word, but it carried a bit of uncertainty.

"I ..."

"What is it?" Bert said.

"I don't want this to sound stupid, and we both know that anything a guy says during sex might well be insincere. But I wanted you to know that what's happening seems somehow — and this is a stupid word, maybe — profound."

He smiled and snuggled tighter to me. "Yeah, I get you. Listen, usually I'm the one who's Daddy, and I can be a damn good one, too. But there's been a need, a deep need in me, that's gone unmet. Being with you is ... well, profound. No matter if it's only for an hour or two."

I smiled and gently pushed his head down toward my crotch.

"Then suck Daddy's cock, boy. Suck it."

"Yes, SIR!" Bert looked up at me, beaming, young again.

As my new son's wet mouth massaged my dick again, I thought about a T-shirt my slightly older ex-lover had given me many years ago, a short while before we broke up. It was black, fit me well, and white lettering over my left tit read "Even Daddies

Need Daddies." At the time, it seemed odd, off base. It would be a few more years before I understood what my boyfriend had been trying to tell me; I'd finally learned it at the feet of a dominant older man. The T-shirt had grown tattered, but I still kept it in the back of my drawer.

I thought about fucking Bert, but turned on as I was, I was honestly unsure I could stay hard enough to do it. Instead, I said, "Come here and let Daddy suck your cock."

He took his mouth away. There was a big grin on his wet mouth. He got to his knees, straddling me, dick right in my face. It was an almost-huge piece of meat, thick and veiny, not boyish at all. But it was my boy's. I pride myself on my cocksucking prowess, but it was a bit of a struggle to wrap my mouth around that big old thing. And though I rarely eat cum — I sometimes think that excessive caution has kept me alive — it wasn't very long till hot cum was coursing down my throat. I swallowed every slightly risky drop.

"Thank you, Daddy," Boy Bert sounded as though he might actually cry. It was alarming, in a way.

"OK, son. Now you can eat Daddy's sperm."

"Yes, SIR!" He sounded happy now, a happy, happy boy. A happy boy who would take his new father's penis in his mouth, suck hard, and gulp down a hot load of the old man's jism. And that's exactly what he did, right before he crawled back up, laid his head on my hairy chest again, and napped blissfully for a while.

And the next day, I washed out that old black T-shirt, folded it carefully, wrapped it in some old Happy Birthday paper I found, and put it aside till the next time father and son got together to make love.

The Contributors

Marcel K. Bromius

Marcel K. Bromius is a frustrated writer. Recent events have violently pulled the author back into reality where he has to work a full-time job in the Baltimore area while going to college part-time in search of an elusive degree in communications. To date, he is the editor of *Dark Sins and Desires Unveiled,* and a published author of erotica and horror erotica short stories that are available in several anthologies: *Erotic Fantasy, Raging Horrormones, Just the Sex, Chance Encounters,* and *Blasphemy,* to name a few.

Tulsa Brown

Tulsa Brown is an escaped novelist from another genre who's been having a ball in erotica since 2003. In 2004, Tulsa's work appeared in 11 anthologies, including *Wet Nightmares, Wet Dreams, Men and Ink: Hot Tattoo Tales,* and *Best SM Erotica 2.*

Dale Chase

Dale Chase has been writing erotica for eight years with over 100 stories published in various magazines and anthologies including translation into German. His first literary effort was recently published in the *Harrington Gay Men's Fiction Quarterly. The Company He Keeps,* his collection of Victorian gentlemen's erotica, is due out in 2007. Chase lives near San Francisco, is at work on a novel, but erotica ultimately prevails.

Jordan M. Coffey

Jordan M. Coffey is the pseudonym of someone who always wanted to be a writer, but took a divergent 20-year path into computers and accounting. After rediscovering the obsessive joy of putting words on paper, Jordan took the plunge into professional publishing and is pleased to still be afloat.

Hank Edwards

Hank Edwards is the author of the novel, *Fluffers, Inc.,* a humorous, erotic mystery. His stories have been published in *Honcho, 100% Beef,* and *American Bear,* as well as various anthologies. He lives in a suburb of Detroit with his partner of many years. Visit his website at www.hankedwardsbooks.com.

Bob Condron

Peter Eros
Australian-born Peter Eros has been a professional journalist since 1954, a veteran of the Gay publishing scene, contributor to *The Advocate* (then a fortnightly newspaper), and managing editor of the original *Zipper Magazine*. He became world affairs correspondent for the London magazine *Ambassador International* in 1975. His gay stories and novellas have appeared in more than twenty STARbooks anthologies. They published his novel *Acolyte Master* in 2003. Peter lives with his lover of 42 years and two mutts in Phoenix, Arizona.

L.P. Gerard
L.P. Gerard is a Haitian American writer living in Miami, Florida. He holds a baccalaureate from the University of Miami, and his work (both fiction and nonfiction) has appeared in an array of publications, including *In Touch*, *Mandate*, *The Miami Herald* and *The Los Angeles Times*.

Ian Hawke
Ian Hawke spends his days writing fiction surrounded by rural North Dakota. His fiction interests range from erotica to history to science fiction. While he continues to write erotic short stories, he is in the process of developing an historical novel and an erotic thriller.

John McFarland
John McFarland has had his work published everywhere from *Cricket Magazine* to *The BadBoy Book of Erotic Poetry*. He has contributed short fiction to the anthologies *CONTRA/DICTION* (Arsenal Pulp Press) and *Wet Nightmares, Wet Dreams* (STARbooks), as well as nonfiction to *The Isherwood Century* (University of Wisconsin Press) and *The Queer Encyclopedia of Music, Dance and Musical Theater* and *The Queer Encyclopedia of the Visual Arts* (Cleis Press). "Encore" is an excerpt from his novel-in-progress *Glancing Blows*. He lives in Seattle.

Tom Lever
Tom Leaver's work has appeared in *Quickies 1*, *2* and *3*, *Bear Book I* and *II*, *American Bear* and various other anthologies. Born in Ireland, he now lives and works in Germany.

Daniel Ritter

Daniel Ritter has written everything from reference work to poetry, and his erotica can also be found in various places online and in print, including *Lovers Who Stay with You* and *Bloodlust*. He lives in the Midwest with an old guitar and a couple of parrots.

Michael Rivers

Michael Rivers was born and raised in Aberdeen, South Dakota (population 26,000). He graduated magna cum laude from Northern State University earning degrees in English and Psychology. In 2001, Rivers moved to Minneapolis to pursue a writing career. The move provided Rivers with the population size, diversity, cultural events and recreational choices that he desired. One year later, he signed his first book contract for *I'll Cover You in $20 Bills*. Rivers continues to work on freelance writing assignments and is always open to new projects for books, short stories, periodicals, films and stage. Visit www.michaelrivers.net

Simon Sheppard

Simon Sheppard is the author of *In Deep and Other Stories* and *Kinkorama: Dispatches from the Front Lines of Perversion*. His next book, *Sex Parties 101*, is due out in early 2005. He's the coeditor of *Rough Stuff and Roughed Up*, and his work appears in over 100 anthologies, including *The Best American Erotica 2005* and *Best Gay Erotica 2005*. He's also the author of the columns "Sex Talk" and "Perv," and loiters shamelessly at www.simonsheppard.com.

Michael Stamp

Michael Stamp's earliest influences were the writings of Gordon Merrick and John Preston, so it's not surprising the New Jersey-based author's own erotica, including the S/M tales, has a decidedly romantic bent. Stamp's stories can be found in the anthologies *Best American Erotica 2002*, *Best Gay Erotica 2001* and *2002*, *Best S/M Erotica*, *Friction 6*, *Casting Couch Confessions*, *Sex Toy Tales*, *Strange Bedfellows*, and the forthcoming *Men of Mystery*, and in magazines like *Inches* and *In Touch*.

Jay Starre

From Vancouver, Jay Starre has written for numerous gay men's magazines including *Men*, *Honcho*, *Torso*, *Mandate*, *Indulge* and *American Bear*. His stories have been included in over 25 gay erotic anthologies including *Lovers Who Stay with You*, *Kink*, *View to A Thrill* and *Wired Hard 3*. His short story "The Four Doors" was nominated for a 2003 Spectrum Award.

Mark Wildyr

Born and raised an Oklahoma, Mark Wildyr presently resides in New Mexico, the setting of many of his stories, which explore developing sexual awareness and intercultural relationships. Approximately 35 of his short stories and novellas have been acquired by Alyson Publications, Arsenal Pulp, Companion Press, Southern Tier Edition of Haworth Press, and STARbooks Press.

Thom Wolf

Thom Wolf is the author of the novels *Words Made Flesh* (Idol 2000) and *The Chain* (Zipper 2003). His stories have appeared in numerous books including several volumes of the popular *Friction* series, *Three the Hard Way*, *Bearotica*, *Bear Lust*, *Twink*, *Manhandled*, *Ultimate Gay Erotica*, the vampire anthology *Blood Lust* and many more. He is proud to have collaborated with author Kevin Killian on "Too Far" for *Frozen Tear II*, a project co-funded by the Arts Council of England. He lives with his boyfriend Liam in North East England and continues to write gay porn.

About the Editor
Bob Condron

Born in the UK, Bob began his career in publishing as co-founder of, and journalist for, the Punk Rock fanzine, *H.G.* It ran to five issues and disappeared without a trace. A mere 20 years later (!) he made his erotic fiction debut courtesy of Bear Magazine. Since then he has authored two homoerotic novels: *Easy Money* (IDOL/Virgin) and *Sweating It Out* (ZIPPER/Millivres) and has contributed to numerous anthologies.

Daddy's Boyz is his first anthology as editor. His second anthology, *Working Stiff: True Blue-Collar Gay Porn* (Alyson Pub.) is due out Fall 2006. Somewhere during his 20 year literary hiatus, he trained as an actor and his work as playwright, director and/or devisor for the theatre has been performed in England, Scotland, Ireland and the United States. His most recent works of erotic fiction appear in *Friction 7*, *Sex Buddies* and *Best Gay Love Stories 2005* (Alyson Pub.).